THE TALES
of
NOSFERATU

SHORT STORIES
SHOWCASING
THE EVOLUTION
OF THE VAMPIRE LEGEND

British Library Cataloguing-in-Publication Data
A catalogue record for this book is available
from the British Library

CONTENTS

The Skeleton Count
Or, The Vampire Mistress

ELIZABETH GREY

*　　*　　*

Count Rodolph, after his impious compact with the prince of darkness, ceased to study alchemy or to search after the elixir of life, for not only was a long lease of life assured him by the demon, but the same authority had declared such pursuits to be vain and delusive. But he still dabbled in the occult sciences of magic and astrology, and frequently passed day after day in fruitless speculation, concerning the origin of matter, and the nature of the soul. He studied the writings of Aristotle, Pliny, Lucretius, Josephus, Iamblicus, Sprenger, Cardan, and the learned Michael Psellus; yet was he as far as ever from attaining a correct knowledge of the things he sought to unveil from the mystery which must ever envelope them. The reveries of the ancient philosophers, of the Gnostics and the Pneaumatologists, only served to plunge him into deeper doubt, and at length he determined to pass from speculation to experiment, and put his half-formed theories to the test of practice.

After keen study of the anatomy of the human frame, and many operations and experiments on the corpse of a malefactor who had been hanged for a robbery and murder, and which he stole from the gibbet in the dead of night, and conveyed to Ravensburg Castle, with the assistance of two wretches whom he had picked up at an obscure hostelry in the town of Heidelberg, he resolved to exhume the corpse of some one recently dead, and attempt its reanimation. The formula of the necromancers for raising the dead did not suffice for their restoration to life, but only for a temporary revivification; but in an old Greek manuscript, which he found in the library of the castle, was an account of how this restored animation might be sustained by means of a miraculous liquid, for the distillation of which a recipe was given.

Count Rodolph gathered the herbs at midnight, which the Greek manuscript prescribed and distilled from them a clear gold-coloured liquid of very little taste, but most fragrant odour, which he preserved in a phial. Having discovered that a peasant's daughter, a·girl of singular beauty, and about sixteen years of age, had died suddenly, and was to be buried on the day following that on which he had prepared his marvellous restorative, he set out on that day to Heidelberg to obtain the assistance of the fellows who had aided him in removing the corpse of the malefactor from the gibbet, and then returned to Ravensburg Castle, to prepare for his strange experiment.

At the solemn hour of midnight he departed secretly from the castle by a door in the eastern tower, of which he retained the key in his own possession, and bent his step to the church-yard of the neighbouring village. It was a fine moonlight night, but all the rustic inhabitants were in the arms of Morpheus, the leaden-eyed god of sleep, and the violator of the sanctity of the grave gained the churchyard unperceived. He found his hired associates waiting for him in the shadow of the wall, which was easily scaled, and being provided with shovels and a sack to contain the corpse, they set to work immediately. The fresh broken earth was soon thrown off from the lid of the coffin, which the resurrectionists removed with a screw-driver, and then the dead was disclosed to their view.

The corpse of the young maiden was lifted from its narrow resting place, and raised in the arms of the ungodly wretches whom Rodolph had hired, who deposited the inanimate clay on the margin of the grave, which they hastily filled up, and then proceeded to enclose in the sack the lifeless remains of the beautiful peasant girl. Having removed every trace of the sacrilegious theft which they had committed, one of them took the sack on his shoulders, and when he was tired his comrade relieved him, and in this manner they reached the castle. Count Rodolph led the way up the narrow stairs which led to his study chamber in the eastern turret, and having deposited the corpse upon the floor, and received their stipulated reward, the two resurrectionists were glad to make a speedy exit from a place which popular rumour began to associate with deeds of darkness and horror.

Having lighted a spirit lamp, which cast a livid and flickering light upon the many strange and mysterious objects which that chamber contained, and made the pale countenance of the corpse appear more ghastly and horrible, Count Rodolph proceeded to denude the body of its grave-clothes, which he carefully concealed, lest the sight of them, when the young maiden returned to life might strike her with a sudden horror which might prove fatal to the complete success of his daring experiment. He then placed the corpse in the centre of a magic circle which he had previously drawn upon the floor of the study, and covered it with a sheet. He had purchased some ready-made female apparel in the town of Heidelberg, and these he placed on the table in readiness for the use of the young girl, whom he felt sanguine of resuscitating.

Bertha had been, as was evidenced by her stark and cold remains, a maiden of surpassing symmetry of form and loveliness of countenance; no painter or sculptor could have desired a finer study, no poet a more inspiring theme. As she lay stretched out upon the floor of the study she looked like some beautiful carving in alabaster, or rather like a waxen figure of most artistical contrivance. Her long black hair was shaded with a purple gloss like the plumage of the raven, and her features were of most exquisite proportion and arrangement. But now her angelic contenance was livid with the pallid hue of death, the iron impress of whose icy hand was visible in every lineament.

Count Rodolph then took in his hand a magic wand, one end of which he placed on the breast of the corpse, and then proceeded to recite the cabalistic words by which necromancers call to life the slumbering tenants of the grave. When he had concluded the impious formula, an awful silence reigned in the turret, and he perceived the sheet gently agitated by the quivering of the limbs, which betokened returning animation. Then a shudder pervaded his frame in spite of himself, as he perceived the eyes of the corpse slowly open, and the dark dilated pupils fix their gaze on him with a strange and stolid glare.

Then the limbs moved, at first convulsively, but soon with a stronger and more natural motion, and then the young girl raised herself to a sitting posture on the floor of the study, and stared about her in a wild and strange manner, which made Rodolph fear that the object of his experiment would prove a wretched idiot or a raving lunatic.

But suddenly he bethought him of the restorative cordial, and snatching the phial from a shelf, he poured down the throat of the resuscitated maiden a considerable portion of the fragrant gold coloured fluid which it contained. Then a ray of that glorious intellect which allies man to the angels seemed to be infused into her mind, and beamed from her dark and lustrous eyes, which rested with a soft and tender expression on the handsome countenance of the young count. Her snowy bosom, from which the sheet had fallen when she rose from her recumbent position on the floor, heaved with the returning warmth of renewed life, and the Count of Ravensburg gazed upon her with mingled sensations of wonder and delight.

As the current of life was restored, and rushed along her veins with tingling warmth, the conscious blush of instinctive modesty mantled on her countenance, and drawing the sheet over her bosom, she rose to her feet, with her long black hair hanging about her shoulders, and her dark eyes cast upon the floor. Count Rodolph then directed her attention to the clothing which he had provided, so sanguine of complete success had the daring experimentalist been, and then he withdrew from the study while the lovely object of his scientific care attired herself.

When the Count of Ravensburg returned to his study, Bertha was sitting before the fire, attired in the garments he had provided for her, and he thought that he had never beheld a more lovely specimen of her sex. She rose when he entered, and kissed his hand, as though he were a superior being, and would have remained standing, with head bowed upon her bosom, as if in the presence of a being of another world, had he not gently forced her to resume the seat from which she had risen, and inquired tenderly the state of her feelings upon a return to life so strange and wonderful. But he found that she retained no remembrance of a previous existence, and all her feelings were new and strange, like those of Eve on bursting into conscious life and being from the hand of the Omnipotent. In her mysterious passage from life to death, and from death to new life, she had lost all her previous ideas and convictions, all her experience of the past, all that she had ever acquired of knowledge; and had become a child of nature, simple and unsophisticated as a denizen of the woods, with all the keen perceptions and untrained instincts of the untutored savage.

The young girl had braided up her flowing tresses of glossy blackness, and on her cheeks dwelt colour that might test a painter's skill, so rich yet delicate its hue, like the rosette tinge of some rare exotic shell, or that which a rose would cast upon an alabaster column. The young count felt himself irresistibly attracted towards the maiden, whom his science had endued with such a mysterious and preternatural existence, and she, on her part, regarded the handsome Rodolph with the wild, yet tender passion of frail humanity, mingled with the gratitude and devotion which she deemed due to one who stood to her in the position of her creator.

Thus the feelings which had so rapidly sprung up in her heart towards the only being of whom she had any conception, partook of a nature of a religious idolatry, but mingled with the grosser feelings of earth, like those which agitated in the bosom of the vestal whose sons founded Rome, or the virgin of Shen-si who was chosen from among all the women of the celestial empire to become the mother of the incarnate Foh.

'Thou art gloriously beautiful, my Bertha!' exclaimed the enamoured count, pressing her in his arms. 'Say that thou wilt be mine, and make me thy happy slave; thou should'st be loving as thou art loveable, beautiful child of mystery!'

'Love thee!' returned Bertha, a soft and tender expression dwelling in the clear depths of her dark eyes. 'I adore thee, my creator; my soul bows itself before thee, yet my heart leaps at thy glance, though I fear it is presumptuous for the work of thy hands to look on thee with eyes of love.'

'Sweet, ingenuous creature!' cried the Count of Ravensburg, kissing her coral lips and glowing cheeks. 'It is I who should worship thee! Thou art mine, Bertha, now and for ever. Henceforth I live only in thy smile!'

'For ever! Shall I remain with thee for ever? Oh, joy incomparable! My heart's idol, I adore thee!' and the beautiful Bertha wound her white arms about his neck, and pressed her lips to his, for in the new existence which she now enjoyed her feelings knew no restraint, and she yielded to every impulse of her ardent nature.

'Come, my Bertha,' said the enraptured Rodolph, 'this solitary turret must not be thy world; come with me, thy Rodolph, and be the mistress of Ravensburg Castle, as thou art already of its owner's heart.'

Passing his arm around the taper waist of the mysterious maiden, Rodolph took up the lamp, and quitting the eastern turret, they proceeded with noiseless steps to his chamber, where the first faint blush of day witnessed the consummation of their desires, nor did the torch of Hymen burn less brightly because no priest blessed their nuptial couch.

The presence in Ravensburg Castle of this young girl, which Rodolph, with that contempt for the opinion of the world which usually marked his actions, took no pains to conceal, became the engrossing topic of conversation in the servants' hall throughout the day, and as Rodolph had never before indulged in any intrigue, either with the peasant girls of the neighbouring village or the courtezans of Heidelburg, the circumstance seemed the more remarkable. But the beautiful Bertha seemed quite unconscious of the equivocal nature of her position in reference to the young count, and though her views of human nature became every moment more enlarged with the sphere of her existence, she still regarded Rodolph as a being of superior mould.

When night again drew his sable mantle over the sleeping earth, Rodolph and the mysterious Bertha sought their couch, and never had shone the inconstant moon on a pair so well matched as regarded physical beauty, or we may add as regarded their strange destiny – one gifted with almost superhuman powers of mind, yet in a few days to undergo so horrible a transformation, and far removed by that strange fate from ordinary mortals; the other endowed with such singular beauty yet doomed to the dreadful existence of one who had passed the boundaries of the grave, and returned to life!

With sonorous and solemn stroke the bell of the castle clock proclaimed the hour of midnight, and then Bertha slowly raised herself from her lover's body and slipping from the bed, attired herself in a half-unconscious state, and stole noiselessly from the room.

Her cheeks were pale, and her eyes had the wild and stolid glare which Rodolph had observed when she awakened from the slumber of the grave; she quitted the castle, and after gazing around her, as if uncertain which way to go, she proceeded towards the village.

She stopped opposite the nearest cottage, and then advanced to the window, and shook the shutters; the fastenings being insecure, they opened with little trouble, and a broken pane of glass enabled Bertha to introduce her hand, and remove the fastenings of the window. Then she cautiously opened the window, and entered the room – she ascended the stairs on tiptoe, and entered a chamber where a little girl was in bed and fast asleep. For a moment she shuddered violently, as if struggling to repress the horrible inclination which is the dread condition of a return to life after passing the portals of death, and then she bent her face down to the child's throat, her hot breath fanned its cheek, and the next moment her teeth punctured its tender skin, and she began to suck its blood to sustain her unnatural existence!

For such is the horrible destiny of the vampire race, of whom we have yet further mysteries and secrets to unfold; and such a being was she whom Count Rodolph had taken from the grave to his bed!

Presently the child awoke with a fearful scream, and its father, leaping from his bed in the next room, hurried to her succour, but Bertha rushed past him in the dark, and escaped from the house. The peasant found the little girl much frightened, and bleeding at the throat; but she had suffered no vital injury, and having ascertained this fact, he snatched up his match-lock, and hurried after the aggressor.

'A vampire!' exclaimed the peasant, turning pale with horror, as he distinctly saw, by the light of the moon, a young female hurrying from the village at a rapid pace.

The man gave chase to the flying Bertha, and gradually gaining ground, came within gun shot, just as she reached the shelving banks of the river, when he raised his weapon to his shoulder, and fired. The report echoed along the banks of the Rhine, and Bertha screamed as the ball penetrated her back, and tumbled headlong into the stream. The peasant hastened back to the village, satisfied that the horrible creature was no more, and the corpse of the vampire floated on the surface of the moonlit river.

The moon was that night at the full, and shed a flood of pearly light over the picturesque scenery of the Rhine, which, throughout its whole course, is a panorama of scenic beauty, every bend revealing some object interesting either for its historical reminiscences or legendary associations. There was the village, but now the scene of a horrible outrage – the castle, thrown into alternate light and shadow by the passing of the light fleecy clouds over the face of the moon – the town of Heidelberg, sloping from the Castle of the Palatine, and spanning the river with its noble bridge – and the Rhine, here shaded by the dark rocks which overhung the opposite bank, and there reflecting the silver light of the moon. The corpse of the vampire floated down the stream for some distance, and then it became arrested in its course by the bending of the river, and lay partly out of the water on the shelving bank.

And now commenced another scene of strange and startling interest – another phase in the fearful existence of the vampire bride! For as the beams of the full moon fell on the inanimate form of that being of mystery and fear, sensation seemed slowly to return, as when the magic spells of the Count of Ravensburg resuscitated her from the grave; her eyes opened, her bosom rose and fell with the warm pulsations of returning life; her limbs moved spasmodically, and then she rose from the bank, and shuddering at the recollection of what had occurred to her, she wrung the water from her saturated garments, and ran towards the castle at a pace accelerated by fear.

Having admitted herself into the castle, she sought the count's chamber with noiseless steps, and having taken off and concealed her wet clothes, she returned to his bed without his being aware that she had ever quitted it. The count was surprised to find that his mistress took no refreshment throughout the day, but he was led to consider it as one of the natural laws of her strange existence, and thought no more about it.

But in the village, the utmost excitement prevailed when it became known that the cottage of Herman Klans had been visited by a vampire during the night, and his little daughter bitten by the horrible creature. All day long the cottage of the mysterious visitation was beset by the wondering villagers, who crossed themselves piously, and wondered who the vampire could have been, and the services of the priest were called into requisition to prevent the little blue-eyed Minna becoming a vampire after death, as is supposed to be the case with those who have the misfortune to be bitten by one of those horrible creatures, just as a person becomes mad after the bite of a mad dog or cat.

According to the terms of the compact which had been entered into between Count Rodolph and the demon, its conditions did not come into operation until seven days after the signing of the dreadful bond, and as day after day flew on, Rodolph dreaded the necessity of acquainting Bertha with the terrible transformation which he must nightly undergo. But he knew how impossible it would be to keep his hideous and appalling metamorphosis a secret from his mistress, and he reflected that if he made her the confidant of his terrible fate it would be the more likely to remain unknown to the rest of the world. He accordingly nerved his mind to the appalling revelation which he had to make, and on the seventh day after his compact with Lucifer, he disclosed to her his awful secret.

'Bertha,' said he, in a sad and solemn tone, 'I am about to entrust thee with a terrible secret; swear to me that thou wilt never divulge it.'

'I swear,' she replied.

'Know, then,' continued the count, lowering his voice to a hoarse whisper, 'that, by virtue of a compact with the infernal powers of evil and of darkness, I am endowed with a term of life and youth amounting almost to the boon of immortality but to this inestimable gift, there is a condition attached which commences this night, and which I almost tremble to impart to thee.'

'Fear not, my Rodolph!' exclaimed his beautiful mistress, twining her round white arms about his neck, 'thy Bertha can never love thee less, and her soul the rather clings to thee more intensely for the preternatural gift which links thy destiny more closely to my own. For mine, too, is a strange and fearful existence, which I owe to thee, and therefore shall I cling to thee the more fondly for the kindred doom which allies us to each other while it lifts us far above ordinary mortals.'

'Then prepare thy ears for a dread revelation, Bertha,' returned the Count of Ravensburg. 'Each night of my future existence, at the hour of sunset, my doom divests me of my mortal shape, and I become a skeleton until sunrise on the morn ensuing. Now, thou knowest all, my Bertha, and be it thy care to prevent the dreadful secret from becoming known.'

'It shall, my brave Rodolph!' exclaimed Bertha, her eyes glittering with a strange expression, as she thought of the facility which her lover's strange doom would allow for her nocturnal absences from the castle. 'No eye but mine shall witness thy transformation, and I will watch over thee until thy return to thy natural shape.'

'Thanks, my Bertha!' returned Rodolph, embracing her. 'The hour draws nigh when I must relinquish for the night my mortal form; come, love, to our chamber, and see that no prying eye beholds the ghastly change.'

Bertha and her lover accordingly repaired to their chamber, and when the luminary of day sank below the horizon, leaving the traces of his splendour on the western sky, the Count Rodolph shrunk to a grisly skeleton, and fell upon the bed. Bertha shuddered as she witnessed the horrid transformation, and they lay down on the bed until midnight, the necessity of secrecy overcoming any repugnance she might otherwise have felt to the horrible contiguity of the skeleton, but when the castle clock proclaimed the hour of midnight with iron tongue, she rose from the bed, and locking the door of the chamber which contained so strange a guest, she stole from the castle to sate her unnatural appetite for human blood.

The moon rode high in the heavens on that night of unfathomable mystery and horror, and her silver beams shone through the chamber-window of Theresa Delmar, one of the loveliest maidens in the village of Ravensburg, revealing a snowy neck, and a white and dimpled shoulder, shaded by the bright golden locks which strayed over the pillow. The maiden's blue eyes were concealed by their thin lids and their long silken fringes, and her snowy bosom gently rose and fell beneath the white coverlet as the thoughts which agitated her by day, mingled in her dreams at night. Silence reigned in the thatched cottage, and throughout the village was only occasionally broken by the barking of some watchful house-dog.

But soon after midnight the silence was broken by a slight noise at the chamber window as if someone was endeavouring to obtain an entrance, and the flood of moonlight which streamed upon the maiden's bed was obscured by the form of a woman standing on the windowsill. Still Theresa slumbered on, nor dreamed of peril so near, for the woman had succeeded in opening the window, and in another moment she stood within the room.

With slow and cautious step she softly approached the bed whereon the maiden reposed so calmly, little dreaming how dread a visitant was near her couch, and then she shuddered involuntarily as she bent over the sleeping girl, and her long dark ringlets mingled with the masses of golden hair which shaded the white shoulder, and the partially exposed bosom of Theresa Delmar. Her lips touched the young girl's neck, her sharp teeth punctured the white skin, and then she began to suck greedily, quaffing the vital fluid which flowed warm and quick in the maiden's veins, and sapping her life to maintain her own!

Still Theresa awoke not, for the puncture made in her throat by the teeth of the horrible creature was little larger than that which would be made by a leech, and the vampire sucked long and greedily, for her long abstinence from blood had sharpened her unnatural appetite. Suddenly Theresa awoke with a start, doubtless caused by some unpleasant transition in her dreams, but she did not immediately cry out, for she felt no pain, and as yet she was scarcely conscious of her danger. But in a few seconds she was thoroughly awake, and her surprise and horror may be more easily imagined than described, when she found bending over her, and sucking her blood, the horrible creature that had but a few nights previously attacked Minna Klaus, and which the child's father thought he had destroyed.

Spell-bound by the glittering eyes of the vampire, she lay without the power to scream, until the appalling horror of her situation became too great for endurance, her quivering nerves were strung to their utmost power of extension, and a wild shriek burst from her lips. Even then the horrible creature did not leave its hold, but continued to suck from her palpitating veins the crimson current of her life, until footsteps were heard hastily approaching the chamber, and the lovely Theresa, whose screams seemed to have broken the fascination which had bound her in its thrall, struggled so violently that Bertha was compelled to relinquish her horrid banquet. Springing to the window, she effected her escape, just as heavy blows resounded on the door of the chamber, and her affrighted victim sank insensible on the bed.

'What is the matter, Theresa? Open the door!' exclaimed her terrified parents; but they received no answer.

Then Delmar broke open the door, and he and his wife rushed into the room and found their daughter lying insensible on the bed, with spots of blood on her throat and bosom, and the window wide open.

'The vampire has come to life again, and has attacked our Theresa!' exclaimed her mother. 'See the blood-marks on her dear neck! Raise the village, Delmar, to pursue the monster.'

'Oh, dear! where am I? Has it gone, mother?' inquired Theresa, as she recovered from her swoon, and gazed in an affrighted manner round the room.

'Yes, it has gone now, dear,' said her mother. 'What was it like?'

'Aye, what was it like?' added old Delmar. 'Perhaps it was not the same one that neighbour Klans shot at the other night.'

'Oh, yes! it was a young woman, and as much like Bertha Kurtel as ever one pea was like another,' replied the young girl, shuddering.

'Holy virgin!' exclaimed her mother, crossing herself with a shudder. 'Bertha Kurtel a vampire, and returned from the grave to prey upon our Theresea! Oh, horrible!'

Delmar hurriedly dressed himself, and catching up an axe, he hastened to call up Klans and others to pursue the vampire, and in a few minutes the whole village was in commotion. About twenty men armed themselves with whatever weapon came first to hand, and followed the direction which the vampire had taken when chased by Herman Klans on a former occasion. They searched every bush all round the village, to which they returned at sunrise without having found any trace of the object of their search. Delmar found his daughter somewhat faint from fright and loss of blood, but not otherwise injured by the vampire's attack. The greatest excitement prevailed in that usually quiet village, and all the morning, groups of men stood about the little street, or clustered round Delmar's cottage, conversing in low and mysterious whispers of the dreadful visitation which the village had a second time received.

'What a shocking thing it would be if a pretty girl like Theresa Delmar was to become a vampire when she dies,' observed one. 'And who knows what may happen now she has been bitten by one of those horrible creatures?'

'And poor little Minna Klaus,' said another.

'Ah, and we do not know how long the list may be if we do not put a stop to it,' added one of the rustic group. 'I have heard Father Ambrose say that they generally attack females and children.'

'Who can it be? that is what I want to know,' said old Klaus.

'Why, Theresa declares it was just like Bertha Kurtel,' returned another, shaking his voice to a whisper.

'Bertha Kurtel!' repeated a youth who had loved her who once bore that name. 'Bertha a vampire! impossible.'

'It is easily ascertained,' observed the gruff voice of the village blacksmith. 'We have only to take up the coffin and see if she is in it, as she ought to be. If we do not find her we shall know what's o'clock.'

'If it was not for her parents' feelings I really should like to be satisfied whether it is Bertha,' remarked old Delmar.

'Feelings!' repeated the smith, in a surly tone. 'Have we not all got our feelings? Are we to have our wives and children attacked in this manner, and all turned into vampires, and let other people's fine feelings prevent us from having satisfaction for it?'

'There is something in that,' observed Delmar, scratching his head with an air of perplexity.

'I would make one if anybody else would go,' said Herman Klaus, after a pause.

'And I will be another,' exclaimed the smith, looking around him. 'Now who will go and have a peep in the churchyard to see whose coffin is empty?'

Several expressed themselves ready, and others following their example the smith proceeded to the churchyard, backed by about twenty of the most resolute of the villagers, to reenact the scene which had taken place there but a few nights since. On arriving at the churchyard the smith and another immediately set to work to throw the earth out of the grave, which was soon accomplished, and amid the most breathless silence the smith proceeded to remove the lid of the coffin.

'Look here, neighbours,' said he, turning pale in spite of himself. 'The lid has been removed, and the coffin is empty!'

'So it is!' exclaimed Herman Klaus.

'Then is it not plain that Bertha is the vampire – the horrible creature that sucked the blood of Theresa Delmar and little Minna Klans?' said the smith, looking round upon the throng which had been swelled during the work of exhumation by idlers from the village.

'But where is she now? that is the question,' observed Herman Klans.

'This must be investigated,' said the smith. 'We must keep watch for the vampire, and catch it; then we must either burn it, or drive a stake through the creature's body, for they say those are the only methods that will effectually fix a vampire.'

The wondering group of peasants returned to the village, and great was the grief of the Kurtels at the horrible discovery that their daughter had become a vampire, and the youth who had so loved Bertha in her human state became delirious on hearing the confirmation of the suspicion which Theresa's assertion had first excited. The ordinary occupations of the villagers were entirely neglected throughout the day, and nothing was talked of but vampires and wehr-wolves, and other human transformations more terrific and appalling than any recorded in the metamorphoses of Ovid. Towards the evening the venerable seneschal of the Count of Ravensburg arrived in the village and had an interview with the Delmars, after which he visited the cottage of Herman Klans, and a vague rumour spread like wildfire from house to house, to the effect that the vampire was an inmate of Ravensburg Castle.

The communication made by the seneschal to Delmar and Klans was to the effect that, on the morning following the interment of Bertha Kurtel, a young female exactly resembling her in form, features, voice, and every individual peculiarity, had appeared in a mysterious manner at the castle, and had resided there ever since in the capacity of the count's mistress. No one knew who she was, where she came from, or how she obtained admission into the castle; and the occurrences in the village having reached the ears of the count's retainers and domestics, accompanied with the suspicion that the vampire was the revived Bertha Kurtel, the seneschal had hastened to the village to report his observations. The abstinence of the count's mistress from food was deemed corroborative of the suspicion that she was a vampire, and the seneschal's report caused the utmost excitement among the villagers. Symptoms of hostile intentions soon became visible, and in less than half an hour, more than a hundred men were proceeding in a disorderly manner towards the castle, armed with every imaginable weapon, and swearing to put an end to the vampire.

Count Rodolph and his beautiful mistress were sitting at a window which commanded a view of the road for some distance, the small white hand of Bertha locked in that of her lover, and whispering words of tenderness and love, when their attention was attracted by a disorderly mob approaching from the village.

'What can this mean?' said Rodolph, rising.

'Oh, this is what I have dreaded!' exclaimed Bertha, turning pale, and clasping her hands in a terrified manner: 'your studies have caused you to be suspected of necromancy, my Rodolph, they come to attack the castle.'

'I fear thou art right, dearest,' said the count: 'but we will give them a warm reception. Ho! a lawless mob menaces the castle with danger: make fast the gates; bar every door; bid my retainers man the battlements to repel the attack.'

'And sunset is approaching,' exclaimed Bertha, with a meaning glance at her lover.

'Do thou retire, sweet love, to thy chamber,' said Rodolph; 'fear not for me; I bear a charmed life, and neither sword nor shot will avail against it. If this lawless rabble be not dispersed when the dread moment comes all hope will be lost, and they shall behold the grisly change. Perhaps they may be struck with a sudden panic, and we may be enabled to fly into another country.'

Bertha retired after embracing the count, and shut herself up in her chamber. Preparations were immediately made to resist the attack of the insurgent villagers, who continued to advance upon the castle, yelling like savages, and breathing vengeance against the vampire mistress of Count Rodolph.

'Down with the vampire!' was the hoarse and sullen cry which rolled like distant thunder from a hundred throats, and then the mob drew up before the castle gates, and the smith struck them heavily with his ponderous hammer.

The count took an arquebuse and fired at the mob, very few of whom were provided with fire-arms; one of the peasants was wounded, and with a shout of rage and defiance a volley of shot, arrows, and stones was directed against the beleaguered castle. The smith continued to batter away at the gate, aided by several stalwart fellows with axes, and though several of the mob were killed by the fire of the men-at-arms, those who were endeavouring to force the gate were protected by the overhanging battlements, and continued to ply their implements with unwearied energy.

Could Rodolph turned pale, and shuddered as he listened to the wild cries of the assailants, not from fear, for apart from his invulnerability he was inaccessible to that feeling, but from the horrible ideas engendered from these shouts, having reference to the beautiful Bertha Kurtel. Had her resuscitation from the grave endowed her with the horrible nature of the vampire? Could that lovely creature sustain her renewed existence with the blood of her former companions? Horrible! yet, had she not hinted at something of the kind when he revealed to her the horrors of his own strange doom? It must be so, then; and he shuddered violently at the appalling idea.

'Down with the vampire!' was still the menacing cry which rose from the assailants, who at length succeeded in breaking down the gates, and rushed tumultuously into the court-yard, shouting and brandishing their weapons.

Undismayed by the fire from the battlements, they commenced an attack on the doors and windows of the castle, and now they were all crowded in the courtyard, Count Rodolph thought the moment favourable for a sally. Drawing his sword, and commanding a score of his armed retainers to follow him, he suddenly opened a door leading into the court-yard, and fell furiously on the flank of the assailants. For a moment they were thrown into confusion, but they quickly rallied, when Count Rodolph and his little party were surrounded and compelled to act on the defensive. The ruddy beams of the setting sun were already purpling the distant hills when the peasants marched upon the castle, and as his broad disk sank below the horizon, the aspect of the Count of Ravensburg suddenly underwent a marvellous change, and much as the insurgents had wondered to see arrows glance off from his body, and their swords rebound as if their stroke fell on a giant oak, how much greater was their astonishment when they beheld him suddenly transformed into a fleshless skeleton!

'It is some devise of Satan! – he is a sorcerer!' cried the stalwart smith, brandishing his huge hammer. 'Come on, mates – down with the vampire!'

'Down with the vampire!' echoed from the mob, and the count's retainers giving way on all sides, as much appalled as the peasants at this horrible metamorphosis, the assailants rushed into the castle by the open door, and marched from room to room, looking in every closet and under every bed, while the terrified Bertha flew from one apartment to another, until she at length sought refuge in the highest apartment of the eastern turret, that chamber which had witnessed her return from death to her renewed state of strange and horrible existence. She had locked and bolted the door of the study, but what availed these obstacles against a furious mob, animated by their success in gaining the castle, and bent upon destruction and revenge? The door cracked, yielded, was forced open, and several men rushed into the little chamber.

'Here she is! – here is the vampire!' cried the foremost, and despite her piercing shrieks and earnest supplications for mercy, the wretched Bertha was dragged out of the study, with her long black hair hanging in wild disorder about her shoulders, and her beautiful countenance pale with overpowering terror.

'Mercy, indeed! What mercy can we feel for a vampire?' cried the peasants, and the terrified creature was dragged down the turret stairs by one or two of the boldest, for few would venture to come in contact with the dreaded being.

As they reached the foot of the stairs a volume of smoke rolled along the passage, and the crackling of burning wood told them that some of their companions had set fire to the castle.

'Now what shall we do with the vampire?' said her remorseless captors.

'Throw her into the Rhine!' suggested one.

'Tie her up and shoot at her!' said another.

'What will be the use of that?' objected a third. 'Nothing but fire or a sharp stake will destroy a vampire. Let us shut her up in the castle, and burn her to ashes!'

'Yes, yes! burn the vampire!' shouted a score of voices.

'No, no! – I say, no!' cried the smith. 'Let us carry her to the churchyard, put her in her coffin again, and peg her down with a stake, so that she can never rise again.'

The suggestion of the smith was approved of, and the wretched Bertha was half-dragged and half-carried, more dead than alive, towards the village church. The flames were bursting forth from all parts of the castle when the lawless spoilers left it, and a red glow hung over its ancient towers; the work of destruction was rapid, and in a few hours nought but the bare and blackened walls were left standing.

On the destroyers of Ravensburg Castle reaching the churchyard, the almost lifeless form of Bertha Kurtel was dragged to the grave, which had been left open, and flung rudely into the coffin. Then a sharp pointed stake was produced, which had been prepared by the way, and the smith plunged it with all the force of his sinewy arms into the abdomen of the doomed vampire. A piercing shriek burst from her pale lips as the horrible thrust aroused her to consciousness, and as her clothes became dabbed with the crimson stream of life, and the smith lifted his heavy hammer and drove the stake through her quivering body, the transfixed wretch writhed convulsively, and the contortions of her countenance were fearful to behold. Thus impaled in her coffin, and while her limbs yet quivered with the last throes of dissolution, the earth was replaced and rammed down by the tread of many feet.

But those strange and terrible scenes were not yet ended. A young peasant of equal curiosity and boldness, and who had been engaged in the attack upon the castle and the horrible tragedy which followed it, was anxious to know more of the strange affair of the skeleton, which had been left in the courtyard where it fell, none of the villagers caring to interfere with so ghastly an object. He therefore stole away a little before midnight, and went towards the castle, where the fire was dying out, though a fiery glow was still reflected from the mouldering embers of beams and rafters. He advanced cautiously through the broken gates of the castle, and shuddered slightly as he perceived the skeleton of the Count of Ravensburg still lying on the pavement of the courtyard.

He determined to watch until daylight, and see what became of the grisly relics of mortality, which a few hours before had been the young and handsome Count of Ravensburg. The hours passed slowly on from midnight to the dawn of another day, and when the rising sun tinged the eastern sky with crimson and gold, a strange spectacle was witnessed by the solitary watcher in the court-yard of Ravensburg Castle.

The skeleton rose slowly from the pavement, and assumed the form of Count Rodolph, just as he appeared at the moment preceding his transformation on the evening before. A cold perspiration bedewed the brow of the peasant, and his hair stood erect with terror, on witnessing this sudden metamorphosis. The count looked up at the dilapidated walls and towers of his castle, and shuddered violently, and crossing the court-yard, passed through the broken gate.

The peasant then hastened to the village, and reported what he had seen, which was a source of much marvel to the rustic inhabitants. The story of the skeleton count, and his vampire mistress, quickly spread all over Germany, but the villagers were no more molested by vampires, for Bertha Kurtel was securely fixed in her coffin, and no ill effects ensued from her attacks upon Theresa Delmar and little Minna Klans.

The Vampyre's Story

JAMES MALCOLM RYMER

* * *

In the reign of the First Charles, I resided in a narrow street, in the immediate neighbourhood of Whitehall. It was a straggling, tortuous thoroughfare, going down to the Thames; it matters little what were my means of livelihood, but I have no hesitation in saying that I was a well-paid agent in some of the political movements which graced and disgraced that period.

London was then a mass of mean-looking houses, with here and there one that looked like a palace, compared with its humbler neighbours. Almost every street appeared to be under the protection of some great house situated somewhere in its extent, but such of those houses as have survived the wreck of time rank now with their neighbours, and are so strangely altered, that I, who knew many of them well, could now scarcely point to the place where they used to stand.

I took no prominent part in the commotions of that period, but I saw the head of a king held up in its gore at Whitehall as a spectacle for the multitude.

There were thousands of persons in England who had aided to bring about that result, but who were the first to fall under the ban of the gigantic power they had themselves raised.

Among these were many of my employers; men, who had been quite willing to shake the stability of a throne so far as the individual occupying it was concerned; but who certainly never contemplated the destruction of monarchy; so the death of the First Charles, and the dictatorship of Cromwell, made royalists in abundance.

They had raised a spirit they could not quell again, and this was a fact which the stern, harsh man, Cromwell, with whom I had many interviews, was aware of.

My house was admirably adapted for the purposes of secrecy and seclusion, and I became a thriving man from the large sums I received for aiding the escape of distinguished loyalists, some of whom lay for a considerable time *perdu* at my house, before an eligible opportunity arrived of dropping down the river quietly to some vessel which would take them to Holland.

It was to offer me so much per head for these royalists that Cromwell sent for me, and there was one in particular who had been private secretary to the Duke of Cleveland, a young man merely, of neither family nor rank, but of great ability, whom Cromwell was exceedingly anxious to capture.

I think there likewise must have been some private reasons which induced the dictator of the Commonwealth to be so anxious concerning this Master Francis Latham, which was the name of the person alluded to.

It was late one evening when a stranger came to my house, and having desired to see me, was shown into a private apartment, when I immediately waited upon him.

'I am aware,' he said, 'that you have been confidentially employed by the Duke of Cleveland, and I am aware that you have been very useful to distressed loyalists, but in aiding Master Francis Latham, the duke's secretary, you will be permitted almost to name your own terms.'

I named a hundred pounds, which at that time was a much larger sum than now, taking into consideration the relative value. One half of it was paid to me at once, and the other promised within four-and-twenty hours after Latham had effected his escape.

I was told that at half-past twelve o'clock that night, a man dressed in common working apparel, and with a broom over his shoulder would knock at my door and ask if he could be recommended to a lodging, and that by those tokens I should know him to be Francis Latham. A Dutch lugger, I was further told, was lying near Gravesend, on board of which, to earn my money, I was expected to place the fugitive.

All this was duly agreed upon; I had a boat in readiness, with a couple of watermen upon whom I could depend, and I was far from anticipating any extraordinary difficulties in carrying out the enterprise.

I had a son about twelve years of age, who being a sharp acute lad, I found very useful upon several occasions, and I never scrupled to make him acquainted with any such affair as this that I am recounting.

Half past twelve o'clock came, and in a very few minutes after that period of time there came a knock at my door, which my son answered, and according to arrangement, there was the person with a broom, who asked to be recommended to a lodging, and who was immediately requested to walk in.

He seemed rather nervous, and asked me if I thought there was much risk.

'No,' said I, 'no more than ordinary risk in all these cases, but we must wait half an hour 'till the tide turns. For just now to struggle against it down the river would really be nothing else but courting observation.'

To this he perfectly agreed, and sat down by my fireside.

I was as anxious as he to get the affair over, for it was a ticklish job, and Oliver Cromwell, if he had brought anything of the kind exactly home to me, would as life order me to be shot as he would have taken his luncheon in the name of the Lord.

I accordingly went down to the water-side to speak to the men who were lying there with the boat, and had ascertained from them that in about twenty minutes the tide would begin to ebb in the centre of the stream, when two men confronted me.

Practised as I was in the habits and appearances of the times, I guessed at once who they were. In fact, a couple of Oliver Cromwell's dismounted dragoons were always well known.

'You are wanted,' said one of them to me.

'Yes, you are particularly wantèd,' said the other.

'But, gentlemen, I am rather busy,' said I. 'In an hour's time I will do myself the pleasure, if you please, of waiting upon you anywhere you wish to name.'

The only reply they made to this was the practical one, of getting on each side of me, and then hurrying me on, past my own door.

I was taken right away to St James's at a rapid pace, being hurried through one of the court yards; we paused at a small door, at which was a sentinel.

My two guides communicated something to him, and he allowed us to pass. There was a narrow passage without any light, and through another door, at which was likewise a sentinel, who turned the glare of a lantern upon me and my conductors. Some short explanation was given to him likewise during which I heard the words His Highness, which was the title which Cromwell had lately assumed.

They pushed me through this doorway, closed it behind me, and left me inside in the dark.

Being perfectly ignorant of where I was, I thought the most prudent plan was to stand stock still, for if I advanced it might be into danger, and my retreat was evidently cut off.

Moreover, those who brought me there must have some sort of intention, and it was better for me to leave them to develop it than to take any steps myself, which might be of a very hazardous nature.

That I was adopting the best policy I was soon convinced, for a flash of light suddenly came upon me, and I heard a gruff voice, say, –

'Who goes there? come this way.'

I walked on, and passed through an open door way into a small apartment, in the centre of which, standing by a common deal table on which his clenched hand was resting, I found Oliver Cromwell himself.

'So, sirrah,' he said, 'royalists and pestilent characters are to ravage the land, are they so? answer me.'

'I have no answer to make, your highness,' said I.

'God's mercy, no answer, when in your own house the Duke of Cleveland's proscribed secretary lies concealed.'

I felt rather staggered, but was certain I had been betrayed by some one, and Cromwell continued rapidly, without giving me time to speak.

'The Lord is merciful, and so are we, but the malignant must be taken by the beloved soldiers of the Commonwealth, and the gospel God-fearing men, who always turn to the Lord, with short carbines, will accompany you. The malignant shall be taken from your house, by you, and the true God-fearing dragoons shall linger in the shade behind. You will take him to the river side, where the Lord willing, there will be a boat with a small blue ensign, on board of which you will place him, wishing him good speed.'

He paused, and looked fixedly upon me by the aid of the miserable light that was in the apartment.

'What then, your highness?' I said.

'Then you will probably call upon us to-morrow for a considerable sum, which will be due to you for this good service to the Common-wealth; yea, it shall be profitable to fight the battles of the Lord.'

I must confess, I had expected a very different result from the interview, which I had been greatly in fear would have resulted, in greatly endangering my liberty. Cromwell was a man not to be tampered with; I knew my danger, and was not disposed to sacrifice myself for Master Latham.

'Your highness shall be obeyed,' I said.

'Ay, verily,' he replied, 'and if we be not obeyed, we must make ourselves felt with a strong arm of flesh. What ho! God-fearing Simpkins, art thon there?'

'Yes, the Lord willing,' said a dragoon, making his appearance at the door.

Cromwell merely made him a sign with his hand, and he laid hold of the upper part of my arm, as though it had been in a vice, and led me out into the passage again where the sentinels were posted.

In the course of a few moments, I was duly in custody of my two guards again, and we were proceeding at a very rapid pace towards my residence.

It was not a very agreeable affair, view it in whatever light I might; but as regarded Cromwell, I knew my jeopardy, and it would be perceived that I had not hesitated a moment in obeying him. Moreover, I considered, for I knew he was generous, I should have a good round sum by the transaction, which added to the fifty pounds I had received from the royalists, made the affair appear to me in a pleasant enough light. Indeed, I was revolving in my mind as I went along, whether it would not be worth while, almost entirely to attach myself to the protector.

'If,' I reasoned with myself, 'I should do that, and still preserve myself a character with the royalists, I should thrive.'

But it will be seen that an adverse circumstance put an end to all those dreams.

When we reached the door of my house, the first thing I saw was my son wiping his brow, as if he had undergone some fatigue; he ran up to me, and catching me by the arm, whispered to me.

I was so angered at the moment, that heedless of what I did, and passion getting the mastery over me, I with my clenched fist struck him to the earth. His head fell upon one of the hard round stones with which the street was paved, and he never spoke again. I had murdered him.

*

I don't know what happened immediately subsequent to this fearful deed; all I can recollect is, that there was a great confusion and a flashing of lights, and it appeared to me as if something had suddenly struck me down to the earth with great force.

When I did thoroughly awaken, I found myself lying upon a small couch, but in a very large apartment dimly lighted, and where, there were many such couches ranged against the walls. A miserable light just enabled me to see about me a little, and some dim dusky-looking figures were creeping about the place.

It was a hospital that the protector had lately instituted in the Strand.

I tried to speak, but could not; my tongue seemed glued to my mouth, and I could not, and then a change came upon my sense of sight, and I could scarcely see at all the dim dusky-looking figures about me.

Some one took hold of me by the wrist, and I heard one say, quite distinctly, –

'He's entirely going, now.'

Suddenly it seemed as if something had fallen with a crushing influence upon my chest, and then a consciousness that I was gasping for breath, and then I thought I was at the bottom of the sea. There was a moment, only a moment, of frightful agony, and then came a singing sound, like the rush of waters, after which, I distinctly felt some one raising me in their arms. I was dropped again, my limbs felt numbed and chill, an universal spasm shot through my whole system, I opened my eyes, and found myself lying in the open air, by a newly opened grave.

A full moon was sailing through the sky and the cold beams were upon my face; a voice sounded in my ears, a deep and solemn voice – and painfully distinct was every word it uttered.

'Mortimer,' it said, for that was my name, 'Mortimer, in life you did one deed which at once cast you out from all hope that anything in that life would be remembered in the world to come to your advantage. You poisoned the pure font of mercy, and not upon such as you can the downy freshness of Heaven's bounty fall. Murderer, murderer of that being sacredly presented to your care by the great Creator of all things, live henceforth a being accused. Be to yourself a desolation and a blight, shunned by all that is good and virtuous, armed against all men, and all men armed against thee, Varney the Vampyre.'

I staggered to my feet, the scene around me was a churchyard, I was gaunt and thin, my clothes hung about me in tattered remnants. The damp smell of the grave hung about them, I met an aged man, and asked him where I was. He looked at me with a shudder, as though I had escaped from some charnel house.

'Why, this is Isledon,' said he.

A peal of bells came merrily upon the night air.

'What means that?' said I.

'Why this is the anniversary of the Restoration.'

'The Restoration! What Restoration?'

'Why of the royal family to the throne, to be sure, returned this day last year. Have you been asleep so long that you don't know that?'

I shuddered and walked on, determined to make further inquiries, and to make them with so much caution, that the real extent of my ignorance should scarce be surmised, and the result was to me of the most astonishing character.

I found that I had been in the trance of death for nearly two years, and that during that period, great political changes had taken place. The exiled royal family had been restored to the throne, and the most remarkable revulsion of feeling that had ever taken place in a nation had taken place in England.

But personally I had not yet fully awakened to all the horror of what I was. I had heard the words addressed to me, but I had attached no very definite meaning to them.

I have already said that I was not yet fully alive to the horror of what I was, but I soon found what the words which had been spoken to me by the mysterious being who had exhumed me meant; I was a thing accursed, a something to be shunned by all men, a horror, a blight, and a desolation.

I felt myself growing sick and weak, as I traversed the streets of the city, and yet I loathed the sight of food, whenever I saw it.

I reached my own house, and saw that it had been burned down; there lay nothing but a heap of charred ruins where it once stood.

But I had an interest in those ruins, for from time to time I had buried considerable sums of money beneath the flooring of the lowest apartments, and I had every reason to believe, as such a secret treasure was only known to myself, that it remained untouched.

I waited until the moon became obscured by some passing clouds, and then having a most intimate knowledge of the locality, I commenced groping about the ruins, and removing a portion of them, until I made my way to the spot where my money was hidden.

The morning came, however, and surprised me at my occupation; so I hid myself among the ruins of what had once been my home for a whole day, and never once stirred from my concealment.

Oh, it was a long and weary day. I could hear the prattle of children at play, an inn or change-house was near at hand, and I could hear noisy drinkers bawling forth songs that had been proscribed in the Commonwealth.

I saw a poor wretch hunted nearly to death, close to where I lay concealed, because from the fashion of his garments, and the cut of his hair, he was supposed to belong to the deposed party.

But the long expected night came at last. It was a dark one, too, so that it answered my purpose well.

I had found an old rusty knife among the ruins, and with that I set to work to dig up my hidden treasure; I was successful, and found it all. Not a guinea had been removed, although in the immediate neighbourhood, there were those who would have sacrificed a human life for any piece of gold that I had hoarded.

I made no enquiries about any one that had belonged to me, I dreaded to receive some horrible and circumstantial answer, but I did get a slight piece of news, as I left the ruins, although I asked not for it.

'There's a poor devil,' said one; 'did you ever see such a wretch in all your life?'

'Why, yes,' said another, 'he's enough to turn one's canary sour, he seems to have come up from the ruins of Mortimer's house. By-the-by did you ever hear what became of him?'

'Yes, to be sure, he was shot by two of Cromwell's dragoons in some fracas or another.'

'Ah, I recollect now, I heard as much. He murdered his son, didn't he?'

I passed on. Those words seemed to send a bolt of fire through the brain, and I dreaded that the speaker might expatiate upon them.

A slow misty rain was falling, which caused the streets to be very much deserted, but being extremely well acquainted with the city, I passed on till I came to that quarter which was principally inhabited by money lenders who I knew would take my money without any troublesome questions being asked me, and also I could procure every accommodation required; and they did so, for before another hour had passed over my head, I emerged richly habited as a chevalier of the period, having really not paid to the conscientious man much more than four times the price of the clothing I walked away with.

And thus I was in the middle of London, with some hundreds of pounds in my pocket, and a horrible uncertainty as to what I was.

I was growing fainter and fainter still, and I feared that unless I succeeded in housing myself shortly, I should become a prey to someone who, seeing my exhausted condition, would, notwithstanding I had a formidable rapier by my side, rob me of all I possessed.

My career has been much too long and too chequered an one even to give the briefest sketch of. All I purpose here to relate is how I became convinced I was a vampyre, and that blood was my congenial nourishment and the only element of my new existence.

I passed on until I came to a street where I knew the houses were large but unfashionable, and that they were principally occupied by persons who made a trade by letting out apartments, and there I thought I might locate myself in safety.

As I made no difficulty about terms, there was no difficulty at all of any sort, and I found myself conducted into a tolerably handsome suite of rooms in the house of a decent-looking widow woman, who had two daughters, young and blooming girls, both of whom regarded me as the new lodger, with looks of anything but favour, considering my awful and cadaverous appearance most probably as promising nothing at all in the shape of pleasant companionship.

This I was quite prepared for – I had seen myself in a mirror – that was enough; and I could honestly have averred that a more ghastly and horrible looking skeleton, attired in silks and broad-cloth, never yet walked the streets of the city.

When I retired to my chamber, I was so faint and ill, that I could scarcely drag one foot after the other; and was ruminating what I should do, until a strange feeling crept over me that I should like – what? Blood! – raw blood, reeking and hot, bubbling and juicy, from the veins of some gasping victim.

A clock upon the stairs struck one. I arose and listened attentively; all was still in the house – still as the very grave.

It was a large old rambling building, and had belonged at one time, no doubt, to a man of some mark and likelihood in the world. My chamber was one of six that opened from a corridor of a considerable length, and which traversed the whole length of the house.

I crept out into this corridor, and listened again for full ten minutes, but not the slightest sound, save my own faint breathing, disturbed the stillness of the house; and that emboldened me so that, with my appetite for blood growing each moment stronger, I began to ask myself from whose veins I could seek strength and nourishment.

But how was I to proceed? How was I to know in that large house which of the sleepers I could attack with safety, for it had now come to that, that I was to attack somebody. I stood like an evil spirit, pondering over the best means of securing a victim.

And there came over me the horrible faintness again, that faintness which each moment grew worse, and which threatened completely to engulf me. I feared that some flush of it would overtake me, and then I should fall to rise no more; and strange as it may appear, I felt a disposition to cling to the new life that had been given to me. I seemed to be acquainted already with all its horrors, but not all its joys.

Suddenly the darkness of the corridor was cleared away, and soft and mellow light crept into it, and I said to myself, –

'The moon has risen.'

Yes, the bright and beautiful moon, which I had felt the soft influence of when I lay among the graves, had emerged from the bank of clouds along the eastern sky, its beams descending through a little window. They streamed right through the corridor, faintly but effectually illuminating it, and letting me see clearly all the different doors leading to the different chambers.

And thus it was that I had light for anything I wished to do, but not information.

The moonbeams playing upon my face seemed to give me a spurious sort of strength. I did not know until after experience what a marked and sensible effect they would always have upon me, but I felt it even then, although I did not attribute it wholly to the influence of the queenly planet.

I walked on through the corridor, and some sudden influence seemed to guide me to a particular door. I know not how it was, but I laid my hand upon the lock, and said to myself –

'I shall find my victim here.'

I paused yet a moment, for there came across me even then, after I had gone so far, a horrible dread of what I was about to do, and a feeling that there might be consequences arising from it that would jeopardise me greatly. Perhaps even then if a great accession of strength had come to my aid – mere bodily aid I mean – I should have hesitated and the victim would have escaped; but, as if to mock me, there came that frightful feeling of exhaustion which felt so like the prelude to another death.

I no longer hesitated; I turned the lock of the door, and I thought that I must be discovered. I left it open about an inch, and then flew back to my own chamber.

I listened attentively; there was no alarm, no movement in any of the rooms – the same death-like stillness pervaded the house, and I felt that I was still safe.

A soft gleam of yellow looking light had come through the crevice of the door when I had opened it. It mingled strangely with the moonlight, and I concluded correctly enough, as I found afterwards, that a light was burning in the chamber.

It was at least another ten minutes before I could sufficiently reassure myself to glide from my own room and approach that of the fated sleeper; but at length I told myself that I might safely do so, and the night was waning fast, and if anything was to be accomplished it must be done at once, before the first beams of early dawn should chase away the spirits of the night, and perhaps should leave me no power to act.

'What shall I be,' I asked myself; 'after another four-and-twenty hours of exhaustion? Shall I have power then to make the election of what I will do or what I will not? No, I may suffer the pangs of death again, and the scarcely less pangs of another revival.'

This reasoning – if it may be called reasoning – decided me; and with cautious and cat-like footsteps, I again approached the bed-room door which I had opened.

I no longer hesitated, but at once crossed the threshold, and looked around me. It was the chamber of the youngest of my landlady's daughters, who, as far as I could judge, seemed to be about sixteen years of age; but they had evidently been so struck with my horrible appearance, that they had placed themselves as little as possible in my way, so that I could not be said to be a very good judge of their ages or of their looks.

I only knew she was the youngest, because she wore her hair long, and wore it in ringlets, which were loose and streaming over the pillow on which she slept, while her sister, I remarked, wore her hair plaited up, and completely off her neck and shoulders.

I stood by the bed-side, and looked upon this beautiful girl in all the pride of her young beauty, so gently and quietly slumbering. Her lips were parted, as though some pleasant images were passing in her mind, and induced a slight smile even in her sleep. She murmured twice, too, a word, which I thought was the name of some one – perchance the idol of her young heart – but it was too indistinct for me to catch it, nor did I care to hear; that which was perhaps a very cherished secret, indeed, mattered not to me. I made no pretensions to her affections, however strongly in a short time I might stand in her abhorrence.

One of her arms, which was exquisitely rounded, lay upon the coverlit; a neck, too, as white as alabaster, was partially exposed to my gaze, but I had no passions – it was food I wanted.

I sprung upon her. There was a shriek, but not before I had secured a draught of life blood from her neck. It was enough. I felt it dart through my veins like fire, and I was restored. From that moment I found out what was to be my sustenance; it was blood – the blood of the young and the beautiful.

The house was thoroughly alarmed, but not before I had retired to my own chamber. I was but partially dressed, and those few clothes I threw off me, and getting into my bed, I feigned to be asleep; so that when a gentleman who slept likewise in the house, but of whose presence I knew nothing, knocked hardly at my door, I affected to awaken in a fright, and called out, –

'What is it? what is it? – for God's sake tell me if it is a fire.'

'No, no – but get up, sir, get up. There's some one in the place. An attempt at murder, I think, sir.'

I arose and opened the door; so by the light he carried he saw that I had to dress myself – he was but half attired himself, and he carried his sword beneath his arm.

'It is a strange thing,' he said; 'but I have heard a shriek of alarm.'

'And I likewise,' said I; 'but I thought it was a dream.'

'Help! help! help!' cried the widow, who had risen, but stood upon the threshold of her own chamber; 'thieves! thieves!'

By this time I had got on sufficient of my apparel that I could make an appearance, and, likewise with my sword in my hand, I sallied out into the corridor.

'Oh, gentlemen – gentlemen,' cried the landlady, 'did you hear anything?'

'A shriek, madam,' said my fellow-lodger; 'have you looked into your daughters' chambers?'

The room of the youngest daughter was the nearest, and into that she went at once. In another moment she appeared on the threshold again with a face as white as a sheet, then she wrung her hands, and said, –

'Murder! murder! – my child is murdered – my child is murdered, Master Harding,' – which I found was the name of my fellow-lodger.

'Fling open one of the windows, and call for the watch,' said he to me, 'and I will search the room, and woe be to any one that I may find within its walls unauthorised.'

I did as he desired, and called the watch, but the watch came not, and then, upon a second visit to her daughter, the landlady found she had only fainted, and that she had been deceived in thinking she was murdered by the sudden sight of the blood upon her neck, so the house was restored to something like quiet again, and the morning being now near at hand, Mr Harding retired to his chamber, and I to mine, leaving the landlady and her eldest daughter assiduous in their attentions to the younger.

How wonderfully revived I felt – I was quite a new creature when the sunlight came dancing into my apartment. I dressed and was about to leave the house, when Mr Harding came out of one of the lowest rooms, and intercepted me.

'Sir,' he said, 'I have not the pleasure of knowing you, but I have no doubt that an ordinary feeling of chivalry will prompt you to do all in your power to obviate the dread of such another night as the past.'

'Dread, sir,' said I, 'the dread of what?'

'A very proper question,' he said, 'but one I can hardly answer; the girl states, she was awakened by some one biting her neck, and in proof of the story she actually exhibits the marks of teeth, and so terrified is she, that she declared that she shall never be able to sleep again.'

'You astonish me.'

'No doubt – it is sufficiently astonishing to excuse even doubts; but if you and I, who are both inmates of the house, were to keep watch to-night in the corridor, it might have the effect of completely quieting the imagination of the young girl, and perhaps result in the discovery of this nocturnal disturber of the peace.'

'Certainly,' said I, 'command me in any way, I shall have great pleasure.'

'Shall it be understood, then, that we meet at eleven in your apartment or in mine.'

'Whichever you may please to consider the most convenient, sir.'

'I mention my own then, which is the furthest door in the corridor, and where I shall be happy to see you at eleven o'clock.'

There was a something about this young man's manner which I did not altogether like, and yet I could not come to any positive conclusion as to whether he suspected me, and therefore I thought it would be premature to fly, when perhaps there would be really no occasion for doing so; on the contrary, I made up my mind to wait the result of the evening, which might or might not be disastrous to me. At all events, I considered that I was fully equal to taking my own part, and if by the decrees of destiny I was really to be, as it were, repudiated from society, and made to endure a new, strange, and horrible existence, I did not see that I was called upon to be particular how I rescued myself from difficulties that might arise.

Relying, then, upon my own strength, and my own unscrupulous use of it, I awaited with tolerable composure the coming of night.

During the day I amused myself by walking about, and noting the remarkable changes which so short a period as two years had made in London. But these happened to be two years most abundantly prolific in change. The feelings and habits of people seemed to have undergone a thorough revolution, which I was the more surprised at when I learned by what thorough treachery the restoration of the exiled family was effected.

The day wore on; I felt no need of refreshment, and I began to feel my own proper position, and to feel that occasionally a draught of delicious life-blood, such as I had quaffed the night before was fresh marrow to my bones.

I could see, when I entered the house where I had made my temporary home, that notwithstanding that I considered my appearance wonderfully improved, that feeling was not shared in by others, for the whole family shrunk from me as though there had been a most frightful contamination in my touch, and as though the very air I had breathed was hateful and deleterious. I felt convinced that there had been some conversation concerning me, and that I was rather more than suspected. I certainly could then have left the place easily and quietly, but I had a feeling of defiance, which did not enable me to do so.

I felt as if I were an injured being, and ought to resist a something that looked like oppression.

'Why,' I said to myself, 'have I been rescued from the tomb to be made the sport of a malignant destiny? My crime was a great one, but surely I suffered enough, when I suffered death as an expiation of it, and I might have been left to repose in the grave.'

The feelings that have since come over me held no place in my imagination, but with a kind of defiant desperation I felt as if I should like to defeat the plan by which I was attempted to be punished, and even in the face of Providence itself, to show that it was a failure entailing far worse consequences upon others than upon me.

This was my impression, so I would not play the coward, and fly upon the first flash of danger.

I sat in my own room until the hour came for my appointment with Mr Harding, and then I walked along the corridor with a confident step, and let the hilt end of my scabbard clank along the floor. I knocked boldly at the door, and I thought there was a little hesitation in his voice as he bade me walk in, but this might have been only my imagination.

He was seated at a table, fully dressed, and in addition to his sword, there was lying upon the table before him a large holster pistol, nearly half the size of a carbine.

'You are well prepared,' said I, as I pointed to it.

'Yes,' he said, 'and I mean to use it.'

'What do they want now?' I said.

'What do who want?'

'I don't know,' I said, 'but I thought I heard some one call you by name from below.'

'Indeed, excuse me a moment, perhaps they have made some discovery.'

There was wine upon the table, and while he was gone, I poured a glass of good Rhenish down the barrel of the pistol. I wiped it carefully with the cuff of my coat, so there was no appearance upon the barrel of anything of the sort, and when he came back, he looked at me very suspiciously, as he said, –

'Nobody called me, how could you say I was called.'

'Because I thought I heard you called; I suppose it is allowable for human nature to be fallible now and then.'

'Yes, but then I am so surprised how you could make such a mistake.'

'So am I.'

It was rather a difficult thing to answer this, and looking at me very steadily, he took up the pistol and examined the priming. Of course, that was all right, and he appeared to be perfectly satisfied.

'There will be two chairs and a table,' he said, 'placed in the corridor, so that we can sit in perfect ease. I will not anticipate that anything will happen, but if it should, I can only say that I will not be backward in the use of my weapons.'

'I don't doubt it,' said I, 'and commend you accordingly. That pistol must be a most formidable weapon. Does it ever miss fire?'

'Not that I know of,' he said, 'I have loaded it with such extraordinary care that it amounts to almost an impossibility that it should. Will you take some wine?'

At this moment there came a loud knocking at the door of the house. I saw an expression of satisfaction come over his face, and he sprung to his feet, holding the pistol in his grasp.

'Do you know the meaning of that knocking,' said I, 'at such an hour?' and at the same time with a sweep of my arm I threw his sword off the table and beyond his reach.

'Yes,' he said, rather excitedly; 'you are my prisoner, it was you who caused the mischief and confusion last night. The girl is ready to swear to you, and if you attempt to escape, I'll blow your brains out.'

'Fire at me,' said I, 'and take the consequences – but the threat is sufficient, and you shall die for your temerity.'

I drew my sword, and he evidently thought his danger imminent, for he at once snapped the pistol in my face. Of course it only flashed in the pan, but in one moment my sword went through him like a flash of light. It was a good blade the money lender had sold me – the hilt struck against his breast bone, and he shrieked.

Bang! bang! bang! came again at the outer door of the house. I withdrew the reeking blade, dashed it into the scabbard just in time to prevent my landlady from opening the door, which she was almost in the act of doing. I seized her by the back of the neck, and hurled her to a considerable distance, and then opening the door myself, I stood behind it, and let three men rush into the house. After which I quietly left it, and was free to continue my existence as – VARNEY, THE VAMPYRE!

The Pale Lady

ALEXANDRE DUMAS & PAUL BOCAGE

* * *

I

Among the Carpathians

I am a Pole by birth, a native of Sandomir, a land where legends
become articles of faith, and where we believe in our family
traditions as firmly as in the Gospel – perhaps more firmly. Not one of
our castles but has its spectre, not one of our cottages but owns its
familiar spirit. Among rich and poor alike, in castle and cot equally,
the two principles of good and ill are acknowledged.

Sometimes the two are at variance and fight one against the other.
Then are heard mysterious noises in passages, howls in old, half-
ruined towers, shakings of walls – so terrible and appalling that cot
and castle are both left desolate, while the inhabitants, whether
peasants or nobles, fly to the nearest church to seek protection from
holy cross or blessed relics, the only preservatives effectual against the
demons that harass our homes.

Moreover in the same land two still more terrible principles, principles still more fierce and implacable, are face to face – to wit, tyranny and freedom.

In the year 1825 broke out between Russia and Poland one of those death struggles that seem bound to drain the life-blood of a people to its last drop, as the blood of a particular family is often exhausted.

My father and two brothers had risen in revolt against the new Czar, and had gone forth to range themselves beneath the flag of Polish independence, so often torn down, so often raised again.

One day I learnt that my younger brother had been killed; another day I was told that my elder brother was mortally wounded; lastly, after a long 24 hours during which I listened with terror to the booming of the cannon coming constantly nearer and nearer, I beheld my father ride in with a hundred horsemen – all that was left of three thousand men under his command. He came to shut himself up in our castle, resolved, if need be, to perish buried beneath its ruins.

Fearless for himself, my father trembled at the fate that threatened me. For him death was the only penalty, for he was firmly resolved never to fall alive into the hands of his enemies: but for me slavery, dishonour, shame might be in store.

From among the hundred men left him my father chose ten, summoned the Intendent of the Estate, handed him all the gold and jewels we possessed, and remembering how, at the date of the second partition of Poland, my mother, then scarcely a child, had found unassailable refuge in the Monastery of Sahastru, situated in the heart of the Carpathian Mountains, bade him conduct me thither. The cloister which had sheltered the mother would doubtless be no less hospitable to the daughter.

Our farewells were brief, notwithstanding the fond love my father bore me. By tomorrow in all likelihood the Russians would be within sight of the castle, so that there was not a moment to lose. Hurriedly I donned a riding-habit which I was in the habit of wearing when following the hounds with my brothers. The most trusty mount in the stables was saddled for me, my father slipped his own pistols, masterpieces of the Toula gunsmiths' art, into my holsters, kissed me and gave the order to start.

That night and next day we covered a score of leagues, riding up the banks of one of the nameless rivers that flow from the hills to join the Vistula. This forced march to begin with had carried us completely out of the reach of our Russian foes.

The last rays of the setting sun showed us the snowy summits of the

Carpathians gleaming through the dusk. Towards the close of next day we arrived at their base, and eventually during the forenoon of the third day we found ourselves winding along a mountain gorge.

Our Carpathian hills differ widely from Western ranges, which are civilised in comparison. All that nature has to show of strange and wild and grand is seen in its completest majesty. Their storm-beaten peaks are lost in the clouds and shrouded in eternal snow; their boundless fir-woods bend over the burnished mirror of lakes that are more like seas, crystal clear waters which no keel has ever furrowed, no fisherman's net ever disturbed.

The human voice is seldom heard in these regions, and then only to raise some rude Moldavian folksong to which the cries of wild animals reply, song and cries blending together to wake the lonely echoes that seem astounded to be roused at all.

Mile after mile you travel beneath the gloomy vaults of the forest interrupted only by the unexpected marvels which the waste reveals to the wayfarer at almost every step, moving his astonishment and admiration.

Danger lurks everywhere, danger compounded of a thousand varying perils; but there is no time to be afraid, the perils are too sublime to admit of common terror. Now it is the sudden formation of cataracts owing to the melting of the ice, which, dashing down from rock to rock, unexpectedly overwhelm the narrow path the traveller is following, a path traced by the sportsman and the game he pursues; now it is the fall of trees undermined by the lapse of time, which tear up their roots from the soil and come crashing down with a sound like that of an earthquake; now it is the onrush of a hurricane which enfolds the climber in storm-clouds riven by the darting zig-zags of the lightning, writhing and coiling like a serpent.

Then, after these Alpine peaks, after these primeval forests, as you have had giant mountains and boundless woods, you next have illimitable steppes, a veritable sea with its waves and tempests, barren, rugged wastes, where the eyes wander and lose themselves on the far-distant horizon. It is not terror now that seizes the spectator, it is irresistible melancholy, a profound sadness. The look of all the countryside, far as the eye can range, is everlastingly the same. You mount only to descend again slopes that are all alike; this you do twenty times over, searching in vain for a beaten track, till finding yourself thus lost in solitude, amid pathless deserts, you deem yourself alone with nature, and your melancholy turns into despair.

Movement seems a vain thing that will advance no whit; you will meet with neither village, nor castle, nor cottage, no smallest trace of human occupation. Only now and again, adding yet another note of sadness to the dreary landscape, a little lake, bare and treeless, without reeds or rushes or brushwood, lying asleep in the bottom of a ravine like another Dead Sea, bars your way with its greenish waters, from which rise at your approach a cloud of aquatic birds uttering long discordant screams. You make a detour; you climb the hill before you, you go down into another valley, you climb another hill, and this goes on and on till finally you come to the end of the range of foothills, which grow gradually lower and lower.

But now, if you make a bend to the south, the landscape recovers all its grandeur again and you catch sight of a new range, higher and more picturesque-looking and more inviting. It is all plumed with woods, and refreshed by countless watercourses. Shade and moisture give back life to the countryside; the tinkle of the hermit's bell is heard, a caravan is seen winding along the hillside. Finally, under the dying rays of the sinking sun, you sight, looking like a covey of white birds crouched side by side, the houses of a village grouped close together to guard against nocturnal attack.

For with life, danger is there again, and it is not now, as in the first range crossed, packs of wolves and bears that are to be feared, but hordes of Moldavian robbers.

However, we drew near our destination in spite of every difficulty. Ten days' constant travelling had sped without accident, and already we could make out the summit of Mount Pion, a giant a whole head taller than his fellow giants, on whose southern slopes lies the Monastery of Sahastru, to which I was bound. Another three days and we stood before the gates.

It was the end of August and the day had been one of blessing heat; the relief was intense when, towards four o'clock, we first began to inhale the fresh evening breeze. We had passed by the ruined towers of Niantzo, and were descending upon a plain just opening to view through a gap in the mountains. We could already, from the point we had reached, trace the course of the Bistriza, and note its banks besprinkled with red water-poppies and great white campanulas. We were making our way along the brink of a precipice at the foot of which rolled the river, as yet no more than a mountain torrent, our path being barely wide enough to allow our beasts to go two abreast.

The guide went first, perched sideways on his horse, singing a native stave to a monotonous air, the words of which I followed with no small interest and pleasure.

The singer was composer too. As for the tune, one must be a born mountaineer to appreciate to the full its wild melancholy and unsophisticated gloom. The words ran thus:

'In the marsh-lands of Stavila,
Where the fight has oft been sore,
    See yonder dead man lying!
'Tis no son of Illyria,
'Tis a brigand, fell and fierce,
Who beguiled a gentle maid,
    And robbed and burned and slew.

'A bullet sped like a hurricane
And struck the robber low,
    In his throat's a yatagan!
But for three long days, oh mystery,
Beneath the grim and lonely pine,
His warm blood wets the ground
    And strains red the Ovigan.

'His blue eyes shine no more;
Let us away, let none come nigh
    The swamp where the dead thief lies.
'Tis a vampire! The wild wolf
Runs howling from the horrid thing!
In terror o'er the bare hillside
    The vulture wings away.'

Suddenly a gun-shot rang out and a musket ball whistled through the air. The song stopped, and our guide rolled mortally wounded down the precipice, while his horse stood shivering on the brink, peering wonderingly into the depths of the abyss into which his master had disappeared.

Simultaneously a great shouting was raised, and we saw ourselves surrounded by a band of brigands, some thirty strong; we were entirely surrounded. All seized their weapons, and though caught unawares, my companions, being old soldiers inured to action, never lost their heads, but returned the fire vigorously. To give an example myself, I grasped a pistol, and seeing how disadvantageous our present position was, cried: 'Forward!' and spurred my horse in the direction of the level country.

But we had to do with mountaineers, who sprang lightly from rock to rock like very demons of the abyss, firing as they leapt, and never losing the menacing position they had taken up on our flank. Moreover, our attempt at escape had been foreseen. At a spot where the road widened and the mountain formed a small plain, a young chief awaited us at the head of ten or a dozen horsemen. On seeing us, they put their horses to a gallop, and dashed forward to charge us in front, while the rest who were pursuing us slipped down the mountain-sides and surrounded us on every side, so as to cut off our retreat completely.

The situation was very serious; yet, inured as I was from childhood to scenes of strife and bloodshed, I could examine my surroundings without a detail escaping me.

Our adversaries were one and all clad in sheepskins and wore enormous round hats garlanded with wild flowers, after the Hungarian fashion. Each carried a long Turkish firepiece; these they brandished in the air after discharging, uttering barbarous shouts the while. In their belts they had besides a curved sabre and a brace of pistols.

Their leader was a young man of barely twenty-two, with a pale face, long dark eyes and hair falling in ringlets about his shoulder. His costume consisted of the flowing Moldavian gown edged with fur and confined at the waist by a scarf of alternate gold and silken stripes. A curved sabre flashed in his hands, and four pistols glittered in his belt.

During the fight he kept up a string of hoarse, inarticulate cries, which scarcely seemed to belong to human speech; yet they sufficiently expressed his orders, for his men obeyed them implicitly, throwing themselves flat on the ground to avoid our fire, springing up anon to deliver their own, bringing down such as were still capable of defence, finishing off the wounded, and presently turning the fight into a mere butchery. Soon I had seen two-thirds of my defenders fall one after the other. Four only were left, who closed about me, never thinking of asking quarter, which they were certain not to receive, hoping one thing only, to sell their lives as dearly as possible.

Then the young chief gave a cry more expressive than ever, pointing his sabre at us. Doubtless the order was to envelop this final handful in a circle of fire, and shoot us down all together, for the long-barrelled Moldavian muskets covered us simultaneously. I felt our last hour was come; I raised my eyes and hands to heaven in a last supplication, and waited for death.

At this supreme moment I saw another young warrior descend – no, *descend* is not the word; I should say dash down, leaping from rock to rock. Then he halted, standing on a boulder, dominating the whole scene like a statue on its pedestal, and pointing to the field of carnage, pronounced the simple word:

'Enough!'

All eyes looked up at the voice. Each man appeared ready to obey this new leader. One bandit only raised his gun to his shoulder again, and fired.

One of our men gave a cry; the ball had broken his left arm. He turned instantly to rush at the man who had wounded him; but before his horse had taken four paces forward, a flash shone out above our heads, and the mutinous brigand rolled over, his skull shattered by a bullet.

Such a press of strong and varying emotions had brought me to the end of my strength, and I fell fainting to the ground.

When I recovered consciousness I was lying on the grass, my head supported against the knees of a man whose hand, very white and covered with rings, I could see about my waist. Standing in front of me, with arms crossed and his sabre under his arm, was the young Moldavian chieftain who had directed the attack against us.

'Kostaki,' my protector was saying in French and with a tone of authority, 'you must go this instant and draw off your men, and leave me to look after the girl.'

'Brother, brother,' replied the individual to whom these words were addressed, and who appeared to find extreme difficulty in containing himself; 'brother, beware of exhausting my patience. I leave you the Castle, leave the Forest to me. Within the Castle you are master, but here I am all-powerful. Here it would need but one word to compel you to obey me.'

'Kostaki, I am the elder – that is to say, I am master everywhere, in the Castle, no less than in the Forest, there as well as here. Oh yes! I am of the blood of the Brankovans as much a you. 'Tis Royal blood and is wont to be obeyed. I order, and I must be obeyed.'

'You order, you, Gregoriska; your lackeys, yes, but not my soldiers.'

'Your soldiers are brigands, Kostaki – brigands I will have hanged from the battlements of our towers, if they do not give me instant obedience.'

'Well, then, order them, and see if they obey!'

Then I felt my supporter draw away his knees and lay my head down softly against a stone. I followed him anxiously with my eyes, and I saw the same young chief who had tumbled, so to speak, from the skies into the middle of the fight, and whom hitherto I had only been able to catch a glimpse of, having swooned at the very instant he had first spoken.

He was a young man of twenty-four, of tall stature, with great blue eyes in which was legible a remarkable endowment of resolution and determination. His long flaxen hair, characteristic of the Slav race, fell about his shoulders like the Archangel Michael's, framing his young, fresh cheeks; his lips parted in a disdainful smile, showing a double row of pearls; his gaze was the eagle's confronting the lightning.

He was dressed in a kind of tunic of black velvet; a little cap, like that which the painter Raphael wears in his portraits, adorned with an eagle's feather, was on his head; he wore tight breeches and embroidered high boots. Round his waist was a sash containing a hunting-knife, while a shoulder-belt carried a short, double-barrelled carbine, the accuracy of which one of the bandits had just been given an opportunity of appreciating.

He extended his arm, and the gesture seemed to command the obedience even of his brother; he pronounced a few words in Moldavian, and these words appeared to produce a profound impression on the brigands.

Then, using the same language, the young chief spoke in his turn, and I could guess that his words were a mixture of threats and imprecations.

But to all his long and fierce harangue the elder of the two brothers vouchsafed not one word of reply.

The brigands bowed before his imperious glance, and, at a gesture from him, ranged themselves behind us.

'Well, so be it, Gregoriska,' said Kostaki, returning to the French tongue. 'The woman shall not be taken to the cavern, then; but she shall be mine none the less. She is to my taste, I have won her in fight, and I will have her.' And with the words, he darted towards me and lifted me in his arms.

'The woman shall be taken to the Castle, I repeat, and given into my mother's care; and I mean to see it is done,' replied my protector.

'My horse, bring me my horse!' cried Kostaki in Moldavian.

A dozen bandits sprang forward to obey, and led up the horse to their chief.

Gregoriska glanced around him, seized a masterless horse by the bridle, and leapt on its back without touching the stirrups.

Kostaki flung himself into the saddle almost as lightly as his brother, although he still held me in his arms, and dashed off at a gallop.

Gregoriska's steed seemed fired with the same spirit, and kept head and flank steadily on a level with the head and flank of Kostaki's mount.

It was a strange sight, the two horsemen speeding side by side, in gloomy silence, never losing one another for a single instant from view, though without seeming to look, giving the rein to their horses, which pursued a wild and desperate course through woods and amid rocks and precipices.

My head was thrown back so as to let me see Gregoriska's fine eyes fixed upon my own. Kostaki, observing this, raised my head, and I could henceforth see only his dark, sombre gaze, devouring my face. I dropped my lids, but in vain; through their shade I could still feel the same piercing glance penetrating to my inmost bosom and lacerating my heart. Then a strange hallucination took possession of me; I thought I was the lost Lenore of Bürger's famous ballad, in the act of being carried off by the spectral horse and horseman, and presently when I felt we were slackening speed, it was with a feeling of sheer terror I opened my eyes, firmly convinced I should see surrounding me only shattered graveyard crosses and open tombs.

What I did behold was hardly less gloomy, to wit, the inner courtyard of a Moldavian castle built in the fourteenth century.

2
The Castle of Brankovan

Then Kostaki let me slip out of his arms on to the ground, and in another moment got down beside me; but, quick as he had been, he had not been quick enough to anticipate Gregoriska. As the latter had said, within the Castle he was undisputed master.

Seeing the arrival of the two young chiefs and the strange woman they had brought along with them, the servants ran eagerly forward, but though their attentions were divided between Kostaki and Gregoriska, it was plain the greatest obsequiousness, the deepest respect, were reserved for the last named.

Two women approached; Gregoriska gave them an order in Moldavian, and signed me to follow them. The gesture was accompanied by a look expressive of so much respect that I did not hesitate to obey. Five minutes afterwards I was in a bedchamber, which, bare and uncomfortable as it must have appeared to the least exacting of mortals, was manifestly the best the Castle contained.

It was a vast, square apartment, provided with a sort of divan covered with green serge, serving as a seat by day and a bed by night.

Five or six great oak settles, an enormous cupboard or wardrobe, and in one corner of the room a canopied chair resembling a great, richly carved church stall, completed the furniture. As to window curtains or bed hangings, such things were out of the question. The way thither was by a staircase adorned with three statues, more than life-size, of dead and gone Brankovans, standing in niches.

In another few minutes the baggage was brought up, my trunks among the rest. The women offered to help me; but while repairing the disorder produced in my costume by the events of the day, I retained my long riding-habit, as better matching my hosts' personal appointments than any other costume I could have adopted.

Scarcely had I completed these little changes of dress when I heard someone knocking softly at the door.

'Come in,' I said, speaking naturally enough in French, French being, as you are aware, a second mother tongue to us Poles.

Gregoriska appeared, saying, 'Ah, madame, I am happy to know that you speak French!'

'And I too, sir,' I replied, 'I am happy to know that language, since, thanks to my doing so, I have been able to appreciate your generous conduct towards me. It was in that tongue you championed me against the evil designs of your brother, and in the same language I now offer you the expression of my heartfelt gratitude.'

'Thank you, madame. It was no more than natural I should take the side of a woman situated as you were. I was hunting in the mountain when I heard irregular but long-continued firing. I knew it must be a question of some attack by armed violence, and made for the scene of action. I arrived in the nick of time, thanks be to God. But may I ask you now, madame, by what strange chance a lady of distinction like yourself came to expose herself to the risks of our wild mountains?'

'I am a Pole, sir,' I replied. 'My two brothers have just been killed in the war against Russia; my father, whom I felt prepared to defend our Castle against the enemy, has doubtless rejoined them by this time. For myself, I was flying to escape from those scenes of massacre, and seeking, by my father's orders, an asylum in the cloister of Sahastru, where my mother in her youth and under similar circumstances, had found a secure refuge.'

'You are the foe of the Russians; so much the better!' cried the young man, 'this will be a strong point in your favour in our Castle here, and we shall require all our strength to sustain the struggle that is brewing. And now, as I know who you are, learn, madame, who we are; the name Brankovan is not unknown to you, is it, madame?'

I bowed assent.

'My mother is the last Princess of the name, the last descendant of that illustrious chief who was done to death by the Cantimirs, the caitiff courtiers of Peter I. My mother married as her first husband my father, Serban Waivady, a Prince as she was a Princess, but of less illustrious race.

'My father had been brought up at Vienna, where he had learnt to appreciate the advantages of civilisation. He resolved to make a European of me, and we started on travels embracing France, Italy, Spain and Germany.

'My mother – it is not a son's part, I know, to tell you what I am going to, but inasmuch as, for your own safety, it behoves you to know us intimately, you will understand the necessity for the revelation – my mother, who, during the earlier years of my father's absence, when I was still quite a child, had had guilty relations with a party chieftain (this,' added Gregoriska with a laugh, 'is what men who have wantonly attacked you are entitled in our country) – my mother, I saw, who had had guilty relations with a certain Count Giordaki Koproli, half Greek, half Moldavian, wrote to my father, confessing all and asking for divorce, declaring in support of her demand that she could not bear, Brankovan as she was, to continue the wife of man who deliberately day by day was making himself more and more of a stranger to his native land. Alas! my father was never called upon to agree to the request – one that may seem extraordinary to you, but which with us is looked upon as the simplest and most natural thing in the world; he had just died of an aneurism, from which he had long suffered, and it was I who received the letter.

'There was nothing for me to do, beyond expressing my heartfelt wishes for my mother's happiness. This I did in a letter, in which I announced to her the news of her widowhood. In the same letter I begged her permission to continue my travels, and this was readily granted.

'My fixed resolution had been to settle in France or Germany, so as to avoid meeting a man who hated me and for whom I could not possibly feel affection for, that is to say, my mother's second husband. But suddenly one day I received news that Count Giordaki Koproli had been assassinated, by all accounts at the hands of the old Cossack troopers of my father's.

'I hurried home; I loved my mother and understood her present isolation and her natural craving to have beside her at such a moment such persons as were bound to her by close ties of kinship. True she had never shown any very tender affection for me, but still she was my mother. One morning, without a word to announce my arrival, I entered the Castle of my ancestors.

'There I found a young man whom I took at first for a stranger, but whom I learnt later was my brother. This was Kostaki, the child of adultery, now legitimised by my mother's second marriage – Kostaki, the untamable being you have yourself seen, whose passions are his only law, who holds nothing sacred in all the world but his mother, who only obeys me as the tiger does the man that has mastered him by sheer force – and this with a never-ceasing growl of protest in vain hope of one day devouring me.

'Inside the Castle, within the home of the Brankovans and Waivadys, I am still master; but once outside its walls, once in the open country, he is again the savage child of the woods and mountains, resolved to make everything bend to his own iron will. How came he to yield today, what made his men obey another? I cannot say; perhaps force of habit, some relic of traditional respect. I should not care to put my authority to a second proof. Stay here, do not quit this room, this court, in a word the circuit of these walls – and I can guarantee your safety; take one step outside the Castle – and I can promise nothing, except to sacrifice my life in your defence.'

'Then cannot I continue my journey to the Monastery of Sahastru, as my father wished?'

'Try if you will; command, and I shall obey; but the end will be – I shall be left a dead man by the wayside, and you will never reach your destination.'

'What is to be done, then?'

'Best stay here and await events; have patience and profit by circumstances. Recognise that you are fallen into a bandit's den, and that your courage alone can save you, your presence of mind alone release you. My mother, despite her preference for Kostaki, the son of her love, is kind and generous. Moreover, she is a Brankovan, in other words a true princess. You shall be presented to her; she will defend you against the brute passions of Kostaki. Place yourself under her protection; you are fair to look upon and she will love you. Indeed,' he went on, looking at me with an indescribable expression on his face, 'who could see you and not love you? Come now to the hall where supper is prepared and where my mother waits you. Show neither embarrassment nor distrust, and speak Polish – no one understands that tongue here; I will translate your words to my mother, and rest assured I will only say what should be said. Above all, not a word of

You do not know yet all the wiles and subterfuges of the most straightforward of my countrymen. Now come.'

I followed him down the staircase I have described, now lighted by pinewood torches burning in iron hands protruding from the walls. Evidently so unusual an illumination had been made in my honour.

Arrived at the great hall, Gregoriska threw open the door and pronounced a Moldavian word, which I learnt subsequently means 'the stranger'. Hereupon a tall, imposing woman came forward to meet us – the Princess Brankovan.

Her white hair was coiled in plaits about her head, on which rested a little cap of sable, surmounted by an aigrette, sign of her princely origin. She wore a sort of tunic of cloth of gold covered with pearls, falling over a long skirt of Turkish material, trimmed with the same fur as her headdress. In her hand she carried a rosary with amber beads, which she was turning rapidly between her fingers.

Beside her stood Kostaki, wearing the magnificent and imposing Magyar costume which lent him a still stranger and more exotic look than ever. It consisted of a gown of green velvet with ample sleeves, falling below the knee, breeches of red cashmere, and Turkish slippers of morocco leather embroidered in gold; his head was uncovered, and his long locks, so black as to be almost blue, tumbled about his bare neck, confined merely by the slender white line of the edging of a silken shirt.

He gave me an awkward bow, and said a few words in Moldavian which I could not understand.

'You can speak French, brother,' Gregoriska said to him. 'Madame is Polish, and understands the language.' Upon this, Kostaki made some remarks in French, which were all but as unintelligible to me as those he had uttered in Moldavian; but the Princess now extended her hand imperiously, and imposed silence on them both. I could plainly see she was telling her sons it was her place to receive me.

Then she began in Moldavian a speech of welcome, which the expression of her face made it easy to gather the drift of. She signed me to the table, offered me a seat by her side, embraced the whole house in a sweeping gesture, as if to tell me it was all at my disposal; then sitting down first with kindly dignity, she made the sign of the cross and began a prayer.

This ended, all took their places – places determined by etiquette, Gregoriska's being next below mine. I was a stranger, and consequently occupied a place of honour next to Kostaki, who sat beside his mother Smerande.

Gregoriska had likewise changed his dress. He now wore the Magyar tunic like his brother; only his was of garnet-red and his breeches of blue cashmere. A magnificent decoration hung at his neck – the Nisham of the Sultan Mahmoud.

The rest of the household supped at the same table, each in the due subordination given him by his position among the friends or dependents of the family.

The meal was a gloomy one; not once did Kostaki address me, though his brother took pains to converse with me and always in French. As for their mother, she offered me some of every dish herself, with the air of grave solemnity which never left her. Gregoriska had said truly, she was a veritable Princess.

After supper, Gregoriska came forward, and approaching his mother, explained to her in Moldavian the desire I must be feeling to be alone, and how needful rest was for me after the emotions of a day such as I had passed. Smerande bowed her head in assent, reached me her hand, kissed me on the brow, as she might have done to a daughter, and wished me a good night and sound repose in her Castle.

Gregoriska was right; I longed eagerly for a moment's solitude. So I thanked the Princess, who led me to the door of the hall, where I found waiting for me the two women who had previously attended me.

I made my bow to the mistress of the house, saluted her two sons, and retired to the same apartment, the room I had quitted an hour before to come down to supper. Meantime the divan had been converted into a bed, the only change that had been effected.

I thanked my tire-women, and informed them by signs that I would undress myself. On this they left the room at once, with marks of respect that showed they had received orders to obey me implicitly.

I was left alone in the vast apartment, which my light was insufficient even to illuminate from end to end; I could only make out bits at a time, as I moved my candle from place to place, never the whole room at once. The light was strangely blended, the moonbeams entering through the curtainless window, and struggling to diminish the glimmer of my taper.

Besides the door by which I had entered, and which opened on to the staircase, my room possessed two others, but massive bolts attached to these and fastening from inside, sufficed to reassure me on this score.

Next I examined the entrance door. Like the others, it was well provided with means of defence. Then I threw open my window, and found a sheer precipice beneath it.

I saw plainly enough that Gregoriska had made a deliberate choice of this particular chamber to ensure me against danger. Presently, coming back to my divan, I discerned a little note lying on a table by my bedside. I opened it and read in Polish:

'Sleep at ease; you will have nothing to fear, so long as you remain within the Castle walls. – *Gregoriska.*'

I followed the advice given me, and, weariness prevailing over all other feelings, I lay down and fell fast asleep.

3
The Two Brothers

Henceforward I was established at the Castle of Brankovan, and from that moment began the drama I am about to relate.

The two brothers both fell in love with me, each in his own peculiar way.

Kostaki did not wait a day before he told me he loved me, declared I should be his or no one's, swore he would kill me sooner than suffer me to belong to another, no matter who.

Gregoriska said nothing; but he lavished infinite care and solicitude upon me. All the resources of a brilliant education, all the recollections of a youth passed at the most famous Courts of Europe, were laid under contribution to please me. Alas! the task was only too easy; at the first sound of his voice, I had felt that he was the chosen one of my soul; at the first look of his eyes, I had felt my heart was his.

At the end of three months, Kostaki had repeated a hundred times over that he loved me. I detested him. At the end of the same period, Gregoriska had never spoken one word of love, and I knew that, ask me when he might, I should be his, heart and soul.

Kostaki had given up his out-of-door life altogether. He never left the Castle now, having for the time being abdicated his authority in favour of a sort of lieutenant, who came to him from time to time for orders, and disappeared to execute them.

Smerande likewise manifested a passionate affection for me, the intensity of which terrified me. She openly championed Kostaki, and seemed to be more jealous of me than he was himself. Only, as she understood neither Polish nor French, while I knew no Moldavian, she could not well make any pressing appeals to me in her boy's favour. Still she had learnt to say three words in French, which she would repeat to me every time her lips were laid upon my forehead:

'Kostaki aime Hedwig' – Kostaki loves Hedwig.

One day I learnt a terrible piece of news, which seemed to crown my misfortunes. The four men who had survived the fight with the brigands had been released, and had returned to Poland, under pledge that one of them should come back within three months to bring me news of my father's fate. One of the four did so come back, only to tell me our Castle had been taken, set fire to, and utterly destroyed, while my father had been killed in trying to defend it.

I was left all alone in the world. Kostaki redoubled his eager appeals and Smerande her tenderness; but I could now urge my mourning for my father as an obstacle. Kostaki only insisted the more, saying that the more lonely and forlorn I was, the more I needed a protector, while his mother was as importunate or perhaps more importunate than himself.

Gregoriska had spoken to me of the power the Moldavians possess over themselves in cases where they desire to keep their true feelings hid; and he was in himself a living example of this faculty. It was impossible to be more certain of the love of a man than I was of his; yet if I had been asked what proof I had to allege for my certainty, I could have given none. No one, in the Castle, had ever seen his hand touch mine, or his eyes seek mine. Jealousy alone could enlighten Kostaki as to his brother's rivalry, as my love alone could inform me of his love.

Nevertheless, I must admit, this excessive self-control of Gregoriska's troubled me. I believed, I felt he loved me, but how could I be sure? I wanted some tangible proof. I was still in this uncertainty, when one evening, just after I had retired to my room for the night, I heard a soft tapping at one of the two doors I have mentioned before as fastening on the inside. From the way the knocks were given, I guessed it was a friend. I went to the door and asked who was there.

'Gregoriska,' replied a voice whose accents there was little fear of my mistaking.

'What do you want with me?' I asked, trembling all over.

'If you trust me,' cried Gregoriska, 'if you believe me to be a man of honour, grant me what I ask.'

'And what is that?'

'Put out your light, as if you had gone to bed, and in half an hour's time open your door to let me in.'

'Come back in half an hour,' was my only and unhesitating answer. Then I put out my light and waited.

My heart beat violently, for I felt sure it was a question of some all-important eventuality. The half hour slipped by, and I heard the taps repeated more softly even than the first time.

Meanwhile I had withdrawn the bolts, so that I had merely to pull the door open.

Gregoriska came in, and, without his saying a word to that effect, I closed the door behind him and shot the bolts. He stood still a moment, mute and motionless, gesturing me to be silent. Then, assured that no immediate danger threatened us, he led me to the middle of the vast apartment, and, seeing from the way I trembled that I could hardly stand, brought me a chair. I sat down, or rather let myself sink helplessly into it.

'God in Heaven!' I exclaimed, 'what is the matter, and why these excessive precautions?'

'Because my life – though that is nothing – because your life, perhaps, depends upon the conversation we are going to have together.'

In great alarm, I seized his hand in mine, which he lifted to his lips, looking into my eyes the while to ask my pardon for such an act of presumption. I dropped my eyes before his – a confession of self-surrender.

'I love you,' he said in a voice as sweet and melodious as a song; 'do you love me?'

'Yes,' I told him.

'Are you ready to be my wife?'

'Yes.'

He drew his hand across his forehead with a deep-drawn sigh of happiness.

'Then you will not refuse to follow me?'

'I will follow you anywhere and everywhere!'

'You understand, of course,' he went on, 'that we can only win happiness by flight.'

'Oh, yes!' I cried, 'let us fly, let us fly!'

'Hush,' he said, shuddering, 'hush.'

'You are right,' and I went up to him trembling.

'This is what I have done,' he said; 'this is why I have been so long without confessing my love to you. It was because I desired, once secure of your affection, that nothing might have power to hinder our union. I am rich, Hedwig, enormously rich, but after the fashion of the Moldavian nobles – rich in lands, in flocks and herds, in serfs. Well, I have sold to the Monastery of Hango a million francs worth of land, cattle and villages. They have given me three hundred thousand francs of the purchase money in precious stones, a hundred thousand francs in gold, the rest in letters of credit upon Vienna. Will a million be enough for you?'

I pressed his hand. 'Your love would have been enough alone, Gregoriska, be sure of that.'

'Well, now, listen; tomorrow I am going to the Monastery of Hango to make my final arrangements with the Superior. He has horses ready for me; these horses will await us at nine o'clock, in hiding, a hundred paces from the Castle. After supper you are to go up to your room the same as today; the same as today you are to put out your light; the same as today you are to open the door and I will come in. But tomorrow, instead of my going out alone, you are to follow me; we will gain the gate opening on the country, we will find our horses, we will spring on their backs, and by next day's dawn we shall be thirty leagues away.'

'Ah! Why is it not next day's dawn already!'

'Hedwig, my darling!' – and Gregoriska pressed me to his heart; our lips met in a long kiss.

He had well said when I opened my chamber door to him that he was a man of honour; was well aware that without possessing my body, he possessed my heart.

The night passed without my having closed an eye. I pictured myself borne away in his arms as I had been by Kostaki. Only now, the ride which had been so fearful, so appalling, so grim, was a sweet, soft, entrancing motion, the very rapidity of which added a voluptuous charm, for speed has a charm and pleasure of its own. Daylight came at last, and I left my room. I seemed to detect something even more morose than usual in the greeting Kostaki vouchsafed me on my appearance. His smile was more than ironical, it was threatening, sinister. As for Smerande, her attitude seemed much as usual.

In the course of breakfast Gregoriska ordered his horses, without Kostaki paying any attention apparently to the circumstance. About eleven, he took leave of us, announcing that he would not be back before evening, and begged his mother not to delay dinner for him. Then, turning to me, he made his excuses for quitting me so suddenly.

He left the great hall, his brother staring after him until he crossed the threshold. As he did so, a lightning flash of hate and malignity shot from Kostaki's eyes that made me shudder.

The day passed amid such fears and anxieties as may be imagined. I had confided our projects to no living soul, hardly in my prayers had I dared to tell God of them; yet I felt as though these plans were known to all the world, that every look cast my way had power to penetrate my heart and read my inmost thoughts.

Dinner was a veritable torture; sombre and silent. Kostaki scarcely opened his mouth. When he did, it was only to address a curt phrase or two to his mother in Moldavian, and every time the tones of his voice made me shudder in spite of myself.

When I rose to go back to my room, Smerande kissed me as usual, and as she kissed me she spoke the sentence which for quite a week now I had not heard her utter:

'Kostaki loves Hedwig.'

The words pursued me like a threat; arrived in my chamber I seemed to hear a voice of fate still murmuring in my ear, 'Kostaki loves Hedwig,' – but Kostaki's love, Gregoriska had told me so, meant death.

About seven in the evening, as twilight was falling, I saw Kostaki cross the castle court; he wheeled round to look in my direction, but I started back to avoid his seeing me. I felt anxious, for as long as the situation of my window allowed me to follow his movements, I had observed that he was making his way towards the stables. I made bold to unbolt my door, and slipped into the next room, from the window of which I could see perfectly what he was about.

Yes, he was going to the stables. Presently he brought out his favourite horse, saddled the animal with his own hands, and this with a minute care that showed he attached the greatest importance to the smallest details. He wore the same costume as on the day I had first seen him, but on this occasion his only weapon was his sabre. His mount saddled, he cast his eyes once more to my window. Then, not seeing me, he leapt into the saddle, rode out by the same gate by which his brother had left the castle and would return, and away at a hard gallop in the direction of the Monastery of Hango.

Then my heart contracted in a spasm of dread; a fatal presentiment told me that Kostaki was going to meet and confront his brother.

I lingered at the window as long as I could make out the track, which a quarter of a league from the Castle made a bend, and disappeared among the first trees of the forest; but darkness was rapidly descending, and every trace of the road soon became invisible.

I lingered on and on. At last the very excess of my disquietude restored my energy, and as it was evidently in the great hall below that I was likely to receive the first tidings of one or other of the two brothers, I went down thither. My first look was for Smerande; but the calmness of her face told me she was under no special apprehension.

She was giving her orders for the customary supper, and places were laid as usual for the two brothers.

I dared not question anyone – indeed, who could I question? Nobody in the Castle, Kostaki and Gregoriska excepted, could speak either of the only two languages I knew myself.

The slightest sound set me trembling.

Nine o'clock was the ordinary hour for the meal. I had come down at half-past eight; I watched anxiously the minute hand, the movement of which was almost visible on the huge face of the Castle clock. Soon the quarter sounded, sad and solemn; then the hand went on its silent way again, and once more I watched the minutes marked off, slowly but surely.

A few minutes before nine I thought I heard a horse gallop into the courtyard. Smerande heard it too, and turned her head towards the window; but the night was too dark for her to see anything.

If she had but cast one glance at me, how easily she might have guessed what was passing in my heart. We heard but one horse only; indeed what else was to be expected? My heart told me only one horseman would return, but which?

Steps sounded in the ante-chamber – slow, heavy steps that seemed to oppress my soul. The door opened. I saw a shadow outlined in the gloom.

The shadow halted on the threshold. My heart trembled in suspense. The shadow came forward, and as it entered further and further into the lighted rooms I breathed again. Another second of such tension and my heart would have stopped beating.

Gregoriska stood before me, but pale as a dead man. To look at him was to see that something dreadful had happened.

'Is it you, my Kostaki?' asked Smerande.

'No, mother,' answered Gregoriska in a hoarse, toneless voice.

'Ah, it is you, is it?' she now said; 'and how long do you expect your mother to wait for you?'

'Why, mother,' protested Gregoriska, glancing at the time-piece, 'it is only nine o'clock.'

And indeed that moment the hour struck.

'Very true,' said Smerande. 'Where is your brother?'

In spite of myself, I could not help thinking it was the same question God had asked of Cain.

Gregoriska said nothing.

'Has no one seen Kostaki?' questioned Smerande.

The Vater (major-domo), after making inquiries of those around him, answered, 'about seven the Count went to the stable, saddled his horse himself, and set out on the road to Hango.'

At that moment my eyes met Gregoriska's. I cannot tell if it was reality or hallucination, but I seemed to see a drop of blood in the middle of his forehead.

I put my finger slowly to my own brow, indicating the spot where I thought I saw the stain. Gregoriska understood me; he took out his handkerchief and wiped his face.

'Yes, yes,' muttered Smerande.

'He must have fallen in with a bear or a wolf, and gone after it for his diversion.'

'Is that a reason for a son to keep his mother waiting? Where did you leave him, Gregoriska? tell me that.'

'Mother,' replied Gregoriska in a startled but firm voice, 'my brother and I did not set out together.'

'Well and good,' ended Smerande. 'Bring in supper, take your places at table, and shut the gates; those who are still outside must sleep outside.'

The first two orders were executed to the letter. Smerande took her place, while Gregoriska seated himself at her right, and myself at her left. Then the serving-men left the hall to carry out the third, that is, to shut the Castle gates.

At that moment a great noise rose from the courtyard and a terrified domestic dashed into the hall crying:

'Princess, Count Kostaki's horse has just galloped into the bailey riderless and dripping with blood.'

'Alas!' faltered Smerande, rising from her seat, pale and menacing, 'it was in like plight his father's horse came back one night.'

I looked at Gregoriska; he was not pale now, he was livid.

The fact is, Count Koproli's horse had dashed one evening into the Castle yard, dripping with blood, and an hour later the retainers had found his body covered with wounds, and brought it home.

Smerande now took a torch from the hands of one of the serving-men, walked to the door, threw it open, and went down the steps into the courtyard.

The horse, in a state of extreme terror, was being held in by main force by three or four grooms, who were doing all they could to soothe the animal. Smerande drew near, looked at the bloodstained saddle, and presently discovered the horse had received a wound in the face.

'Kostaki has been killed by a blow in front,' she said, 'in a duel, and by a single adversary. Search for the body, my lads; afterwards we will search till we find his murderer.'

As the horse had come back by the Hango gate of the Castle, all the men hurried out the same way, and soon we could see their torches flitting about the fields and diving into the forest, just as the fire-flies flash and gleam on a fine summer's evening in the plains about Nice or Pisa.

Smerande, as though convinced the search would soon be success-ful, stood waiting under the archway. Not a tear flowed from the eyes of the bereaved mother; yet it was plain that despair was tearing her entrails.

Gregoriska was behind her and I was next Gregoriska. On leaving the great hall he had made as if to offer me his arm, but had hesitated, and finally given up the intention, apparently afraid.

In about a quarter of an hour we saw a single torch reappear at the turning of the road, then two more, and finally the whole number. Only now, instead of being dispersed about the country, they were massed round a common centre – which it soon became manifest consisted of a litter and a man stretched upon it.

The funereal band advanced slowly but surely, and in another ten minutes was at the gateway. On observing the unhappy mother waiting for her dead son, the bearers uncovered instinctively, and marched sad and silent into the Castle yard.

Smerande joined the procession, and we came after her. In this order we all reached the great hall, where they laid down the body.

Then, with a gesture of supreme dignity, Smerande beckoned all to draw back, and, going up to the dead man, knelt down before him, parted the long hair which fell like a veil before his face, gazed long at his features, with dry eyes still, then, opening the Moldavian gown he wore, lifted the blood-stained shirt.

The wound was in the right side of the breast, and must have been made by a straight blade and a double-edged one. I remembered I had noticed that very day in Gregoriska's belt the long hunting-knife that served as a bayonet for his carbine.

I looked for the weapon now; but it had disappeared.

Smerande called for water, dipped her handkerchief in it and washed the wound. A gush of bright, fresh, scarlet blood welled up and reddened the lips of the gash.

The whole scene was at once odious and sublime. The vast gloomy hall, thick with the smoke of pine torches, the wild faces, the fiercely gleaming eyes, the strange dresses, the mother gazing at the still warm blood, and reckoning how long her son had been dead, the deep silence, only broken by the sobs of the bandits whose chief Kostaki had been, all was impressive and awe-inspiring to the last degree.

Lastly, Smerande put her lips to her son's brow; then, rising to her full height and tossing back the long coils of her white hair which had become unfastened, she cried, 'Gregoriska, Gregoriska!'

Gregoriska shuddered, shook his head, and coming out of his lethargy, answered, 'Yes, mother?'

'Come here, son, and hear me.'

Gregoriska obeyed with a shudder, but obey he did. The nearer he approached the corpse, the more abundantly did the red blood gush from the wound. Happily Smerande was not looking that way, for at sight of this accusing flood, she would have had no need to look further for the murderer.

'Gregoriska,' she went on, 'I know very well that you and Kostaki were enemies. I know quite well that you are a Waivady by your father, and he a Koproli by his; but through your mother you are both of you Brankovans. I know that you are a man of the Western cities, he a child of the Eastern hills; but still, by virtue of the womb that bore you both, you are brothers. Well! Gregoriska, I would know this, if you mean to lay your brother to rest beside his father without the oath of vengeance having been pronounced; if I may weep my dead in peace and confidence as a woman should, putting my trust in you to punish as a man's part is?'

'Tell me the name of my brother's murderer, madame, and command me; I swear that ere an hour is past, if you so order, he shall have ceased to live.'

'Nay! swear, Gregoriska, swear, under penalty of my curse, do you hear my son? swear the murderer shall die, that you will not leave one stone upon another of his house, that his mother, children, brothers, his wife or his betrothed, shall perish by your hand. Swear, invoking the anger of Heaven upon your head, if you fail to keep the sacred obligation. If you break the oath, be prepared for wretchedness, the execration of your friends, your mother's malediction.'

Gregoriska laid his hand upon the corpse. 'I swear the murderer shall die,' he said.

On this strange oath, of which I and the dead man alone perhaps could grasp the true sense, I saw, or I thought I saw, an appalling progidy follow.

The dead man's eyes opened and fixed themselves on mine with a keener look than I had ever seen in them, and as though the double ray they shot had been a material thing, I felt a red-hot iron pierce to my very heart.

It was more than my strength could bear, and I swooned away.

4
The Cloister of Hango

When I came to myself, I was in my chamber, lying upon my bed, while one of my two tire-women was watching beside me.

I asked where Smerande was, and was told she was praying beside her son's body. Then I asked where Gregoriska was, and learned that he was at the Monastery of Hango.

Flight was needless, for was not Kostaki dead? Marriage was impossible; I could never wed a fratricide.

Three days and three nights dragged by, filled with strange and fantastic dreams. Awake or asleep, I could never lose sight of those two eyes glaring alive and eager in the dead face – a horrid vision!

On the third day Kostaki was to be buried, and early on that day they brought me a full suit of widow's weeds, saying Smerande sent them me. I dressed myself and came downstairs.

The rooms seemed utterly empty; every soul was in the Castle chapel. I made my way thither; and as I crossed the threshold, Smerande, whom I had not seen for three days, came forward to meet me in the doorway.

She looked like a carven image of Grief. Slow as a statue she laid her icy lips on my forehead, and in a voice that seemed to come from the tomb, she pronounced her customary phrase: 'Kostaki loves you.'

You can form no conception of the effect these words produced on me. This declaration of love, made in the present instead of in the past tense, this *loves you* instead of *loved you*, this passion from the world of the dead singling me out among the living, made a profound and terrible impression on my mind.

At the same time a strange, uncanny feeling crept over me that in very deed I was the wife of the dead man, and not the betrothed of the living brother. The coffin yonder drew me to him in spite of myself; I was attracted reluctantly and painfully, as they say a bird is fascinated by a serpent. I looked for Gregoriska, and saw him standing, pale and sad, beside a pillar. His eyes were raised to Heaven; I cannot say if he saw me.

The monks from Hango surrounded the bier, singing the funeral psalms of the Greek rite, sometimes melodious enough, more often harsh and monotonous. I longed to pray too, but the words died upon my lips; my mind was so confounded I seemed to be present at a consistory of demons rather than among a company of priests of God.

When they lifted the body to carry it to the grave, I tried to follow; but my strength failed me. I felt my limbs bend under me, and I leant against the doorway for support. Then Smerande approached me, signing to Gregoriska, who also came up in obedience to the gestures. Smerande addressed me in Moldavian.

'My mother bids me repeat to you word for word what she is going to say,' put in Gregoriska.

Smerande resumed, and when she had ended, he said:

'These are my mother's words,' and, translating into French:

'You weep my son, Hedwig; you loved him, did you not? I thank you for your tears and for your love; henceforward you are my daughter as truly as if Kostaki had been your husband – henceforth you have a country, a mother, a home. We will shed the guerdon of tears we owe the dead, then we will both remember our dignity and show ourselves worthy of him who is no more . . . I, his mother, you his wife! Farewell! return to your chamber; for myself, I will follow my son to his last resting-place. When I come back, I shall shut myself up with my grief, and when you see me again, I shall have conquered it. Rest assured I shall kill it, for I will not have it kill me.'

I could only reply by a groan to those affecting words. I returned to my room, and the funeral procession started and presently disappeared at the bend of the road. The Cloister of Hango was only half a league from the Castle as the crow flies; but irregularities of the ground forced the road to make wide detours, and to anyone following the highway, it was pretty nearly a two hours' journey.

We were in the month of November, and the days were short and chilly. At five in the afternoon it was quite dark. About seven I saw the torches reappear and the mourners returning. All was over; the dead man lay in the tomb of his fathers.

I have already described the strange fancy which had persistently possessed my mind ever since the fatal event which had put us all in mourning, and more particularly since I had seen those eyes, which death had closed, re-open and fix themselves on mine. Tonight, worn out by the emotions of the day, I felt more depressed than ever. I listened to the hours one after the other sounding on the Castle clock, and grew sadder and sadder the nearer the flight of time brought me to the minute when Kostaki must have died.

I heard a quarter to nine strike. Then an extraordinary sensation came over me, a sort of shuddering horror that ran over my whole body and froze it; then along with this an invincible drowsiness obscured my senses, weighed down my bosom and darkened my eyes. I stretched out my arms and stepped backwards to my bed, on which I fell in a half swoon.

Still my senses were not so completely deadened as to prevent my hearing a footstep approaching the door of my chamber. I seemed to notice the door opening, after which I neither saw nor heard anything more.

But I felt a sharp throb of pain at my neck, before I finally relapsed into complete unconsciousness.

At midnight I awoke, to find my lamp still burning. I tried to rise, but I was so weak I had to repeat the effort before I succeeded. However, I fought down this feebleness, and still feeling the same pricking sensation in my neck now that I was awake as I had felt in my sleep, I dragged myself along the walls as far as the mirror and looked at myself.

A pin-prick, or something like it, marked the carotid artery. I thought some insect had bitten me in my sleep, and as I was worn out with fatigue, I lay down and went to sleep again.

Next morning I awoke as usual; and as usual I made to spring out of bed the moment my eyes were open; but I experienced a feeling of extreme exhaustion such as I had felt only once before in my lfe, on the morning after I had been bled. I looked at my face in the glass, and I was struck with my own pallor.

The hours dragged by sad and sombre, and all day long I had an unaccustomed and unaccountable craving to stay where I was, every change of place or position being a weariness of the flesh.

Night came, and they brought me my lamp. My women, or so I understood from their signs, offered to stay with me; but I refused with thanks, and they left me to myself.

At the same time as before I began to feel the same sensations. I endeavoured this time to rise and summon help; but I could not get as far as the door. I heard vaguely the sound of the clock chiming a quarter to nine; then came footsteps, and the door opened. But I could neither hear nor see anything more; as on the first evening, I had fallen back fainting on my bed.

As before I felt a sharp pain at the side of my neck; as before, I roused at midnight, only now I awoke weaker and paler than ever.

Next day the same horrid fancy held undisputed possession of my mind. I had made up my mind to go down to Smerande, weak and feeble as I was, when one of my women came into my room, uttering the name of Gregoriska, who followed her across the threshold.

I tried to get up from my chair to receive him, but fell back again exhausted by the efforts. He gave a cry at the sight, and dashed forward to my assistance; but I had still strength enough left to wave him off.

'What are you come here for?' I asked him.

'Alas!' he said, 'I was coming to bid you farewell! I was coming to tell you that I am leaving a world that is intolerable to me without your love and your presence; I was coming to tell you I am retiring to a cell in the Monastery of Hango!'

'You must forego my presence, but my love is yours still, Gregoriska,' I returned. 'Alas! I love you still, and my great grief is, that henceforth such love is next door to a crime.'

'Then I may hope you will pray for me, Hedwig?'

'Yes; only I shall not have long to pray,' I added.

'What is wrong with you, tell me, and why are you so pale?'

'Wrong – wrong! Nay! doubtless God is taking pity on me, calling me to him.'

Gregoriska came near and took my hand, which I had not the strength to withdraw, and, looking me hard in the face, said:

'This pallor is not natural, Hedwig; what does it mean?'

'If I were to tell you what I think, Gregoriska, you would deem me mad.'

'No, no! tell me, Hedwig. I beseech you, tell me. We are here in a country that is like no other country, in a family that is like no other family. Tell me, tell me all, I beseech you.'

So I told him all – the strange hallucination which came over me at the hour when Kostaki must have died, the horror, the drowsiness, the icy chill, the prostration that laid me fainting on my bed, the sound of footsteps I seemed to hear, the opening door I seemed to see, and then the sharp pang of pain followed by a pallor and exhaustion growing greater day by day.

I had supposed my narrative would strike Gregoriska as merely the first stage of mania, and I concluded it with some natural timidity; but I saw, on the contrary, that he was profoundly impressed by what I had said.

He reflected a moment.

'So you fell asleep,' he asked, 'every evening at a quarter to nine?'

'Yes – in spite of all the efforts I make to resist the drowsiness.'

'Then, you seem to see the door open?'

'Yes – although I always bolt it.'

'Then, you feel a sharp pain in the neck?'

'Yes – though my neck shows scarcely any trace of a wound.'

'Will you let me see this trace?' he asked next.

In reply, I bent my head sideways so as to show the place, which he examined carefully.

'Hedwig,' he said, after a moment's silence, 'Hedwig, do you trust me?'

'Can you ask!' I cried indignantly.

'Do you believe my word?'

'As I believe in the Holy Gospels.'

'Very well, then, Hedwig; on my word, I swear you have not a week to live, unless you agree to do this very day what I am going to tell you . . .'

'And if I agree?'

'If you agree, you will be saved, perhaps.'

'Perhaps?'

But he would say no more.

'Come what may, Gregoriska,' I resumed, 'I will do whatever you bid me to do.'

'Then listen,' he said, 'and above all do not be too much alarmed. In your country, as in Hungary, there is a tradition.'

I shuddered, for I remembered the tradition in question.

'Ah!' he went on, 'then you know what I mean?'

'Yes!' I told him, 'yes, in Poland I have seen persons subject to this horrible fate.'

'You allude to vampires, do you not?'

'Yes, in my childhood I saw a dreadful sight in the cemetery of a village belonging to my father – the exhumation of forty peasants who had died one after the other, all in a fortnight, without an explanation of the cause of death. Seventeen exhibited all the marks of vampirism, that is to say, their bodies were found fresh, rosy, and looking as if still alive; the remainder were their victims.'

'And what was done to deliver the countryside from the scourge?'

'A stake was driven through their hearts, and this done, the bodies burned.'

'Yes, that is what is ordinarily done, but in your case it is not enough. To deliver you from the phantom, I must first know who it is, and, by God! I will know. Yes, if need be, I will fight hand to hand with him, be he who he may.'

'Oh, Gregoriska, you terrify me!' I cried in alarm.

'I said, "be he who he may", and I repeat it. But to bring this awful enterprise to a good end, you must agree to everything I am going to ask you to do.'

'Say on.'

'Be ready at seven this evening; come down to the chapel – and come alone. You must conquer your weakness, Hedwig, you *must*. There we will receive the nuptial benediction. Agree to this, beloved; to defend you efficiently, I must have the right, before God and men, to watch over your safety. We will return here when the rite is complete, and then – and then . . .'

'Oh! Gregoriska,' I ejaculated. 'If it is he, if it is Kostaki, he will kill you!'

'Have no fear, my beloved, my Hedwig; only agree.'

'You may rest assured I shall do whatever you ask.'

'Till tonight, then.'

'Yes, do you whatever is needful; I will second you to the best of my powers. Now go.'

He left me; and a quarter of an hour later, I saw a horseman bounding along the road to the Monastery, and knew it was Gregoriska.

No sooner had he vanished from my sight than I knelt down and prayed such prayers as are never uttered in your lukewarm irreligious Western land; thus occupied, I awaited seven o'clock, offering up to God and the Saints the holocaust of my meditations. I only rose from my knees as the clock struck the hour.

I was weak as a dying woman, pale as the sheeted dead. I threw a long, black veil over my head, and descended the stairs, supporting myself by the walls. I reached the chapel without having encountered a living soul.

Gregoriska was waiting for me there, along with Father Basil, Superior of the Cloister of Hango. My betrothed wore by his side a holy sword, heirloom of an old Crusader who had been at the taking of Constantinople with Villehardouin and Baldwin of Flanders.

'Hedwig,' he said, striking his hand upon his sword, 'with God's good help, here is a weapon will break the spell that threatens your life. Come boldly hither; this holy man is ready, after hearing my confession, to receive and sanctify our marriage vows.'

The ceremony began; never perhaps before had it been performed in simpler and at the same time more solemn guise. The Priest, or *Pope* according to the phraseology of the Greek Church, had neither acolyte nor assistant; with his own hands he placed the wedding crowns upon our heads. Both clad in mourning raiment, we marched about the altar, taper in hand; then Father Basil pronounced the ceremonial words, adding further:

'And now go, my children, and God give you force and courage to wrestle with the Enemy of Mankind. You are armed in your innocence and the justice of your cause; you will overcome the Demon. Go, and Heaven's blessing go with you.'

We kissed the holy books and left the chapel; then for the first time I rested on Gregoriska's arm, and at the touch of his valiant arm, at the contact of his noble heart, life seemed to flow back again into my veins. I felt confident of victory, now that Gregoriska was with me.

Half past eight struck. At the sound, Gregoriska spoke.

'Hedwig,' he said, 'we have no time to lose. Will you go to sleep as usual and slumber through it all? or will you remain up and dressed and see everything?'

'By your side I fear nothing; I will stay awake, I prefer to see it all.'

Gregoriska drew from his bosom a twig of box consecrated by the priest and still wet with holy water, and gave it me.

'Take this branch, ' said he, 'lie down on your bed, repeat thy prayers to the Virgin and wait. Fear nothing, God is with us. Above all, never quit hold of your talisman; with it you can command even the powers of hell. Do not cry nor call for help; pray, wait and hope.'

I lay down on the bed and crossed my hands over my bosom, on which I placed the branch the priest had blessed.

Meantime Gregoriska concealed himself behind the great canopied chair I have described before, which cut off a corner of the room.

I counted the minutes, one by one, and no doubt Gregoriska did the same. The clock struck the three quarters.

Instantly I felt the old drowsiness, the same sensations of horror and icy cold, creeping over me; but I put the holy branch to my lips, and found relief.

Then I heard distinctly the noise of slow and measured footsteps sounding on the stairs and coming nearer and nearer to the door. It opened slowly and noiselessly as if moved by a supernatural force, and then . . .

And then I beheld Kostaki, pale as I had seen him lying on the litter; his long dark hair falling about his shoulders dripped with blood; he wore his usual dress, only it was open at the breast, showing the bleeding wound.

He was dead, a corpse. Flesh, clothes, bearing, were those of a dead man; only the eyes, those awful eyes, were alive.

At the sight, strange to say, instead of an increase of terror, I felt fresh courage. Doubtless God gave me His courage that I might judge my position calmly, and defy the Powers of Evil. At the first step the spectre took towards my bed, I fixed my eyes boldly on his leaden orbs and held out the holy branch at him.

The phantom strove to advance, but a power stronger than his own held him rooted to the spot; he hesitated, muttering:

'Oh, she is not asleep, she knows all.'

He spoke in Moldavian, and yet I understood the sense of his words, as if they had been uttered in a tongue I was familiar with.

We stood face to face, and I could not withdraw my eyes from his. Presently, without needing to turn my head in his direction, I saw Gregoriska come out from behind the canopied stall, looking like the Angel of Destruction, and holding his sword in his right hand. With the left he made the sign of the cross and stepped slowly forwards, his sword's point threatening the spectre. On seeing his brother, Kostaki too drew his sabre with a screech of eldritch laughter; but scarcely had his sabre touched the consecrated steel ere the phantom arm fell back powerless and inert.

Kostaki heaved a sigh full of hatred and despair.

'What would you of me?' he asked his brother.

'In the name of the living God, I adjure you,' said Gregoriska, 'to answer my questions.'

'Speak,' replied the phantom, gnashing his teeth.

'Did I lay wait for you?'

'No.'

'Did I attack you?'

'No.'

'Did I strike you?'

'No.'

'You threw yourself upon my sword point and nothing else. Therefore in the eyes of God and men I am innocent of the crime of fratricide; therefore you have not received a divine mission, but an infernal behest; therefore you have left the tomb, not as a holy shade, but an accursed spectre. I command you, return to your tomb.'

'With her, yes!' cried Kostaki, making a supreme effort to reach and seize me.

'No! alone!' thundered Gregoriska in reply, 'this woman is mine.'
And as he pronounced the words, he touched with the point of his consecrated sword the raw wound in his brother's breast. Kostaki uttered a scream as if a falchion of fire had seared him, and, putting his left hand to his bosom, he took a step back.

Simultaneously, and keeping step by step with his ghostly adversary, Gregoriska advanced upon him; then, his eyes upon the dead man's eyes, his sword at his brother's breast, he began to drive the spectre before him slowly, sternly, solemnly. It was something like the passage of Don Juan and the Commendatore – the spectre recoiling before the consecrated blade and the irresistible will of God's Champion, the latter following him up pace for pace without a word. Both were breathless, both ghastly pale, the living man pushing the dead before him, forcing him to forsake the Castle that was his home in the past, for the tomb, his abiding place henceforth.

Oh, it was a horrid sight, a dreadful, dreadful sight!

And yet, urged by a superior force, a force mysterious, unknown, invisible, not knowing myself what I did, I rose from the bed and followed them. We descended the staircase, our only light Kostaki's blazing eye-balls. We traversed the gallery and the Castle yard; we passed the gate at the same measured pace – the phantom stepping backwards, Gregoriska with outstretched arm, myself behind them both.

The fantastic procession continued for a full hour. The dead man had to be led back to his tomb; only, instead of the beaten road, Kostaki and Gregoriska went straight to their end, paying scant heed to hindrances and obstacles. Indeed these had ceased to exist; beneath their feet rough places grew smooth, torrents dried up, trees fell back, rocks flew open. The same miracle worked for me as for them; but the heavens seemed to my eyes shrouded in a veil of darkness; moon and stars had disappeared and all I could see in the gloom was the flashing of the vampire's eyes of fire.

In this fashion we reached Hango, in this fashion we passed through the hedge of arbutus which fenced in the cemetery. The moment we were inside, I made out through the obscurity the tomb of Kostaki, side by side with his father's. Nothing was hid from me that night. At the edge of the open grave Gregoriska halted, saying,

'Kostaki, all is not yet over for you; a voice from Heaven tells me you will be pardoned if you repent. Promise to go back into your tomb, promise to leave it no more, promise to give God the devotion you have vowed to Hell.'

'Never,' replied Kostaki.

'Repent,' reiterated Gregoriska.

'Never.'

'For the last time, Kostaki, I appeal to you.'

'Never.'

'Well, then, call Satan to your help, as I call God to mine, and we shall see yet once again who will be victorious.'

Two cries rang out simultaneously and the swords crossed amid a myriad sparks; the fight lasted a minute, which seemed a century to me.

Kostaki fell; I saw the terrible sword whirl in the air, I saw it plunged into his body, nailing it to the freshly upturned earth. A last blood-curdling scream, which had nothing human about it, rent the air.

Gregoriska stood still over his adversary, but faintly and staggering. I ran up and caught him in my arms.

'Are you wounded?' I asked him anxiously.

'No,' he answered me, 'but in such a contest, dear Hedwig, 'tis not the wound that kills but the stress and struggle. I have striven with Death, and to Death I belong.'

'Beloved, beloved,' I cried, 'begone from here, and life will come back, perhaps.'

'No,' he said solemnly, 'here is my tomb, Hedwig. But waste no time, take a handful of this earth saturated with his blood and lay it on the bite he gave you; it is the only means to guard you in the future against his odious love.'

I shuddered, but obeyed. Stopping to gather up the blood-stained mould, I saw Kostaki's corpse pinned to the earth; the holy sword was through his heart, and an abundant jet of rich black blood gushed from the wound, as if he had died but an instant before. I kneaded a little mould with the blood, and applied the horrid talisman to my neck.

'Now, Hedwig, my adored Hedwig,' faltered Gregoriska in a thin, weak voice, 'listen heedfully to my last behests. Leave the country at the earliest opportunity; in distance lies your only safety. Father Basil had received my last instructions today, and he will carry them out. Hedwig, a kiss, the last, the only kiss, my Hedwig, before I die' – and with these words on his lips, Gregoriska fell dead beside his brother.

Under any other circumstances, in a graveyard, beside an open tomb, with two corpses lying side by side, I should have gone mad; but, I have already said so, God had given me a strength to match the terrible occurrences which He made me not only witness but play a part in.

I looked about me in search of help, and at that moment I saw the cloister door open, and the monks, Father Basil at their head, advancing towards me, two by two, carrying lighted torches and chanting the prayers of the dead.

Father Basil had just returned to the Monastery, and, foreseeing what had befallen, he had come straight to the cemetery, all his monks with him.

He found me, a living woman, standing over two dead men.

Kostaki's face was disfigured by a last hideous convulsion; but Gregoriska wore a calm and almost smiling aspect. As he had directed, the latter was buried by his sinful brother's side – God's servant keeping watch and ward over the Devil's.

Smerande, when she heard of this fresh calamity and the part I had played in it, desired to see me. She came to visit me at the Cloister of Hango, and learnt from my lips all that had happened that dreadful night.

I told her the fantastic history in all its dreadful details, but she heard me, as Gregoriska had, without a great surprise or horror.

'Hedwig,' she said to me, when I had finished, after a moment's silence, 'strange as the story is you have just told me, yet you have spoken only the plain truth. The race of the Brankovans is accursed to the third and fourth generation, because a Brankovan once killed a priest. But the curse is now run out; for though a wife, you are a virgin, and I am the last of my race. If my son has bequeathed you a million, take it. When I am gone, except for the few pious legacies I propose to leave, you shall have the remainder of my fortune. Now follow your bridegroom's advice, and return with all haste to the countries where God does not suffer the accomplishment of these appalling prodigies. I need no one to help me mourn my sons. Farewell. Take no more heed of me; my lot to come concerns only myself and my God.'

And, kissing me on the brow as of old, she left me, to shut herself up in her bedchamber in the Castle of Brankovan.

A week later I started for France. As Gregoriska had hoped, my nights presently ceased to be haunted by the dreadful phantom. Health returned, and the only penalty remaining from my hideous adventure is this deathly pallor, which accompanies to the tomb every living creature that has once felt the embrace of a Vampire.

The Grave of Ethelind Fionguala

JULIAN HAWTHORNE

*   *   *

One cool October evening – it was the last day of the month, and unusually cool for the time of year – I made up my mind to go and spend an hour or two with my friend Keningale. Keningale was an artist (as well as a musical amateur and poet), and had a very delightful studio built onto his house, in which he was wont to sit of an evening. The studio had a cavernous fire-place, designed in imitation of the old-fashioned fire-places of Elizabethan manor-houses, and in it, when the temperature out-doors warranted, he would build up a cheerful fire of dry logs. It would suit me particularly well, I thought, to go and have a quiet pipe and chat in front of that fire with my friend.

I had not had such a chat for a very long time – not, in fact, since Keningale (or Ken, as his friends called him) had returned from his visit to Europe the year before. He went abroad, as he affirmed at the time, 'for purposes of study,' whereat we all smiled, for Ken, so far as we knew him, was more likely to do anything else than to study. He was a young fellow of buoyant temperament, lively and social in his habits, of a brilliant and versatile mind, and possessing an income of twelve or fifteen thousand dollars a year; he could sing, play, scribble, and paint very cleverly, and some of his heads and figure-pieces were really well done, considering that he never had any regular training in art; but he was not a worker. Personally he was fine-looking, of good height and figure, active, healthy, and with a remarkably fine brow, and clear, full-gazing eye. Nobody was surprised at his going to Europe, nobody expected him to do anything there except amuse himself, and few anticipated that he would be soon again seen in New York. He was one of the sort that find Europe agree with them. Off he went, therefore; and in the course of a few months the rumour reached us that he was engaged to a handsome and wealthy New York girl whom he had met in London. This was nearly all we did hear of him until, not very long afterward, he turned up again on Fifth Avenue, to every one's astonishment; made no satisfactory answer to those who wanted to know how he happened to tire so soon of the Old World; while, as to the reported engagement, he cut short all allusion to that in so peremptory a manner as to show that it was not a permissible topic of conversation with him. It was surmised that the lady had jilted him; but, on the other hand, she herself returned home not a great while after, and, though she had plenty of opportunities, she has never married to this day.

Be the rights of that matter what they may, it was soon remarked that Ken was no longer the careless and merry fellow he used to be; on the contrary, he appeared grave, moody, averse from general society, and habitually taciturn and undemonstrative even in the company of his most intimate friends. Evidently something had happened to him or he had done something. What? Had he committed a murder? or joined the Nihilists? or was his unsuccessful love affair at the bottom of it? Some declared that the cloud was only temporary, and would soon pass away. Nevertheless, up to the period of which I am writing, it had not passed away, but had rather gathered additional gloom, and threatened to become permanent.

Meanwhile I had met him twice or thrice at the club, at the opera, or in the street, but had as yet had no opportunity of regularly renewing my acquaintance with him. We had been on a footing of more than common intimacy in the old days, and I was not disposed to think that he would refuse to renew the former relations now. But what I had heard and myself seen of his changed condition imparted a stimulating tinge of suspense or curiosity to the pleasure with which I looked forward to the prospects of this evening. His house stood at a distance of two or three miles beyond the general range of habitations in New York at this time, and as I walked briskly along in the clear twilight air

I had leisure to go over in my mind all that I had known of Ken and had divined of his character. After all, had there not always been something in his nature – deep down, and held in abeyance by the activity of his animal spirits – but something strange and separate, and capable of developing under suitable conditions into – into what? As I asked myself this question I arrived at his door; and it was with a feeling of relief that I felt the next moment the cordial grasp of his hand, and his voice bidding me welcome in a tone that indicated unaffected gratification at my presence. He drew me at once into the studio, relieved me of my hat and cane, and then put his hand on my shoulder.

'I am glad to see you,' he repeated, with singular earnestness – 'glad to see you and to feel you; and to-night of all nights in the year.'

'Why to-night especially?'

'Oh, never mind. It's just as well, too, you didn't let me know beforehand you were coming; the unreadiness is all, to paraphrase the poet. Now, with you to help me, I can drink a glass of whisky and water and take a bit draw of the pipe. This would have been a grim night for me if I'd been left to myself.'

'In such a lap of luxury as this, too!' said I, looking round at the glowing fire-place, the low, luxurious chairs, and all the rich and sumptuous fittings of the room. 'I should have thought a condemned murderer might make himself comfortable here.'

'Perhaps; but that's not exactly my category at present. But have you forgotten what night this is? This is November-eve, when, as tradition asserts, the dead arise and walk about, and fairies, goblins, and spiritual beings of all kinds have more freedom and power than on any other day of the year. One can see you've never been in Ireland.'

'I wasn't aware till now that you had been there, either.'

'Yes, I have been in Ireland. Yes – ' He paused, sighed, and fell into a reverie, from which, however, he soon roused himself by an effort, and went to a cabinet in a corner of the room for the liquor and tobacco. While he was thus employed I sauntered about the studio, taking note of the various beauties, grotesquenesses, and curiosities that it contained. Many things were there to repay study and arouse admiration; for Ken was a good collector, having excellent taste as well as means to back it. But, upon the whole, nothing interested me more than some studies of a female head, roughly done in oils, and, judging from the sequestered positions in which I found them, not intended by the artist for exhibition or criticism. There were three or four of these studies, all of the same face, but in different poses and costumes. In one the head was enveloped in a dark hood, over-shadowing and partly concealing the features; in another she seemed to be peering duskily through a latticed casement, lit by a faint moonlight; a third showed her splendidly attired in evening costume, with jewels in her hair and ears, and sparkling on her snowy bosom. The expressions were as various as the poses; now it was demure penetration, now a subtle inviting glance, now burning passion, and again a look of elfish and elusive mockery. In whatever phase, the countenance possessed a singular and poignant fascination, not of beauty merely, though that was very striking, but of character and quality likewise.

'Did you find this model abroad?' I inquired at length. 'She has evidently inspired you, and I don't wonder at it.'

Ken, who had been mixing the punch, and had not noticed my movements, now looked up, and said: 'I didn't mean those to be seen. They don't satisfy me, and I am going to destroy them; but I couldn't rest till I'd made some attempts to reproduce – What was it you asked? Abroad? Yes – or no. They were all painted here within the last six weeks.'

'Whether they satisfy you or not, they are by far the best of yours I have ever seen.'

'Well, let them alone, and tell me what you think of this beverage. To my thinking, it goes to the right spot. It owes its existence to your coming here. I can't drink alone, and those portraits are not company, though, for aught I know, she might have come out of the canvas to-night and sat down in that chair.' Then, seeing my inquiring look, he added, with a hasty laugh, 'It's November-eve, you know, when anything might happen, provided it's strange enough. Well, here's to ourselves.'

We each swallowed a deep draught of the smoking and aromatic liquor, and set down our glasses with approval. The punch was excellent. Ken now opened a box of cigars, and we seated ourselves before the fire-place.

'All we need now,' I remarked, after a short silence, 'is a little music. By-the-by, Ken, have you still got the banjo I gave you before you went abroad?'

He paused so long before replying that I supposed he had not heard my question. 'I have got it,' he said, at length, 'but it will never make any more music.'

'Got broken, eh? Can't it be mended? It was a fine instrument.'

'It's not broken, but it's past mending. You shall see for yourself.'

He arose as he spoke, and going into another part of the studio, opened a black oak coffer, and took out of it a long object wrapped up in a piece of faded yellow silk. He handed it to me, and when I had unwrapped it, there appeared a thing that might once have been a banjo, but had little resemblance to one now. It bore every sign of extreme age. The wood of the handle was honey-combed with the gnawings of worms, and dusty with dry-rot. The parchment head was green with mould, and hung in shrivelled tatters. The hoop, which was of solid silver, was so blackened and tarnished that it looked like dilapidated iron. The strings were gone, and most of the tuning-screws had dropped out of the decayed sockets. Altogether it had the appearance of having been made before the Flood, and been forgotten in the forecastle of Noah's Ark ever since.

'It is a curious relic, certainly,' I said. 'Where did you come across it? I had no idea that the banjo was invented so long ago as this. It certainly can't be less than two hundred years old, and may be much older than that.'

Ken smiled gloomily. 'You are quite right,' he said; 'it is at least two hundred years old, and yet it is the very same banjo that you gave me a year ago.'

'Hardly,' I returned, smiling in my turn, 'since that was made to order with a view of presenting it to you.'

'I know that; but the two hundred years have passed since then. Yes; it is absurd and impossible, I know, but nothing is truer. That banjo, which was made last year, existed in the sixteenth century, and has been rotting ever since. Stay. Give it to me a moment, and I'll convince you. You recollect that your name and mine, with the date, were engraved on the silver hoop?'

'Yes; and there was a private mark of my own there, also.'

'Very well,' said Ken, who had been rubbing a place on the hoop with a corner of the yellow silk wrapper; 'look at that.'

I took the decrepit instrument from him, and examined the spot which he had rubbed. It was incredible, sure enough; but there were the names and the date precisely as I had caused them to be engraved; and there, moreover, was my own private mark, which I had idly made with an old etching point not more than eighteen months before. After convincing myself that there was no mistake, I laid the banjo across my knees, and stared at my friend in bewilderment. He sat smoking with a kind of grim composure, his eyes fixed upon the blazing logs.

'I'm mystified, I confess,' said I. 'Come; what is the joke? What method have you discovered of producing the decay of centuries on this unfortunate banjo in a few months? And why did you do it? I have heard of an elixir to counteract the effects of time, but your recipe seems to work the other way – to make time rush forward at two hundred times his usual rate, in one place, while he jogs on at his usual gait elsewhere. Unfold your mystery, magician. Seriously, Ken, how on earth did the thing happen?'

'I know no more about it than you do,' was his reply. 'Either you and I and all the rest of the living world are insane, or else there has been wrought a miracle as strange as any in tradition. How can I explain it? It is a common saying – a common experience, if you will – that we may, on certain trying or tremendous occasions, live years in one moment. But that's a mental experience, not a physical one, and one that applies, at all events, only to human beings, not to senseless things of wood and metal. You imagine the thing is some trick or jugglery. If it be, I don't know the secret of it. There's no chemical appliance that I ever heard of that will get a piece of solid wood into that condition in a few months, or a few years. And it wasn't done in a few years, or a few months either. A year ago to-day at this very hour that banjo was as sound as when it left the maker's hands, and twenty-four hours afterward – I'm telling you the simple truth – it was as you see it now.'

The gravity and earnestness with which Ken made this astounding statement were evidently not assumed. He believed every word that he uttered. I knew not what to think. Of course my friend might be insane, though he betrayed none of the ordinary symptoms of mania; but, however that might be, there was the banjo, a witness whose silent testimony there was no gainsaying. The more I meditated on the matter the more inconceivable did it appear. Two hundred years – twenty-four hours; these were the terms of the proposed equation. Ken and the banjo both affirmed that the equation had been made; all worldly knowledge and experience affirmed it to be impossible. What was the explanation? What is time? What is life? I felt myself beginning to doubt the reality of all things. And so this was the mystery which my friend had been brooding over since his return from abroad. No wonder it had changed him. More to be wondered at was it that it had not changed him more.

'Can you tell me the whole story?' I demanded at length.

Ken quaffed another draught from his glass of whisky and water and rubbed his hand through his thick brown beard. 'I have never spoken to any one of it heretofore,' he said, 'and I had never meant to speak of it. But I'll try and give you some idea of what it was. You know me better than any one else; you'll understand the thing as far as it can be understood, and perhaps I may be relieved of some of the oppression it has caused me. For it is rather a ghastly memory to grapple with alone, I can tell you.'

Hereupon, without further preface, Ken related the following tale. He was, I may observe in passing, a naturally fine narrator. There were deep, lingering tones in his voice, and he could strikingly enhance the comic or pathetic effect of a sentence by dwelling here and there upon some syllable. His features were equally susceptible of humorous and of solemn expressions, and his eyes were in form and hue wonderfully adapted to showing great varieties of emotion. Their mournful aspect was extremely earnest and affecting; and when Ken was giving utterance to some mysterious passage of the tale they had a doubtful, melancholy, exploring look which appealed irresistibly to the imagination. But the interest of his story was too pressing to allow of noticing these incidental embellishments at the time, though they doubtless had their influence upon me all the same.

'I left New York on an Inman Line steamer, you remember,' began Ken, 'and landed at Havre. I went the usual round of sight-seeing on the Continent, and got round to London in July, at the height of the season. I had good introductions, and met any number of agreeable and famous people. Among others was a young lady, a countrywoman of my own – you know whom I mean – who interested me very much, and before her family left London she and I were engaged. We parted there for the time, because she had a Continental trip still to make, while I wanted to take the opportunity to visit the north of England and Ireland. I landed at Dublin about the 1st of October, and, zigzagging about the country, I found myself in County Cork about two weeks later.

'There is in that region some of the most lovely scenery that human eyes ever rested on, and it seems to be less known to tourists than many places of infinitely less picturesque value. A lonely region too: during my rambles I met not a single stranger like myself, and few enough natives. It seems incredible that so beautiful a country should be so deserted. After walking a dozen Irish miles you come across a group of two or three one-roomed cottages, and, like as not, one or more of those will have the roof off and the walls in ruins. The few peasants whom one sees, however, are affable and hospitable, especially when they hear you are from that terrestrial heaven whither most of their friends and relatives have gone before them. They seem simple and primitive enough at first sight, and yet they are as strange and incomprehensible a race as any in the world. They are as superstitious, as credulous of marvels, fairies, magicians, and omens, as the men whom St Patrick preached to, and at the same time they are shrewd, sceptical, sensible, and bottomless liars. Upon the whole, I met with no nation on my travels whose company I enjoyed so much, or who inspired me with so much kindliness, curiosity and repugnance.

'At length I got to a place on the sea-coast, which I will not further specify than to say that it is not many miles from Ballymacheen, on the south shore. I have seen Venice and Naples, I have driven along the Cornice Road, I have spent a month at our own Mount Desert, and I say that all of them together are not so beautiful as this glowing, deep-hued, soft-gleaming, silvery-lighted, ancient harbour and town, with the tall hills crowding around it and the black cliffs and headlands planting their iron feet in the blue, transparent sea. It is a very old place, and has had a history which it has outlived ages since. It may once have had two or three thousand inhabitants; it has scarce five or six hundred to-day. Half the houses are in ruins or have disappeared; many of the remainder are standing empty. All the people are poor, most of them abjectly so; they saunter about with bare feet and uncovered heads, the women in quaint black or dark-blue cloaks, the men in such anomalous attire as only an Irishman knows how to get together, the children half naked. The only comfortable-looking people are the monks and the priests, and the soldiers in the fort. For there is a fort there, constructed on the huge ruins of one which may have done duty in the reign of Edward the Black Prince, or earlier, in whose mossy embrasures are mounted a couple of cannon, which occasionally sent a practice-shot or two at the cliff on the other side of the harbour. The garrison consists of a dozen men and three or four officers and non-commissioned officers. I suppose they are relieved occasionally, but those I saw seemed to have become component parts of their surroundings.

'I put up at a wonderful little old inn, the only one in the place, and took my meals in a dining-saloon fifteen feet by nine, with a portrait of George I (a print varnished to preserve it) hanging over the mantel-piece. On the second evening after dinner a young gentleman came in – the dining-saloon being public property of course – and ordered some bread and cheese and a bottle of Dublin stout. We presently fell into talk; he turned out to be an officer from the fort, Lieutenant O'Connor, and a fine young specimen of the Irish soldier he was. After telling me all he knew about the town, the surrounding country, his friends, and himself, he intimated a readiness to sympathise with whatever tale I might choose to pour into his ear; and I had pleasure in trying to rival his own outspokenness. We became excellent friends; we had up a half-pint of Kinahan's whisky, and the lieutenant expressed himself in terms of high praise of my countrymen, my country, and my own particular cigars. When it became time for him to depart I accompanied him – for there was a splendid moon abroad – and bade him farewell at the fort entrance, having promised to come over the next day and make the acquaintance of the other fellows. "And mind your eye, now, going back, my dear boy," he called out, as I turned my face homeward. "Faith, 'tis a spooky place, that graveyard, and you'll as likely meet the black woman there as anywhere else!"

'The graveyard was a forlorn and barren spot on the hill-side, just the hither side of the fort: thirty or forty rough head-stones few of which retained any semblance of the perpendicular, while many were so shattered and decayed as to seem nothing more than irregular natural projections from the ground. Who the black woman might be I knew not, and did not stay to inquire. I had never been subject to ghostly apprehensions, and as a matter of fact, though the path I had to follow was in places very bad going, not to mention a hap-hazard scramble over a ruined bridge that covered a deep-lying brook, I reached my inn without any adventure whatever.

'The next day I kept my appointment at the fort, and found no reason to regret it; and my friendly sentiments were abundantly reciprocated, thanks more especially, perhaps, to the success of my banjo, which I carried with me, and which was as novel as it was popular with those who listened to it. The chief personages in the social circle besides my friend the lieutenant were Major Molloy, who was in command, a racy and juicy old campaigner, with a face like a sunset, and the surgeon, Dr Dudeen, a long, dry, humorous genius, with a wealth of anecdotical and traditional lore at his command that I have never seen surpassed. We had a jolly time of it, and it was the precursor of many more like it. The remains of October slipped away rapidly, and I was obliged to remember that I was a traveller in Europe, and not a resident in Ireland. The major, the surgeon, and the lieutenant all protested cordially against my proposed departure, but, as there was no help for it, they arranged a farewell dinner to take place in the fort on All-halloween.

'I wish you could have been at that dinner with me! It was the essence of Irish good-fellowship. Dr Dudeen was in great force; the major was better than the best of Lever's novels; the lieutenant was overflowing with hearty good-humour, merry chaff, and sentimental rhapsodies anent this or the other pretty girl of the neighbourhood. For my part I made the banjo ring as it had never rung before, and the others joined in the chorus with a mellow strength of lungs such as you don't often hear outside of Ireland. Among the stories that Dr Dudeen regaled us with was one about the Kern of Querin and his wife, Ethelind Fionguala – which being interpreted signifies "the white-shouldered." The lady, it appears, was originally betrothed to one O'Connor (here the lieutenant smacked his lips), but was stolen away on the wedding night by a party of vampires, who, it would seem, were at that period a prominent feature among the troubles of Ireland. But as they were bearing her along – she being unconscious – to that supper where she was not to eat but to be eaten, the young Kern of Querin, who happened to be out duck-shooting, met the party, and emptied his gun at it. The vampires fled, and the Kern carried the fair lady, still in a state of insensibility, to his house. "And by the same token, Mr Keningale," observed the doctor, knocking the ashes out of his pipe, "ye're after passing that very house on your way here. The one with the dark archway underneath it, and the big mullioned window at the corner, ye recollect, hanging over the street as I might say – "

' "Go 'long wid the house, Dr Dudeen, dear," interrupted the lieutenant; "sure can't you see we're all dying to know what happened to sweet Miss Fionguala, God be good to her, when I was after getting her safe up-stairs – "

' "Faith, then, I can tell ye that myself, Mr O'Connor," exclaimed the major, imparting a rotary motion to the remnants of whiskey in his tumbler. " 'Tis a question to be solved on general principles, as Colonel O'Halloran said that time he was asked what he'd do if he'd been the Dook o' Wellington, and the Prussians hadn't come up in the nick o' time at Waterloo. "Faith," says the colonel, "I'll tell ye – "

' "Arrah, then, major, why would ye be interruptin' the doctor, and Mr Keningale there lettin' his glass stay empty till he hears – The Lord save us! the bottle's empty!"

'In the excitement consequent upon this discovery, the thread of the doctor's story was lost; and before it could be recovered the evening had advanced so far that I felt obliged to withdraw. It took some time to make my proposition heard and comprehended; and a still longer time to put it in execution; so that it was fully midnight before I found myself standing in the cool pure air outside the fort, with the farewells of my boon companions ringing in my ears.

'Considering that it had been rather a wet evening in-doors, I was in a remarkably good state of preservation, and I therefore ascribed it rather to the roughness of the road than to the smoothness of the liquor, when, after advancing a few rods, I stumbled and fell. As I picked myself up I fancied I had heard a laugh, and supposed that the lieutenant, who had accompanied me to the gate, was making merry over my mishap; but on looking round I saw that the gate was closed and no one was visible. The laugh, moreover, had seemed to be close at hand, and to be even pitched in a key that was rather feminine than masculine. Of course I must have been deceived; nobody was near me: my imagination had played me a trick, or else there was more truth than poetry in the tradition that Halloween is the carnival-time of disembodied spirits. It did not occur to me at the time that a stumble is held by the superstitious Irish to be an evil omen, and had I remembered it it would only have been to laugh at it. At all events, I was physically none the worse for my fall, and I resumed my way immediately.

'But the path was singularly difficult to find, or rather the path I was following did not seem to be the right one. I did not recognize it; I could have sworn (except I knew the contrary) that I had never seen it before. The moon had risen, though her light was as yet obscured by clouds, but neither my immediate surroundings nor the general aspect of the region appeared familiar. Dark, silent hill-sides mounted up on either hand, and the road, for the most part, plunged downward, as if to conduct me into the bowels of the earth. The place was alive with strange echoes, so that at times I seemed to be walking through the midst of muttering voices and mysterious whispers, and a wild, faint sound of laughter seemed ever and anon to reverberate among the passes of the hills. Currents of colder air sighing up through narrow defiles and dark crevices touched my face as with airy fingers. A certain feeling of anxiety and insecurity began to take possession of me, though there was no definable cause for it, unless that I might be belated in getting home. With the perverse instinct of those who are lost I hastened my steps, but was impelled now and then to glance back over my shoulder, with a sensation of being pursued. But no living creature was in sight. The moon, however, had now risen higher, and the clouds that were drifting slowly across the sky flung into the naked valley dusky shadows, which occasionally assumed shapes that looked like the vague semblance of gigantic human forms.

'How long I had been hurrying onward I know not, when, with a kind of suddenness, I found myself approaching a graveyard. It was situated on the spur of a hill, and there was no fence around it, nor anything to protect it from the incursions of passers-by. There was something in the general appearance of this spot that made me half fancy I had seen it before; and I should have taken it to be the same that I had often noticed on my way to the fort, but that the latter was only a few hundred yards distant therefrom, whereas I must have traversed several miles at least. As I drew near, moreover, I observed that the head-stones did not appear so ancient and decayed as those of the other. But what chiefly attracted my attention was the figure that was leaning or half sitting upon one of the largest of the upright slabs near the road. It was a female figure draped in black, and a closer inspection – for I was soon within a few yards of her – showed that she wore the calla, or long hooded cloak, the most common as well as the most ancient garment of Irish women, and doubtless of Spanish origin.

'I was a trifle startled by this apparition, so unexpected as it was, and so strange did it seem that any human creature should be at that hour of the night in so desolate and sinister a place. Involuntarily I paused as I came opposite her, and gazed at her intently. But the moonlight fell behind her, and the deep hood of her cloak so completely shadowed her face that I was unable to discern anything but the sparkle of a pair of eyes, which appeared to be returning my gaze with much vivacity.

' "You seem to be at home here," I said, at length. "Can you tell me where I am?"

'Hereupon the mysterious personage broke into a light laugh, which, though in itself musical and agreeable, was of a timbre and intonation that caused my heart to beat rather faster than my late pedestrian exertions warranted; for it was the identical laugh (or so my imagination persuaded me) that had echoed in my ears as I arose from my tumble an hour or two ago. For the rest, it was the laugh of a young woman, and presumably of a pretty one; and yet it had a wild, airy, mocking quality, that seemed hardly human at all, or not, at any rate, characteristic of a being of affections and limitations like unto ours. But this impression of mine was fostered, no doubt, by the unusual and uncanny circumstances of the occasion.

' "Sure, sir," she said, "you're at the grave of Ethelind Fionguala."

'As she spoke she rose to her feet, and pointed to the inscription on the stone. I bent forward, and was able, without much difficulty, to decipher the name, and a date which indicated that the occupant of the grave must have entered the disembodied state between two and three centuries ago.

' "And who are you?" was my next question.

' "I'm called Elsie," she replied. "But where would your honour be going on November-eve?"

'I mentioned my destination, and asked her whether she could direct me thither.

' "Indeed, then, 'tis there I'm going myself," Elsie replied; "and if your honour 'll follow me, and play me a tune on the pretty instrument, 'tisn't long we'll be on the road."

'She pointed to the banjo which I carried wrapped under my arm. How she knew it was a musical instrument I could not imagine; possibly, I thought, she may have seen me playing on it as I strolled about the environs of the town. Be that as it may, I offered no opposition to the bargain, and further intimated that I would reward her more substantially on our arrival. At that she laughed again, and made a peculiar gesture with her hand above her head. I uncovered my banjo, swept my fingers across the strings, and struck into a fantastic dance-measure, to the music of which we proceeded along the path, Elsie slightly in advance, her feet keeping time to the airy measure. In fact, she trod so lightly, with an elastic, undulating movement, that with a little more it seemed as if she might float onward like a spirit. The extreme whiteness of her feet attracted my eye, and I was surprised to find that instead of being bare, as I had supposed, these were incased in white satin slippers quaintly embroidered with gold thread.

' "Elsie," said I, lengthening my steps so as to come up with her, "where do you live, and what do you do for a living?"

' "Sure, I live by myself"; she answered; "and if you'd be after knowing how, you must come and see for yourself."

' "Are you in the habit of walking over the hills at night in shoes like that?"

' "And why would I not?" she asked, in her turn. "And where did your honour get the pretty gold ring on your finger?"

'The ring, which was of no great intrinsic value, had struck my eye in an old curiosity-shop in Cork. It was an antique of very old-fashioned design, and might have belonged (as the vender assured me was the case) to one of the early kings or queens of Ireland.

' "Do you like it?" said I.

' "Will your honour be after making a present of it to Elsie?" she returned, with an insinuating tone and turn of the head.

' "Maybe I will, Elsie, on one condition. I am an artist; I make pictures of people. If you will promise to come to my studio and let me paint your portrait, I'll give you the ring, and some money besides."

' "And will you give me the ring now?" said Elsie.

' "Yes, if you'll promise."

' "And will you play the music to me?" she continued.

' "As much as you like."

' "But maybe I'll not be handsome enough for ye," said she, with a glance of her eyes beneath the dark hood.

' "I'll take the risk of that," I answered, laughing, "though, all the same, I don't mind taking a peep beforehand to remember you by." So saying, I put forth a hand to draw back the concealing hood. But Elsie eluded me, I scarce know how, and laughed a third time, with the same, airy mocking cadence.

' "Give me the ring first, and then you shall see me," she said, coaxingly.

' "Stretch out your hand, then," returned I, removing the ring from my finger. "When we are better acquainted, Elsie, you won't be so suspicious."

'She held out a slender, delicate hand, on the forefinger of which I slipped the ring. As I did so, the folds of her cloak fell a little apart, affording me a glimpse of a white shoulder and of a dress that seemed in that deceptive semi-darkness to be wrought of rich and costly material; and I caught, too, or so I fancied, the frosty sparkle of precious stones.

' "Arrah, mind where ye tread!" said Elsie, in a sudden, sharp tone.

'I looked round, and became aware for the first time that we were standing near the middle of a ruined bridge which spanned a rapid stream that flowed at a considerable depth below. The parapet of the bridge on one side was broken down, and I must have been, in fact, in imminent danger of stepping over into empty air. I made my way cautiously across the decaying structure; but, when I turned to assist Elsie, she was nowhere to be seen.

'What had become of the girl? I called, but no answer came. I gazed about on every side, but no trace of her was visible. Unless she had plunged into the narrow abyss at my feet, there was no place where she could have concealed herself – none at least that I could discover. She had vanished, nevertheless; and since her disappearance must have been premeditated, I finally came to the conclusion that it was useless to attempt to find her. She would present herself again in her own good time, or not at all. She had given me the slip very cleverly, and I must make the best of it. The adventure was perhaps worth the ring.

'On resuming my way, I was not a little relieved to find that I once more knew where I was. The bridge that I had just crossed was none other than the one I mentioned some time back; I was within a mile of the town, and my way lay clear before me. The moon, moreover, had now quite dispersed the clouds, and shone down with exquisite brilliance. Whatever her other failings, Elsie had been a trustworthy guide; she had brought me out of the depth of elf-land into the material world again. It had been a singular adventure, certainly; and I mused over it with a sense of mysterious pleasure as I sauntered along, humming snatches of airs, and accompanying myself on the strings. Hark! what light step was that behind me? It sounded like Elsie's; but no, Elsie was not there. The same impression or hallucination, however, recurred several times before I reached the outskirts of the town – the tread of an airy foot behind or beside my own. The fancy did not make me nervous; on the contrary, I was pleased with the notion of being thus haunted, and gave myself up to a romantic and genial vein of reverie.

'After passing one or two roofless and moss-grown cottages, I entered the narrow and rambling street which leads through the town. This street a short distance down widens a little, as if to afford the wayfarer space to observe a remarkable old house that stands on the northern side. The house was built of stone, and in a noble style of architecture; it reminded me somewhat of certain palaces of the old Italian nobility that I had seen on the Continent, and it may very probably have been built by one of the Italian or Spanish immigrants of the sixteenth or seventeenth century. The moulding of the projecting windows and arched doorway was richly carved, and upon the front of the building was an escutcheon wrought in high relief, though I could not make out the purport of the device. The moonlight falling upon this picturesque pile enhanced all its beauties, and at the same time made it seem like a vision that might dissolve away when the light ceased to shine. I must often have seen the house before, and yet I retained no definite recollection of it; I had never until now examined it with my eyes open, so to speak. Leaning against the wall on the opposite side of the street, I contemplated it for a long while at my leisure. The window at the corner was really a very fine and massive affair. It projected over the pavement below, throwing a heavy shadow aslant; the frames of the diamond-paned lattices were heavily mullioned. How often in past ages had that lattice been pushed open by some fair hand, revealing to a lover waiting beneath in the moonlight the charming countenance of his high-born mistress! Those were brave days. They had passed away long since. The great house had stood empty for who could tell how many years; only bats and vermin were its inhabitants. Where now were those who had built it; and who were they? Probably the very name of them was forgotten.

'As I continued to stare upward, however, a conjecture presented itself to my mind which rapidly ripened into a conviction. Was not this the house that Dr Dudeen had described that very evening as having been formerly the abode of the Kern of Querin and his mysterious bride? There was the projecting window, the arched doorway. Yes, beyond a doubt this was the very house. I emitted a low exclamation of renewed interest and pleasure, and my speculations took a still more imaginative, but also a more definite turn.

'What had been the fate of that lovely lady after the Kern had brought her home insensible in his arms? Did she recover, and were they married and happy ever after; or had the sequel been a tragic one? I remembered to have read that the victims of vampires generally became vampires themselves. Then my thoughts went back to that grave on the hill-side. Surely that was unconsecrated ground. Why had they buried her there? Ethelind of the white shoulder! Ah! why had not I lived in those days; or why might not some magic cause them to live again for me? Then would I seek this street at midnight, and standing here beneath her window, I would lightly touch the strings of my bandore until the casement opened cautiously and she looked down. A sweet vision indeed! And what prevented my realizing it? Only a matter of a couple of centuries or so. And was time, then, at which poets and philosophers sneer, so rigid and real a matter that a little faith and imagination might not overcome it? At all events, I had my banjo, the bandore's legitimate and lineal descendant, and the memory of Fionguala should have the love-ditty.

'Hereupon, having retuned the instrument, I launched forth into an old Spanish love-song, which I had met with in some mouldy library during my travels, and had set to music of my own. I sang low, for the deserted street re-echoed the lightest sound, and what I sang must reach only my lady's ears. The words were warm with the fire of the ancient Spanish chivalry, and I threw into their expression all the passion of the lovers of romance. Surely Fionguala, the white-shouldered, would hear, and awaken from her sleep of centuries, and come to the latticed casement and look down! Hist! see yonder! What light – what shadow is that that seems to flit from room to room within the abandoned house, and now approaches the mullioned window? Are my eyes dazzled by the play of the moonlight, or does the casement move – does it open? Nay, this is no delusion; there is no error of the senses here. There is simply a woman, young, beautiful, and richly attired, bending forward from the window, and silently beckoning me to approach.

'Too much amazed to be conscious of amazement, I advanced until I stood directly beneath the casement, and the lady's face, as she stooped toward me, was not more than twice a man's height from my own. She smiled and kissed her finger-tips; something white fluttered in her hand, then fell through the air to the ground at my feet. The next moment she had withdrawn, and I heard the lattice close.

'I picked up what she had let fall; it was a delicate lace handkerchief, tied to the handle of an elaborately wrought bronze key. It was evidently the key of the house, and invited me to enter. I loosened it from the handkerchief, which bore a faint, delicious perfume, like the aroma of flowers in an ancient garden, and turned to the arched doorway. I felt no misgiving, and scarcely any sense of strangeness. All was as I had wished it to be, and as it should be; the mediæval age was alive once more, and as for myself, I almost felt the velvet cloak hanging from my shoulder and the long rapier dangling at my belt. Standing in front of the door I thrust the key into the lock, turned it, and felt the bolt yield. The next instant the door was opened, apparently from within; I stepped across the threshold, the door closed again, and I was alone in the house, and in darkness.

'Not alone, however! As I extended my hand to grope my way it was met by another hand, soft, slender, and cold, which insinuated itself gently into mine and drew me forward. Forward I went, nothing loath; the darkness was impenetrable, but I could hear the light rustle of a dress close to me, and the same delicious perfume that had emanated from the handkerchief enriched the air that I breathed, while the little hand that clasped and was clasped by my own alternately tightened and half relaxed the hold of its soft cold fingers. In this manner, and treading lightly, we traversed what I presumed to be a long, irregular passageway, and ascended a staircase. Then another corridor, until finally we paused, a door opened, emitting a flood of soft light, into which we entered, still hand in hand. The darkness and the doubt were at an end.

'The room was of imposing dimensions, and was furnished and decorated in a style of antique splendour. The walls were draped with mellow hues of tapestry; clusters of candles burned in polished silver sconces, and were reflected and multiplied in tall mirrors placed in the four corners of the room. The heavy beams of the dark oaken ceiling crossed each other in squares, and were laboriously carved; the curtains and the drapery of the chairs were of heavy-figured damask.

At one end of the room was a broad ottoman, and in front of it a table, on which was set forth, in massive silver dishes, a sumptuous repast, with wines in crystal beakers. At the side was a vast and deep fireplace, with space enough on the broad hearth to burn whole trunks of trees. No fire, however, was there, but only a great heap of dead embers; and the room, for all its magnificence, was cold – cold as a tomb, or as my lady's hand – and it sent a subtle chill creeping to my heart.

'But my lady! how fair she was! I gave but a passing glance at the room; my eyes and my thoughts were all for her. She was dressed in white, like a bride; diamonds sparkled in her dark hair and on her snowy bosom; her lovely face and slender lips were pale, and all the paler for the dusky glow of her eyes. She gazed at me with a strange, elusive smile; and yet there was, in her aspect and bearing, something familiar in the midst of strangeness, like the burden of a song heard long ago and recalled among other conditions and surroundings. It seemed to me that something in me recognized her and knew her, had known her always. She was the woman of whom I had dreamed, whom I had beheld in visions, whose voice and face had haunted me from boyhood up. Whether we had ever met before, as human beings meet, I knew not; perhaps I had been blindly seeking her all over the world, and she had been awaiting me in this splendid room, sitting by those dead embers until all the warmth had gone out of her blood, only to be restored by the heat with which my love might supply her.

' "I thought you had forgotten me," she said, nodding as if in answer to my thought. "The night was so late – our one night of the year! How my heart rejoiced when I heard your dear voice singing the song I know so well! Kiss me – my lips are cold!"

'Cold indeed they were – cold as the lips of death. But the warmth of my own seemed to revive them. They were now tinged with a faint colour, and in her cheeks also appeared a delicate shade of pink. She drew fuller breath, as one who recovers from a long lethargy. Was it my life that was feeding her? I was ready to give her all. She drew me to the table and pointed to the viands and the wine.

' "Eat and drink," she said. "You have travelled far, and you need food."

' "Will you eat and drink with me?" said I, pouring out the wine.

' "You are the only nourishment I want," was her answer. "This wine is thin and cold. Give me wine as red as your blood and as warm, and I will drain a goblet to the dregs."

'At these words, I know not why, a slight shiver passed through me.

She seemed to gain vitality and strength at every instant, but the chill of the great room struck into me more and more.

'She broke into a fantastic flow of spirits, clapping her hands, and dancing about me like a child. Who was she? And was I myself, or was she mocking me when she implied that we had belonged to each other of old? At length she stood before me, crossing her hands over her breast. I saw upon the forefinger of her right hand the gleam of an antique ring.

' "Where did you get that ring?" I demanded.

'She shook her head and laughed. "Have you been faithful?" she asked. "It is my ring; it is the ring that unites us; it is the ring you gave me when you loved me first. It is the ring of the Kern – the fairy ring, and I am your Ethelind – Ethelind Fionguala."

' "So be it," I said, casting aside all doubt and fear, and yielding myself wholly to the spell of her inscrutable eyes and wooing lips. "You are mine, and I am yours, and let us be happy while the hours last."

' "You are mine, and I am yours," she repeated, nodding her head with an elfish smile. "Come and sit beside me, and sing that sweet song again that you sang to me so long ago. Ah, now I shall live a hundred years."

'We seated ourselves on the ottoman, and while she nestled luxuriously among the cushions, I took my banjo and sang to her. The song and the music resounded through the lofty room, and came back in throbbing echoes. And before me as I sang I saw the face and form of Ethelind Fionguala, in her jewelled bridal dress, gazing at me with burning eyes. She was pale no longer, but ruddy and warm, and life was like a flame within her. It was I who had become cold and bloodless, yet with the last life that was in me I would have sung to her of love that can never die. But at length my eyes grew dim, the room seemed to darken, the form of Ethelind alternately brightened and waxed indistinct, like the last flickerings of a fire; I swayed toward her, and felt myself lapsing into unconsciousness, with my head resting on her white shoulder.'

Here Keningale paused a few moments in his story, flung a fresh log upon the fire, and then continued:

'I awoke, I know not how long afterward. I was in a vast, empty room in a ruined building. Rotten shreds of drapery depended from the walls, and heavy festoons of spiders' webs grey with dust covered the windows, which were destitute of glass or sash; they had been boarded up with rough planks which had themselves become rotten with age, and admitted through their holes and crevices pallid rays of light and chilly draughts of air. A bat, disturbed by these rays or by my own movement, detached himself from his hold on a remnant of mouldy tapestry near me, and after circling dizzily around my head, wheeled the flickering noiselessness of his flight into a darker corner. As I arose unsteadily from the heap of miscellaneous rubbish on which I had been lying, something which had been resting across my knees fell to the floor with a rattle. I picked it up, and found it to be my banjo – as you see it now.

'Well, that is all I have to tell. My health was seriously impaired; all the blood seemed to have been drawn out of my veins; I was pale and haggard, and the chill – Ah, that chill,' murmured Keningale, drawing nearer to the fire, and spreading out his hands to catch the warmth – 'I shall never get over it; I shall carry it to my grave.'

Let Loose

MARY CHOLMONDELEY

*   *   *

A few years ago I took up architecture, and made a tour through Holland, studying the buildings of that interesting country. I had one companion on this expedition, who has since become one of the leading architects of the day. He was a tall grave man, slow of speech, absorbed in his work, and with a certain quiet power of overcoming obstacles which I have seldom seen equalled. A more careless man as to dress I have rarely met, and yet, in all the heat of July in Holland, I noticed that he never appeared without a high starched collar which had not even fashion to commend it at that time.

I often chaffed him about his splendid collars, and asked him why he wore them, but without eliciting any response. One evening as we were walking back to our lodgings in Middleberg I attacked him for about the thirtieth time on the subject.

'Why on earth do you wear them?' I said.

'You have, I believe, asked me that question many times,' he replied, in his slow, precise utterance; 'but always on occasions I was occupied. I am now at leisure, and I will tell you.'

And he did.

I have put down what he said, as nearly in his own words as I can remember them.

Ten years ago, I was asked to read a paper on English Frescoes at the Institute of British Architects. I was determined to make the paper as good as I possibly could, down to the slightest details; and I consulted many books on the subject, and studied every fresco I could find. My father, who had been an architect, had left me, at his death, all his papers and note-books on the subject of architecture. I searched them diligently, and found in one of them a slight unfinished sketch of nearly forty years ago, that specially interested me. Underneath was noted, in his clear small hand – *Frescoed east wall of crypt. Parish Church. Wet Waste-on-the-Wolds, Yorkshire (viâ Pickering).'*

The sketch had such a fascination for me that at last I decided to go there and see the fresco for myself. I had only a very vague idea as to where Wet Waste-on-the-Wolds was, but I was ambitious for the success of my paper; it was hot in London, and I set off on my long journey not without a certain degree of pleasure, with my dog Brian, a large nondescript brindled creature, as my only companion.

I reached Pickering, in Yorkshire, in the course of the afternoon, and then began a series of experiments on local lines which ended, after several hours, in my finding myself deposited at a little out-of-the-world station within nine or ten miles of Wet Waste. As no conveyance of any kind was to be had, I shouldered my little portmanteau, and set out on a long white road, that stretched away into the distance over the bare, treeless wold. I must have walked for several hours, over a waste of moorland patched with heather, when a doctor passed me, and gave me a lift to within a mile of my destination. The mile was a long one, and it was quite dark by the time I saw the feeble glimmer of lights in front of me, and found that I had reached Wet Waste. I had considerable difficulty in getting any one to take me in; but at last I persuaded the owner of the public-house to give me a bed, and quite tired out, I got into it as soon as possible, for fear he should change his mind, and fell asleep to the sound of a little stream below my window.

I was up early next morning, and inquired directly after breakfast for the way to the clergyman's house, which I found was close at hand. At Wet Waste everything was close at hand. The whole village seemed composed of a straggling row of one-storied grey stone houses, the same colour as the stone walls that separated the few fields enclosed from the surrounding waste, and as the little bridges over the beck that ran down one side of the grey wide street. Everything was grey. The church, the low tower of which I could see at a little distance, seemed to have been built of the same stone; so was the parsonage when I came up to it, accompanied on my way by a mob of rough, uncouth children, who eyed me and Brian, with half-defiant curiosity.

The clergyman was at home, and after a short delay I was admitted. Leaving Brian in charge of my drawing materials I followed the servant into a low panelled room in which at a latticed window a very old man was sitting. The morning light fell on his white head bent low over a litter of papers and books.

'Mr Er—?' He said looking up slowly, with one finger keeping his place in a book.

'Blake.'

'Blake,' he repeated after me, and was silent.

'I told him that I was an arhictect; that I had come to study a fresco in the crypt of his church; and asked for the keys.

'The crypt,' he said, pushing up his spectacles and peering hard at me. 'The crypt has been closed for thirty years. Ever since—' and he stopped short.

'I should be much obliged for the keys,' I said again.

He shook his head.

'No,' he said. 'No one goes in there now.'

'It is a pity,' I remarked, 'for I have come a long way with that one object,' and I told him about the paper I had been asked to read, and the trouble I was taking with it.

He became interested. 'Ah!' he said, laying down his pen, and removing his finger from the page before him, 'I can understand that. I also was young once, and fired with ambition. The lines have fallen to me in somewhat lonely places, and for forty years I have held the cure of souls in this place, where truly I have seen but little of the world, though I myself may be not unknown in the paths of literature. Possibly you may have read a pamphlet, written by myself, on the Syrian version of the Three Authentic Epistles of Ignatius?'

'Sir,' I said, 'I am ashamed to confess that I have not time to read even the most celebrated books. My one object in life is my art. *Ars longa, vita brevis*, you know.'

'You are right, my son,' said the old man, evidently disappointed, but looking at me kindly. 'There are diversities of gifts, and if the Lord has entrusted you with a talent, look to it. Lay it not up in a napkin.'

I said I would do so if he would lend me the keys of the crypt. He seemed startled by my recurrence to the subject and looked undecided.

'Why not?' he murmured to himself. 'The youth appears a good youth. And superstition! What is it but distrust in God!'

He got up slowly, and taking a large bunch of keys out of his pocket opened with one of them an oak cupboard in the corner of the room.

'They should be here,' he muttered, peering in; 'but the dust of many years deceives the eye. See, my son, if among these parchments there be two keys; one of iron and very large, and the other steel, and of a long and thin appearance.'

I went eagerly to help him, and presently found in a back drawer two keys tied together, which he recognised at once.

'Those are they,' he said. 'The long one opens the first door at the bottom of the steps which go down against the outside wall of the church hard by the sword graven in the wall. The second opens (but it is hard of opening and of shutting) the iron door within the passage leading to the crypt itself. My son, is it necessary to your treatise that you should enter this crypt?'

I replied that it was absolutely necessary.

'Then take them,' he said; 'and in the evening you will bring them to me again.'

I said I might want to go several days running, and asked if he would not allow me to keep them till I had finished my work, but on that point he was firm.

'Likewise,' he added, 'be careful that you lock the first door at the foot of the steps before you unlock the second, and lock the second also while you are within. Furthermore, when you come out lock the iron inner door as well as the wooden one.'

I promised I would do so, and, after thanking him, hurried away, delighted at my success in obtaining the keys. Finding Brian and my sketching materials waiting for me in the porch, I eluded the vigilance of my escort of children by taking the narrow private path between the parsonage and the church which was close at hand, standing in a quadrangle of ancient yews.

The church itself was interesting, and I noticed that it must have arisen out of the ruins of a previous edifice, judging from the number of fragments of stone caps and arches, bearing traces of very early carving, now built into the walls. There were incised crosses, too, in some places, and one especially caught my attention, being flanked by a large sword. It was in trying to get a nearer look at this that I stumbled, and looking down saw at my feet a flight of narrow stone steps, green with moss and mildew. Evidently this was the entrance to the crypt. I at once descended the steps, taking care of my footing, for they were damp and slippery in the extreme. Brian accompanied me, as nothing would induce him to remain behind. By the time I had reached the bottom of the stairs I found myself almost in darkness, and I had to strike a light before I could find the keyhole and the proper key to fit into it. The door, which was of wood, opened inwards fairly easily, although an accumulation of mould and rubbish on the ground outside showed it had not been used for many years. Having got through it, which was not altogether an easy matter, as nothing would induce it to open more than about eighteen inches, I carefully locked it behind me, although I should have preferred to leave it open, as there is to some minds an unpleasant feeling in being locked in anywhere, in case of a sudden exit seeming advisable.

I kept my candle alight with some difficulty, and after groping my way down a low and of course exceedingly dank passage, came to another door. I noticed that it was of iron, and had a long bolt, which, however, was broken. Without delay I fitted the second key into the lock, and pushing the door open after considerable difficulty, I felt the cold breath of the crypt upon my face. I must own I experienced a momentary regret at locking the second door again as soon as I was well inside, but I felt it my duty to do so. Then, leaving the key in the lock, I seized my candle and looked round. I was standing in a low vaulted chamber with a groined roof, cut out of the solid rock. It was difficult to see where the crypt ended, as further light thrown on any point only showed other rough archways or openings, cut in the rock, which had probably served at one time for family vaults. A peculiarity of the Wet Waste crypt, which I had not noticed in other places of that description, was the beautiful arrangement of skulls and bones which were packed about four feet high on either side. The skulls were symmetrically built up to within a few inches of the top of the low archways on my left, and the shin bones were arranged in the same manner on my right. *But the fresco!* I looked round for it in vain. Perceiving at the further end of the crypt a very low and very massive archway, the entrance to which was not filled up with bones, I passed under it, and found myself in a second much smaller chamber. Holding my candle above my head, the first object its light fell upon was – the fresco, and at a glance I saw that it was unique. Setting down some of my things with a trembling hand on a rough stone shelf hard by, which had evidently been a credence table, I examined the work more closely. It was a reredos over what had probably been the altar at the time the priests were proscribed. The fresco belonged to the earliest part of the fifteenth century, and was so perfectly preserved that I could almost trace the limits of each day's work in the plaster, as the artist had dashed it on, and smoothed it out with his trowel. The subject was the Ascension, gloriously treated. I can hardly describe my elation as I stood and looked at it, and reflected that this magnificent specimen of English fresco painting would be made known to the world by myself. Recollecting myself at last, I opened my sketching bag, and, lighting all the candles I had brought with me, set to work.

Brian walked about near me, and though I was not otherwise than glad of his company in my rather lonely position, I wished several times I had left him behind. He seemed restless, and even the sight of so many bones appeared to exercise no soothing effect upon him. At last, however, after repeated commands, he lay down watchful but motionless on the stone floor.

I must have worked for several hours, and I was pausing to rest my eyes and hands when I noticed for the first time the intense stillness that seemed to surround me. No sound from the outer world reached me. No sound from *me* could reach the outer world. The church clock which had clanged out so loud and ponderously as I went down the steps, had not since sent the faintest whisper of its iron tongue down to me below. All was silent as the grave. This *was* the grave. Those who had come here had indeed gone down into silence. I repeated the words to myself, or rather they repeated themselves to me.

Gone down into silence.

I was awakened from my reverie by a faint sound. I sat still and listened. Bats occasionally frequent vaults and underground places.

The sound continued, a faint, stealthy, rather unpleasant sound. I do not know what kinds of sounds bats make, whether pleasant or otherwise. Suddenly there was a noise as of something falling, a momentary pause – and then – an almost imperceptible but distinct jangle as of a key.

I had left the key in the lock after I had turned it, and I now regretted having done so. I got up, took one of the candles, and went back into the larger crypt, for though I hope I am not made nervous by hearing a noise for which I cannot instantly account, still, on occasions of this kind, I must honestly say I would rather they did not occur. As I came towards the iron door, there was another distinct (I had almost said hurried) sound. The impression on my mind was one of great haste. When I reached the door, and held the candle near the lock to take out the key, I perceived that the other one, which hung by a short string to its fellow, was vibrating slightly. I should have preferred not to find it vibrating, as there seemed no occasion for such a course; but I put them both into my pocket, and turned to go back to my work. As I turned I saw on the ground what had occasioned the louder noise I had heard, namely, a skull which had evidently just slipped from its place on the top of one of the walls of bones, and had rolled almost to my feet. There, disclosing a few more inches of the top of an archway behind, was the place from which it had been dislodged. I stooped to pick it up, but fearing to displace any more skulls by meddling with the pile, and not liking to gather up its scattered teeth, I let it lie, and went back to my work, in which I was soon so completely absorbed that I was only roused at last by my candles beginning to burn low and go out one after another.

Then, with a sigh of regret, for I had not nearly finished, I turned to go. Poor Brian, who had never quite reconciled himself to the place, was almost beside himself with delight. As I opened the iron door he pushed past me, and a moment later I heard him whining and scratching, and I had almost added beating, against the wooden one. I locked the iron door, and hurried down the passage as quickly as I could, and almost before I had got the other one ajar there seemed to be a rush past me into the open air, and Brian was bounding up the steps and out of sight. As I stopped to take out the key I felt quite deserted and left behind. When I came out once more into the sunlight there was a vague sensation all about me in the air of exultant freedom.

It was quite late in the afternoon, and, after I had sauntered back to the parsonage to give up the keys, I persuaded the people of the public house to let me join in the family meal which was spread out in the kitchen. The inhabitants of Wet Waste were primitive people, with the frank, unabashed manner that flourishes still in lonely places, especially in the wilds of Yorkshire; but I had no idea that, in these days of penny posts and cheap newspapers, such entire ignorance of the outer world could have existed in any corner, however remote, of Great Britain.

When I took one of the neighbour's children on my knee, a pretty little girl with the palest aureole of flaxen hair I had ever seen, and began to draw pictures for her of the birds and beasts of other countries, I was instantly surrounded by a crowd of children, and even grown-up people, whilst others came to their doorways and looked on from a distance, calling to each other in the strident unknown tongue which I have since discovered goes by the name of 'Broad Yorkshire.'

The following morning as I came out of my room, I perceived that something was amiss in the village. A buzz of voices reached me as I passed the bar, and in the next house I could hear through the open window a high-pitched wail of lamentation.

The woman who brought me in my breakfast was in tears, and in answer to my questions told me that the neighbour's child, the little girl whom I had taken on my knee the evening before, and plaything of the village, had died in the night.

I felt sorry for the general grief that the little thing's death seemed to cause, and the uncontrolled wailing of the poor mother took my appetite away.

I hurried off early to my work, calling on my way for the keys, and with Brian for my companion descended once more into the crypt, and drew and measured with an absorption that gave me no time that day to listen for sounds real or fancied. Brian, too, on this occasion seemed quite content, and slept peacefully beside me on the stone floor. When I had worked as long as I could, I put away my books with regret that even then I had not quite finished as I had hoped to do. It would be necessary to come again for a short time on the morrow. When I returned the keys late that afternoon, the old clergyman met me at the door, and asked me to come in and have tea with him.

'And has the work prospered?' he asked as we sat down in the long, low room, into which I had just been ushered, and where he seemed to live entirely.

I told him it had, and showed it to him.

'You have seen the original of course?' I said.

'Once,' he replied, gazing fixedly at it. He evidently did not care to be communicative, so I turned the conversation to the age of the church.

'All here is old,' he said. 'When I was young, forty years ago, and came here because I had no means of mine own, and was much moved to marry at that time, I felt oppressed that all was so old; and that this place was so far removed from the world, for which I had at times longings grievous to be borne; but I had chosen my lot, and with it I was forced to be content. My son, marry not in youth, for love, which truly in that season is a mighty power, turns away the heart from study, and young children break the back of ambition. Neither marry in middle life when the talk of a woman is become a weariness, so, you will not be burdened with a wife in your old age.'

I asked if the neighbouring villages were as antiquated as Wet Waste.

'Yes, all about here is old,' he repeated. 'The paved road leading to Dyke Fens is an ancient park road, made even in the time of the Romans. Dyke Fens which is very near here, a matter but of four or five miles, is likewise old, and forgotten by the world. The Reformation never reached it. It stopped here. And at Dyke Fens they still have a priest and a bell, and bow down before the saints. It is a damnable heresy, and weekly I expound it as such to the people, showing them true doctrine; and I have heard that this same priest has so far yielded himself to the Evil One that he has preached against me as withholding Gospel truths from my flock; but I take no heed of it, neither of his pamphlet touching the Clementine Homilies, in which he vainly contradicts that which I have plainly set forth and proven beyond doubt, concerning the word *Asaph*.'

The old man was fairly off on his favourite subject, and it was some time before I could get away. As it was he followed me to the door, and I only escaped because the old clerk hobbled up at that moment, and claimed his attention.

The following morning I went for the keys the third and last time. I had decided to leave early the next day. I was tired of Wet Waste, and a certain gloom seemed to my fancy to be gathering over the place. There was a sensation of trouble in the air, as if, although the day was bright and clear, a storm were coming.

This morning to my astonishment the keys were refused to me when I asked for them. I did not however take the refusal as final, and after a little delay I was shown into the room where as usual the clergyman was sitting, or rather on this occasion was walking up and down.

'My son,' he said with vehemence. 'I know wherefore you have come, but it is of no avail. I cannot lend the keys again.'

I replied that, on the contrary, I hoped he would give them to me at once.

'It is impossible,' he repeated. 'I did wrong, exceeding wrong. I will never part with them again.'

'Why not?'

He hesitated, and then said, slowly –

'The old clerk, Abraham Kelly, died last night.' He paused and then went on: 'The doctor has just been here to tell me of that which is a mystery to him. I do not wish the people of the place to know it, and only to me he has mentioned it, but he has discovered plainly on the throat of the old man, and also, but more faintly on the child's, marks as of strangulation. None but he has observed it, and he is at a loss how to account for it. I, alas! can account for it but in one way, but in one way.'

I did not see what all this had to do with the crypt, but to humour the old man, I asked what that way was.

'It is a long story, and haply to a stranger, it may appear but foolishness, but I will even tell it, for I perceive that unless I furnish a reason for withholding the keys you will not cease to entreat me for them.

'I told you at first when you inquired of me concerning the crypt, that it had been closed these thirty years, and so it was. Thirty years ago a certain Roger Despard, even the lord of the manor of Wet Waste and Dyke Fens, the last of his family, which is now, thank the Lord, extinct, died. He was an evil man of a vile life, neither fearing God nor regarding man, and the Lord appeared to have given him over to the tormentors even in this world, for he suffered many things of his vices, more especially from drunkenness, in which seasons, and they were many, he was as one possessed by seven devils, being an abomination to his household, and a root of bitterness to all, both high and low.

'And at last the cup of his iniquity being full to the brim he came to die, and I went to exhort him on his death-bed, for I heard that terror had come upon him, and that evil imaginations encompassed him so thick on every side, that few of them that were with him could abide his presence. But when I saw him I perceived that there was no place of repentance left for him, and he scoffed at me and my superstition, even as he lay dying, and swore there was no God and no angel, and all were damned even as he was. And the next day towards evening the pains of death came upon him, and he raved the more exceedingly, inasmuch as he said he was being strangled by the evil one. Now on his table was his hunting knife, and with his last strength he crept and laid hold upon it, no man withstanding him, and swore a great oath that if he went down to burn in hell, he would leave one of his hands behind on earth, and that it would never rest until it had drawn blood from the throat of another, and strangled him, even as he himself was being strangled. And he cut off his own right hand at the wrist, and no man dared go near him to stop him, and the blood went through the floor, even down to the ceiling of the room below, and thereupon he died.

'And they called me in the night, and told me of his oath, and I counselled that no man should speak of it, and I took the dead hand which none had ventured to touch, and I laid it beside him in his coffin; for I thought it better he should take it with him, so that he might have it, if haply some day after much tribulation he should perchance be moved to stretch forth his hands towards God. But the story got spread about, and the people were affrighted, so when he came to be buried in the place of his fathers, he being the last of his family, and the crypt likewise full, I had it closed, and kept the keys myself, and suffered no man to enter therein any more; for truly he was a man of an evil life, and the devil is not yet wholly overcome, not cast chained into the lake of fire. So in time the story died out, for in thirty years much is forgotten. And when you came and asked me for the keys I was at the first minded to withhold them, but I thought it was a vain superstition, and I perceived that you do but ask a second time for what is first refused; so I let you have them, seeing it was not an idle curiosity, but a desire to improve the talent committed to you, that led you to require them.'

The old man stopped, and I remained silent, wondering what would be the best way to get them just once more.

'Surely, sir,' I said at last, 'one so cultivated and deeply read as yourself cannot be biassed by an idle superstition.'

'I trust not,' he replied, 'and yet – it is a strange thing that since the crypt was opened two people have died, and the mark is plain upon the throat of the old man, and visible on the young child. No blood was drawn, but the second time the grip was stronger than the first. The third time, perchance – '

'Superstition such as that,' I said with authority, 'is an entire want of faith in God. You once said so yourself.'

I took a high moral tone which is often efficacious with conscientious humble-minded people.

He agreed, and accused himself of not having faith as a grain of mustard seed, but even when I had got him as far as that, I had a severe struggle for the keys. It was only when I finally explained to him that if any malign influence *had* been let loose the first day, at any rate, it was out now for good or evil, and no further going or coming of mine could make any different, that I finally gained my point. I was young, and he was old; and, being somewhat shaken by what had occurred, he gave in at last, and I wrested the keys from him.

I will not deny that I went down the steps that day with a vague, undefinable repugnance, which was only accentuated by the closing of the two doors behind me. I remembered then, for the first time, the faint jangling of the key, and other sounds which I had noticed the first day, and how one of the skulls had fallen. I went to the place where it still lay. I have already said these walls of skulls were built up so high as to be within a few inches of the top of the low archways that led into more distant portions of the vault. The displacement of the skull in question had left a small hole, just large enough for me to put my hand through. I noticed for the first time, over the archway above it, a carved coat of arms, and the name, now almost obliterated, of Despard. This, no doubt, was the Despard vault. I could not resist moving a few more skulls and looking in, holding my candle as near the aperture as I could. The vault was full. Piled high, one upon another, were old coffins, and remnants of coffins, and strewn bones. I think when I come to die, I would rather go home to the earth, than try to keep up appearances in a vault. The coffin nearest the archway alone was intact, save for a large crack across the lid. I could not get a ray from my candle to fall on the brass plates, but I felt no doubt this was the coffin of the wicked Sir Roger. I put back the skulls, including the one which had rolled down, and carefully finished my work. I was not there much more than an hour, but I was glad to get away.

If I could have left Wet Waste that day, I should have done so, for I had a totally unreasonable longing to leave the place; but I found that only one train stopped during the day at the station from which I had come, and that it would not be possible to be in time for it that day.

Accordingly I submitted to the inevitable, and wandered about with Brian for the remainder of the afternoon, and until late into the evening, sketching and smoking. The day was oppressively hot, and even after the sun had set across the burnt stretches of the wolds, it seemed to grow very little cooler. Not a breath stirred. In the evening, when I was tired of loitering in the lanes, I went up to my own room, and, after contemplating afresh my finished study of the fresco, I suddenly set to work to write the part of my paper bearing upon it. As a rule I write with difficulty, but that evening words came to me with winged speed, and with them a hovering impression that I must make haste, that I was much pressed for time. I wrote and wrote, until my candles guttered out, and left me trying to finish by the day.

I had to put away my MS., and feeling it was too early to go to bed, for the church clock was just counting out ten, I sat down by the open window and leaned out to try and catch a breath of air. It was a lovely night, and as I looked out my nervous haste and hurry of mind died down. The moon was sailing clear and tranquil over a fleckless sky; was touching the rugged village, the mist-dimmed trees, and ghostly wolds beyond, with a glory of her own.

The little stream below my window was not all that a stream should be. In the day time, fleets of unseaworthy refuse constantly hurried down it; it owned to dead kittens in the shallow places; but to-night it looked innocent and clear, under the loving eye of the moon that saw it, not as it was, but as it ought to be.

I sat a long time leaning against the window-sill. The heat was still intense. I am not, as a rule, easily elated or ready cast down, but as I sat that night in the lonely village on the moors, with Brian's head against my knee, how or why I know not, a great depression gradually came upon me.

My mind went back to the crypt and the countless dead who had been laid there. The sight of the goal to which all human life, and strength, and beauty, travel in the end, had not affected me at the time, but now, the very air about me seemed heavy with death.

What was the good, I asked myself, of working and toiling, and grinding down my heart and youth in the mill of long and strenuous effort; seeing that in the grave folly and talent, idleness and labour lie together, and are alike forgotten. Labour seemed to stretch before me till my heart ached to think of it, to stretch before me even to the end of life, and then came, as the recompense of my labour – the grave. Even if I succeeded, if after wearing my life threadbare with toil, I succeeded, what remained to me in the end? The grave. A little sooner, while the hands and eyes were still strong to labour, or a little later when all power and vision had been taken from them; sooner or later only – *the grave.*

I roused myself at last, when the moon came to look in upon me where I sat, and, leaving the window open, I pulled myself together, and went to bed.

I fell asleep almost immediately, but I do not fancy I could have been asleep very long when I was wakened by Brian. He was growling in a low muffled tone, as he sometimes did in his sleep, when his nose was buried in his rug. I called out to him to shut up, and as he did not do so, turned in bed to find my match box or something to throw at him. The moonlight was still in the room, and as I looked at him, I saw him raise his head and evidently wake up. I admonished him, and was just on the point of falling asleep when he began to growl again in a low savage manner that waked me most effectually. Presently he shook himself and got up, and began prowling about the room. I sat up in bed and called to him, but he paid no attention. Suddenly I saw him stop short in the moonlight; he showed his teeth, and crouched down, his eyes following something in the air. I looked at him in horror. Was he going mad? His eyes were glaring and his head moved slightly as if he were following the rapid movements of an enemy. Then with a furious snarl, he suddenly sprang from the ground, and rushed in great leaps across the room towards me, dashing himself against the furniture, his eyes rolling, snatching and tearing wildly in the air with his teeth. I saw he had gone mad. I leaped out of bed, and rushing at him caught him by the throat. The moon had gone behind a cloud, but in the darkness I felt him turn upon me, felt him rise up, and his teeth close in my throat. I was being strangled. With all the strength of despair I kept my grip of his neck, and dragging him across the room tried to crush in his head against the iron rail of my bedstead. It was my only chance. I felt the blood running down my neck. I was suffocating. After one moment of frightful struggle I beat his head against the bar, and heard his skull give way. I felt him give one strong shudder, a groan, and then I fainted away.

When I came to myself I was lying on the floor, surrounded by the people of the house, my reddened hands still clutching Brian's throat. Some one was holding a candle towards me, and the draught from the window made it flare and waver. I looked at Brian. He was stone dead. The blood from his great battered head was trickling slowly over my hands. His great jaw was fixed in something that – in the uncertain light – I could not see.

They turned the light a little.

'Oh God!' I shrieked. 'There! Look! look!'

'He's off his head,' said some one, and I fainted again.

I was ill for about a fortnight without regaining consciousness, a waste of time of which even now I cannot think without poignant regret. When I did recover consciousness I found I was being carefully nursed by the old clergyman and the people of the house. I have often heard the unkindness of the world in general inveighed against, but for my part I can honestly say that I have received many more kindnesses than I have time to repay. Country people especially are remarkably attentive to strangers in illness.

I could not rest until I had seen the doctor who attended me, and had received his assurance that I should be equal to reading my paper on the appointed day. This pressing anxiety removed, I told him of what I had seen before I fainted the second time. He listened attentively, and then assured me, in a manner than was intended to be soothing, that I was suffering from an hallucination, due, no doubt, to the shock of my dog's sudden madness.

'Did you see the dog after it was dead?' I asked.

He said he did. The whole jaw was covered with blood and foam; the teeth certainly seemed convulsively fixed, but the case being evidently one of extraordinary virulent hydrophobia, owing to the intense heat, he had had the body buried immediately.

My companion stopped speaking as we reached our lodgings, and went upstairs. Then, lighting a candle, he slowly turned down his collar.

'You see I have the marks still,' he said; 'but I have no fear of dying of hydrophobia. I am told such peculiar scars could not have been made by the teeth of a dog. If you look closely you see the pressure of the five fingers. That is the reason why I wear high collars.'

A True Story of a Vampire

COUNT ERIC STENBOCK

*   *   *

Vampire stories are generally located in Styria; mine is also. Styria is by no means the romantic kind of place described by those who have certainly never been there. It is a flat, uninteresting country, only celebrated for its turkeys, its capons, and the stupidity of its inhabitants. Vampires generally arrive at night, in carriages drawn by two black horses.

Our Vampire arrived by the commonplace means of the railway train, and in the afternoon. You must think I am joking, or perhaps that by the word 'Vampire' I mean a financial vampire. No, I am quite serious. The Vampire of whom I am speaking, who laid waste to our hearth and home, was a *real* vampire.

Vampires are generally described as dark, sinister-looking, and singularly handsome. Our Vampire was, on the contrary, rather fair, and certainly was not at first sight sinister-looking, and though decidedly attractive in appearance, not what one would call singularly handsome.

Yes, he desolated our home, killed my brother – the one object of my adoration – also my dear father. Yet, at the same time, I must say that I myself came under the spell of his fascination, and, in spite of all, have no ill-will towards him now.

Doubtless you have read in the papers *passim* of 'the Baroness and her beasts'. It is to tell how I came to spend most of my useless wealth on an asylum for stray animals that I am writing this.

I am old now; what happened then was when I was a little girl of about thirteen. I will begin by describing our household. We were Poles; our name was Wronski: we lived in Styria, where we had a castle. Our household was very limited. It consisted, with the exclusion of domestics, of only my father, our governess – a worthy Belgian named Mademoiselle Vonnaert – my brother, and myself. Let me begin with my father: he was old and both my brother and I were children of his old age. Of my mother I remember nothing: she died in giving birth to my brother, who was only one year, or not as much, younger than myself. Our father was studious, continually occupied in reading books, chiefly on recondite subjects and in all kinds of unknown languages. He had a long white beard, and wore habitually a black velvet skull-cap.

How kind he was to us! It was more than I could tell. Still it was not I who was the favourite. His whole heart went out to Gabriel – Gabryel as we spelt it in Polish. He was always called by the Russian abbreviation – Gavril – I mean, of course, my brother, who had a resemblance to the only portrait of my mother, a slight chalk sketch which hung in my father's study. But I was by no means jealous: my brother was and has been the only love of my life. It is for his sake that I am now keeping in Westbourne Park a home for stray cats and dogs.

I was at that time, as I said before, a little girl; my name was Carmela. My long tangled hair was always all over the place, and never would be combed straight. I was not pretty – at least, looking at a photograph of me at that time, I do not think I could describe myself as such. Yet at the same time, when I look at the photograph, I think my expression may have been pleasing to some people: irregular features, large mouth, and large wild eyes.

I was by way of being naughty – not so naughty as Gabriel in the opinion of Mlle Vonnaert. Mlle Vonnaert, I may intercalate, was a wholly excellent person, middle-aged, who really did speak good French, although she was a Belgian, and could also make herself understood in German, which, as you may or may not know, is the current language of Styria.

I find it difficult to describe my brother Gabriel; there was something about him strange and superhuman, or perhaps I should rather say praeterhuman, something between the animal and the divine. Perhaps the Greek idea of the Faun might illustrate what I mean; but that will not do either. He had large, wild, gazelle-like eyes: his hair, like mine, was in a perpetual tangle – that point he had in common with me, and indeed, as I afterwards heard, our mother having been of gipsy race, it will account for much of the innate wildness there was in our natures. I was wild enough, but Gabriel was much wilder. Nothing would induce him to put on shoes and stockings, except on Sundays – when he also allowed his hair to be combed, but only by me. How shall I describe the grace of that lovely mouth, shaped verily 'en arc d'amour'. I always think of the text in the Psalm, 'Grace is shed forth on thy lips, therefore has God blessed thee eternally' – lips that seemed to exhale the very breath of life. Then that beautiful, lithe, living, elastic form!

He could run faster than any deer: spring like a squirrel to the topmost branch of a tree: he might have stood for the sign and symbol of vitality itself. But seldom could he be induced by Mlle Vonnaert to learn lessons; but when he did so, he learnt with extraordinary quickness. He would play upon every conceivable instrument, holding a violin here, there, and everywhere except the right place: manufacturing instruments for himself out of reeds – even sticks. Mlle Vonnaert made futile efforts to induce him to learn to play the piano. I suppose he was what was called spoilt, though merely in the superficial sense of the word. Our father allowed him to indulge in every caprice.

One of his peculiarities, when quite a little child, was horror at the sight of meat. Nothing on earth would induce him to taste it. Another thing which was particularly remarkable about him was his extraordinary power over animals. Everything seemed to come tame to his hand. Birds would sit on his shoulder. Then sometimes Mlle Vonnaert and I would lose him in the woods – he would suddenly dart away. Then we would find him singing softly or whistling to himself, with all manner of woodland creatures around him – hedgehogs, little foxes, wild rabbits, marmots, squirrels, and such like. He would frequently bring these things home with him and insist on keeping them. This strange menagerie was the terror of poor Mlle Vonnaert's heart. He chose to live in a little room at the top of a turret; but which, instead of going upstairs, he chose to reach by means of a very tall chestnut-tree, through the window. But in contradiction of all this, it was his custom to serve every Sunday Mass in the parish church, with hair nicely combed and with white surplice and red cassock. He looked as demure and tamed as possible. Then came the element of the divine. What an expression of ecstasy there was in those glorious eyes!

Thus far I have not been speaking about the Vampire. However, let me begin with my narrative at last. One day my father had to go to the neighbouring town – as he frequently had. This time he returned accompanied by a guest. The gentleman, he said, had missed his train, through the late arrival of another at our station, which was a junction, and he would therefore, as trains were not frequent in our parts, have had to wait there all night. He had joined in conversation with my father in the too-late-arriving train from the town: and had consequently accepted my father's invitation to stay the night at our house. But of course, you know, in those out-of-the-way parts we are almost partriarchal in our hospitality.

He was announced under the name of Count Vardalek – the name being Hungarian. But he spoke German well enough: not with the monotonous accentuation of Hungarians, but rather, if anything, with a slight Slavonic intonation. His voice was peculiarly soft and insinuating. We soon afterwards found out he could talk Polish, and Mlle Vonnaert vouched for his good French. Indeed he seemed to know all languages. But let me give my first impressions. He was rather tall with fair wavy hair, rather long, which accentuated a certain effeminacy about his smooth face. His figure had something – I cannot say what – serpentine about it. The features were refined; and he had long, slender, subtle, magnetic-looking hands, a somewhat long sinuous nose, a graceful mouth, and an attractive smile, which belied the intense sadness of the expression of the eyes. When he arrived his eyes were half closed – indeed they were habitually so – so that I could not decide their colour. He looked worn and wearied. I could not possibly guess his age.

Suddenly Gabriel burst into the room: a yellow butterfly was clinging to his hair. He was carrying in his arms a little squirrel. Of course he was bare-legged as usual. The stranger looked up at his approach; then I noticed his eyes. They were green: they seemed to dilate and grow larger. Gabriel stood stock-still, with a startled look, like that of a bird fascinated by a serpent. But nevertheless he held out his hand to the newcomer. Vardalek, taking his hand – I don't know why I noticed this trivial thing – pressed the pulse with his forefinger. Suddenly Gabriel darted from the room and rushed upstairs, going to his turret-room this time by the staircase instead of the tree. I was in terror what the Count might think of him. Great was my relief when he came down in his velvet Sunday suit, and shoes and stockings. I combed his hair, and set him generally right.

When the stranger came down to dinner his appearance had somewhat altered; he looked much younger. There was an elasticity of the skin, combined with a delicate complexion, rarely to be found in a man. Before, he had struck me as being very pale.

Well, at dinner we were all charmed with him, especially my father. He seemed to be thoroughly acquainted with all my father's particular hobbies. Once, when my father was relating some of his military experiences, he said something about a drummer-boy who was wounded in battle. His eyes opened completely again and dilated: this time with a particularly disagreeable expression, dull and dead, yet at the same time animated by some horrible excitement. But this was only momentary.

The chief subject of his conversation with my father was about certain curious mystical books which my father had just lately picked up, and which he could not make out, but Vardalek seemed completely to understand. At dessert-time my father asked him if he were in a great hurry to reach his destination: if not, would he not stay with us a little while: though our place was out of the way, he would find much that would interest him in his library.

He answered, 'I am in no hurry. I have no particular reason for going to that place at all, and if I can be of service to you in deciphering these books, I shall be only too glad.' He added with a smile which was bitter, very very bitter: 'You see I am a cosmopolitan, a wanderer on the face of the earth.'

After dinner my father asked him if he played the piano. He said, 'Yes, I can a little,' and he sat down at the piano. Then he played a Hungarian csardas – wild, rhapsodic, wonderful.

That is the music which makes men mad. He went on in the same strain.

Gabriel stood stock-still by the piano, his eyes dilated and fixed, his form quivering. At last he said very slowly, at one particular motive – for want of a better word you may call it the relâche of a csardas, by which I mean that point where the original quasi-slow movement begins again – 'Yes, I think I could play that.'

Then he quickly fetched his fiddle and self-made xylophone, and did, actually alternating the instruments, render the same very well indeed.

Vardalek looked at him, and said in a very sad voice, 'Poor child! you have the soul of music within you.'

I could not understand why he should seem to commiserate instead of congratulate Gabriel on what certainly showed an extraordinary talent.

Gabriel was shy even as the wild animals who were tame to him. Never before had he taken to a stranger. Indeed, as a rule, if any stranger came to the house by any chance, he would hide himself, and I had to bring him up his food to the turret chamber. You may imagine what was my surprise when I saw him walking about hand in hand with Vardalek the next morning, in the garden, talking livelily with him, and showing his collection of pet animals, which he had gathered from the woods, and for which we had had to fit up a regular zoological gardens. He seemed utterly under the domination of Vardalek. What surprised us was (for otherwise we liked the stranger, especially for being kind to him) that he seemed, though not noticeably at first – except perhaps to me, who noticed everything with regard to him – to be gradually losing his general health and vitality. He did not become pale as yet; but there was a certain languor about his movements which certainly there was by no means before.

My father got more and more devoted to Count Vardalek. He helped him in his studies: and my father would hardly allow him to go away, which he did sometimes – to Trieste, he said: he always came back, bringing us presents of strange Oriental jewellery or textures.

I knew all kinds of people came to Trieste, Orientals included. Still, there was a strangeness and magnificence about these things which I was sure even then could not possibly have come from such a place as Trieste, memorable to me chiefly for its necktie shops.

When Vardalek was away, Gabriel was continually asking for him and talking about him. Then at the same time he seemed to regain his old vitality and spirits. Vardalek always returned looking much older, wan, and weary. Gabriel would rush to meet him, and kiss him on the mouth. Then he gave a slight shiver: and after a while began to look quite young again.

Things continued like this for some time. My father would not hear of Vardalek's going away permanently. He came to be an inmate of our house. I indeed, and Mlle Vonnaert also, could not help noticing what a difference there was altogether about Gabriel. But my father seemed totally blind to it.

One night I had gone downstairs to fetch something which I had left in the drawing-room. As I was going up again I passed Vardalek's room. He was playing on a piano, which had been specially put there for him, one of Chopin's nocturnes, very beautifully: I stopped, leaning on the banisters to listen.

Something white appeared on the dark staircase. We believed in ghosts in our part. I was transfixed with terror, and clung to the banisters. What was my astonishment to see Gabriel walking slowly down the staircase, his eyes fixed as though in a trance! This terrified me even more than a ghost would. Could I believe my senses? Could that be Gabriel?

I simply could not move. Gabriel, clad in his long white night-shirt, came downstairs and opened the door. He left it open. Vardalek still continued playing, but talked as he played.

He said – this time speaking in Polish – *Nie umiem wyrazic jak ciechi kocham* – 'My darling, I fain would spare thee; but thy life is my life, and I must live, I who would rather die. Will God not have any mercy on me? Oh! Oh! life; oh, the torture of life!' Here he struck one agonized and strange chord, then continued playing softly, 'O Gabriel, my beloved! my life, yes *life* – oh, why life? I am sure this is but a little that I demand of thee. Surely thy superabundance of life can spare a little to one who is already dead. No, stay,' he said now almost harshly, 'what must be, must be!'

Gabriel stood there quite still, with the same fixed vacant expression, in the room. He was evidently walking in his sleep. Vardalek played on: then said, 'Ah!' with a sign of terrible agony. Then very gently, 'Go now, Gabriel; it is enough.' And Gabriel went out of the room and ascended the staircase at the same slow pace, with the same unconscious stare. Vardalek struck the piano, and although he did not play loudly, it seemed as though the strings would break. You never heard music so strange and so heart-rending!

I only know I was found by Mlle Vonnaert in the morning, in an unconscious state, at the foot of the stairs. Was it a dream after all? I am sure now that it was not. I thought then it might be, and said nothing to anyone about it. Indeed, what could I say?

Well, to let me cut a long story short, Gabriel, who had never known a moment's sickness in his life, grew ill: and we had to send to Gratz for a doctor, who could give no explanation of Gabriel's strange illness. Gradual wasting away, he said: absolutely no organic complaint. What could this mean?

My father at last became conscious of the fact that Gabriel was ill. His anxiety was fearful. The last trace of grey faded from his hair, and it became quite white. We sent to Vienna for doctors. But all with the same result.

Gabriel was generally unconscious, and when conscious, only seemed to recognize Vardalek, who sat continually by his bedside, nursing him with the utmost tenderness.

One day I was alone in the room: and Vardalek cried suddenly, almost fiercely, 'Send for a priest at once, at once,' he repeated. 'It is now almost too late!'

Gabriel stretched out his arms spasmodically, and put them round Vardalek's neck. This was the only movement he had made for some time. Vardalek bent down and kissed him on the lips. I rushed downstairs: and the priest was sent for. When I came back Vardalek was not there. The priest administered extreme unction. I think Gabriel was already dead, although we did not think so at the time.

Vardalek had utterly disappeared; and when we looked for him he was nowhere to be found; nor have I seen or heard of him since.

My father died very soon afterwards: suddenly aged, and bent down with grief. And so the whole of the Wronski property came into my sole possession. And here I am, an old woman, generally laughed at for keeping, in memory of Gabriel, an asylum for stray animals – and – people do not, as a rule, believe in Vampires!

Grettir at Thorhall-Stead

FRANK NORRIS

*   *   *

I

Glamr

Thornhall the bonder had been to the great Thingvalla, or annual fair of Iceland, to engage a shepherd, and was now returning. It had been a good two-days' journey home, for his shaggy little pony, though sure-footed, was slow. For the better part of three hours on the evening of the second day he had been picking his way cautiously among the great boulders of black basalt that encumbered the path. At length, on the summit of a low hill, he brought the little animal to a standstill and paused a moment, looking off to the northward, a smile of satisfaction spreading over his broad, sober face. For he had just passed the white stone that marked the boundary of his own land. Below him opened the little valley named the Vale of Shadows, and in its midst, overshadowed by a single Norway pine, black, wind-distorted, was the stone farmhouse, the byre, Thorhall's home.

Only an Icelander could have found pleasure in that prospect. It was dreary beyond expression. Save only for the deformed pine, tortured and warped by its unending battle with the wintry gales, no other tree relieved the monotony of the landscape. To the west, mountains barred the horizon – volcanic mountains, gashed, cragged, basaltic, and still blackened with primeval fires. Bare of vegetation they were – sombre, solitary, empty of life. To the eastward, low, rolling sand dunes, sprinkled thinly with gorse, bore down to the sea. They shut off a view of the shore, but farther on the horizon showed itself, a bitter, inhospitable waste of grey water, blotted by fogs and murk and sudden squalls. Though the shore was invisible, it nonetheless asserted itself. With the rushing of the wind was mingled the prolonged, everlasting thunder of the surf, while the taint of salt, of decaying kelp, of fish, of seaweed, of all the pungent aromas of the sea, pervaded the air on every hand.

Black gulls, sharply defined against the grey sky, slanted in long tacking flights hither and thither over sea and land. The raucous bark of the seal hunting mackerel off the shore made itself occasionally heard. Otherwise there was no sign of life. Veils of fine rain, half fog, drove across the scene between ocean and mountain. The wind blew incessantly from off the sea with a steady and uninterrupted murmur.

Thorhall rode on, inclining his head against the gusts and driving wind. Soon he had come to the farmhouse. The servants led the pony to the stables and in the doorway Thorhall found his wife waiting for him. They embraced one another and – for they were pious folk – thanked God for the bonder's safe journey and speedy return. Before the roaring fire of drift that evening Thorhall told his wife of all that had passed at the Thingvalla, of the wrestling, and of the stallion fights.

'And did you find a shepherd to your liking?' asked his wife.

'Yes, a great fellow with white teeth and black hair. Rather surly, I believe, but strong as a troll. He promised to be with me by the beginning of the winter night. His name is Glamr.'

But the summer passed, the sun dipped below the horizon not to reappear for six months, the winter night drew on, snow buried all the landscape, hurricanes sharp as boarspears descended upon the Vale of Shadows; in their beds the dwellers in the byre heard the grind and growl of the great bergs careering onward through the ocean, and many a night the howl of hunger-driven wolves startled Thorhall from his sleep; yet Glamr did not come.

Then at length and of a sudden he appeared; and Thorhall on a certain evening, called hastily by a frightened servant, beheld the great figure of him in the midst of the kitchen floor, his eyebrows frosted yet scowling, his white teeth snapping with cold, while in a great hoarse voice, like the grumble of a bear, he called for meat and drink.

From thenceforward Glamr became a member of Thorhall's household. Yet seldom was he found in the byre. By day he was away with the sheep; by night he slept in the stables. The servants were afraid of him, though he rarely addressed them a word. He was not only feared, but disliked. This aversion was partly explained by Glamr's own peculiar disposition – gloomy, solitary, uncanny, and partly by a fact that came to light within the first month of his coming to the Vale of Shadows.

He was an unbeliever. Never did his broad bulk darken the lich-gate of the kirk; the knolling of the matin and the vesper-bell put him in a season of even deeper gloom than usual. It was noticed that he could not bear to look upon a cross; the priest he abhorred as a pestilence. On holy days he kept far from home, absenting himself upon one pretext or another, withdrawing up into the chasms and gorges of the hills.

So passed the first months of the winter.

Christmas day came, and Christmas night. It was bitter, bitter cold. Snow had fallen since second cockcrow the day before, and as night closed in such a gale as had not been known for years gathered from off the Northern Ocean and whirled shrieking over the Vale of Shadows. All day long Glamr was in the hills with the sheep, and even above the roaring of the wind his bell-toned voice had occasionally been heard as he called and shouted to his charges. At the candle-lighting time he had not returned. The bonder and his family busked themselves to attend the Christmas mass.

Some two hours later they were returning. The wind was going down, but even yet shreds of torn seaweed and scud of foam, swept up by the breath of the gale, drove landward across the valley. The clouds overhead were breaking up, and between their galloping courses one saw the sky, the stars glittering like hoar frost.

The bonder's party drew near the farmhouse, and the servants, going before with lanthorns and pine torches, undid the fastenings of the gate. The wind lapsed suddenly, and in the stillness between two gusts the plunge of the surf made itself heard.

Then all at once Thorhall and his wife stopped and her hand clutched quickly at his wrist.

'Hark! what was that?'

What, indeed? Was it an echo of the storm sounding hollow and faint from some thunder-split crag far off there in those hills toward which all eyes were suddenly turned; was it the cry of a wolf, the clamour of a falcon, or was it the horrid scream of human agony and fury, vibrating to a hoarse and bell-like note that sounded familiar in their ears?

'Glamr! Where is Glamr?' shouted Thorhall, as he entered the byre. But those few servants who had been left in charge of the house reported he had not yet returned.

Night passed and no Glamr; and in the morning the search-party set out toward the hills. Half way up the slope, the sheep – a few of them – were found, scattered, half buried in drifts; then a dog, dead and frozen hard as wood. From it led a track up into the higher mountains, a strange track indeed, not human certainly, yet whether of wolf or bear no one could determine. Some had started to follow when a lad who had looked behind the shoulder of a great rock raised a cry.

There was the body of Glamr. The shepherd was stretched upon his back, dead, rigid. The open eyes were glazed, the face livid; the tongue protruding from the mouth had been bitten through in the last agony. All about the snow was trampled down, and the bare bushes crushed and flattened out. Even the massive boulder near which the body had been found was moved a little from its place. A fearful struggle had been wrought out here, yet upon the body of Glamr was no trace of a wound, no mark of claw or hand. Only among his footprints was mingled that strange track that had been noticed before, and as before it led straight up toward the high part of the mountains.

The young men raised the body of the shepherd and the party moved off toward the kirk and the graveyard. Even though Glamr had shunned the mass, the priest might be prevailed upon to bury him in consecrated ground. But soon the young men had to pause to rest. The body was unexpectedly heavy. Once again, after stopping to breathe, they raised the bier upon their shoulders. Soon another helper was summoned, then another; even Thorhall aided. Ten strong men though they were, they staggered and trembled under that earthly weight. Even in that icy air the perspiration streamed from them. Heavier and still heavier grew the burden; it bore them to the earth. Their knees bowed out from under them, their backs bent. They were obliged to give over.

Later in the day they returned with oxen and a sledge. They repaired to the spot where the body had been left; then stared at each other with paling faces. In the snow at their feet there was the impression made by the great frame of the shepherd. But that was all; the body was gone, nor was there any footprint in the snow other than they themselves had made.

A cairn was erected over the spot, and for many a long day the strange death of the shepherd of the Vale of Shadows was the talk of the countryside. But about a month or so after the death of Glamr a strange sense of uneasiness seemed to invade the household of the byre. By degrees it took possession of first one and then another of the servants and family. No one spoke about this. It was not a thing that could be reduced to words, and for the matter of that, each one believed that he or she was the only one affected. This one thought himself sick; that one believed himself merely nervous. But nevertheless a certain perplexity, a certain disturbance of spirit was in the air.

One evening Thorhall and his wife met accidentally in the passage between the main body of the house and the dairy. They paused and looked at each other for no reason that they could imagine. Thus they stood for several seconds.

'Well,' said Thorhall at length, 'what is it?'

'Ay,' responded his wife, 'Ay, what *is* it?'

'Nothing,' he replied; and she, echoing his words, also answered 'Nothing.'

Then they laughed nervously, yet still looking fixedly into each other's eyes for all that.

'I believe,' said Thorhall the next day, 'that I am to be sick. I cannot tell – I feel no pain – no fever – and yet – '

'And I, too,' declared his wife. 'I am – no, not sick – but distressed. I – I am troubled. I cannot tell what it is. I sometimes think I am *afraid*.'

A week later, on a certain evening just after curfew, the whole family was aroused by a wild shriek as of someone in mortal terror. Thorhall and his wife rushed into the dairy whence the cry came and found one of the maids in a fit upon the floor.

When she recovered she cried out that she had seen at one of the windows the face of Glamr.

II

Grettir

The cold, bright Icelandic summer shone over Thorhall's byre and the Vale of Shadows. There was no cloud in the sky. The void and lonely ocean was indigo blue. But still the prospect was barren, inhospitable. Only a few pallid flowers, hardy bluebells and buttercups, appeared here and there on the sand dunes in the hollows beneath the gorse and bracken. In the lower hills, on the far side of the valley, a tenuous skim of verdure appeared. At times a ptarmigan fluttered in and out of the crevices of these hills searching for blueberries; at times on the surfaces of the waste of dunes a sandpiper uttered its shrill and feeble piping. Always, as ever, the wind blew from off the ocean; always, as ever, the solitary pine by the farmhouse writhed and tossed its gaunt arms; always the gorse and bracken billowed and weltered under it. The sand drifted like snow, encroaching forever upon the cultivated patches around the house. Always the surf – surge on surge – boomed and thundered on the shore, casting up broken kelp and jetsam of wreck. Always, always forever and forever, the monotony remained. The bleakness, the wild, solitary stretches of sea and sky and land turned to the eye their staring emptiness. At long intervals the figure of a servant, a herdsman or at times Thorhall himself moved – a speck of black on the illimitable grey of nature – across the landscape. Ponies, shagged, half wild, their eyes hidden under tangled forelocks, sometimes wandered down upon the shore – their thick hair roughing in the wind – to snuff at the salty seaweeds. The males sometimes fought on the shore, their hoofs thudding on the resounding beach, their screams mingling with the incessant roar of the breakers.

Once even, at Eastertide, during a gale, an empty galley drove ashore, a *snekr* with dragon prow, the broken oars dangling from the thole-pins; and in the waist of her a Viking chieftain, dead, the salt rime rusting on his helmet.

With the advent of summer the mysterious trouble at the farmhouse in the Vale of Shadows disappeared. But the fall equinox drew on, the nights became longer; soon the daylight lasted but a few hours and the sun set before it could be said to have actually risen.

As the winter darkness descended upon the farmhouse the trouble recommenced. During the night the tread of footsteps could be heard making the rounds of the byre. The fumbling of unseen fingers could be distinguished at the locks. The low eaves of the house were seized in the grip of strong hands and wrenched and pulled till the rafters creaked. Outhouses were plucked apart and destroyed, fences uprooted. After nightfall no one dared venture abroad.

Thorhall had engaged a new shepherd, one Thorgaut, a young man, who professed himself fearless of the haunted sheep-walks and farmyard. He was as popular where Glamr had been disliked. He made love to the housemaids, helped in the butter-making, and rode the children on his back. As to the Vampire, he snapped his fingers and asked only to meet him in the open.

The snow came in August, and was followed by sleet and icy rains and blotting sea-fogs. As the time went on the nightly manifestations increased. Windows were broken in; iron bars shaken and wrenched; sheep and even horses killed.

At length one night a terrible commotion broke out in the stables – the shrill squealing of the horses and the tramping and bellowing of cows, mingled with deep tones of a dreadful voice. Thorhall and his people rushed out. They found that the stable door had been riven and splintered, and they entered the stable itself across the wreckage. The cattle were goring each other, and across the stone partition between the stalls was the body of Thorgaut, the shepherd, his head upon one side, his feet on the other, and his spine snapped in twain.

It chanced that about this time Grettir, well known and well beloved throughout all Iceland, came into that part of the country and one eventide drew rein at Thorhall's farmhouse. This was before Grettir had been hunted from the island by the implacable Thorbjorn, called The Hook, and driven to an asylum and practical captivity upon the rock of Drangey.

He was at this time in the prime of his youth and of a noble appearance. His shoulders were broad, his arms long, his eye a bright blue, and his flaxen hair braided like a Viking's. For cloak he wore a bearskin, while as for weapons he carried nothing but a short sword.

Thorhall, as may be easily understood, welcomed the famous outlaw, but warned him of Glamr.

Grettir, however, was not to be dissuaded from remaining overnight at the byre.

'Vampire or troll, troll or vampire, here bide I till daybreak,' he declared.

Yet despite the bonder's fears the night passed quietly. No sound broke the stillness but the murmur of the distant surf, no footfall sounded around the house, no fingers came groping at the doors.

'I have never slept easier,' announced Grettir in the morning.

'Good; and Heaven be praised,' declared the bonder fervently.

They walked together toward the stables, Thorhall instructing Grettir as to the road he should follow that day. As they drew near, Grettir whistled for his horse, but no answering whicker responded.

'How is this?' he muttered, frowning.

Thorhall and the outlaw hurried into the building, and Grettir, who was in the advance, stopped stock-still in the midst of the floor and swore a great oath.

His horse lay prone in the straw of his stall, his eyeballs protruding, the foam stiff upon his lips. He was dead. Grettir approached and examined him. Between shoulder and withers, the back – as if it had been a wheat-straw – was broken.

'Never mind,' cried the bonder eagerly, 'I have another animal for you, a piebald stallion of Norway stock, just the beast for your weight. Here is your saddle. On with it. Up you go and a speedy journey to you.'

'Never!' exclaimed Grettir, his blue eyes flashing. 'Here will I stay till I meet Glamr face to face. No man did me an injury that he did not rue it. I sleep at the byre another night.'

Dark as a wolf's mouth, silent as his footfalls, the night closed down. There was no moon as yet, but the heavens were bright. Steadily as the blast of some great huntsman's horn, the wind held from the northeast. The sand skimming over the dunes and low hills near the coast was caught up and carried landward and drifted in at crevice and door-chink of the farmhouse. A young seal, lost, no doubt, from the herd that had all day been feeding in the offing – barked and barked incessantly from a rock in the breakers. In the pine tree by the house a huge night-bird, owl or hawk, stirred occasionally with a prolonged note. By and by the weather grew colder, the ground began to freeze and crack. Inside in the main hall of the house, covered by his bearskin cloak, Grettir lay wakeful and watching. He reclined in such a manner – his head pillowed on his arm – that he could see the door. At the other end of the hall the fire of drift was dying down upon the flags. On the other side of the partition, in the next room, lay the bonder, alternately dozing and waking.

The time passed heavily, slowly. From far off toward the shore could be heard the lost seal raising from time to time his hoarse, sobbing bark.

Then at length a dog howled, and an instant after the bonder spoke aloud. He had risen from his bed and stood in the door of his room.

'Hark! Did you not hear something?'

'I hear the barking of the seal,' said Grettir, 'the baying of the hound, the cry of the night-bird, and the break of the surges; nothing else.'

'No. This was a footstep. There. Listen!'

A heavy footfall sounded crunching in the snow from without and close by. It passed around and in front of the house; and the wooden shutter of a window of the hall was plucked at and shaken. Then an outhouse was attacked – a shed where in summertime the calves were fed. Grettir could hear the snap and rasp of splintering boards.

'It has a strong arm,' he muttered.

Once more the tread encircled the house. In a very short time it sounded again in front of the byre.

'It has a long stride,' said Grettir.

The tread ceased. For a long moment there was silence, while the scurrying sand rattled delicately against the house like minute hailstones. Suddenly a corner eave was seized. Something tugged at it, wrenching, and the thatch gave with the long swish of rent linen.

'It has a tall figure,' said Grettir.

For nearly a quarter of an hour these different sounds continued, now distinct, now confused, now distant, now near at hand. Suddenly from overhead there came a jar and a crash, and Grettir felt the dust from the rafters descend upon his face; the Vampire was on the roof. But soon he leaped down and now the footsteps came straight to the door of the hall. The door itself was gripped with colossal strength. In the crescent-shaped openings of the upper panels a hand appeared, black against the faint outside light, groping, picking. It seized upon the edge of the board in the lower bend of the crescent and pulled. The board gave way, ripped to the very door-sill; then an arm followed the hand, reaching for one of the two iron bars with which the door was fenced. Evidently it could not find these, for the effort was soon abandoned and another panel was split and torn away. The cross-panel followed, the nails shrieking as they were drawn out from the wood. Then at last the door, shattered to its very hinges, gave way, leaving only the bars set in the stone sockets of the jamb, and against the square of grey light of the entrance stood, silhouetted, the figure of a monster. Stood but for a moment, for almost at once the bars were pulled out.

The Vampire was within the house, the light from the smouldering logs illuminating the face.

Glamr's face was livid. The pupils of the eyes were white, the hair matted and thick. The whole figure was monstrously enlarged, bulked like a *jotun*, and the vast hands, white as those of the drowned, swung heavily at his sides.

Once in the hall, he stood for a long moment looking from side to side, then moved slowly forward, reaching his great arms overhead, feeling and fumbling with the roofbeams with his fingers, and guiding himself thus from beam to beam.

Grettir, watching, alert, never moved, but lay in his place, his eyes fixed upon the monster.

But at length Glamr made out the form stretched upon the couch and came up and laid hold of a flap of the bearskin under Grettir's shoulders and tugged at it. But Grettir, bracing his feet against the footboard of the couch, held back with all his strength. Glamr seized the flap in both hands and set his might to pull, till the tough hide fetched away, and he staggered back, the corner of skin still in his grip. He looked at it stupidly, wondering, bewildered.

Then suddenly the bonder, listening from within his bolded door, heard the muffled crashing shock of the onset. The rafters cracked, the byre shook, the shutters rocked in their grooves, and Grittir, eyes alight, hair flying like a torch, thews rigid as iron, leaped to the attack.

Down upon the hero's arms came the numbing, crushing grip of the dead man's might. One instant of that inhuman embrace and Grettir knew that now peril of his life was toward. Never in all his days of battle and strength had such colossal might risen to match his own. Back bore the wrestlers, back, back toward the sides of the hall. Benches ironed to the wall were overturned, wrenched like paper from their fastenings. The great table crashed and splintered beneath their weight. The floor split with their tramping, and the fire was scattered upon the hearth. Now forward, now back, from side to side and from end to end of the wrecked hall drove the fight. Great of build though the fighters were, huge of bone, big of muscle, they yet leaped and writhed with the agility, the rapidity of young lambs.

But fear was not in Grettir. Never in his life had he been afraid. Only anger shook him, and fine, above-board fury, and the iron will to beat his enemy.

All at once Grettir, his arms gripped about the Vampire's middle, his head beneath the armpit, realized that the creature was dragging him toward the door. He fought back from this till the effort sent the blood surging in his ears, for he knew well that ill as the fight had fared within the house it must go worse without. But it was all one that he braced his feet against the broken benches, the wreck of the table, the every unevenness of the floor. The Vampire had gripped him close and dragged and clutched and heaved at his body, so that the white nails drove into his flesh, and the embrace of those arms of steel shut in the ribs till the breath gushed from the nostrils in long gasps of agony.

And now they swayed and grappled in the doorway. Grettir's back was bent like a bow and Grettir's arms at fullest stretch strained to their sockets, till it seemed as though the very tendons must tear from off the bones. And ever the foul thing above him drew him farther and yet farther from out the entrance-way of the house.

'God save you, Grettir!' cried the bonder, 'God save you, brave man and true. Never was such a fight as this in all Iceland. Are you spent, Grettir?'

Muffled under the arms of his foe, the voice of Grettir shouted: 'Stand from us. I am much spent, but I fear not.'

Then with the words, feeling the half-sunk stone of the threshold beneath his feet, he bowed his knees, and with his shoulder against the Vampire's breast drove, not, as hitherto, back, but forward, and that with all the power of limb and loin.

The Vampire reeled from the attack. His shoulder crashed against the outer doorcase, and with that gigantic shock the roof burst asunder. Down crushed and roared the frozen thatch, and then in that hideous ruin of splintering rafters, grinding stones, and wreck of panel and beam the Vampire fell backward and prone to the ground, while Grettir toppled down upon him till his face was against the dead man's face, his eye to his dead eye, his forehead to his front, and the grey bristle of his beard between his teeth.

The moon was bright outside, and all at once, lighted by her rays, Grettir for the first time saw the Vampire's face.

Then the soul of him shrank and sank, and the fear that all his days he had not known leaped to life in his heart. Terror of that glare of the dead man's gaze caught him by the throat, till his grip relaxed, and his strength dwindled away and he crouched there motionless but for his trembling, looking, looking into those blind, white, dead eyes.

And the Vampire began to speak:

'Eagerly has thou striven to match thyself with me, and ill hast thou done this night. Now thou art weak with the fear and the rigor of this fight, yet never henceforth shalt thou be stronger than at this moment. Till now thou hast won much fame by great deeds, yet henceforth ill-luck shall follow thee and woe and man-slayings and untoward fortune. Outlawed shalt thou be, and thy lot shall be cast in lands far from thine home. Alone shalt thou dwell and in that loneliness, this weird I lay upon thee: Ever to see these eyes with thine eyes, till the terror of the Dark shall come upon thee and the fear of night, and the twain shall drag thee to thy death and thy undoing.'

As the voice ceased, Grettir's wits and strength returned, and suddenly seizing the hair of the creature in one hand and his short sword in the other, he hewed off the head.

But within the heart of him he knew that the Vampire had said true words, and as he stood looking down upon the great body of his enemy and saw the glazed and fish-like eyes beneath the lids, he could for one instant look ahead to the days of his life yet to be, to the ill-fortune that should dog him from henceforth, and knew that at the gathering of each night's dusk the eyes of Glamr would look into his.

Thorhall came out when the fight was done, praising God for the issue, and he and Grettir together burned the body and, wrapping the ashes in a skin, buried them in a corner of the sheep-walks.

In the morning Thorhall gave Grettir the piebald horse and new clothes and set him a mile on his road. They rode through the Vale of

Shadows and kissed each other farewell on the shore where the road led away toward Waterdale.

The clouds had gathered again during the dawn and the rain was falling, driven landward by the incessant wind. The seals again barked and hunted in the offing, and the rough-haired ponies once more wandered about on the beach snuffing at the kelp and seaweed.

Long time Thorhall stood on the ridge watching the figure of Grettir grow small and indistinct in the waste of north country and under the blur of the rain. Then at last he turned back to the byre.

But Grettir after these things rode on to Biarg, to his mother's house, and sat at home through the winter.

The Blood Fetish

MORLEY ROBERTS

*   *   *

Outside the tent the forest was alive and busy, as it is for ever in the tropics of Africa. Birds called with harsh strange notes from dark trees, for, though the forest was even more full of creeping shadows, the sun had not yet sunk beyond the western flats through which the Kigi ran to the sea. Monkeys chattered and howled: and beneath this chorus was the hum of a million insects, that voice of the bush which never ceases. The sick man in the tent moved uneasily and looked at his companion.

'Give me something to drink, doctor,' he said.

The doctor supported his head while he drank.

'Were there any of your drugs in it?' asked the patient.

'No, Smith,' said the doctor.

'My taste is morbid,' said Smith. 'I shan't last long, old chap.'

Dr Winslow looked out into the forest, into the night, for now it was night very suddenly.

'Nonsense,' said Winslow. 'You'll live to take your collection home and be more famous than you are now.'

'Am I famous?' asked Simcox Smith. 'I suppose I am in my way. I'm thought to know more than most about this country and the devilish ways of it. Every one acknowledges that, or everyone but Hayling.'

He frowned as he mentioned the name.

'He's no better than an ignorant fool,' he remarked. 'But we see strange things here, doctor.'

The doctor sighed.

'I suppose so,' he said, 'but what fools we are to be here at all.'

The dying man shook his head.

'No, no, I've learnt a lot, old chap. I wish I could teach Hayling. I meant to, and now I can't. He'll spend all his time trying to discredit my – my discoveries.'

'Lie quiet,' said the doctor, and for long minutes Simcox Smith and the anthropologist said nothing. He lay thinking. But he spoke at last.

'I've not bought that thing from Suja,' he said.

'Don't,' said Winslow.

'You think it's a fraud?'

'I'm sure of it,' said Winslow.

Simcox Smith laughed.

'You are as bad as Hayling.'

He put out his hand and drew Winslow closer to him.

'Suja showed me what it did,' he said. 'I saw it myself.'

'On what?' asked Winslow quickly.

'On a prisoner, one who was killed when you were away.'

'And it did – '

'Did something! My God, yes,' said the anthropologist, shivering.

'What?' asked the doctor curiously, but with drawn brows.

'He grew pale and it got red. I thought I saw the wrist,' said Simcox Smith. 'I thought I saw it. I *did* see it.'

Winslow would have said it was all a delusion if Smith had been well. He knew how men's minds went in the rotten bush of the West Coast. He had had seen intellects rot, and feared for his own.

'Oh,' said Winslow.

The sick man lay back in his bed.

'I'll buy it and send it to Hayling.'

'Nonsense,' said Winslow; 'don't.'

'You don't believe it, so why shouldn't I send it? I will. I'll show Hayling! He's a blind fool, and believes there are no devilish things in this world. What is this world, old chap, and what are we? It's all horrible and ghastly. Fetch Suja, old chap.'

'Nonsense, lie down and be quiet,' said Winslow.

'I want Suja, the old rascal, I want him,' said Smith urgently. 'I must have it for Hayling. I'd like Hayling or some of his house to grow pale. They'll see more than the wrist. Oh God! what's the head like?'

He shivered.

'I want Suja,' he said moaning, and presently Winslow went out and sent a boy for Suja, who came crawling on his hands and knees, for he was monstrously old and withered and weak. But his eyes were alive. They looked like lamps in a gnarled piece of wood. He kneeled on the floor beside Smith's bed. Smith talked to him in his own tongue that Winslow could not understand, and the two men, the two dying men, talked long and eagerly while Winslow smoked. Suja was dying, had been dying for twenty, for fifty years. His people said they knew not how old he was. But Smith would die next day, said Winslow. Suja and Smith talked, and at last they came to an agreement. And then Suja crawled out of the tent.

'Get me a hundred dollars out of my chest,' said Smith. 'And when I am dead you will give him my clothes and blankets; all of them.'

'All right if you say so,' said Winslow. He got the hundred dollars out, and presently the old sorcerer came back. With him he brought a parcel done up in fibre and a big leaf, and over that some brown paper on which was a label in red letters, 'With great care.' It was a precious piece of paper, and not a soul thereabouts but Suja would have touched it. The red letters were some dreadful charm, so Suja had told the others.

'This is it,' said Suja.

'Give him the money,' said Smith eagerly.

He turned to Suja and spoke quietly to him in his own tongue.

'It's not mine, Suja, but John Hayling's. Say it.'

Winslow heard Suja say something, and then he heard the words, 'Shon 'Aylin'.'

Simcox Smith looked up at Winslow.

'He gives it to Hayling, Winslow,' he said triumphantly.

'Is that part of the mumbo jumbo?' asked Winslow, half contemptuously. But somehow he was not wholly contemptuous. The darkness of the night and the glimmer of the lamp in the darkness, and the strange and horrible aspect of the sorcerer affected him.

'Shon 'Aylin',' mumbled Suja, as he counted his dollars.

'Yes, it's part of it,' said Smith. 'It won't work except on the one who owns it and on his people. It must be transferred. We gave it to the slave who died.'

'It's a beastly idea,' said Winslow.

'You'll send it for me,' said Smith. 'You must.'

'Oh, all right,' said Winslow.

With trembling hands Smith put the packet into a biscuit tin.

Old Suja crept out into the darkness.

'I believe anything with that old devil in the tent,' said Winslow. Smith giggled.

'It's true, and it's Hayling's. I always meant to send it to him, the unbelieving beast,' he said. 'I wish I was going to live to see it. You'll send it, Winslow?'

'Yes.'

'You promise on your word of honour?' insisted Smith.

Reluctantly enough, Winslow gave his word of honour, and Smith was satisfied. And at ten o'clock that night he died in his sleep.

Winslow packed up all his papers and collections, and sent him down to the coast by carriers and canoe. The packet containing the fetish which Smith had bought from the ancient sorcerer he sent by post to England. He addressed it to A. J. Hayling, 201 Lansdown Road, St John's Wood. By this time Winslow had recovered his tone. He believed nothing which he could not see. He was angry with himself for having been affected by what Smith and old Suja had said and done.

'It's absurd, of course,' said Winslow, with bent brows. He added, 'but it's a beastly idea.'

When he sent the fetish away he wrote a letter to go with it, saying that Simcox Smith had often spoken to him of his rival in England. He described briefly what had occurred at the time of Smith's death, and gave some brief details of old Suja. He was obviously very old, and all the natives for miles round were frightened of him. Nevertheless, there was, of course, nothing in the thing. Latterly the climate and overwork had obviously affected Smith's mind. 'I should not send it if he had not made me promise to do so on my word of honour,' wrote Winslow.

He dismissed the matter from his mind, and the parcel and letter went home by the next Elder Dempster boat.

Mr Hayling was rather pleased than otherwise to hear of Simcox Smith's decease, although he said 'poor fellow,' as one must when a scientific enemy and rival dies. They had quarrelled for years when they met at the Society's rooms, and had fought in the scientific journals. Hayling was an anthropological Mr Gradgrind. He wanted facts, and nothing but facts. He believed he was a Baconian, as he knew nothing of Bacon. It had never occurred to him that there was any mystery in anything. There was nothing but ignorance, and most men were very ignorant. The existence of men, of things, of the universe, of matter itself, were all taken for granted by him, in the same way they are taken for granted by the average man. What made Simcox Smith (who had a *penchant* for metaphysics) once jokingly called the

Me-ness of the Ego was an absurdity. It was idiocy. When a man begins to think what made himself an Ego and what constitutes his 'Me,' he is the on the verge of insanity unless he is a great philosopher.

'Simcox Smith is an ass,' said Hayling, quite oblivious to the fact that Smith had done good work in many directions and offered some conjectural hypotheses to the world which had much merit and might some day rank as theories. 'Simcox Smith is an ass. He believed in occultism. He believed, I am prepared to swear, in witchcraft. He mistook the horrible ideas of a savage race for realities. Would you believe it, he even said that everything believed in utter and simple faith had a kind of reality? He said this was a law of nature!'

Obviously Simcox Smith had been mad. But some easily affected and imaginative people said it was a dreadful idea, just as Winslow had said the notion of Suja's blood fetish was a beastly one. Imagine for an instant that the idea was true! It meant that the frightful imaginations of madmen had a quasi existence at least! It meant that there was a dreadful element of truth (for who knew what truth was?) in any conceived folly. A man had but to imagine something to create it. One of Smith's friends really believed this. He was an atheist, he said, but he believed (in a way, he added, as he laughed) that mankind had really created a kind of anthropomorphic deity, with the passions and feelings attributed to him by belief and tradition. No wonder, said this friend of Smith's, that the world was a horrible place to any one who could grasp its misery and had ears for its groans.

It must be acknowledged that this idea of Simcox Smith's was a horrible one. It really affected some men. One tried it on a child (he was very scientific, and believed in experiments he could more or less control) and the child saw things which threw it into a fit and injured it for life. Nevertheless, it was a very interesting experiment, for something happened to the child (there were odd marks on it) which looked like something more than suggestion, unless it is all true that we hear of stigmata. Perhaps it is, but personally I have an idea (I knew Smith) that there is something in his damnable creating theory.

But to return to Hayling. He got the parcel from the Coast, and he read Winslow's letter.

'Poor fellow,' said Hayling; 'so he's dead at last. Well, well! And what is this that he sends? A blood fetish? Ah, he thinks he can convert me at the last, the poor mad devil.'

He opened the parcel, and inside the matting and the leaves, which smelt of the West Coast of Africa (the smell being muddy and very distinctive to those who have smelt it), he found a dried black hand, severed at the wrist joint. There was nothing else, only this hand.

'Humph,' said Hayling, who had nerves which had never been shaken by the bush and the fevers of the bush, and had never heard black men whispering dreadfully of the lost souls of the dead. 'Humph.'

He picked it up and looked at it. It was an ordinary hand, a right hand, and there was nothing remarkable about it at first. On a further look the nails seemed remarkably long, and that gave the hand a rather cruel look. Hayling said 'humph,' again. He examined it carefully and saw that it was very deeply marked on the palm.

'Very interesting,' said Hayling. Curiously enough (or rather it would have been curious if we didn't know that the strongest of us have our weak spots), he had a belief or some belief in palmistry. He had never acknowledged it to a soul but a well-known palmist in the west of London. 'Very interesting. I wonder what Sacconi would say of these lines?'

Sacconi was the palmist. He was an Irishman.

'I'll show it to Sacconi,' said Hayling. He packed it up in its box again and put it in a cupboard, which he locked up. He dismissed the matter, for he had a good deal to do. He had to write something about Simcox Smith, for instance, and he was working on totemism. He hardly thought of the dried hand for some days.

Hayling was a bachelor, and lived with a niece and a housekeeper. He was a nice man to live with unless one knew anything about anthropology and totems and such like, and Mary Hayling knew nothing about them whatever. She said 'Yes, uncle dear,' and 'No, uncle dear,' just as she ought to do, and when he abused Simcox Smith, or Robins-Gunter, or Williams, who were rivals of his, she was always sympathetic and said it was a shame.

'What's a shame?' asked Hayling.

'I don't know, dear uncle,' said Mary Hayling.

And Hayling laughed.

Then there was the housekeeper. She was fair, stout and ruddy, and very cheerful in spite of the fact that skulls and bones and specimen things in bottles made her flesh creep. She knew nothing whatever about them, and wondered what they mattered. Why Mr Hayling raged and rumbled about other men's opinions on such horrid subjects she didn't know. However, she took everything easily, and only remonstrated when the fullness of the house necessitated skulls being exposed to public view. The passage even had some of them and the maids objected to dusting them, as was only natural. Hayling said he didn't want 'em dusted, but what would any housekeeper who was properly constituted think of that? She made the girls dust them, though she herself shivered. She even saw that they wiped glass bottles with awful things inside them. She and the housemaid cleaned up Mr Hayling's own room and opened the cupboard where the hand was. The girl gave a horrid squeak as she put her hand in and touched it.

'Oh, law, ma'am, what is it?' asked Kate.

'Don't be a fool, girl,' said Mrs Farwell, with a shiver. 'It's only a hand.'

'Only – oh Lord! I won't touch it,' said the girl. 'There's a dead mouse by it.'

'Then take out the dead mouse,' said the housekeeper. The girl did so, and slammed the cupboard door to and locked it. The mouse was a poor shrivelled little thing, but how interesting it would have been to dead Simcox Smith neither Kate nor the housekeeper knew. It went into the dustbin as if it did not bear witness to a horror.

That afternoon Mrs Farwell spoke to Hayling.

'If you please, sir, there's a hand in that cupboard, and I couldn't get Kate to clean it out.'

'A hand! Oh yes, I remember,' said Hayling. 'The girl's a fool. Does she think it will hurt her? How did she know it was there? I wrapped it up. Some one's been meddling.'

'I don't think so, sir,' said Mrs Farwell, with dignity. 'She is much too frightened to meddle, and so am I.'

'Mrs Farwell, you are a fool,' said Hayling.

'Thank you, sir,' said Mrs Farwell.   When Mrs Farwell had sailed out of the room Hayling opened the cupboard and found the hand out of its package.

'Some one *has* been meddling,' growled Hayling. 'They pretend that they are frightened and come hunting here to get a sensation. I know 'em. They're all savages, and so are all of us. Civilization!'

He gave a snort when he thought of what civilization was. That is an anthropological way of looking at it. It's not a theological way at all.

He looked at the hand. It was a curious hand.

'It's contracted a little,' said Hayling. 'The fist has closed, I think. Drying unequally. But it's interesting; I'll show it to Sacconi.'

He put the hand into its coverings, and took it that very afternoon to Sacconi.

Personally Hayling believed in chiromancy. As I have said, it really was his only weakness. I never used to believe it when he argued with me, but now I have my doubts. When Sacconi took the thing into his own white and beautiful hands and turned it over to look at the palm, his eyebrows went up in a very odd way. Hayling said so.

'This, oh, ah,' said Sacconi. His real name was Flynn. He came from Limerick. 'This is very odd – very – '

'Very what?' asked Hayling.

'Horrible, quite horrible,' said Sacconi.

'Can you read it, man?'

Sacconi grunted.

'Can I read the *Times*? I can, but I don't. I've half a mind not to read this. It's very horrible, Hayling.'

'The devil,' said Hayling; 'what d'ye mean?'

'This is a negro's hand.'

'Any fool can see that,' said Hayling rudely.

'A murderer's hand.'

'That's likely enough,' said Hayling.

'A cannibal's hand.'

'You don't say so!' said Hayling.

'Oh, worse than that.'

'What's worse?'

Sacconi said a lot that Hayling denounced as fudge. Probably it was fudge. And yet –

'I'd burn it,' said Sacconi, with a shiver, as he handed it back to Hayling, and went to wash his hands. 'I'd burn it.'

'There's a damn weak spot in you, Sacconi,' said the anthropologist.

'Perhaps,' said Sacconi, 'but I'd burn it.'

'Damn nonsense,' said Hayling. 'Why should I?'

'I believe a lot of things you don't,' said Sacconi.

'I disbelieve a lot that you don't,' retorted Hayling.

'You see, I'm a bit of a clairvoyant,' said Sacconi.

'I've heard you say that before,' said Hayling, as he went away.

When he got home again he put the hand in the cupboard. He forgot to lock it up. And he locked the cat up in his room when he went to bed.

There was an awful crying of cats, or a cat, in the middle of the night. But cats fight about that time.

And when Kate opened the door of Hayling's working-room in the morning she saw the hand upon the hearthrug, and gave a horrid scream. It brought Mrs Farwell out of the drawing-room, and Hayling out of the bathroom in a big towel.

'What the devil – ' said Hayling.

'What is it, Kate?' cried Mrs Farwell.

'The hand! the hand!' said Kate. 'It's on the floor.'

Mrs Farwell saw it. Hayling put on his dressing-gown, and came down and saw it, too.

'Give that fool a month's notice,' said Hayling. 'She's been meddling again.'

'I haven't,' said Kate, sobbing. And then Mrs Farwell saw the cat lying stretched out under Hayling's desk.

'It was the cat. There she is,' said Mrs Farwell.

'Damn the cat,' said Hayling. He took Kate's broom and gave the cat a push with it.

The cat was dead.

'I don't want a month's notice,' said Kate, quavering, 'I'll go now.'

'Send the fool off,' said Hayling angrily. He took up the cat, of which he had been very fond, and put it outside, and shut the door on the crying girl and Mrs Farwell. He picked up the hand and looked at it.

'Very odd,' said Hayling.

He looked again.

'Very beastly,' said Hayling. 'I suppose it's my imagination.'

He looked once more.

'Looks fresher,' said Hayling. 'These fools of women have infected me.'

He put the hand down on his desk by the side of a very curious Maori skull, and went up-stairs again to finish dressing.

That morning the scentific monthlies were out, and there was so much of interest in them that Hayling forgot all about the hand. He had an article in one of them abusing Robins-Gunter, whose views on anthropology were coloured by his fanaticism in religion. 'Imagine a man like that thinking he is an authority on anything scientific,' said Hayling. It was a pleasure to slaughter him on his own altar, and indeed this time Hayling felt he had offered Robins-Gunter up to the outraged deity of Truth.

'It's a massacre,' said Hayling; 'it's not a criticism – it's a massacre.'

He said 'Ha-ha!' and went to town to hear what others had to say about it. They had so much to say that he remained at the club till very late, and got rather too much wine to drink. Or perhaps it was the whisky-and-soda. He left his working-room door open and unlocked.

Kate had gone, sacrificing a fortnight's wages. Mrs Farwell said she was a fool. Kate said she would rather be a fool outside that house. She also said a lot of foolish things about the hand, which had a very silly effect upon the housekeeper. For how else can we account for what happened that night? Kate said that the beastly hand was alive, and that it had killed the cat. Uneducated superstitious girls from the country often say things as silly. But Mrs Farwell was a woman of nerves. She only went to sleep when she heard her master come in.

She woke screaming at three o'clock, and Hayling was still so much under the influence of Robins-Gunter's scientific blood and the club whisky that he didn't wake. But Mary Hayling woke and so did the cook, and they came running to Mrs Farwell's room. They found her door open.

'What's the matter? what's the matter?' screamed Mary Hayling. She brought a candle and found Mrs Farwell sitting up in bed.

She was as white as a ghost, bloodlessly white. 'There's been a horrible thing in my room,' she whispered.

The cook collapsed on a chair; Mary Hayling sat on the bed and put her arms round the housekeeper.

'What?'

'I saw it,' whispered Mrs Farwell. 'A black man, reddish black, very horrible – '

She fainted, and Mary laid her down.

'Stay with her,' said Mary. 'I'll go and wake my uncle.'

The cook whimpered, but she lighted the gas and stayed, while Mary hammered on Hayling's door. He thought it was thunderous applause at a dinner given him by the Royal Society. Then he woke.

'What is it?'

Mary opened the door and told him to get up.

'Oh, these women,' he said.

His head ached. He went up-stairs cursing and found Mrs Farwell barely conscious. The cook was shaking like a jelly, and Hayling thrust her aside. He had some medical training before he turned to anthropology, and he took hold of the housekeeper's wrist, and found her pulse a mere running thread.

'Go and bring brandy,' said Hayling, 'and fetch Dr Sutton from next door.'

He was very white himself. So far as he could guess she looked as if she were dying of loss of blood. But she didn't die. Sutton, when he came in, said the same.

'She's not white only from fainting, she's blanched,' he declared.

He turned back her nightgown, and found a very strange red patch on her shoulder. It was redder than the white skin, and moist. He touched it with a handkerchief, and the linen was faintly reddened. He turned and stared at Hayling.

'This is very extraordinary,' he said, and Hayling nodded.

He tried to speak and could not. At last he got his voice. It was dry and thick.

'Don't you think the patch is the shape of a hand?' asked Hayling.

'Yes, rather,' replied Sutton; 'somewhat like it, I should say.'

They were all in the room then: Mary Hayling and the cook. There was no other person in the house. They could have sworn that was a fact. They heard a noise below.

'What's that?' asked Hayling.

'Some one gone out of the front door, sir,' said the trembling cook.

'Nonsense,' said Hayling.

But the door slammed. When he ran down he found no one about. He went up-stairs again shaking. For he had looked for something in his own room and had not found it.

The next day there was a curious paragraph in all the evening papers.

'The freshly severed hand of a negro was picked up early this morning in Lansdown Road, St John's Wood, just outside the residence of the well-known anthropologist, Mr A. J. Hayling. The police are investigating the mystery.'

But Hayling destroyed the article in which he proposed to massacre poor credulous Simcox Smith.

The Land of the Time-Leeches

GUSTAV MEYRINK

*   *   *

In the churchyard of the secluded and out-of-the-world little town of Runkel my grandfather's body is laid 'to eternal rest.' His gravestone is thickly overgrown with moss and the date well-nigh obliterated; but below it, standing out in gilt[1] and as fresh as though they were cut yesterday, are four letters ranged round a cross, thus:

'VIVO' – 'I live.' Such was the meaning I was told, when as a boy I read the inscription for the first time. The word at once impressed itself as deeply on my soul as if the dead had uttered it from underneath the sod.

'VIVO' – 'I live,' a strange watch-word for a tombstone! Even to-day it re-echoes in my heart; whenever I think of it, I feel as I felt long since when first I stood before that grave. In my imagination I see my grandfather – though I had never known him in the flesh – lying there, untouched by decay, with folded hands, eyes open clear as crystal, motionless; like one who has escaped corruption in the midst of the realm of mould, with silent patience awaiting resurrection.

[1] Cp. the Golden Gate of the Osiric Garden, end of *Der Golem.*

I have since visited many a churchyard of many a town; ever have my steps been directed there by a vague desire, for which I could not account, to read once more that word on some chance stone. Twice only have I found it – that cross-encircling 'VIVO' – once in Danzig, once in Nuremburg. In both cases Time's finger has rubbed out the name; in both the 'VIVO' shines out fresh and untouched as if instinct with life.

I had been told in my youth, and had always believed, that my grandfather had not left behind a single line in his own writing. All the more excited was I then when one day I discovered in a secret drawer of an old writing-desk – an ancient family heirloom – a packet of notes which had evidently been written by him. They were enclosed in a book-cover, on which I read the strange sentence:

'How shall man escape death if not by ceasing to wait and hope?'

At once I felt light up within me that mysterious 'VIVO,' which had ever throughout my life accompanied me with a faint shimmer, dying away a thousand times only to revive without any apparent outer cause in dreams or waking moments. If I had at times believed some chance had put that 'VIVO' on his tombstone – a parson's choice perhaps – now, with this sentence on the book-cover before me, I knew for sure and certain the 'VIVO' must have had a deeper meaning for him; must doubtless hint at something that filled the whole life of my father's father. And indeed, as I read on, page after page of his bequest to me confirmed my first intuition.

Most of the notes are of too private a nature to have their contents revealed to other eyes. It must suffice if I touch lightly on those details which led to my acquaintance with Johann Hermann Obereit.

It appeared from these memoirs that my grandfather was a member of a society called the 'Philadelphians,' an order claiming that its roots go back to ancient Egypt and hailing as its founder the legendary Hermes Trismegistus. Even the secret grips and signs of recognition were given. The name of Johann Hermann Obereit frequently occurred. He was a chemist and apparently an intimate friend of my grandfather's; indeed he seemed to have lived in the same house with him at Runkel. I wished naturally to learn more about the life of my extraordinary ancestor and about that hidden world-renouncing philosophy the spirit of which spoke out of every line he had written. I accordingly decided to go to Runkel to find out whether by chance any descendants of Obereit were still there and if they had any family records.

One can scarcely imagine anything more dream-like than this tiny little town of Runkel, slumbering away in spite of the screams and cries of Time, like some forgotten relic of the Middle Ages, with its crooked streets and passages, silent as the dead, and grass-grown, rugged cobble-stones, beneath the shadow of the ancient rock-built castle of Runkelstein, the ancestral seat of the Princes of Wied.

The very first morning after my arrival I felt myself irresistibly drawn to the little churchyard. There the days of my youth woke again to memory, as I stepped from one flower-carpeted mound to another in the sweet sunshine and read mechanically from the stones the names of those who slumbered beneath. Already from afar I recognized my grandfather's with its glittering mystic inscription. But on drawing near I found I was no longer alone.

An old white-haired, clean-shaven man of sharp-cut features was sitting there, with his chin resting on the ivory handle of his walking-stick. As I approached he glanced at me with strangely vivid eyes, as of one in whom the likeness to a well-remembered face had awakened a host of memories. He was dressed in old-fashioned clothes, high collar and stock – one might almost have said like a family portrait in Louis Philippe or early Victorian style.

I was so astonished at a sight so out of keeping with present-day surroundings, moreover my brooding thoughts were so deeply sunk in what I had gathered from my grandfather's writings, that scarcely knowing what I did I uttered half-aloud the name 'Obereit.'

'Yes, my name is Johann Hermann Obereit,' said the old gentleman without showing the least surprise. I nearly stopped breathing. And what I learned from the conversation that followed was even less calculated to diminish my astonishment.

It is indeed not an every-day experience to find oneself face to face with a man to all appearances not much older than oneself yet who had lived so long – some century and a half, he said! I felt like a youth in spite of my already white hair, as we paced side by side, while he spoke of Napoleon and historic persons he had known long years ago, as one would speak of people who had died the other day.

'In Runkel,' he said with a smile, 'I am believed to be my own grandson.' He pointed to a tomb we were passing and which bore the date 1798. 'By right I should be lying there,' he continued. 'I had the date put on to avoid the curiosity of the crowd for a modern Methuselah. The "VIVO",' he added, as if divining my thought, 'will be put on only when I am dead for good.'

Almost at once we became intimate friends; and he soon insisted on my staying with him. A month thus passed; and we sat up many a night engaged in deep discourse. But always when I would have asked the purport of the sentence on the book-cover that contained my grandsire's papers, he deftly turned the conversation. 'How shall a man escape death if not by ceasing to wait and hope?' What could it mean?

One evening – indeed the last we passed together – our talk had turned on the old witch-trials. I was contending that they must all have been highly hysterical women, when suddenly he said: 'So you do not believe a man may leave his body and travel, say, to Blocksberg?' 'Shall I show you now?' he asked, looking sharply at me.

I shook my head. 'I admit only this much,' I said, laughing. 'The so-called witches got into a kind of trance by taking narcotic drugs, and were then firmly persuaded they rode through the air on broomsticks!'

He remained sunk in thought. 'You will perhaps say that I too travelled only in imagination,' he murmured half aloud, and relapsed again into meditation.

After a while he rose slowly, went to his desk and returned with a small book.

'Perhaps you may be interested in what I wrote down here when first I made the experiment many long years ago. I must tell you I was still very young and full of hopes.'

I saw from his indrawn look that his memory was going back to far-off days.

'I believed in what men call life, till blow after blow fell on me. I lost whatever one may value most on earth – my wife, my children – all. Then fate brought about my meeting with your grandfather. It was he who taught me to understand what our desires are, what waiting is, what expectation, what hope is; how they are interlocked with one another; how one may tear the mask off the faces of those ghostly vampires. We called them the Time-leeches; for like blood-suckers they drain from our hearts Time, the very sap of life. It was here in this room that he taught me the first step on the way towards the conquest of death and how to strangle the vipers of hope. And then . . .' – he hesitated for a moment. 'And then I became like a block of wood that does not feel whether it be touched gently or split asunder, plunged into water or thrown into fire. Since then there has been, as it were, a certain void within me. No more have I looked for consolation; no more have I needed it. Wherefore should I seek it? I know I *am*. Since then only is it that I *live*. There is a fundamental difference between "I live" and "*I live*." '

'You say that so simply; and yet it is terrible,' I interrupted, deeply moved.

'It only seems to be so,' he assured me smilingly. 'Out of this heart-stableness there streams a sense of beatitude of which you can scarcely dream. It is like a sweet melody that never ceases – this "I am." Once born it cannot die – neither in sleep, nor when the outer world wakes our senses for us again, nor even in death.

'Shall I tell you why men now die so early and no longer live for a thousand years as it is written of the patriarchs in the scriptures? They are like the green watery shoots of a tree. They have forgotten that they belong to the trunk, and so they wither away the first autumn. But I wanted to tell you how I first left my body.

'There is an old, old doctrine, as ancient as mankind itself. It has been handed on from mouth to ear until this day; but few know it. It teaches how to step over the threshold of death without losing consciousness. He who can rightly do so is henceforth master of himself. He has gained a new self, and what till then seemed his self becomes henceforth a tool just as now our hands and feet are organs for us.

'Heart-beat and breath are stilled as in a corpse when the newly rediscovered spirit goes forth – when we go forth as once did Israel from the fleshpots of Egypt, and the waters of the Red Sea stood as walls on either side.

'Long and oft had I to practise, nameless and excruciating were the tortures I had to undergo, before I succeeded finally in freeing myself consciously from the body. At first I felt myself, as it were, hovering – just as we think ourselves able to fly in dreams – with knees drawn up yet moving quite easily.

'Suddenly I began gliding down. I found myself in a black stream running as it were from the south to the north. In our language we call it the flowing backwards of the Jordan. There was a roaring of waters, a buzzing of blood in the ears. In great excitement many voices – though I could not see their owners – cried out on me to turn back. A trembling seized upon me, and in dumb fear I swam towards a cliff that rose from the waters before me. Standing there in the moonlight was a naked child. But the signs of sex were absent, and in its forehead it had a third eye, like Polyphemus of old. It stood stock still, pointing with its hand to the interior of the island.

'I advanced through a wood on a smooth white road, but without feeling the ground beneath my feet. When I tried to touch the trees and shrubs around me I could not feel them. It was as though there were a thin layer of air between them and me which I could not penetrate. A phosphorescence as from decaying wood covered every object and made seeing possible. But their outlines seemed vague and and loose and soft like molluscs, and all seemed strangely over-sized. Featherless birds, with round staring eyes, swollen like fattened geese and huddled together in a huge nest, hissed down at me. A fawn, scarce able to walk yet as big as a full-grown deer, lay in the moss and lazily turned its fat pug-dog-like head towards me.

'There was a toad-like sluggishness in every creature I happened to see.

'By and by the knowledge of where I was dawned on me – in a land as real as our own world and yet but a reflection of it, in the realm of those unseen doubles that thrive upon the marrow of their terrestrial counterparts, that exploit their originals and grow into ever huger shapes, the more the latter eat themselves up in vain hoping and waiting for happiness and joy. If the mothers of young animals are shot off and their little ones waste and waste away longing in faith for their food until they die in the tortures of starvation, spectral doubles grow up in this accursed spirit-land, and like spiders suck up the life that trickles from the creatures of our world. The life-powers of all that thus wane away in vain hopes, become gross shapes and luxurious weeds in this Leech-land, the very soil of which is impregnated by the fattening breath of time spent in vain waiting and wasting.

'As I wandered on I came to a town full of people. Many of them I knew on earth. I reminded myself of their countless vain and abortive hopes; how they walked more and more bowed down year after year, yet could not drive out of their hearts the vampires – their own demonic selves that devoured their Life and their Time. Here I saw them staggering about swollen into spongy monsters with huge bellies, bulging eyes and cheeks puffed with fat.

'First I noticed a bank which displayed in its windows the announcement:

FORTUNA
LOTTERY OFFICE
EVERY TICKET
WINS
THE FIRST PRIZE

Out of it came thronging a grinning crowd carrying sacks of gold, smacking their puffed lips in greasy contentment – phantoms in fat and jelly of all who waste their lives on earth in the insatiable hunger for a gambler's gains.

'I entered a vast hall; it seemed like a colossal temple whose columns reached the sky. There, on a throne of coagulated blood, sat a monstrous four-armed figure. Its body was human but its head a brute's – hyæna-like, with foam-flecked jaws and snout. It was the war-god of the still savage superstitious nations who offer it their prayers for victory over their foes.

'Filled with horror and loathing I fled out of the atmosphere of decay and corruption which filled the place, back into the streets, but only to be dumbfounded again at the sight of a palace which surpassed in splendour any I had ever seen. And yet every stone, every gable, mullion, ornament, seemed strangely familiar; it was as if I had once built it all up in fancy for myself. I mounted the broad white marble steps. On the door-plate before me I read . . . my own name – JOHANN H. OBEREIT! I entered. Inside I saw myself clad in purple sitting at a table groaning with luxuries and waited on by thousands of fair women slaves. Immediately I recognized them as the women who had pleased my senses in life, though most of them but as a passing moment's whim.

'A feeling of indescribable hatred filled me when I realized that this foul double of mine had wallowed and revelled here in lust and luxury my whole life; that it was I myself who had called him into being and lavished riches on him by the outflow of the magic power of my own self, drained from me by the vain hopes and lusts and expectations of my soul.

'With terror I saw that my whole life had been spent in waiting and in waiting only – as it were an unstaunchable bleeding to death; that the time left me for feeling the *present* amounted to only a few hours.

'Like a bubble burst before me whatever I had hitherto thought to be the content of my life. I tell you that whatever we seem to finish on earth ever generates new waiting and hoping. The whole world is pervaded by the pestiferous breath of the decay of a scarcely-born present. Who has not felt the enervating weakness that seizes on one when sitting in the waiting-room of a doctor or lawyer or official? What we call life is the waiting-room of death!

'Suddenly I realized then and there what Time is. We ourselves are forms made out of Time – bodies that seem to be matter, but are no more than coagulated Time. And our daily withering away towards the grave – what is it but our returning unto Time again, waiting and hoping being but the symptoms of this process, even as ice on a stove hisses away as it changes back to water again?

'I now saw that, as this knowledge woke in my mind, trembling seized upon my double, and that his face was contorted with terror. Then I knew what I had to do; to fight unto the death with every weapon against those phantoms that suck our life away like vampires.

'Oh! they know full well why they remain invisible for man, why they hide themselves from our eyes – those parasites of our life! – even as it is the devil's most foul device to act as if he did not exist. Since then I have for ever rooted out of my life the two ideas of hoping and waiting.'

'I am sure,' I said, when the old gentleman fell to silence, 'I should break down at the first step, if I tried to tread the terrible way along which you have walked. I can well believe that by incessant labour a man may benumb the feeling of waiting and hoping in his soul; but . . .'

'Yes, but only *benumb* it,' he interrupted. 'Within you the waiting still remains alive. You must put the axe to the root. Become as an automaton in this world, as one dead though seemingly alive. Never reach out after a tempting fruit, if there is to be the shortest waiting for it. Do not stir a hand; and all will fall ripe into your lap. At the beginning, and for long perchance, it may be like a wandering through desert plains void of all consolation; but suddenly there will be a brightness round you and you will see all things – beautiful and ugly – in a new and unexpected splendour. Then will there be no more "importance" and "unimportance" for you; every event will be equally "important" and "unimportant." You will become "horned" by drinking the dragon's blood, and be able to say of yourself: I fare forth into the shoreless sea of an unending life with snow-white sails.'

These were the last words Johann Hermann Obereit spoke to me. I have not seen him again.

Many years have passed since then and I have tried as well as I could to follow his doctrine; but waiting and hoping will not wane from my heart.

I am too weak, alas! to root out these weeds; and so I no longer wonder that on the countless gravestones so very seldom does one find the legend:

$$\begin{array}{c|c} V & I \\ \hline V & O \end{array}$$

The Elder Brother

CHARLES CALDWELL DOBIE

*   *   *

Last week my landlady said in the midst of the evening meal, 'You must see to it that you are early to your dinner to-morrow night, Josef Vitek, for I have a great treat in store for you.'

Now hearing my landlady talk thus I felt sure that she was planning some brave dish, and so to plague her I answered:

'I am not sure that I shall be here at all. My Greek friend is to celebrate his name-day and he has said something to me about a feast.'

'His name-day!' cried my landlady in scorn, for she cares little for my Greek friend. 'And what unmannerly thing is that, I should like to know? In Alsace we have no such foolishness.'

'Nor in my country, either . . . But it seems it stands in place of a birthday. And it falls upon the day called after the saint a man is named for.'

'Do not tell me,' my landlady cried out, 'that such a stupid lout is named for a saint!'

'Well,' I retorted gravely, 'since he is a Christian what else is left? . . . You would not have him named for the devil?'

At this my landlady put two hands upon her hips and wagged her old head from one side to another. 'Christian, indeed! Then why does he not have a birthday like decent folks?'

'Perhaps he does,' I answered. 'That I do not know. But is there anything to prevent one having a name-day, too? . . . And think how many, being named for the same saint, feast upon the same day? It is almost as good as Easter or Christmas . . . No, I do not agree with you: for my part I think it is a good arrangement. And what is more, I should say that any excuse for feasting serves a good turn.'

'To hear you talk, Josef Vitek, one would fancy that you were worn down to a shadow with lean living . . . I do not know what sort of outlandish fare your Greek friend can provide you, but if you are willing to risk it I suppose there is no more to be said.'

I looked at my landlady out of the corner of my eye. Her face was very red and in a moment I thought she might have wept from her disappointment and anger. Yet the longer her vexation, the more happily I knew she would smile in the end, so I said:

'I know some of the things he will serve me: broth of chicken with a taste of lemon and little bitter-sweet olives in the Greek fashion. And like as not, lamb baked with eggplant. And rice fried in butter. And in the end a curd of goat's milk.'

'And you call that a feast? Lamb and bitter olives and goat's-milk curd? . . . Shall I tell you what you would have at my table? Well then, a roast duck with noodles for one thing. And a batter pudding with all manner of preserves in the centre for another. To say nothing of nuts and raisins and little red apples with your coffee. If you can match that anywhere in San Francisco, well and good. But for my part I would not trade so much as the little red apples for anything you have named me.'

Now my landlady had named everything that she knew was my delight and there was so much sorrow bound up in her anger that I put up my finger as if an idea suddenly had come to me, and I replied:

'Now that I think on it, my Greek friend's name-day is a week from to-morrow! So I shall have both feasts!' And I threw back my head, laughing.

With that my landlady gave me a merry box on the ears and cried out gayly:

'Josef Vitek, you are a trial and no mistake! Fancy what a scare you gave me! Here was I, with a duck all dressed and ready for tomorrow's roasting, and noodles freshly rolled and cut into thin strips, and a guest all invited! Well, that which ends happily ends best.'

'A guest!' cried I. 'Now that is as it should be. And pray what is his name?'

'*His* name! Do you not think that one man at my table is worry enough? Besides I have only a single duck. Nay, this guest which I have invited is a woman. Not just any woman, mind you, but one who has a rare gift. For if everything is as it should be with her, at the end of the meal she can look into your teacup and tell you whatever the future has in store for you.'

'What!' I exclaimed. 'Can it be that you are asking a gipsy to sup with you?'

At this my landlady's face grew red again. 'Do you think I am quite a fool, Josef Vitek? I have not lived a decent life these many years to end by sitting at the same table with a thieving witch.'

'Well,' I answered, 'I am glad of that. But in Bohemia we have gipsies for such traffic. Although there was once an old woman in Polna, where I was born, who could tell marvelous things with a strand cut from your hair . . . In a teacup, did you say? Yes, come to think of it, gipsies look at your palm or they spread out cards before them.'

'As my guest can do also if she has the mind for it. Indeed, there are no end to the pleasant things she can tell you, any way she chooses.'

'If they be only pleasant things then it is well,' said I. 'But I remember that once my mother sent the strand from a lock of my sister's hair to the woman I told you of. And she sent back word: In less than a twelvemonth the child will die. And so it was.'

'Well, what better can one expect from one who tells a fortune from a strand of human hair?' demanded my landlady. 'For my part I should say that such a creature was in league with the devil. Doubtless she bewitched this sister of yours. And you must know, Josef Vitek, that there are such things as vampires.'

'Vampires!' I repeated. 'And what are they, pray?'

And with that my landlady told me so many stories concerning them that I forgot to eat the apple tart which she had set before me and I had to run all the way to my evening baking.

I was so late to my task that all my comrades were at their places when I entered, short of breath from my running, and my Greek friend who worked beside me looked up and said:

'What is the matter, Josef Vitek? One would think that you had seen your grandfather's ghost.'

'Well,' I answered, laughing, 'and if I had, I should certainly not run from it. For, as I remember, my grandfather was a kindly old man and his ghost would be a very gentle ghost, I am sure. But,' I went on, recalling my landlady's tales, 'I could not have run faster if I had met a vampire.'

At this my Greek friend turned pale. 'Hush, Josef Vitek!' he cried. 'It is not good for a Christian to so much as mention such creatures. For you must have heard the dreadful things they do.'

'Ah, then you have them in Greece, too! And are they the same sort that my landlady talks of: lost souls who rise up from their graves at midnight to drain the heart's blood from a man?'

'Yes,' whispered my Greek friend, 'they are the same in every country. And the worst of it is, you could not guess it if you saw one. At midnight, did you say? . . . Josef Vitek, they may *rise* from their graves at that hour but when they return is another matter. They are abroad at all seasons and they are always very beautiful, so that a man loses his heart to them . . .'

'Can you mean,' asked I, 'that there are no ugly ones, nor any men among them?'

'If there are I have yet to hear of it. I have a friend who has great knowledge of them. He is a seventh son and has the gift of discerning things that others cannot see. If one can trust his report, their lips are always red and their eyes two burning coals. And when all other wiles fail they let down great strands of blue-black hair to lure a man with its perfume. And they have little sharp white teeth.'

'Barring the little sharp white teeth,' said I, 'they have a pleasant sound.'

'They have, indeed!' replied my Greek friend, turning away with a shudder.

And with that I whipped off my coat and began to toss from the mixing pails enough dough for my first kneading.

All night as I plied my trade I thought about fortune tellers, and seventh sons, and vampires with little sharp white teeth, until these things were all mixed up in my mind like the very dough which finally I pushed into the oven. I wondered what this friend of my landlady would be like: an old gnarled witchlike creature or something dark and flashing in the manner of a young gipsy? And I watched my Greek friend going about his tasks with the bitter smile that is usually on his red lips turned to grave silence.

All this made me solemn also, but in the end I said to myself:

'Josef Vitek, do not be a fool! There are no such things as vampires abroad. This landlady of yours is full of such old-wives' tales. And as for your Greek friend, he is a sly dog and has stooped to many a trick to give himself a laugh at the expense of another. Even now he is probably thinking, "What sport to watch this simpleton from Polna swallow however large a dish of lies I set before him!" '

And I went home in the early morning light, misty as it usually is in San Francisco, whistling gaily; so that my landlady, meeting me at the threshold, said:

'That is right, my son. Be happy while there is time for it. For no one knows what is in the future.'

To which I replied, laughing:

'But to-night, at your table, I shall learn everything.'

'So much the more reason,' she answered, 'that you sing now at daybreak.'

'But I thought this friend of yours told only pleasant things.'

My landlady looked at me and shook her head. 'When you are as old as I am, Josef Vitek, you will learn that bitterness lies at the bottom of every sweet cup.'

'If there is only sweetness at the beginning,' I said, 'I shall be content.'

To which she made answer:

'So think we all until the draught is drained.'

Now this friend of my landlady who told only pleasant fortunes was neither a gnarled old witch nor a brown gipsy. She was very beautiful, with flashing eyes and bright red lips and hair as sleek and shining as the wing of a blackbird.

Her name was Elena and when she looked into my teacup she said:

'Josef Vitek, there is much sweetness in store for you . . . And a tear or two!' And she smiled in a curious way that hid her teeth.

But teacup fortunes were not to her taste, so she called to my landlady for a deck of cards.

'Now, Josef Vitek,' she commanded, 'shuffle these cards and cut them three times and make a wish, and then we shall see what we shall see.'

To shuffle the cards and to cut them was no great matter, but when it came to wishing there was much time wasted; for at once a flood of wishes crowded in upon me and, try as I would, I could not tell which to decide upon.

'Come, now,' said my landlady impatiently, 'you are holding everything back! There must be a thousand things a youth like you can wish for!'

'That is just it!' I cried. 'A thousand things to wish for and only one wish!'

But in the end I said to myself, 'Josef Vitek, if you wish just to be happy you will do well. For to be happy is to get every wish no matter how many.' And I laughed to myself, thinking how clever I was, and straight-way I cut the cards three times.

Then Elena spread out the cards before her and from the beginning she began to see marvellous things: journeys by land and water, pieces of money, an envious friend, and much feasting. I kept my counsel until she named this last circumstance and at once I cried out to my landlady.

'See, this is the name-day of my Greek friend which has turned up in the cards. Now if that is not wonderful I should like to know what is!'

To which the landlady replied:

'Not a bit more wonderful than the envious friend. If he is not that heathenish Greek, then I have never heard a fortune told in my life.'

As for Elena, she kept on sorting and discarding and turning up cards, and all the while finding astonishing things. But when it came to the matter of my wish she shook her head, saying:

'Sometimes your wish seems in your hand and then it vanishes . . . No, I have never seen quite the like of it before – to come and go in this fashion!'

'Well,' thought I, 'nobody can be always happy!' And I remembered Miriam whom I had loved. And I sighed as I had done that first evening when she had let me buy her a sweet-meat in the Greek coffee-house where she had danced.

As I sighed, the woman before me threw away the cards and looked straight into my eyes so that I felt a pleasant chill run over me. And she said again, smiling her discreet smile that concealed her teeth:

'Josef Vitek, give me your hands palms upwards. For your real fortune is withheld from the cards as it was from the teacup.'

So I gave her my hands palms upward, and she bent them back with her cool touch, and again that pleasant chill ran over me, and again she turned two burning eyes upon me as she said:

'You have a cold heart, Josef Vitek. And there are many women who will weep because of you. But there is one woman that stands out from all the rest: she shall sit at table with you one night as I do here. And she shall hold your hand thus and her heart will beat fast, as mine does!'

With that she brought my hands up to her breast and I felt the beating of her heart, and at once the pleasant chill which had swept me changed to fire and I felt my cheeks burn as I heard my landlay saying in a cold voice:

'Come, drink your coffee, Josef Vitek! . . . We have had enough of fortune telling for one evening.'

Now as soon as my landlady had spoken thus I remembered that it was time to go to work and I rose from the table. And at once Elena rose also, saying:

'If you are going in my direction, Josef Vitek, I shall walk with you.'

At these words my landlady frowned, motioning me with her head against the invitation. But I thought to myself, 'What concern can it be of hers whom I walk with to my work? I am no goose to be herded hither and thither!'

So I answered without looking at my landlady:

'Whatever is your direction is mine!'

And I waited while she covered herself in a cloak coloured like a flame.

We went out into the night, but my landlady did not so much as follow us to the door. I felt ashamed to see her treat a guest so, and at the foot of the stairs I said to my companion:

'My landlady never follows anyone to the door at night. The chill air is not good for her.'

'Night is for youth, Josef Vitek!' she replied. And I felt her hand touch mine.

I felt her hand touch mine and it was as if Miriam had touched me, only with a difference: this touch set me shivering. Yet I did not feel cold. And while I was still pondering this strange circumstance, she said:

'Josef Vitek, which way shall we walk?'

'Wherever you will!' I answered, scarcely knowing what I said.

We turned our steps in the opposite direction from what should have been my course. But somehow my night's task at the bakery where I work seemed very far away, like a tale that had been told. And presently we stood upon the top of a hill in a little public square with a plume of cypress trees upon its crest. And San Francisco lay before us, twinkling its thousand eyes.

Then Elena said to me softly, 'Josef Vitek, you are a cold youth and no mistake . . . Come closer.'

But instead of obeying her, I drew back as if a cold wind had touched me. And with that she gave a toss of her head as one does who is displeased and her blue-black hair fell in a dark shower over her shoulders. Her blue-black hair fell in a dark shower over her shoulders and a strange perfume filled the air and I heard her say again:

'Come closer, Josef Vitek, there is nothing to fear!'

And at that moment I felt two burning lips against my throat.

I came home at my appointed hour, in the chill of morning, and as usual my landlady was waiting for me at the head of the stairs. Her face had a stern look and she said coldly:

'Josef Vitek, already your Greek friend has been here asking for you. He came almost at daybreak and there was nothing to do but lie concerning you. So I said, "He is sleeping now after a night of pain."

And he went away with an unsatisfied look upon his face as if he knew that I had deceived him. If he comes again I shall bring him to you.'

And having said her say, she went into her room, closing the door. All the time I have lived with my landlady she had never spoken so coldly to me. Yet in my room everything was as it always was – a plate of fruit on the table before my bed, and a little mound of spice cakes near it such as are my delight, and the coverlet turned down. And I thought:

'She must love you still, Josef Vitek, or she would not put apples and spice cakes upon your table. She must love you still, Josef Vitek, or she would not tell a lie for you.'

And I remembered my mother, almost as I had last seen her on that day I fled my country – standing in the door with an Austrian officer opposite her, saying, 'No, my son Josef Vitek is not here . . . Only this morning he went out into the fields with his father' – while all the time I was peering at her from a huge chest in which she had once stored her linen.

And thinking it all over, I said aloud to myself, 'My landlady is not my mother and my Greek friend is not an Austrian officer. And the lie that was told this morning was not to save me from fighting for an enemy. But it was told to spare me unpleasantness, and in that they were both alike . . . Yes, Josef Vitek, there are beautiful lies just as there are beautiful women.' And as I said this I shut my eyes and the vision of that public square, plumed with cypress trees, rose before me and I smelled the strange perfume of unbound hair.

As I stood there a knock came on my door, and before I could answer my Greek friend pushed his way into my room.

Yes, before I could answer, my Greek friend pushed his way into my room and his little glinting eyes travelled from the cap upon my head to the untouched bed, and he said bitingly:

'Ah, Josef Vitek, and have you been in such pain that you could not rest except upon your two feet?'

I drew myself up proudly. 'I have not been in pain at all, my friend . . . In fact, everything has been as it should with me. You see, my landlady was mistaken.'

At that my Greek friend smiled a knowing smile. 'Josef Vitek,' he said, 'there are three things that keep a man from his daily task: being sick, or drunk with wine, or under the spell of a woman . . . Now your own testimony sets at naught the first circumstance, and the testimony of my eyes sets at naught the second. There remains only the third excuse . . . Well, we are all human, Josef Vitek, and you are young in the bargain. I was once so myself.'

And for a moment a shadow crossed his face and I knew that he too was thinking of Miriam, for had he not loved her also? . . . As for me, I felt the hot blood rising to my cheeks and the laughter of my Greek friend filled the room.

When my Greek friend had departed I threw myself on my bed, but my sleep was filled with strange dreams; so I awoke at my appointed time feeling as tired as when I had first lain down. And instead of going into my landlady's kitchen for the evening meal, I tiptoed out into the night, thinking:

'To-morrow she will be better humoured . . . Besides, I must be beforehand to my task, to make up for my absence. I shall not even take time to eat.' For, if the truth were known, I did not feel hungry.

But it seemed that I was not to go to my task that night, for as I turned the first corner whom should I see but Elena, standing with her flame-coloured cloak blowing in the wind. And suddenly I felt cold all over and my teeth chattered and I said to myself, 'I must go roundabout before she sees me!' But ere I could retrace my steps I felt her eyes upon me and I heard her voice say:

'Ah, Josef Vitek, so there you are! And whither do you go at such an early hour?'

'To my task,' I answered as coldly as I could in spite of my beating temples.

'To your task, Josef Vitek? . . . *To your task?* . . . On such a night as this, with the moon just rising and the stars waiting to be fanned into a flame? . . . Come, this is not a night for *work*, Josef Vitek!' And as she spoke my night's task seemed very far away, and yet a voice within me made me answer:

'What are a rising moon and flaming stars to me, who must labour and sweat? . . . A man must eat, and unless he be a rich man or a king, he must earn it.'

'Be a king, then, for to-night, Josef Vitek!' she cried, touching me with a finger that burned in spite of its chill. And at that moment all my strength went out of me and I felt my resolution fall as a ripe field before a shining sickle.

On that night we did not climb upward to the public square with its crest of plumed cypresses, but instead we rode out to the sea; for the air was clear and there was no mist to chill us. And we sat in the yellow sand with the perfume of lupines mingling with the wet smell of the ocean, while far off in the west, hanging above the water, the evening star burned so brightly that even the moon could not shame it. And again Elena's teeth flashed in the dusk, and again she let down her blue-black hair, and again her two lips burned my throat. And again I forgot everything that was or ever had been. For it was as if the sea crept in and covered us.

When morning came Elena rose, shaking the sand from her tangled hair, and she left me without a word. And with her going it was as if the sea fell back also, uncovering me, and I remembered everything that was or ever had been. I thought of my native village and my landlady and my nightly task. But the thing that I thought of more than any of these was the monastery near Polna where once I plied my trade as baker. And I recalled the rose garden in which the pious men walked in the noon sunlight and where the bees grew heavy with sweetness, and the hush and peace that fell on the old grey walls at evening, and the tinkling of bells. Yes, I once had plied my trade in such a place even before I knew that trade perfectly, for my good mother had said, 'My son Josef is but a lad – and where better can a lad be than in the shelter of a holy place? Perhaps, who knows, he may end it by being a holy man.' And remembering her hopes for me, I wept, burying my face in the sand.

Thus I lay until noon, and then I rose and went back to the crowded town and to my lodgings. But my landlady was not at the door to greet me, neither were there apples nor spice cakes upon my table; and the coverlet had not been turned down.

Again I rose from sleep at the appointed time, thinking to be beforehand to my task, and again I went out softly so that I might escape the ill-humour of my landlady, and again Elena stood upon the corner waiting. And again when she spoke to me and touched me with her cool fingers I felt my resolution fall as a ripe field before a shining sickle.

And thus the days passed, with my nightly task at the bakery where I work growing farther and farther away, like a tale that had been told. And in all this time I saw nothing of my landlady: for in the morning she was not on hand to greet me and at night I stole out without breaking bread at her table. Only my Greek friend came with news from my comrades, and yet I cared for no word he uttered. It was as if nothing in life mattered except the coming of night and Elena in her flame-coloured cloak. Not even when he said to me, 'Josef Vitek, you cannot go on thus forever . . . presently you will return to find your place taken at the bakery,' did I feel the least uneasiness. If the truth were known, I but laughed at him, and the next day he said:

'If you do not work, Josef Vitek, how shall you live? . . . Who will pay your landlady if you earn no money, and where will you find lodgings?'

'Once I thought of these things,' I returned, 'but what are food and lodgings to me now?'

And looking at me sharply, he said:

'Josef Vitek, you are talking like one already dead. It must be that a woman has bewitched you . . . Come, is she more beautiful than Miriam?'

'She is different,' I answered. 'When Miriam was near I felt a *sweet* pain in my heart.'

He turned away with a hard laugh and presently he said:

'To-morrow is my name-day, Josef Vitek. Have you forgotten that you are pledged to my feast?'

'I cannot come without Elena,' I answered.

'As you will,' returned my Greek friend. 'At a name-day feast there is always room for whatever guests come at the eleventh hour.'

So he departed with my promise. But once he was gone, I thought: 'What will Elena say to a feast? Perhaps she will not like the idea.' And I was disturbed. But that night when I told her of it, she said:

'A feast, did you say? And will there be men there?'

'Yes,' I answered, remembering my Greek friend's last name-day, 'scores of them.'

A strange ravenous look came into her eyes and her lips smiled a discreet smile, concealing her teeth.

'Come let us make haste, Josef Vitek!' she breathed softly. 'For if there is one thing I like above anything in the world, it is a feast.'

And with that her lips grew fuller and more red.

Truly, in spite of many faults, my Greek friend is a brave giver of feasts. Even if my landlady had been minded to provide fare for threescore guests she could not have done better. For the most part it was all as I had prophesied: broth of chicken with a dash of lemon, little bitter-sweet olives, lamb baked with eggplant, and at the end a curd of goat's milk. Only there was chicken as well, fried in sweet butter, and sea bass for those who wished it. And with every course strange and warming drinks: mastica, and mavro-daphne, and retzina, and cognac. And between the courses melancholy music to which the men danced, holding one another's hands in a long line, with the women sitting at the snow-white tables looking on. Yes, between the courses the men danced together, and Elena at my side said:

'What a strange custom! Do you do thus in Bohemia?'

'Nay,' I answered, 'in my country we dance to gay music with the skirts of our partners flying in the breeze.'

'Then let us dance together, Josef Vitek,' she cried, 'when all this sad gliding is finished.'

'As you will,' I replied. And as soon as they had finished I threw a coin to the musicians and I called to them:

'Can you not play us a gay tune? Come, play us a gay tune and *we* shall dance for you!'

With that the feasters broke into a laugh and clapped their hands and the head musician, striking his bow against the strings, began a wild tune that set my pulses leaping. I looked down into Elena's eyes and I said:

'Are you ready? Are you ready to dance with me, knowing nothing of a single measure which I shall tread?'

For answer she rose, pressing her body against mine, and I heard her say between closed teeth:

'Dance, Josef Vitek! Dance and leave such things as measures to Greeks and fools!'

So we danced, and to this day I cannot say what steps were traced by us. For we were like two leaves blown in the wind and I could not even say who led or who followed. But at once I thought:

'It is thus that witches upon broomsticks dance!'

And I felt the hot breath of Elena in my face and I said to myself:

'Josef Vitek, this is not a gay dance! This is not a gay dance for there is something terrible in it!'

And thus we whirled and leaped and swayed and presently the music stopped and I heard the company crying out their pleasure. And with that we stood still . . . We stood still, with the company crying out their pleasure, and presently a press of men swept us toward our table and I felt the hand of my Greek friend upon my shoulder, and I heard his voice saying:

'Come with me, Josef Vitek, for I have something to say to you.'

And though I was loth to leave Elena even for a moment, I went with him and stood apart.

'Josef Vitek,' he said, 'such dancing and such a woman are not for you.'

I felt the blood warm in my face. 'You are right!' I answered in my pride. 'But for that matter there is not a man among us who can measure up to her.'

He looked at me sharply and this time he laughed. 'Josef Vitek, you are a child and no mistake . . . At your age all men are fools!'

I was about to speak when a laugh like silver broke in upon me. Elena stood at my elbow.

'At his age, did you say? . . . Tell me, pray, at what age then are they wise?' And she threw a glance of fire at my Greek friend and I felt my heart grow cold.

She threw a glance of fire at my Greek friend and his little eyes became two points of flame, and he reached over to a near-by table and poured amber wine into an empty glass and gave it to her. She held the glass almost to her lips, then dashed it to the floor. 'Give me red wine or nothing!' she cried.

An ugly look came over the face of my Greek friend and I saw him set his teeth together. Yet he did as she commanded, and presently she stood before us, sipping at red wine in a strange manner which left me shuddering. And as she stained her red lips further with the last drop, she said to my Greek friend:

'Let *us* dance together!'

To which he replied:

'I dance only in the fashion of my country.'

'And I,' she answered, 'in the fashion of any who will pay the piper!'

With that my Greek friend tossed a coin upon the platform where the players sat gossiping and at once they caught up their instruments and began a slow melancholy tune. Then Elena and my Greek friend stepped out upon the floor and she danced in *his* fashion with little snakelike glidings, until she seemed herself just such a creature intent on charming whom she would. And as the music quickened my Greek friend leaped before her like some spellbound thing, and her black hair tumbled in a dark shower about her shoulders, and her smile became wider and wider until I saw her teeth unguarded for the first time.

I saw her teeth unguarded for the first time and I turned away shuddering: *for they were small and sharp and pointed!*

They sat all night, Elena and my Greek friend, at a table which had no third seat; while I stood in a far corner of the room – sick with dread and envy and I know not what. And all night long Elena sipped red wine, and my Greek friend, wine the colour of amber. And neither turned eyes in my direction.

And at dawn Elena rose, slipping on her cloak of flame, and my Greek friend followed after her. They halted for a moment before the door and I thought:

'Shall I warn him against her? Shall I tell him what manner of woman she is to drain the heart's blood from a man?'

But almost at once I grew bitter and I said to myself: 'Has he no eyes of his own?'

And so I let them go together out into the dawn.

For myself, I turned my steps in the direction of my lodgings. The morning air was dank and misty and I felt sick and weary and full of strange confusion. At one moment I longed again for Elena and in the next I hated her. And in the moments that I hated her I thought of my Greek friend, wondering what was to become of him and whether I had done right to let him go thus without protest. But always, in the end, bitterness had its way and I would mutter:

'Does a man who is despoiled warn the thief?'

Thus I came to my lodgings, still at odds with myself. And no landlady stood upon the threshold to greet me. And my room was clean and cold and unadorned, so that I thought of my cell back in that monastery near Polna where I had once plied my trade. Yes, in the grey morning light it seemed as if it might well be that very place, except that here there was no peace. And shivering, I lay down to wait the appointed hour for me to go to my task.

I rose at evening, still sick at heart, and I went softly out into the dusk lest my landlady should hear me. And as I turned in the direction of the bakery where I work – whose shadow should cross my path but the shadow of my Greek friend! For a moment I drew back, but he said quickly:

'Ah, Josef Vitek, I have been waiting for you! . . . Come, let us go to our task together.'

I felt my heart beat fast, but there was nothing to do but go with him and thus we walked in silence, and I thought:

'Is he laughing, Josef Vitek? Or does he repent the wrong he did you?'

And looking at his face, as dark as a shuttered house, I could not answer.

But when we reached the bakery, entering the narrow wash-room where the men gather, I felt his hand upon my shoulder. I felt his hand upon my shoulder in the fashion of an elder brother, and at that moment every one pressed forward full of questions concerning my absence, and I heard my Greek friend say:

'Do not bother him! Cannot you see how pale and spent he is? For a week or more he has been in the hands of the devil. Yes, for a week he has been in the hands of the devil and it is only by a miracle that you have him with you to-night.'

And suddenly, looking at my Greek friend, I understood everything, and I said to as many as could hear me:

'Comrades, he is only half right . . . For a week or more I *have* been in the hands of the devil. But it was not a miracle that saved me. Instead, I was saved by nothing so truly as by this friend of mine, himself.'

And with that my Greek friend broke out into his old laugh, half bitterness and half scorn, but his fingers gripped my shoulder in a way which told me that my words had pleased him.

When morning came my Greek friend walked back with me to my lodgings, and I thought:

'Yes, he has become like an elder brother, indeed. Even now he will not trust me to danger. I might be a child in my first week at school.'

And the thought pleased me because I had always fancied this Greek friend of mine a man without affection. And walking home in the cool grey dawn, I said to him:

'Did you not mark her red lips last night when you danced with her?'

'Yes,' he answered.

'And her eyes like two burning coals?'

'Yes.'

'And her blue-black hair with its perfume?'

'Yes.'

'And at the end, her little sharp white teeth?'

'Yes.'

'Then, did you not fear that she would drain your heart's blood?'

My Greek friend shook his head. 'There is little wine in a cracked jug, Josef Vitek.'

At that moment we both looked up and I felt my Greek friend's hand in mine: a cloak of flame was billowing in the morning air and Elena stood waiting on the corner near my lodgings.

For a moment my heart beat fast. And I heard my Greek friend say between his teeth:

'Courage, brother!'

And we passed her swiftly and her taunting laugh floated after us.

My Greek friend halted at the foot of the stairs to my lodgings and I said farewell to him. But he did not go at once. Instead I saw him standing, as I mounted upward, like the keeper to some forbidden gate.

I entered the house and at the door to my landlady's room I stopped and beat upon it.

'Who is there?' I heard her cracked voice call out.

'It is Josef Vitek,' I cried back.

'Well?'

'I have come home again,' I said, and I went swiftly to my room.

I went swiftly to my room and laid myself down, closing my eyes. And presently I heard the door open gently. I lay quite still, pretending I was fast asleep; and between my half-opened lids I saw my landlady creep gently in and place spice cakes and red apples and grapes upon my table.

As she left again, closing the door softly, a single tear dropped upon my pillow. And I gave a happy sigh and fell into a deep sleep.

I, The Vampire

HENRY KUTTNER

I

The Chevalier Futaine

The party was dull. I had come too early. There was a preview that night at Grauman's Chinese, and few of the important guests would arrive until it was over. Indeed, Jack Hardy, ace director at Summit Pictures, where I worked as assistant director, hadn't arrived – yet – and he was the host. But Hardy had never been noted for punctuality.

I went out on the porch and leaned against a pillar, sipping a cocktail and looking down at the lights of Hollywood. Hardy's place was on the summit of a hill overlooking the film capital, near Falcon Lair, Valentino's famous turreted castle. I shivered a little. Fog was sweeping in from Santa Monica, blotting out the lights to the west.

Jean Hubbard, who was an ingenue at Summit, came up beside me and took the glass out of my hand.

'Hello, Mart,' she said, sipping the liquor. 'Where've you been?'

'Down with the *Murder Desert* troupe, on location in the Mojave,' I said. 'Miss me, honey?'

I drew her close. She smiled up at me, her tilted eyebrows lending a touch of diablerie to the tanned, lovely face. I was going to marry Jean, but I wasn't sure just when.

'Missed you lots,' she said, and held up her lips. I responded.

After a moment I said, 'What's this about the vampire man?'

She chuckled. 'Oh, the Chevalier Futaine. Didn't you read Lolly Parsons' write-up in *Script*? Jack Hardy picked him up last month in Europe. Silly rot. But it's good publicity.'

'Three cheers for publicity,' I said. 'Look what it did for *Birth of a Nation*. But where does the vampire angle come in?'

'Mystery man. Nobody can take a picture of him, scarcely anybody can see him. Weird tales are told about his former life in Paris. Going to play in Jack's *Red Thirst*. The kind of build-up Universal gave Karloff for *Frankenstein*. The Chevalier Futaine' – she rolled out the words with amused relish – 'is probably a singing waiter from a Paris café. I haven't seen him – but the deuce with him, anyway. Mart, I want you to do something for me. For Deming.'

'Hess Deming?' I raised my eyebrows in astonishment. Hess Deming, Summit's biggest box-office star, whose wife, Sandra Colter, had died two days before. She, too, had been an actress, although never the great star her husband was. Hess loved her, I knew – and now I guessed what the trouble was. I said, 'I noticed he was a bit wobbly.'

'He'll kill himself,' Jean said, looking worried. 'I – I feel responsible for him somehow, Mart. After all, he gave me my start at Summit. And he's due for the D.Ts any time now.'

'Well, I'll do what I can,' I told her. 'But that isn't a great deal. After all, getting tight is probably the best thing he could do. I know if I lost you, Jean – '

I stopped. I didn't like to think of it.

Jean nodded. 'See what you can do for him, anyway. Losing Sandra that way was – pretty terrible.'

'What way?' I asked. 'I've been away, remember. I read something about it, but – '

'She just died,' Jean said. 'Pernicious anemia, they said. But Hess told me the doctor really didn't know what it was. She just seemed to grow weaker and weaker until – she passed away.'

I nodded, gave Jean a hasty kiss, and went back into the house. I had just seen Hess Deming walk past, a glass in his hand.

He turned as I tapped his shoulder. 'Oh, Mart,' he said, his voice just a bit fuzzy. He could hold his liquor, but I could tell by his bloodshot eyes that he was almost at the end of his rope. He was a handsome devil, all right, well-built, strong-featured, with level grey eyes and a broad mouth that was usually smiling. It wasn't smiling now. It was slack, and his face was bedewed with perspiration.

'You know about Sandra?' he asked.

'Yeah,' I said. 'I'm sorry, Hess.'

He drank deeply from the glass, wiped his mouth with a grimace of distaste.

'I'm drunk, Mart,' he confided. 'I had to get drunk. It was awful – those last few days. I've got to burn her up.'

I didn't say anything.

'Burn her up. Oh, my God, Mart – that beautiful body of hers, crumbling to dust – and I've got to watch it! She made me promise I'd watch to make sure they burned her.'

I said, 'Cremation's a clean ending, Hess. And Sandra was a clean girl, and a damned good actress.'

He put his flushed face close to mine. 'Yeah – but I've got to burn her up. It'll kill me, Mart. Oh, God!' He put the empty glass down on a table and looked around dazedly.

I was wondering why Sandra had insisted on cremation. She'd given an interview once in which she stressed her dread of fire. Most write-ups of stars are applesauce, but I happened to know that Sandra did dread fire. Once, on the set, I'd seen her go into hysterics when her leading man lit his pipe too near her face.

'Excuse me, Mart,' Hess said. 'I've got to get another drink.'

'Wait a minute,' I said, holding him. 'You want to watch yourself, Hess. You've had too much already.'

'It still hurts,' he said. 'Just a little more and maybe it won't hurt so much.' But he didn't pull away. Instead he stared at me with the dullness of intoxication in his eyes. 'Clean,' he said presently. 'She said that too, Mart. She said burning was a clean death. But, God, that beautiful white body of hers – I can't stand it, Mart! I'm going crazy, I think. Get me a drink, like a good fellow.'

I said, 'Wait here, Hess. I'll get you one.' I didn't add that it would be watered – considerably.

He sank down in a chair, mumbling thanks. As I went off I felt sick. I'd seen too many actors going on the rocks to mistake Hess's symptoms. I knew that his box-office days were over. There would be longer waits between pictures, and then personal appearances, and finally Poverty Row and serials. And in the end maybe a man found dead in a cheap hall bedroom on Main Street, with the gas on.

*

There was a crowd around the bar. Somebody said, 'Here's Mart. Hey, come over and meet the vampire.'

Then I got a shock. I saw Jack Hardy, my host, the director with whom I'd worked on many a hit. He looked like a corpse. And I'd seen him looking plenty bad before. A man with a hangover, or a marijuana jag, isn't a pretty sight, but I'd never seen Hardy like this. He looked as though he was keeping going on his nerve alone. There was no blood in the man.

I'd last seen him as a stocky, ruddy blond, who looked like nothing so much as a wrestler, with his huge biceps, his ugly, good-natured face, and his bristling crop of yellow hair. Now he looked like a skeleton, with skin hanging loosely on the big frame. His face was a network of sagging wrinkles. Pouches bagged beneath his eyes, and those eyes were dull and glazed. About his neck a black silk scarf was knotted tightly.

'Good God, Jack!' I exclaimed. 'What have you been doing to yourself?'

He looked away quickly. 'Nothing,' he said brusquely. 'I'm all right. I want you to meet the Chevalier Futaine – this is Mart Prescott.'

'Pierre,' a voice said. 'Hollywood is no place for titles. Mart Prescott – the pleasure is mine.'

I faced the Chevalier Pierre Futaine.

We shook hands. My first impression was of icy cold, and a slick kind of dryness – and I let go of his hand too quickly to be polite. He smiled at me.

A charming man, the Chevalier. Or so he seemed. Slender, below medium height, his bland, round face seemed incongruously youthful. Blond hair was plastered close to his scalp. I saw that his cheeks were rouged – very deftly, but I know something about make-up. And under the rouge I read a curious, deathly pallor that would have made him a marked man had he not disguised it. Some disease, perhaps, had blanched his skin – but his lips were not artificially reddened. And they were as crimson as blood.

He was clean-shaved, wore impeccable evening clothes, and his eyes were black pools of ink.

'Glad to know you,' I said. 'You're the vampire, eh?'

He smiled. 'So they tell me. But we all serve the dark god of publicity, eh, Mr Prescott? Or – is it Mart?'

'It's Mart,' I said, still staring at him. I saw his eyes go past me, and an extraordinary expression appeared on his face – an expression of amazement, disbelief. Swiftly it was gone.

I turned. Jean was approaching, was at my side as I moved. She said, 'Is this the Chevalier?'

Pierre Futaine was staring at her, his lips parted a little. Almost inaudibly he murmured, 'Sonya.' And then, on a note of interrogation, 'Sonya?'

I introduced the two. Jean said, 'You see, my name isn't Sonya.'

The Chevalier shook his head, an odd look in his black eyes.

'I once knew a girl like you,' he said softly. 'Very much like you. It is strange.'

'Will you excuse me?' I broke in. Jack Hardy was leaving the bar. Quickly I followed him.

I touched his shoulder as he went out the French windows. He jerked out a startled oath, turned a white death-mask of a face to me.

'Damn you, Mart!' he snarled. 'Keep your hands to yourself.'

I put my hands on his shoulders and swung him around.

'What the devil has happened to you?' I asked. 'Listen, Jack, you can't bluff me or lie to me. You know that. I've straightened you out enough times in the past, and I can do it again. Let me in on it.'

His ruined face softened. He reached up and took away my hands. His own were ice-cold, like the hands of the Chevalier Futaine.

'No,' he said. 'No use, Mart. There's nothing you can do. I'm all right, really. Just – overstrain. I had too good a time in Paris.'

I was up against a blank wall. Suddenly, without volition, a thought popped into my mind and out of my mouth before I knew it.

'What's the matter with your neck?' I asked abruptly.

He didn't answer. He just frowned and shook his head.

'I've a throat infection,' he told me. 'Caught it on the steamer.'

His hand went up and touched the black scarf.

There was a croaking, harsh sound from behind us – a sound that didn't seem quite human. I turned. It was Hess Deming. He was swaying in the portal, his eyes glaring and bloodshot, a little trickle of saliva running down his chin.

He said in a dead, expressionless voice that was somehow dreadful, 'Sandra died of a throat infection, Hardy.'

Jack didn't answer. He stumbled back a step. Hess went on dully.

'She got all white and died. And the doctor didn't know what it was, although the death certificate said anaemia. Did you bring back some filthy disease with you, Hardy? Because if you did I'm going to kill you.'

'Wait a minute,' I said. 'A throat infection? I didn't know – '

'There was a wound in her throat – two little marks, close together. That couldn't have killed her, unless some loathsome disease – '

'You're crazy, Hess,' I said. 'You know you're drunk. Listen to me: Jack couldn't have had anything to do with – that.'

Hess didn't look at me. He watched Jack Hardy out of his bloodshot eyes. He went on in that low, deadly monotone:

'Will you swear Mart's right, Hardy? Will you?'

Jack's lips were twisted by some inner agony. I said, 'Go on, Jack. Tell him he's wrong.'

Hardy burst out, 'I haven't been near your wife! I haven't seen her since I got back. There's – '

'That's not the answer I want,' Hess whispered. And he sprang for the other man – reeled forward, rather.

Hess was too drunk, and Jack too weak, for them to do each other any harm, but there was a nasty scuffle for a moment before I separated them. As I pulled them apart, Hess's hand clutched the scarf about Jack's neck, ripped it away.

And I saw the marks on Jack Hardy's throat. Two red, angry little pits, white-rimmed, just over the left jugular.

2

The Cremation of Sandra

It was the next day that Jean telephoned me.

'Mart,' she said, 'we're going to run over a scene for *Red Thirst* tonight at the studio – Stage 6. You've been assigned as assistant director on the pic, so you should be there. And – I had an idea Jack might not tell you. He's been – so odd lately.'

'Thanks, honey,' I said. 'I'll be there. But I didn't know you were in the flicker.'

'Neither did I, but there's been some wire-pulling. Somebody wanted me in it – the Chevalier, I think – and the big boss phoned me this morning and let me in on the secret. I don't feel up to it, though. Had a bad night.'

'Sorry,' I sympathized. 'You were okay when I left you.'

'I had a – nightmare,' she said slowly. 'It was rather frightful, Mart. It's funny, though, I can't remember what it was about. Well – you'll be there to-night?'

I said I would, but as it happened I was unable to keep my promise. Hess Deming telephoned me, asking if I'd come out to his Malibu place and drive him into town. He was too shaky to handle a car himself, he said, and Sandra's cremation was to take place that afternoon. I got out my roadster and sent it spinning west on Sunset. In twenty minutes I was at Deming's beach house.

The house-boy let me in, shaking his head gravely as he recognized me.

'Mist' Deming pretty bad,' he told me. 'All morning drinking gin – straight – '

From upstairs Hess shouted, 'That you, Mart? Okay – I'll be down right away. Come up here, Jim!'

The Japanese, with a meaning glance at me, pattered upstairs.

I wandered over to a table, examining the magazines upon it. A little breath of wind came through the half-open window, fluttering a scrap of paper. A word on it caught my eye, and I picked up the note. For that's what it was. It was addressed to Hess, and after one glance I had no compunction about scanning it.

'Hess dear,' the message read. 'I feel I'm going to die very soon. And I want you to do something for me. I've been out of my head, I know, saying things I didn't mean. Don't cremate me, Hess. Even though I were dead I'd feel the fire – I know it. Bury me in a vault in Forest Lawn – and don't embalm me. I shall be dead when you find this, but I know you'll do as I wish, dear. And, alive or dead, I'll always love you.'

The note was signed by Sandra Colter, Hess's wife. This was odd. I wondered whether Hess had seen it yet.

There was a little hiss of indrawn breath from behind me. It was Jim, the house-boy. He said, 'Mist' Prescott – I find that note last night. Mist' Hess not seen it. It Mis' Colter's writing.'

He hesitated, and I read fear in his eyes – sheer, unashamed fear. He put a brown forefinger on the note.

'See that, Mist' Prescott?'

He was pointing to a smudge of ink that half obscured the signature. I said, 'Well?'

'I do that, Mist' Prescott. When I pick up that note. The ink – not dry.'

I stared at him. He turned hastily at the sound of footsteps on the stairs. Hess Deming was coming down, rather shakily.

I think it was then that I first realized the horrible truth. I didn't believe it, though – not then. It was too fantastic, too incredible; yet something of the truth must have crept into my mind, for there was no other explanation for what I did then.

Hess said, 'What have you got there, Mart?'

'Nothing,' I said quietly. I crumpled the note and thrust it into my pocket. 'Nothing important, anyway. Ready to go?'

He nodded, and we went to the door. I caught a glimpse of Jim staring after us, an expression of – was it relief? – in his dark, wizened face.

The crematory was in Pasadena, and I left Hess there. I would have stayed with him, but he wouldn't have it. I knew he didn't want anyone to be watching him when Sandra's body was being incinerated. And I knew it would be easier for him that way. I took a short cut through the Hollywood hills, and that's where the trouble started.

I broke an axle. Recent rains had gullied the road, and I barely saved the car from turning over. After that I had to hike miles to the nearest telephone, and then I wasted more time waiting for a taxi to pick me up. It was nearly eight o'clock when I arrived at the studio.

The gateman let me in, and I hurried to Stage 6. It was dark. Cursing under my breath, I turned away, and almost collided with a small figure. It was Forrest, one of the cameramen. He let out a curious squeal, and clutched my arm.

'That you, Mart? Listen, will you do me a favour? I want you to watch a print – '

'Haven't time,' I said. 'Seen Jean around here? I was to – '

'It's about that,' Forest said. He was a shrivelled, monkey-faced little chap, but a mighty good cameraman. 'They've gone – Jean and Hardy and the Chevalier. There's something funny about that guy.'

'Think so? Well, I'll phone Jean. I'll look at your rushes tomorrow.'

'She won't be home,' he told me. 'The Chevalier took her over to the Grove. Listen, Mart, you've *got* to watch this. Either I don't know how to handle a grinder any more, or that Frenchman is the damnedest thing I've ever shot. Come over to the theatre, Mart – I've got the reel ready to run. Just developed the rough print myself.'

'Oh, all right,' I assented, and followed Forrest to the theatre.

I found a seat in the dark little auditorium, and listened to Forrest moving about in the projection booth. He clicked on the amplifier and said, 'Hardy didn't want any pictures taken – insisted on it, you know. But the boss told me to leave one of the automatic cameras going– not to bother with the sound – just to get an idea how the French guy would screen. Lucky it wasn't one of the old rattler cameras, or Hardy would have caught on. Here it comes, Mart!'

I heard a click as the amplifier was switched off. White light flared on the screen. It faded, gave place to a picture – the interior of Stage 6.

The set was incongruous – a mid-Victorian parlour, with overstuffed plush chairs, gilt-edged paintings, even a particularly hideous what-not. Jack Hardy moved into the range of the camera. On the screen his face seemed to leap out at me like a death's-head, covered with sagging, wrinkled skin. Following him came Jean, wearing a tailored suit – no one dresses for rehearsals – and behind her –

I blinked, thinking that my eyes were tricking me. Something like a glowing fog – oval, tall as a man – was moving across the screen. You've seen the nimbus of light on the screen when a flash-light is turned directly on the camera? Well – it was like that, except that its source was not traceable. And, horribly, it moved forward at about the pace a man would walk.

The amplifier clicked again. Forrest said, 'When I saw it on the negative I thought I was screwy, Mart. I saw the take – there wasn't any funny light there. Look – ' The oval, glowing haze was motionless beside Jean, and she was looking directly at it, a smile on her lips. 'Mart, when that was taken, Jean was looking right at the French guy!'

I said, somewhat hoarsely, 'Hold it, Forrest. Right there.'

The images slowed down, became motionless. Jean's left profile was toward the camera. I leaned forward, staring at something I had glimpsed on the girl's neck. It was scarcely visible save as a tiny, discoloured mark on Jean's throat, above the jugular – but unmistakably the same wound I had seen on the throat of Jack Hardy the night before!

I heard the amplifier click off. Suddenly the screen showed blindingly white, and then went black.

I waited a moment, but there was no sound from the booth.

'Forrest,' I called. 'You okay?'

There was no sound. The faint whirring of the projector had died. I got up quickly and went to the back of the theatre. There were two entrances to the booth, a door which opened on stairs leading down to the alley outside, and a hole in the floor reached by means of a metal ladder. I went up this swiftly, an ominous apprehension mounting within me.

Forrest was still there. But he was no longer alive. He lay sprawled on his back, his wizened face staring up blindly, his head twisted at an impossible angle. It was quite apparent that his neck had been broken almost instantly.

I sent a hasty glance at the projector. The can of film was gone! And the door opening on the stairway was ajar a few inches.

I stepped out on the stairs, although I knew I would see no one. The white-lit, broad alley between Stages 6 and 4 was silent and empty.

The sound of running feet came to me, steadily growing louder. A man came racing into view. I recognized him as one of the publicity gang. I hailed him.

'Can't wait,' he gasped, but slowed down nevertheless.

I said, 'Have you seen anyone around here just now? The – Chevalier Futaine?'

He shook his head. 'No, but – ' His face was white as he looked up at me. 'Hess Deming's gone crazy. I've got to contact the papers.'

Ice gripped me. I raced down the stairs, clutched his arm.

'What do you mean?' I snapped. 'Hess was all right when I left him. A bit tight, that's all.'

His face was glistening with sweat. 'It's awful – I'm not sure yet what happened. His wife – Sandra Colter – came to life while they were cremating her. They saw her through the window, you know – screaming and pounding at the glass while she was being burned alive. Hess got her out too late. He went stark, raving mad. Suspended animation, they say – I've got to get to a phone, Mr Prescott!'

He tore himself away, sprinted in the direction of the administration buildings.

I put my hand in my pocket and pulled out a scrap of paper. It was the note I had found in Hess Deming's house. The words danced and wavered before my eyes. Over and over I was telling myself, 'It can't be true! Such things can't happen!'

I didn't mean Sandra Colter's terrible resurrection during the cremation. That, alone, might be plausibly explained – catalepsy, perhaps. But taken in conjunction with certain other occurrences, it led to one definite conclusion – and it was a conclusion I dared not face.

What had poor Forrest said? That the Chevalier was taking Jean to the Cocoanut Grove? Well –

The taxi was still waiting. I got in.

'The Ambassador,' I told the driver grimly. 'Twenty bucks if you hit the green lights all the way.'

3
The Black Coffin

All night I had been combing Hollywood – without success. Neither the Chevalier Futaine nor Jean had been to the Grove, I discovered. And no one knew the Chevalier's address. A telephone call to the studio, now ablaze with excitement over the Hess Deming disaster and the Forrest killing, netted me exactly nothing. I went the rounds of Hollywood night life vainly. The Trocadero, Sardi's, all three of the Brown Derbies, the smart, notorious clubs of the Sunset eighties – nowhere could I find my quarry. I telephoned Jack Hardy a dozen times, but got no answer. Finally, in a 'private club' in Culver City, I met with my first stroke of good luck.

'Mr Hardy's upstairs,' the proprietor told me, looking anxious. 'Nothing wrong, I hope, Mr Prescott? I heard about Deming.'

'Nothing,' I said. 'Take me up to him.'

'He's sleeping it off,' the man admitted. 'Tried to drink the place dry, and I put him upstairs where he'd be safe.'

'Not the first time, eh?' I said, with an assumption of lightness. 'Well, bring up some coffee, will you? Black. I've got to – talk to him.'

But it was half an hour before Hardy was in any shape to understand what I was saying. At last he sat up on the couch, blinking, and a gleam of realization came into his sunken eyes.

'Prescott,' he said, 'can't you leave me alone?'

I leaned close to him, articulating carefully so he would be sure to understand me. 'I know what the Chevalier Futaine is,' I said.

And I waited for the dreadful, impossible confirmation, or for the words which would convince me that I was an insane fool.

Hardy looked at me dully. 'How did you find out?' he whispered.

An icy shock went through me. Up to that moment I had not really believed, in spite of all the evidence. But now Hardy was confirming the suspicions which I had not let myself believe.

I didn't answer his question. Instead, I said, 'Do you know about Hess?'

He nodded, and at sight of the agony in his face I almost pitied him. Then the thought of Jean steadied me.

'Do you know where he is now?' I asked.

'No. What are you talking about?' he flared suddenly. 'Are you mad, Mart? Do you – '

'I'm not mad. But Hess Deming is.'

He looked at me like a cowering, whipped dog.

I went on grimly: 'Are you going to tell me the truth? How you got those marks on your throat? How you met this – creature? And where he's taken Jean?'

'Jean!' He looked genuinely startled. 'Has he got – I didn't know that, Mart – I swear I didn't. You – you've been a good friend to me, and – and I'll tell you the truth – for your sake and Jean's – although now it may be too late – '

My involuntary movement made him glance at me quickly. Then he went on.

'I met him in Paris. I was out after new sensations – but I didn't expect anything like that. A Satanist club – devil-worshippers, they were. The ordinary stuff – cheap, furtive blasphemy. But it was there that I met – him.

'He can be a fascinating chap when he tries. He drew me out, made me tell him about Hollywood – about the women we have here. I bragged a little. He asked me about the stars, whether they were really as beautiful as they seemed. His eyes were hungry as he listened to me, Mart.

'Then one night I had a fearful nightmare. A monstrous, black horror crept in through my window and attacked me – bit me in the throat, I dreamed, or thought I did. After that –

'I was in his power. He told me the truth. He made me his slave, and I could do nothing. His powers – are not human.'

I licked dry lips. Hardy continued:

'He made me bring him here, introducing him as a new discovery to be starred in *Red Thirst* – I'd mentioned the picture to him, before I – knew. How he must have laughed at me! He made me serve him, keeping away photographers, making sure that there were no cameras, no mirrors near him. And for a reward – he let me live.'

I knew I should feel contempt for Hardy, panderer to such a loathsome evil. But somehow I couldn't.

I said quietly, 'What about Jean? Where does the Chevalier live?'

He told me. 'But you can't do anything, Mart. There's a vault under the house, where he stays during the day. It can't be opened, except with a key he always keeps with him – a silver key. He had a door specially made, and then did something to it so that nothing can open it but that key. Even dynamite wouldn't do it, he told me.'

I said, 'Such things – can be killed.'

'Not easily. Sandra Colter was a victim of his. After death she, too, became a vampire, sleeping by day and living only at night. The fire destroyed her, but there's no way to get into the vault under Futaine's house.'

'I wasn't thinking of fire,' I said. 'A knife – '

'Through the heart,' Hardy interrupted almost eagerly. 'Yes – and decapitation. I've thought of it myself, but I can do nothing. I – am his slave, Mart.'

I said nothing, but pressed the bell. Presently the proprietor appeared.

'Can you get me a butcher-knife?' I measured with my hands. 'About so long? A sharp one?'

Accustomed to strange requests, he nodded. 'Right away, Mr Prescott.'

As I followed him out, Hardy said weakly, 'Mart.'

I turned.

'Good luck,' he said. The look on his wrecked face robbed the words of their pathos.

'Thanks,' I forced myself to say. 'I don't blame you, Jack, for what's happened. I – I'd have done the same.'

I left him there, slumped on the couch, staring after me with eyes that had looked into hell.

It was past daylight when I drove out of Culver City, a long, razor-edged knife hidden securely inside my coat. And the day went past all too quickly. A telephone call told me that Jean had not yet returned home. It took me more than an hour to locate a certain man I wanted – a man who had worked for the studio before on certain delicate jobs. There was little about locks he did not know, as the police had sometimes ruefully admitted.

His name was Axel Ferguson, a bulky, good-natured Swede, whose thick fingers seemed more adapted to handling a shovel than the mechanisms of locks. Yet he was as expert as Houdini – indeed, he had at one time been a professional magician.

The front door of Futaine's isolated canyon home proved no bar to Ferguson's fingers and the tiny sliver of steel he used. The house, a modern two-story place, seemed deserted. But Hardy had said *below* the house.

We went down the cellar stairs and found ourselves in a concrete-lined passage that ran down at a slight angle for perhaps thirty feet. There the corridor ended in what seemed to be a blank wall of bluish steel. The glossy surface of the door was unbroken, save for a single keyhole.

Ferguson set to work. At first he hummed under his breath, but after a time he worked in silence. Sweat began to glisten on his face. Trepidation assailed me as I watched.

The flashlight he had placed beside him grew dim. He inserted another battery, got out unfamiliar-looking apparatus. He buckled on dark goggles, and handed me a pair. A blue, intensely brilliant flame began to play on the door.

It was useless. The torch was discarded after a time, and Ferguson returned to his tools. He was using a stethoscope, taking infinite pains in the delicate movements of his hands.

It was fascinating to watch him. But all the time I realized that the night was coming, that presently the sun would go down, and that the life of the vampire lasts from sunset to sunrise.

At last Ferguson gave up. 'I can't do it,' he told me, panting as though from a hard race. 'And if I can't, nobody can. Even Houdini couldn't have broken this lock. The only thing that'll open it is the key.'

'All right, Axel,' I said dully. 'Here's your money.'

He hesitated, watching me. 'You going to stay here, Mr Prescott?'

'Yeah,' I said. 'You can find your way out. I'll – wait awhile.'

'Well, I'll leave the light with you,' he said. 'You can let me have it sometime, eh?'

He waited, and, as I made no answer, he departed, shaking his head.

Then utter silence closed around me. I took the knife out of my coat, tested its edge against my thumb, and settled back to wait.

Less than half an hour later the steel door began to swing open. I stood up. Through the widening crack I saw a bare, steel-lined chamber, empty save for a long, black object that rested on the floor. It was a coffin.

The door was wide. Into view moved a white, slender figure – Jean, clad in a diaphanous, silken robe. Her eyes were wide, fixed and staring. She looked like a sleep-walker.

A man followed her – a man wearing impeccable evening clothes. Not a hair was out of place on his sleek blond head, and he was touching his lips delicately with a handkerchief as he came out of the vault.

There was a little crimson stain on the white linen where his lips had brushed.

I, *The Vampire*

Jean walked past me as though I didn't exist. But the Chevalier Futaine paused, his eyebrows lifted. His black eyes pierced through me.

The handle of the knife was hot in my hand. I moved aside to block Futaine's way. Behind me came a rustle of silk, and from the corner of my eye I saw Jean pause hesitatingly.

The Chevalier eyed me, toying negligently with his handkerchief. 'Mart,' he said slowly. 'Mart Prescott.' His eyes flickered toward the knife, and a little smile touched his lips.

I said, 'You know why I'm here, don't you?'

'Yes,' he said. 'I – heard you. I was not disturbed. Only one thing can open this door.'

From his pocket he drew a key, shining with a dull silver sheen.

'Only this,' he finished, replacing it. 'Your knife is useless, Mart Prescott.'

'Maybe,' I said, edging forward very slightly. 'What have you done to Jean?'

A curious expression, almost of pain, flashed into his eyes. 'She is mine,' he shot out half angrily. 'You can do nothing, for – '

I sprang then, or, at least, I tried to. The blade of the knife sheared down, straight for Futaine's white shirtfront. It was arrested in midair. Yet he had not moved. His eyes had bored into mine, suddenly, terribly, and it seemed as though a wave of fearful energy had blasted out at me – paralyzing me, rendering me helpless. I stood rigid. Veins throbbed in my temples as I tried to move – to bring down the knife. It was useless. I stood as immovable as a statue.

The Chevalier brushed past me.

'Follow, he said almost casually, and like an automaton I swung about, began to move along the passage. What hellish hypnotic power was this that held me helpless?

Futaine led the way upstairs. It was not yet dark, although the sun had gone down. I followed him into a room, and at his gesture dropped into a chair. At my side was a small table. The Chevalier touched my arm gently, and something like a mild electric shock went through me. The knife dropped from my fingers, clattering to the table.

Jean was standing rigidly near by, her eyes dull and expressionless. Futaine moved to her side, put an arm about her waist. My mouth felt as though it were filled with mud, but somehow I managed to croak out articulate words.

'Damn you, Futaine! Leave her alone!'

He released her, and came toward me, his face dark with anger.

'You fool, I could kill you now, very easily. I could make you go down to the busiest corner of Hollywood and slit your throat with that knife. I have the power. You have found out much, apparently. Then you know – my power.'

'Yes,' I muttered thickly. 'I know that. You devil – Jean is mine!'

The face of a beast looked into mine. He snarled, 'She is not yours. Nor is she – *Jean*. She is Sonya!'

I remembered what Futaine had murmured when he had first seen Jean. He read the question in my eyes.

'I knew a girl like that once, very long ago. That was Sonya. They killed her – put a stake through her heart, long ago in Thurn. Now that I've found this girl, who might be a reincarnation of Sonya – they are so alike – I shall not give her up. Nor can anyone force me.'

'You've made her a devil like yourself,' I said through half-paralyzed lips. 'I'd rather kill her – '

Futaine turned to watch Jean. 'Not yet,' he said softly. 'She is mine – yes. She bears the stigmata. But she is still – alive. She will not become – *wampyr* – until she has died, or until she has tasted the red milk. She shall do that tonight.'

I cursed him bitterly, foully. He touched my lips, and I could utter no sound. Then they left me – Jean and her master. I heard a door close quietly.

The night dragged on. Futile struggles had convinced me that it was useless to attempt escape – I could not even force a whisper through my lips. More than once I felt myself on the verge of madness – thinking of Jean, and remembering Futaine's ominous words. Eventually agony brought its own surcease, and I fell into a kind of coma, lasting for how long I could not guess. Many hours had passed, I knew, before I heard footsteps coming toward my prison.

Jean moved into my range of vision. I searched her face with my eyes, seeking for some mark of a dreadful metamorphosis. I could find none. Her beauty was unmarred, save for the terrible little wounds on her throat. She went to a couch and quietly lay down. Her eyes closed.

The Chevalier came past me and went to Jean's side. He stood looking down at her. I have mentioned before the incongruous youthfulness of his face. That was gone now. He looked old – old beyond imagination.

At last he shrugged and turned to me. His fingers brushed my lips again, and I found that I could speak. Life flooded back into my veins, bringing lancing twinges of pain. I moved an arm experimentally. The paralysis was leaving me.

The Chevalier said, 'She is still – clean. I could not do it.'

Amazement flooded me. My eyes widened in disbelief.

Futaine smiled wryly. 'It is quite true. I could have made her as myself – undead. But at the last moment I forbade her.' He looked toward the windows. 'It will be dawn soon.'

I glanced at the knife on the table beside me. The Chevalier put out a hand and drew it away.

'Wait,' he said. 'There is something I must tell you, Mart Prescott. You say that you know who and what I am.'

I nodded.

'Yet you cannot know,' he went on. 'Something you have learned, and something you have guessed, but you can never know me. You are human, and I am – the undead.

'Through the ages I have come, since first I fell victim to another vampire – for thus is the evil spread. Deathless and not alive, bringing fear and sorrow always, knowing the bitter agony of Tantalus, I have gone down through the weary centuries. I have known Richard and Henry and Elizabeth of England, and ever have I brought terror and destruction in the night, for I am an alien thing. I am the undead.'

The quiet voice went on, holding me motionless in its weird spell.

'I, the vampire, I, the accursed, the shining evil, *negotium perambulans in tenebris* . . . but I was not always thus. Long ago in Thurn, before the shadow fell upon me, I loved a girl – Sonya. But the vampire visited me, and I sickened and died – and awoke. Then I arose.

'It is the curse of the undead to prey upon those they love. I visited Sonya. I made her my own. She, too, died, and for a brief while we walked the earth together, neither alive nor dead. But that was not Sonya. It was her body, yes, but I had not loved her body alone. I realized too late that I had destroyed her utterly.

'One day they opened her grave, and the priest drove a stake through her heart, and gave her rest. Me they could not find, for my coffin was hidden too well. I put love behind me then, knowing that there was none for such as I.

'Hope came to me when I found – Jean. Hundreds of years have passed since Sonya crumbled to dust, but I thought I had found her again. And – I took her. Nothing human could prevent me.'

The Chevalier's eyelids sagged. He looked infinitely old.

'Nothing human. Yet in the end I found that I could not condemn her to the hell that is mine. I thought I had forgotten love. But, long and long ago, I loved Sonya. And, because of her, and because I know that I would only destroy, as I did once before, I shall not work my will on this girl.'

I turned to watch the still figure on the couch. The Chevalier followed my gaze and nodded slowly.

'Yes, she bears the stigmata. She will die, unless' – he met my gaze unflinchingly – 'unless I die. If you had broken into the vault yesterday, if you had sunk that knife into my heart, she would be free now.' He glanced at the windows again. 'The sun will rise soon.'

Then he went quickly to Jean's side. He looked down at her for a moment.

'She is very beautiful,' he murmured. 'Too beautiful for hell.'

The Chevalier swung about, went toward the door. As he passed me he threw something carelessly on the table, something that tinkled as it fell. In the portal he paused, and a little smile twisted the scarlet lips. I remembered him thus, framed against the black background of the doorway, his sleek blond head erect and unafraid. He lifted his arm in a gesture that should have been theatrical, but, somehow, wasn't.

'And so farewell. I who am about to die – '

He did not finish. In the faint greyness of dawn I saw him striding away, heard his footsteps on the stairs, receding and faint – heard a muffled clang as of a great door closing. The paralysis had left me. I was trembling a little, for I realized what I must do soon. But I knew I would not fail.

I glanced down at the table. Even before I saw what lay beside the knife, I knew what would be there. A silver key . . .

The Bride of the Isles

'LORD BYRON'

(James Robinson Planche)

*　　*　　*

There is a popular superstition *still extant* in the southern isles of Scotland, but not with the force as it was a century since, that the souls of persons, whose actions in the mortal state were so wickedly attrocious as to deny all possibility of happiness in that of the next;

were doomed to everlasting perdition, but had the power given them by infernal spirits to be for awhile the scourge of the living.

This was done by allowing the wicked spirit to enter the body of another person at the moment their own soul had winged its flight from earth; the corpse was thus reanimated – the same look, the same voice, the same expression of countenance, with physical powers to eat and drink, and partake of human enjoyments, but with the most wicked propensities, and in this state they were called Vampires. This second existence, as it may not improperly be termed, is held on a tenure of the most horrid and diobolical nature. Every *All-Hallow E'en*, he must wed a lovely virgin, and slay her, which done, he is to catch her warm blood and drink it, and from this draught he is renovated for *another* year, and free to take *another* shape, and pursue his Satannic course; but if he failed in procuring a wife at the appointed time, or had not opportunity to make the sacrifice before the moon set, the Vampire *was no more* – he did not turn into a skeleton, but literally vanished into air and nothingness.

One of these demoniac sprites, Oscar Montcalm, of infamous notoriety in the Scotch annals of crime and murder, (who was decapitated by the hands of the common executioner), was a most successful Vampire, and many were the poor unfortunate maidens who had been sacrificed to support his supernatural career, roving from place to place, and every year changing his shape as opportunity presented itself, but always choosing to enter the corpse of some man of rank and power, as by that means his voracious appetite for luxury was gratified.

Oscar Montcalm had seen, and distantly adored in his mortal state, the superior beauty of the Lady Margaret, daughter of the Baron of the Isles, the good Lord Ronald; but, such was his situation, he had not dared to address her; however, he did not forget her in his Vampire state, but marked her out for one of his victims, in revenge for the scorn with which he had been treated by her father.

Lady Margaret, though lovely and well proportioned, entered her twentieth year unmarried, nor had she ever been addressed by a suitor whom she could regard with the least partiality, and with much anxiety she sought to know whether she should ever enter into wedlock, and what sort of person her future lord would be. With credulity pardonable to the times in which she lived, and the narrow education then given to females, even of rank, she consulted Sage Seer and Witch, as to this important event; but it is not to be wondered at that she met with many contradictions, every one telling a different tale. At length urged on by the irresistible desire to pry into futurity, she repaired with her two maidens, Effie and Constance, to the CAVE of FINGAL, where, cutting off a lock of her hair, and joining it to a ring from her finger, she cast it into the well, according to the directions she had received from Merna, the Hag of the mountains, who had instructed the fair one as to this expedition.

No sooner was the ring flung into well than a dreadful storm arose; the torches, which the attendant maidens had borne, were extinguished, and the immense cave was in utter darkness: loud and dreadful was the thunder, accompanied by a horrid confusion of sounds, which beggars description.

Margaret and her companions sunk on their knees; but they were too stupified with horror: to pray, or to endeavour to retrace their way out of this den of horrors. Of a sudden, the cave was brilliantly illuminated. But with no visible means of light, for there were neither torch, lamp, or candle. Solemn music was heard, slow and awfully grand, and in a few minutes two figures appeared, one heavy morose in countenance, and clad in dark robes, who announced herself as Uno, the spirit of the storm, and touching a sable curtain, discovered to the view of Margaret the figure of a noble young warrior, Ruthven, earl of Marsden, who had accompanied her father to the wars. Again the storm resounded, the curtain closed, and the cave resumed its darkness; but this was only transient – the brilliant light returned – Una was gone, and the light figure, dressed in transparent robes, sprinkled over with spangles remained. With her wand she pulled aside the curtain, and a young man of interesting appearance was visible, but his person was a stranger to the fair one. Ariel, the spirit of the Air, then waved her hand to the entrance of the cave, as a signal for them to depart, and bowing low, they withdrew, amid strains of heart thrilling harmony, rejoiced to find themselves once more in an open space, and they happily returned in safety to the baron's castle. The Lady Margaret was well pleased with what she had seen, as promising her two husbands, though she was somewhat puzzled by calling to mind a couplet that Ariel had repeated three or four times, while the curtain remained undrawn.

> 'But once, fair maid, will you be wed,
> 'You'll know no second bridal bed.'

What could this mean? Surely she would never stoop to illicit desires or intrigue? She thought she knew her own heart too well.

The Vampire had seen into the designs of Margaret to visit the Cave of Fingal, and he sought out Ariel and Uno, to whom, by virtue of his supernatural rights, he had easy access. The spirit of the air would not befriend him, but the spirit of the storm assisted him to pry into futurity; and to suit his views, she presented the figure of Ruthven, earl of Marsden. In the mean time, Marsden had the good fortune to save Lord Ronald's life in the battle, and the wars being ended, or at least suspended for a time, he invited the gallant youth home with him to his castle, to pass a few months amid the social rites of hospitality and the pleasures of the chase.

The Lady Margaret received her father with dutiful affection, and gratitude to providence for his safe return, and she beheld young Marsden with secret delight; but when informed that he had preserved the baron from overpowering enemies, her gratitude knew no bounds, and she looked so beautiful and engaging, while returning her thankful effusions for the service he had rendered her father, that the earl could not resist the impulse, and from that hour became deeply enamoured of the lovely fair one.

Marsden's rank and birth were unexceptionable but his fortune was very inadequate to support a title, which made him (added to the love of military glory) enter into the profession of arms, of which he was an ornament.

Margaret was an only child, and her father abounding in wealth and honours; it might therefore be presumed that an ambition might lead him to form very exalted views for the aggrandizement of his heiress; and so he had, but perceiving how high his preserver stood in the good graces of his darling child, and that the passion was becoming mutual, he resolved not to give any interruption to their happiness, but if Marsden could win Margaret to let him have her, as a rich reward for the service he had performed amid the clang of arms.

Parties were daily formed by the baron for the chace, hawking, or fishing, while the evening was given to the festive dance, or the minstrels tuned their harps in the great hall, and sang the deeds of scottish chiefs, long since departed, amongst whom the heroic Wallace was not forgot.

The loves of Ruthven and Lady Margaret were now generally known throughout the islands and congratulations poured in from every quarter.

A day was fixed for the nuptials, and magnificent preparations were made at the castle for the celebration of the ceremony, when the sudden and severe illness of the baron caused a delay. He wished them not to defer their marriage on his account; but the young people, in this instance, would not obey him, declaring their joys would be incomplete without his revered presence.

The baron blessed them for this instance of love and filial duty, but he still felt a strong desire to have the marriage concluded.

The baron was scarce recovered, when he and Ruthven were summoned to the field of battle, a war having broke out in Flanders, and the marriage was deferred till their return; and taking a most affectionate leave of the Lady Margaret, the father and lover left the castle, and the fair one in the charge of old Alexander, the faithful steward, with many commands and cautions respecting the edifice and the Lady, whom they both regarded as a gem of inestimable value, with whom they were loath to part, but imperious duty and the calls of honour allowed no alternative.

Robert, the old Steward's son, attended the baron abroad; and Marsden took his own servant the faithful Gilbert. They were successful in several skirmishes with the enemy, but in the final engagement Ruthven lost his life, dying in the arms of the Lord of the Isles, who mourned over him as for a beloved son, and he ordered Robert and Gilbert, who were on the spot, to convey the body to a place beyond the carnage, that when the battle was over he might see it, (if he himself survived,) and have the valued remains interred in a manner that became an earl and a soldier, dying in defending his country's cause.

The battle ended, for the glory and success of Great Britain, and the good Baron of the Isles was unhurt, so was Robert, but Gilbert was amongst the slain.

Lord Ronald, fatigued with the sharp action of the day, in which he had borne his part with a vigour surprising to his time of life, for his head was now silvered over with the honourable badge of age, repaired to his tent to take some refreshment and an hour's rest on his couch, to invigorate his frame. The couch eased his weary limbs, but his eyes closed not, and all his thoughts were on Ruthven, and the distress the sad news would give to his dear child. He arose, and with trembling fingers penned a letter to her, describing the melancholy event, and exhorting her, for the sake of her father, to support this trial with resignation and patience, and bow to the dispensations of Providence, who orders all things eventually for the best, however severe and distressing they seem at the time. He ended his letter by observing that he should return to the castle of the Isles without delay, being anxious to fold her in his arms, and that he should bring the corpse of the brave Marsden to his native land.

The letter being sent off expressly by one of his retainers, the baron ordered some soldiers to attend with a bier, and taking Robert for their guide they went to fetch the body of Ruthven, and in the mean time he had a small tent erected for its reception, surmounted by a sable flag.

But this posthumous attention of the good baron was all in vain, for after a long absence, Robert and the soldiers returned, with the unwelcome news that the body of the gallant Scot was not to be found, but the spot where it had been deposited by the servants was still marked with the blood that had flowed from his gaping wounds and it was presumed that the enemy had found the corpse, and had conveyed it away to some obscure hole out of revenge for the slaughter he had dealt among their leaders before his fall. This event added materially to Ronald's regret and sorrow, for the natives of the Isles of Escotia held a traditional superstition, that while the body lay unburied the spirit wandered denied of rest. He offered rewards for the body without success, and was at length obliged, though with much reluctance, to drop the affair.

The baron was obliged to pay his duty in England to his sovereign before he repaired to the Isles. Unexpected events detained him two months at the British court, but he at last effected his departure to his long wished for home.

A courier made known his approach, and Lady Margaret, attended by the whole household, dressed in their best array, came forth to meet him, headed by the aged minstrel, and they received their lord with joyous shouts and lively strains, about half a mile from the gates of the castle.

Lord Ronald, as the carriage descended a steep hill that led into the valley, had a full view of the party approaching to meet him, and his heart felt elate at the compliment. He could discern his daughter; but how came it she was not in sables? Surely Ruthven, her betrothed lover, deserved that mark of respect to his memory! But he could observe that she was gaily dressed, and her high plume of feathers waving in the light breeze that adulated the air. The baron cast a look on his own deep mourning, and sighed; he was not pleased – but worse and worse. As he gained a nearer view, he perceived that his daughter was handed along, most familiarly by a knight. I had hoped, said he to himself, that Margaret would have rose superior to the inconstancy and caprice attributed to her sex. Can it be possible, that she has so soon forgot the valiant accomplished Ruthven! Oh, woman! woman! are ye all alike? As the vehicle entered the valley, Ronald quitted it, to receive the welcome of his child and retainers.

Powers of astonishment! was it, or was it not, illusion? By what miracle did he behold Ruthven, earl of Marsden, standing before him, and Lady Margaret hanging with chaste expressions of delight on his arm; there was a scar on his forehead, and he was much paler than before the battle, but no other alteration was visible. As for Robert, he stood aghast, his hair bristled up and his joints trembled, and altogether would have served as a good model of horror to a painter or statuary.

Ruthven stretched forth his hand – 'You seem astonished, my good lord,' said he, 'to find me here before you, or, indeed to find me here at all. I was discovered by some peasants returning from their daily labour, nearly covered with fern and leaves, ['Yes' said Robert, 'that was Gilbert's work and mine.'] by means of a little dog, who had scented out my body from its purposed concealment. They were very poor, and my clothes and decorations were a strong temptation, to which they yielded, they agreed to strip me, sell the clothes, and divide the spoil. While they were thus occupied, they perceived signs of life, and their humanity prevailed over every other consideration, I was conveyed to one of their cottages, and well attended. The man had a wonderful skill in herbs and simples, therefore my cure was rapid, but previous to my leaving them, I well rewarded every one who had been instrumental in my preservation and freely forgave the intended plunder they had confessed to me, as it was the means directed by fate to prolong my existence, and restore me to my angelic Margaret.

'When I recovered, I found the British forces had quitted Flanders, but I could not learn which direction my friend the baron (you my dear lord) had taken; so I hastened to Scotland with all the speed my situation would admit of, and we were retarded at sea by adverse winds. I found my dear betrothed, and her fair damsels, in deep mourning for my supposed loss; but I soon changed her tears for smiles, and her sables for gayer vestments: but at first her surprise, like yours, Lord Ronald, was too great to admit of utterance, but in time we became composed and grateful, and we agreed not to inform you of my existence, but astonish you on your arrival.'

The baron greeted his young friend most warmly and testified his hope that no more ill-omened events would disappoint the nuptials of the brave earl and Margaret, whom he tenderly clasped to his bosom, and kissing each cheek, remarked that she was the living image of his dear departed wife. He then turned to the old harper, and bidding him strike up a lively strain, proceeded to the castle, where all was joy and festivity; again resounded the song, and again the damsels, with their swains shewed off their best reels *a-la Caledonia*.

In the old steward's room a plenteous board was spread, for the upper servants and retainers of the hospitable Lord of the isles, who ordered flowing bowls and well replenished horns to the health of Ruthven and Margaret.

Some of the party were remarking on the wonderful preservation of Marsden's earl by the Flemish peasants, instead of plundering and leaving him to perish, as many would have done to an almost expiring enemy.

'*Almost expiring!*' said Robert, whose cheeks had not yet recovered their usual hue since the meeting in the valley with Ruthven.

'*Almost Expiring!*' he repeated; 'I am certain the body of the earl was dead – aye, as dead as my great grandsire – when I and Gilbert carried him from the field of battle; and when we left him under the fern he was as cold as ice, and the blood from his wounds coagulated – No, no, he never came to life again; this Ruthven you have here must be a Vampire.'

'*A Vampire! a Vampire!*' resounded from all the company, with loud shouts of laughter at poor Robert's simplicity. 'Perhaps you are a *Vampire*,' said his sweetheart, Effie, joining in the mirth, 'so I shall take care how I trust myself in your power.'

Robert did not reply, and all the rest of the night he had to stand the bantering jests of his companions.

But Robert was right; Marsden's earl died on the field of battle, and the moment the servants quitted the corpse, the Vampire, wicked Montcalm, whose relics lay smouldering beneath a stone in Fingal's cave, watching the moment, took possession, and reanimated the body; the wounds instantly healed, but the face wore a pallid hue, the invariable case with the Vampires, their blood not flowing, in that free circulation which belong to real mortals.

The story told by the Vampire was a fabrication, respecting the peasants, to impose on Lord Ronald and the Lady Margaret as to the appearance of the supposed Ruthven, and he well succeeded.

On previously consulting the Spirit of the Storm, the Vampire had discovered that Margaret would be courted by Ruthven, earl of Marsden; he also discovered, in his peep into futurity, that the young hero would be slain in battle, and this seemed to him a glorious opportunity to obtain possession of the lovely Margaret, and make her his victim, renovate his Vampireship, and go on in the most diabolical career, hurling destruction on the human race, and drawing them into crime after crime, till they sunk into the gulph of eternal infamy.

It now wanted a month to All Hallow E'en and it so chanced, that in that year the next coming moon would set on that very eve from its full orbit. The Vampire repaired to the cave of Fingal, and by magic means, which he well knew how to put in execution, he raised up some infernal spirits, whom he asked for orders. They told him they would consult their ruler Beelzebub, and he was to come on the third eve from thence for an answer.

This, then, was the decree – he must wed a virgin, destroy her, and drink her blood, before the setting of the moon on All Hallow E'en, or terminate into mere non-entity; and if the maid was unchaste, the charm was dissolved. If he succeeded he was to quit the form of earl Marsden and get egress into some other corpse to give it animation.

The supposed death of Ruthven had caused Margaret to imbibe the idea that the two figures she had seen in Fingal's cave, and Ariel's couplet prophetic but of one marriage, now made out by his fall, he being only a betrothed lover, and the stranger knight she regarded as her future spouse; but the return of the earl again puzzled her, and she knew not what to think, but at length resolved on another visit to the mystic cavern. Possibly ashamed of confessing this weakness to her maidens, or, what is more probable, conscious that from the terrors they had experienced in attending her there, she could not persuade them to go a second time, she went alone, and soon after midnight, when all the castle was hushed in sound repose, save the Vampire, who beheld from the lofty casement, the temporary flight of the enterprising Margaret. How did he thirst for her blood – how willingly would he have immolated the lovely maid that moment, and paid the infernal tribute, but for one clause that interposed and saved her from his fangs. This was the necessity of his being first legally married, in all due form, to the intended victim. He regarded her with a diabolical and malicious scowl, while, by as bright a star light as ever illumined the heavens, he saw her tripping through the park's wide avenues of stately firs. He wondered where she was going, and felt apprehensive that some event was in agitation that might deprive him of his bride. The Vampire had just concluded to follow her, when a heaviness, he could neither resist or shake off, overpowered him and sealed his eyes in a deep sleep.

Margaret, in much perturbation and a beating heart, gained the way to the cave; but the interior was so dark that she was obliged to grope on her hands and knees to the magic well, and cast in the accustomed charm. The thunder rolled, and the storm commenced, but with not one quarter of the violence as on her preceding visit. The music followed in an harmonious strain, and the spirits of the storm and air soon stood before her. The beauty, the innocence, of the noble maid, her virtues and her benevolence, had interested these mystical beings in her behalf – yes, even the stern and oft obdurate Una felt for Margaret, and wished to save her. They could not alter the decree of fate, nor had they power over the Vampires; the only thing that remained was to warn the inquirer, if possible, of her danger. For this purpose, they unfolded the curtain, and presented to her view, the real Ruthven on the field of battle, bleeding and a corpse. She heard his last sigh, saw his last convulsive motion; – *a grizzly fleshless skeleton stood by his side, and at that moment entered his corpse, which sprung up reanimated.* Margaret knew well the traditional tales of the Vampires, and shudderd as she beheld one before her; for what could be more plain? No further vision was shewn her – she was warned from the cave, and the fair one returned to the castle, dejected and spiritless. What did this mean? Ruthven, her adored Ruthven, could be no Vampire – impossible – so accomplished, so clever, superior in most things to others of his rank. – She past the intervening hours in a very restless state, till they met at their morning repast in the small saloon. The Vampire handed her to a chair; she remembered the scene in the cave, and shrank back with a feeling of disgust; but this was not lasting; the labours of the spirit of the storm and the air had not their intended effect; like advice given to young maidens that accords not with the inclination, it sank before the fascination of the object beloved, and she regarded what had been shewn her as wayward spite in Una and Ariel; so ready are we to twist circumstances to act in conformity with our own inclination.

The dews of night, the chilling breeze, the damp of the magic cave of Fingal, joined to the fatigue and agitation of the noble maiden, caused a fever which confined her to her chamber several days, and again delayed the marriage. The Vampire grew impatient, and before the Lady Margaret was scarce convalescent, he began to press for the nuptial ceremony, with what the good baron thought indecorous haste, though he made all possible allowance for repeated disappointments and youthful passions.

Robert, much better read than the warrior, his master, in the traditional tales of his country, and its popular superstitions, had not yet got the better of his shock at the re-appearance of Ruthven in his native valley, when he felt convinced that marsden's earl died of his wounds on the field of battle at Flanders. 'Aye, by the holy rood, he did,' would the youth often mutter to himself – 'May I never live to be married to my gentle Effie, and it wants but three days and three nights to that happy morn, if I did not see Ruthven's eye-strings crack, and heart's veins burst asunder: this is a Vampire, and this is the moon when those foul fiends pay their tribute, and now he is all impatience to wed my young mistress, forsooth – Yes, yes, 'tis plain enough: but what is the use of saying any thing about it, my father and all the servants laugh at me; even my intended turns into ridicule, any thing I advance on that subject, and calls me Robert, the Vampire hunter: but I will not be deterred from doing my duty like an honest servant, let them jeer as they will. I am resolved to tell the baron all that I know, that is, all I think of his guest, and then he may please himself, and come what will, my conscience will be clear.'

Robert had courage to face a cannon, and never turned his back on the bravest foe, but he felt daunted at the disclosure he meant to make to Lord Ronald; the subject was awkward, and the Vampire (if Vampire he was) might take a summary revenge on him for his interference. Yet his resolution was not shaken, and seeking the cellar-man he procured a glass of cordial and a horn of ale to revive his spirits, and then, finding himself what he called his own man again, he sought the baron, whom he happened to find a one and taking his evening walk in the grounds, while Margaret and her lover were sitting at their music.

Robert told his tale with much hesitation and faultering, but the baron heard him with more patience than he expected, and made him recount every particular of his suspicions. ' 'Tis strange! 'Tis marvellous strange!' replied the good Lord Ronald; 'for I have seen many persons from Flanders, and yet they never heard of the earl of Marsden being saved by the peasants: one would have thought such news would have spread like wildfire.'

'Neither does he go to mass or prayer,' observed Robert, 'as a christian warrior ought to do; nor does he take salt on his trencher.* And All-Hallow-E'en is fast approaching,' continued Robert: 'this is the fatal moon, and my young mistress –'

'Shall never be his,' exclaimed the baron 'till the moon sets, and the night, so tragic and pregnant of evil to many a spotless maid, is gone by; then if Ruthven is Marsden's true earl, he may have my Margaret. She shall then be his, and I will turn all my fish-ponds into bowls for whiskey punch, and the great fountain in the fore court shall flow with ale till not a Scot around can stand upon his legs, or he is no well-wisher to me or mine; but if he is an infernal Vampire, his reign will be

---

* This remark of Robert's was another popular Superstition of the Isles.

over. Faith, by St. Andrew, I know not what to think, but I have had fearful dreams, portentous of evil to my ancient house.'

The baron dismissed Robert with a present, and many encomiums on his fidelity and zeal for him and the Lady Margaret. 'My father,' said the honest fellow, 'has lived with you from youth to age: I was born within these walls, and my deceased mother suckled your amiable heiress; treachery in me would be double guilt: No, I would die to serve the house of Ronald!'

When the baron entered his daughter's appartment, a groupe met his eyes, very ill calculated to give him pleasure in his present frame of mind full of supernatural ideas, and teeming with dread suspicions; Margaret had changed her robes of plaid silk for virgin white, her neck chain, bracelets, and other ornaments of filagree silver, most exquisitely wrought. Ruthven was also dressed with elegance. The fair one's attendants were also in their best. The steward and the physician of the household were present, and the chaplain stood with the sacred book in his hand.

'We were waiting for you, my dear Lord Baron,' said the Vampire, Ruthven; 'I have persuaded my lovely betrothed to be mine this very evening. We have been so very unfortunate, that I dread further delay, and think every hour teeming with evil till she is mine irrevocably.'

'You have no rival,' answered the baron, much alarmed and piqued: 'you are secure in Margaret's love and my consent. My friends and tenants will ill brook such privacy; they have been accustomed to see the daughters of the Lord of the Isles wedded in public pomp and magnificence, and to share in the festive and abundant hospitalities. – No, by the shades of my ancestors, I will have no such doings.'

Ruthven pleaded hard, but the baron heeded not his arguments or eloquence, for the more he seemed bent on espousing Margaret then, the old lord thought more on Robert's report and his own suspicions. Margaret, infatuated by the spell that cast an illusion over her senses, seemed to forget her proper dignity and the delicate decorum of her sex, and joined in the solicitations of her lover. 'My dear father,' said the beauteous maiden, 'Ruthven and myself are in unison with each other's sentiments: we seek not in pomp and glare for happiness; we place our prospects of future bliss in elegant retirement and domestic pleasures. Allow us to be now united, I entreat you, and you can afterwards treat your neighbours, retainers, and servants, as plenteously as you like, but I shrink from the idea of a public marriage.'

Ruthven took the hand of his betrothed, which she presented to him with the most endearing smiles, while her eyes were modestly bent down and her cheeks covered with roseate blushes, and never did Lady Margaret look so irresistibly captivating as at that moment.

The baron, while she was speaking, trembled with emotion – Not for a single hour, said he, mentally, would I defer their happiness on account of bridal pomp, if I thought all was right; but I will not risk the sacrificing so much loveliness, and that my only child, the image of my lost Cassandra, to a Vampire; but he did not like to disclose the suspicions he had imbibed, for if they were founded in error, how grossly ridiculous would he appear, and he resolved to delay the nuptials, and stay the test of the moon. He therefore said, 'It is my pleasure to give a full month to splendid preparation, 'tis but a short delay, and let me have the satisfaction to have the nuptials as I would wish them to be, in honour of Marsden's earl and Ronald's daughter.'

The baron observed the lover give a start at the words 'a full month,' and his eyes shot forth a most malicious glance. He still held Margaret's hand. 'Nonsense! my good friend,' said he, – 'this is not fair, from one warrior to another – Chaplain, begin the ceremony.'

The enraged baron flung off his guard, snatched the book from the hands of the priest, and bade Margaret retire with her maidens to another room, accusing Ruthven of being a Vampire.

This was strongly resented by the accused, and, indeed, every one took his part, and laughed at the suggestion. This raised his passion so high that he was declared by the physician to be insane, and they coercively conveyed him to his chamber, and barred him in, where he was on the point of becoming frantic indeed, from the thoughts that the marriage might now take place in spite of his injunctions, for he was more convinced than ever of Ruthven being a supernatural imposter, or he would never have acted so uncourteous to a knight in his own castle.

Robert having heard from his father, the old steward, of the interruption of the marriage, through the baron's mania, in thinking the Earl of Marsden a Vampire, and his lord's confinement in the western turret, observed that he supposed the nuptials then were all off – His parent answered no, that the young people were not forced to obey such whims; that Lady Margaret was retired for an hour to regain her composure, and the chaplain would then perform the ceremony. 'And who is to be the bride's father?' said Robert. 'I am to have that honour,' replied the steward. – 'And much good may it do you,' said the son; 'but if I was you, I'd cater better for the noble lady Margaret than to give her to an evil spirit' – 'Go to, for an ungracious bird,' exclaimed Alexander; 'you are as mad as your master; poor Effie will have but a crazy husband at the best of it.' 'Better a crazy one, than a blood thirsty Vampire, father,' observed Robert, who quitted the room, vexed at the loud peal of laughter, which was now set up against him.

Robert went out into the park, but returned privately into the castle by a bye path and a private door, of which he had a key, having procured it some time before he went to the wars, for he was then a rakish youth, and loved to steal out to the village dance or festival, after he was supposed to retire to rest for the night; but now, he was contracted to the languishing blue-eyed Effie he was reformed, and voluntarily relinquished all such stolen delights. The key was now regarded by him as a treasure. 'It helped me,' said he to himself, to sow my wild oats; 'it shall now aid me to perform a more laudable purpose. Little did I think to see the good Baron of the Isles a captive in his own castle; and for what, but that he is in too much possession of his senses to sacrifice his lovely virgin daughter to a Vampire, for such, by the holy rood, is this fine Earl of Marsden. Why his face is the image of death itself, and his eyes glare; yet my Lady Margaret forsooth! thinks him very handsome, now she is under the influence of the wicked spell; the real Ruthven looked not so when he came to woo the noble fair one; but he says 'tis through his wounds in battle: I think by St. Cuthbert, he has had time enough to get his complexion again, and he eats and drinks voraciously, it makes me sick to see him as I stand in waiting, and no salt – faugh!'

This long soliloquy brought the faithful youth to the door of the baron's prison; he drew the bolts and entered; his Lord was pacing the chamber with unmeasured strides, and beating his forehead, while heavy sighs burst from his aged bosom. He started and stood still on Robert's entrance.

'Friend or foe,' said he. 'Friend,' replied Robert, 'and when I prove otherwise to my most noble master and commander, may I be siezed by the foul fiend and made food for vulture.'

'I am not mad,' said the good old veteran, 'but I think I may say, I am distracted with grief;' 'You are no more mad than I my lord; I do not join in that absurd tale; but hasten and arm yourself? The marriage is to take place almost immediately – let us hasten and prevent it, ere it is too late.'

Lord Ronald was doubly shocked – his suspicions of the Vampire was increased by this obstinate persisting in the nuptials against his command, and the want of tenderness and filial love testified by his daughter. How changed was Margaret! did she choose for her bridal hours those of confinement to her sire – had she not supposed him insane, it is not to be thought she would have suffered him to be thus treated; this then was her season for connubial joys – the sudden insanity of her only surviving parent, he who had so ardently strove not only to fulfil his own duties, but to supply the place as far as possible of the late lady Cassandra, his amiable wife, and he felt there was no sting so keen as a child's ingratitude. The barbed arrow seemed to touch his very vitals, and for the first time in his life the brave Ronald shed tears.

'Take courage, my lord,' said Robert, 'if they dare still to oppose your authority, this trusty falchion, this well tried steel, shall prove if Ruthven is common flesh and blood or no.'

'Moderation! moderation! Robert,' replied the Baron, as he led the way to Lady Margaret's apartment, where he did not arrive one minute too soon – the ceremony was on the point of commencing, and 'tis possible a few of the first words had been pronounced by the priest.

The Baron's entrance caused a universal consternation – the maidens shrieked, and the Vampire began to bluster, but Lord Ronald took prompt measures. He solemnly protested that he was in the full use and exercise of his senses, and charged his daughter, on the penalty of incurring his curse, not to enter into wedlock with Marsden's Earl till he sanctioned it. She did not choose to disobey on such an awful threat, but casting a look of anguish and tenderness on her lover, she burst into tears, and leaning on the arms of her sympathizing maidens, withdrew to her chamber, where throwing herself on a couch, gave way to a full tide of sorrow. 'Cruel father,' she exclaimed! 'ridiculous superstition! I feel I never shall be the bride of my truly adored and adoring Ruthven, so many fatal interruptions seem as if the fates forbid our union – spirits of the storm and air, are ye not too in league against me?'

The Vampire now besought the baron's forgiveness and friendship, attributing his recent behaviour to excess of love, that did not brook delay; he also interceded for the chaplain, whom Lord Ronald was about to dismiss for his presumption, and peace was again restored in the Castle of the Isles.

Wine was called for, and a repast was spread and the Vampire so artfully strove against the suspicions of the Baron, that the prejudices of the latter were nearly done away; and Robert blamed for his credulous folly; yet the false Earl could not obtain from the old nobleman a promise to allow him to wed before the setting of the moon, for Ronald still adhered to that test, nor would abridge, aught of a term that now waxed very short.

The Vampire concealed his chagrin and feigned content; he thought it best to keep a firm footing in the castle, as some chance might still operate in his favour, founding his hopes on the spell he had obtained over Lady Margaret, and the strong affection with which she beheld him, and he scarcely admitted a doubt of success, if he could get the Baron and Robert out of the way; for no one else in the castle had the least doubt of his being the real Earl of Marsden.

The Baron, however, watched with great vigilance, and Robert never stirred from a station he had taken that commanded a view of the door of Lady Margaret's chamber. Time seemed to ride on swift pinions with the Vampire – his fears were stronger than his hopes – he had never been so foiled before in his attempts, and he thought it best to provide against the coming danger, and leave the mistress alone for her allegiance to Robert, persuade her to wed himself, and then sacrifice her to pay his annual demoniac tribute. This would serve two purposes, renew his Vampire-ship, and be a deadly revenge on the interfering Robert, on whom he longed to wreak his diabolical rage.

It seemed rather a difficult achievement to gain the affections of a young and certainly most virtuous maiden, (who was to be married in a few hours to the object of her first choice) from that object, but the Vampire's case grew desperate, and he resolved to try if the charm would operate.

While Robert was watching the lady the Vampire resolved to seize on the more ignoble prize, and he assailed Effie with every alluring temptation. He told the poor girl that he was tired of pursuing the match with Lady Margaret, and abhorred the thoughts of allying himself to such a piece of dotage as the credulous Baron, who was grown superannuated, and only fit to sit amongst the old wives a-spinning, and tell legendary tales of hobgoblins, and water sprites. He said Effie's beauty and innocence had charmed him – that she wanted nothing but dress and rank to be level with her mistress, and that would be hers by marrying Marsden's Earl.

'But I am ignorant, and can neither play music, sing, dance, or do the honours of a table, like Lady Margaret.' This reply pleased the Vampire; it seemed one of a very yielding nature, if she had no scruples but what arose from a fear of her own demerits.

'All these can soon be taught,' said the deceiver. 'I must seek some lady of fallen fortune, but elegant accomplishments, to polish your native gracefulness; she shall be your companion in my absence, and your tutoress, and I will join in the delightful task; therefore that can be no objection.' Effie raised several other difficulties, but all were successfully combated, and the Vampire Earl promised to make the forsaken Robert amends for the loss of his bride by a noble sum and a pretty damsel from off his own estate.

Effie yielded; and though by this act she justly incurred censure and reproach, yet we must do her the justice to remember, that the Vampire had a tongue to charm his victims, and eyes that are described like the fascination of a basilisk; and to have a powerful Earl sighing for her love, might have tempted a higher maid than the simple Effie, the mere child of nature.

Having gained her consent, he hastened to secure his prize; he persuaded her that they must instantly flee, lest the lynx-eyed Robert should grow jealous, and interrupt their promised happiness; he therefore told her, to meet him in an hour, at the end of the long avenue in the castle park, and he would be prepared with a horse to convey her to the next convent, (about five miles distant,) where the priest could join their hands.

That he intended to wed Effie was too true; in that promise lurked no deceit, but the ceremony over, he meant to take her into an adjacent wood, offer up his sacrifice by immolating her with his own hands, and drinking her heart's blood; then seek out some noble form just departed – enter it – and woo Lady Margaret in a new character, and finally triumph over the Baron, for he hated all who opposed him in his designs.

Poor unsuspecting Effie, thy head ran on nothing but the glare of thy expected coronet, and thou felt no pity for thy so lately loved Robert, or thy kind and generous mistress, though both were to be betrayed by this clandestine step.

She was true to her appointment and crossed the park with light steps – the Vampire was in waiting – he assisted her to mount the horse, and then sprung up behind her – The steed bounded off like lightning. In an instant Robert rushed from a copse and cried out for the fugitives to stop, but instead of obeying him the Vampire spurred his horse to quicken him on. The Baron had taken Robert's post to watch the Lady Margaret while the latter made an excursion for air; his gun was loaded, and vengeance nerved the young soldier's arm with so sure an aim that the corporeal part of the Vampire fell mortally wounded to the ground, dragging Effie after it loudly shrieking, and all her new raised love extinguished – for the illusion had vanished, and the image of Robert again filled her virgin heart. Most happily for her future peace the secret of her consenting to the supposed Earl's passion was known to her alone – there had been no witness of that degrading incident so fatal to her integrity; and Robert, believing she was carried off against her will all ended well – she was espoused to her faithful suitor at the appointed time, and made an excellent wife; for her direliction had made her watchful over herself – she often thought of the precipice on which she had stood and trembled. Her beauty long after her marriage gained her admirers, but they were soon dismissed with spirit, and taught to keep at a proper distance, for Effie was now proof against seduction.

But to return to the Vampire. He lay bleeding on the ground, while Robert conveyed Effie to the castle, cautioning her to secrecy as she valued his life, for he knew not what might be the result of this act, if it was indeed Marsden's Earl he had slain. He sought the Baron who was much vexed at the recital, though he acknowledged that Robert had much provocation, and Ruthven's elopement with Effie was an insult on the Lady Margaret not to be borne. The Lord of the Isles and his faithful follower repaired to the spot where the latter had left the treacherous Earl.

'I wonder,' said Robert, as they proceeded hither, and calling to mind the scene in Flanders, 'whether we shall find his lordship there, or whether Beelzebub has given him a second lift.' The Vampire, however, was there, bleeding copiously, but in full possession of his senses. He declared life to be ebbing fast, and that he forgave Robert his death wound; also, he ascribed his carrying off Effie as a mere frolic to alarm her and that he had intended to convey her back in safety to the castle. 'I do not like such jests,' said the indignant Robert, 'and you have paid for an act you had better have left alone.'

The false earl then proceeded to state, on the oath of a dying man, that he was no Vampire. This gave a sad pang both to the baron and Robert, and the former testified his regret at the conduct such suspicions had given rise to. He then demanded of Ruthven if he had any commission to charge him with, and it should be punctually executed.

'Swear it,' exclaimed the Vampire, eagerly.

The baron drew forth his sword and swore on it.

'Give me that topaz ring from off your finger,' said the Vampire; 'let me die with it on, in token of your renewed amity, and allow it to be buried with me.' To this the Lord Ronald most readily consented.

'Next' said the Vampire, drawing it forth from his bosom, where it hung extended by an hair chain, 'take this ring of twisted gold, and cast it into a well that stands on the north side of Fingal's Cave – 'tis a charm given by the mighty Stuffa. I shall thus have a vow performed that will give peace to my soul, and save it from wandering after it has quitted its mortal clay-built tenement. In a few minutes I shall be no more – draw my body aside into the copse, and to-morrow at your return you can seek it, and give me burial; but for the present conceal my death from all you meet: name it not until the ring is in the cave.'

In a few minutes the Vampire seemed to die with a heavy groan, and the afflicted baron and his attendant proceeded to obey the last injunction thus-received, both conscience-stricken at having thus treated Marsden's Earl, and feeling assured, from the manner of his death, that he was a mortal man. They returned to the castle to prepare for their journey to the cave; but mentioned not the decease of Ruthven; and even Effie was imposed on to believe that the wounds, though they had bled much, were but trifling. This gave much comfort to the damsel, as it cleared her Robert of a deed of blood.

The Baron and Robert set out as soon as it dawned, for the cave of Fingal, to perform what they thought an imperious duty, for as such they considered a posthumous request made under such distressing circumstances.

Little did the credulous pair suspect that they were now made the agents of the wicked Vampire, for this is the true story of the magic ring.

The outer part of the Vampire was not subject to disease, and it was invincible to the sword. If they could contrive to have Stuffa's ring flung into the well of the cave of Fingal within twenty-four hours after the death wound it was restored to its vile career for the appointed time, and for that season the malignant spirit hovered round the body.

The good Lord of the Isles and Robert arrived safe there, and with little difficulty found the well, for report had spread its situation far and wide owing to its magic qualities. Lord Ronald cast in the ring – instantaneously a hissing, as if of snakes, followed, but soon all was silent as the grave.

They left the cavern and found themselves in the midst of a pelting storm, and their horses, which they had left tied to a tree, were unloosened and they sought in vain for them. As they continued their search a sweet musical voice was heard by the wanderers.

'Tis Ariel bids you haste away,
'Tis Ariel warns you not to stay;
Hie and stop a horrid scene,

'Tis the fatal *Hallow E'en*,
Haste and save the destined fair
From the treacherous Vampire's snare!'

'Robert,' said the Baron, 'did you hear ought or do my ears deceive me? – again was the verse repeated with this additional stanza –

'Lose not time but quickly see
Whose the triumph is to be,
Margaret must be no more,
Or the Vampire's reign is o'er'

'Tis plane enough, my lord; Ariel, who is always reckoned a benign spirit, warns us – We are deceived – Oh this cursed Vampire! I see it now, he made us tools for his own purpose.'

'Nonsense, my good fellow,' said the Baron, 'it must be some new plot against my peace – a real Vampire, for we left Marsden's Earl quite dead.'

'Oh, he was dead enough in Flanders,' observed Robert, 'but he seems to have as many lives as the Witch of Endor's tabby cat. My mind forbodes horrid things – No harm, however, in getting home quick.'

But they were involved in the intricacies of the forest, and it required both patience and perseverence to find the right track; at length they succeeded, and walked on with rapid strides, for the evening wore away. At this juncture some horsemen overtook them – It was quite dusk and objects scarce discernible.

'Hoy, Holla, my good foresters! can you put us in the way for Baron Ronald's castle; the Lord of the Isles we mean, said the foremost of the caveliers?'

'What want you there?' replied the Baron, (himself) 'let us know ere we guide you, for we are going thither.'

'I am Hildebrand, Lord Gowen's sister's son, sent by my mother to pay my respects and duty to him as becomes a nephew and a godson, nor has he seen me since my infancy.'

'Welcome! Welcome!' exclaimed the Baron, 'son of my beloved Ellen, I am thy uncle, but by some strange accidents, here on foot with one single follower.'

' 'Tis lucky, replied the youth, springing from his steed and embracing the Baron, that we have some led horses in our train.' Lord Ronald and Robert were glad to hear of this seasonable supply, and mounting the noble beasts, set off at full speed.

Hildebrand; as they rode along, was made acquainted with recent events by his worthy uncle – he was struck with terror, and felt much interested for the Lady Margaret; for young Gowen had imbibed from the Countess, (his mother) a strong belief of the existence of Vampires, and he intimated, though respectfully, to his venerable uncle, that he had done wrong by throwing the ring into the well, as by that means it was most probable, the wicked sprite had acquired reanimation.

Again the storm arose and served to retard their progress, for the steeds affrighted at the vivid and incessant lighting, could with difficulty be got forward. At length they arrived at the copse, and Robert with two of Earl Gowen's serving men dismounted to seek for the body, but it was not there. 'Just as I thought to find it,' said the former, 'beshrew me it is an industrious sprite; but the moon will soon set,' and as the benign Ariel sang –

> 'Let's haste and save the destin'd fair
> From the treacherous Vampire's snare.'

They spurred their horses, and the storm having made a temporary stop they were soon across the park. Music was sounding – they could distinguish the harper's strain – the great hall was lighted up most brilliantly – a sumptuous altar had been erected at one end – and for the third time, the marriage ceremony was about to begin, when the Baron, Lord Gowen and Robert rushed in and secured the intended bride, who fainted immediately, for in the person of her noble cousin she beheld the form shewn her by Una and Ariel in the cave of Fingal, and the Vampire's charm vanished away like snow before the meridian sun.

The Vampire seemed armed with supernatural strength – he resisted all their efforts to subdue him – and their swords made no impression – he struggled hard to bear away the Lady Margaret from the midst of her protectors, and the amazing efforts of the Vampire spread horror and alarm, for that he was an evil sprite no one now doubted. He had returned to the castle that evening, and said he came with the Baron's consent, (who had undertaken a sudden journey) to wed the Lady Margaret, and had brought her father's ring as a token. All was now bustle, preparation and joy, till the unexpected entrance of the Lord of the Isles and his companions, and had it not been for the providence of Gowen seeking the castle that night, the fiend would have triumphed, for they could not have got home on foot time enough to save her.

But the fiend was not to be overpowered – he jumped on the temporary altar sword in hand (after having wounded and bit with his teeth several of the domestics) insisting he would yet have his bride. In an instant the scene changed – the moon set – the thunder rolled over the castle, and the bolt fell on the Vampire – he rolled lifeless upon the floor, and after a terrific yell, melted into air, incorporeal and invisible to every eye. Thus ended the wicked sprite.

Some months after this event Margaret was happily united to Earl Gowen, with whom she led a happy life till they both sunk into the grave, venerable with age, making good the prediction of the spirits of the cave of Fingal –

> 'Ne'er but once was she to wed,
> Or have a second bridal bed.'

Les Vampires

EUGENE SUE

*   *   *

The dark and damp staircase seemed doubly dingy on this gloomy winter's day. The entrance to each of the apartments of this house had, to the observant eye, a physiognomy peculiar to itself. Thus, the door which led to the commander's abode was freshly painted of a brown colour, grained in imitation of wainscot; a copper-gilt handle shone on the lock, and a handsome bell-rope, with a red silk tassel, was in striking contrast with the mouldy antiquity of the walls.

The door of the second story, inhabited by the fortune-teller and pawnbroker, presented a singular aspect. A stuffed owl, a bird signally cabalistic and symbolical, was nailed over the room-door by the feet and wings; and a little wicket, latticed with iron wire, enabled those within to examine their visitors previous to admitting them.

The dwelling of the Italian quack doctor, who was suspected of pursuing a frightful avocation, was also distinguished by the strangeness of the entrance. His name was done in horses' teeth, inlaid on a tablet of black wood, screwed on the panels; and the bell-rope, instead of the classic termination of a hare's or a deer's foot, was appended to the wire by the dried fore-arm of an ape; this withered limb, with its five articulated fingers and its perfect nails, had something of the horrible in its appearance. One might have taken it for the hand of a child!

As Rudolph passed by this ominous-looking door, he fancied that he heard the sound of smothered sobs; then, all at once, an agonized, convulsive, horrible cry, which seemed as if wrung from the inmost soul of some wretched sufferer, awakened the echoes of that silent house. Rudolph shuddered: then, quick as thought, he rushed to the door, and pulled the bell violently.

'What ails you, sir?' asked the astonished porter.

'That cry!' said Rudolph; 'did you not hear it?'

'Yes sir, I heard it; no doubt it is one of M. Cæsar's patients having a tooth drawn – or perhaps two.'

This explanation seemed plausible, but it did not satisfy Rudolph. He had rung the bell violently; yet no one came to answer him. He could hear several doors shut in succession; and through a glass bull's-eye which was above the door, Rudolph indistinctly saw a haggard, cadaverous, and pallid countenance. A perfect forest of wild, red hair crowned that hideous visage, which was fringed below by a long beard of the same colour. This hideous face disappeared in a moment. Rudolph felt completely petrified.

Brief as had been the vision, he believed that he recognized those features. Those green eyes, that shone bright as aqua-marine beneath those staring and yellow eyebrows – that livid paleness – that slender and prominent aquiline nose, the nostrils of which, strangely dilated and arched outward, exposed the nasal septum – reminded him in a fearful manner of a certain Polidori, whose name had been so execrated by Murphy in his conversation with Baron de Graun. Although Rudolph had not seen Polidori for sixteen or seventeen years, he had a thousand reasons for not forgetting him: the only thing that contradicted his remembrance was, that the man, whom he fancied he saw in the person of this fair-skinned and red-haired quack, was extremely dark. If Rudolph (supposing his conjectures to be correct) felt no surprise at finding a man whose learning, great talent, and intelligence, he knew, fallen to such a state of degradation, perhaps of infamy – it was because he also knew that these rare and noble gifts were allied to so much perversity, such wild, unbridled passions, desires so foul, and, beyond all, to such an affected scorn and contempt of the world, as might induce this man, when overtaken by want, to prefer degraded and dishonourable modes of subsistence; nay, even to enjoy a fiendish satisfaction that he was hiding beneath his ignoble pursuits the precious treasures of a highly-gifted mind. But, we must repeat that, although he had last seen Polidori in the prime of life, and although he must be about the same age as the charlatan, there were still between the two persons certain differences so remarkable, that Rudolph remained in great doubt as to whether they were one and the same person. At length turning to Pipelet, he inquired – 'Has M. Bradamanti long resided in this house?'

'About a year, sir; now I recollect, he came in January quarter. He is a very punctual lodger; he cured my dreadful rheumatism – '

'Mrs Pipelet tells me that there are certain horrible reports about him.'

'She has told you of them?'

'Make yourself quite easy; I am very discreet.'

'Well, sir, I don't believe there's the least truth in these reports – and I never will believe it – I trust I have too much modesty to do anything of the kind,' rejoined Pipelet, blushing, and preceding his new lodger to the next landing-place.

More than ever resolved to clear up his doubts – feeling that Polidori's presence in the same house might greatly interfere with his projects, and experiencing a growing inclination to put the worst interpretation on the horrible cry he had heard, Rudolph resolved to assure himself of this man's identity, and followed the porter to the upper story, where was situated the apartment he wished to rent.

Miss Dimpleton's lodging, next-door neighbour to the chamber for which Rudolph was in treaty, was easily recognized, thanks to a charming gallantry of the painter who has been described as the mortal foe of Pipelet. Half-a-dozen chubby little Cupids, very freely and spiritedly painted in the style of Watteau, were grouped about a shield. One held a thimble, another a pair of scissors, another a flat-iron, and another a hand-glass; and in the midst of them, in pink letters on a sky-blue ground, was 'Miss Dimpleton, dressmaker;' the whole being surrounded by a garland of flowers, which stood out in admirable relief from the sea-green colour of the door. This beautiful little panel had all the better effect from its strong contrast with the filthiness of the staircase.

At the risk of opening afresh Alfred's wounds, Rudolph said, pointing to the door: 'That, I suppose, is the work of M. Cabrion?'

'Yes, sir; he took the liberty of spoiling the painting of the door, by daubing it over with those fat, indecent brats, stark naked, which he called 'Coopids.' If it hadn't been for the entreaties of Miss Dimpleton, and M. Red Arms' weakness, I would have scratched all that out, as I also would this palette, filled with horrid-looking monsters, amongst whom you may detect their equally abominable creator – you may know him by his sugar-loaf hat.'

And, there, sure enough, on the door of the room Rudolph was about to engage, might be seen a palette surrounded by all sorts of odd, strange-looking figures, the witty conceit of which might have done honour to Callot. Rudolph followed the porter into a good-sized room, which communicated with a small bed-room, and was lighted by two windows which opened upon the Rue du Temple. Some wild fancies, which had been painted on the same door, had been scrupulously respected by M. Germain. Rudolph had many reasons for wishing to occupy this apartment; therefore, modestly placing in the porter's hand forty *sous*, he said to him: –

'This apartment exactly suits me; here is the deposit. I will send my furniture in to-morrow. But let me beg of you not to efface that palette. It is so very funny. Don't you think so?'

'Funny! Oh, sir! I have seen every one of those monsters in my nightmares; hunting me, sir, in my dreams, with Cabrion at the head of them, till I have awoke in a cold sweat: oh, there was a horrid chase!'

'I can imagine that they were not pleasant visitors. But tell me, have I any need to see your M. Red Arm about the hiring of this apartment?'

'No, sir; he seldom comes here, except now and then on business with Mother Burette. I always treat directly with the lodgers. I will only further trouble you for your name?'

'Rudolph.'

'Rudolph what?'

'Plain Rudolph, M. Pipelet.'

'I am satisfied, sir; I did not ask from idle curiosity – names and inclinations are free.'

'Tell me, M. Pipelet, cannot I call to-morrow upon poor Morel, as a next neighbour, to ask if I can be of any use to him, since my predecessor, M. Germain, was so good to him?'

'Oh, yes, sir, that can be done; it is true that will not be of much use to him, as they are to be turned out; but still it will ease his mind.' Then, as if struck with a sudden thought, Pipelet, looking slyly at his new lodger, said: 'I understand, I understand: it is a beginning, so that you can also call by-and-by, with a good grace, upon the little neighbour next door!'

'Oh! I reckon upon that as certain.'

'There is no harm in that, sir – it is the custom – understand, I mean honourably; and I am sure Miss Dimpleton has heard us in the room, and is in a fever to see us go down again. I will make a noise on purpose with the key, and if you look behind, you will see her watching us.' And, sure enough, Rudolph perceived that the door, which was so handsomely decorated with the Cupids à la Watteau, was ajar, and, through the narrow opening, he could see the turn-up tip of a little rosy nose, and a large inquisitive black eye; but, as he slackened his step, the door suddenly slammed to. 'Did I not tell you, sir, that she was watching us?' said the porter; then he added: 'Pray excuse me, one moment, while I step into my warehouse.'

'Where is that?'

'At the top of that ladder is the landing upon which opens the door of Morel's garret, and behind a panel of the wainscot is a little dark hole, where I keep my leather; the partition is so warped and full of cracks, that I can see and hear there as if I was in their room. It is not, God, knows, that I wish to act the spy upon them – on the contrary. But pray excuse me for a minute or two, sir, while I get my bit of leather. If you will be good enough to step down stairs, I will rejoin you.'

And so saying, Pipelet began to mount the crazy ladder, an ascent which seemed perilous at his years.

Rudolph threw a last glance at Miss Dimpleton's door, as he reflected that that young girl, the companion of poor Goualeuse, was doubtless acquainted with the retreat of the Schoolmaster's son, when he heard some one in the lower story come out of the apartment of the charlatan; he distinguished the light step of a female, and the rustle of a silk dress. Rudolph stopped for an instant, lest he should intrude. Hearing no more, he went down. Arrived at the second landing-place, he saw and picked up a handkerchief that lay upon the lower stair – doubtless it belonged to the female who had just left the lodging of Polidori. He took it to one of the narrow-stair-case windows, and examined it. It was magnificently trimmed with costly lace, and embroidered in one of the corners were the initials D. N., surmounted by a ducal coronet. The handkerchief was literally soaked with tears. Rudolph's first impulse was to follow the person from whose hand this mute evidence of grief had fallen, with the intention of restoring it; but reflecting that such a step might be taken for impertinent curiosity, he determined to keep it as the first link in the chain of a mysterious adventure, in which he had found himself suddenly and unintentionally involved. On arriving at the porter's lodge, he said to Mrs Pipelet: 'Did not a female come down stairs just now?'

'No, sir – but a very fine *lady*, tall and slender, in a large black veil did. She came from the apartment of M. Bradamanti. Little Hoppy went for a coach, in which the lady has just gone away. But what astonished me was to see that little blackguard get up behind the coach. I dare say, though, it was to see where the lady goes to; for he is as mischievous as a magpie, and active as a ferret, spite of his club-foot.'

'So, then,' thought Rudolph, 'the charlatan will most likely discover this lady's name and address, since doubtless it is he who has ordered Hoppy to follow her.'

'Well, sir, does your room suit you?' asked the portress. 'It suits me excellently! I have hired it: to-morrow I will send in my furniture.'

'May heaven bless you for coming by our door, sir; we shall have one good lodger the more.'

'I hope so, Mrs Pipelet. It is understood that you will see to my little domestic affairs. To-morrow my goods will be brought. I will see them arranged myself.' And Rudolph left the lodge.

The results of the visit to the house of the Rue du Temple were sufficiently important, alike to the solution of the mystery he hoped to penetrate, and to the noble curiosity with which he found out every occasion of doing good, and of preventing evil. On reflection, he thought he had achieved the following results: That Miss Dimpleton *must* be acquainted with the residence of François Germain, the

Schoolmaster's son. A young woman, who, according to some appearances, might unfortunately be the Marchioness d'Harville, had made, for the morrow, an appointment with the Commander, which might ruin her for ever; and, for a thousand reasons, Rudolph took a most lively interest in his friend D'Harville, whose peace and honour seemed so cruelly compromised.

An honest and laborious artizan, crushed by the most frightful misery, was about to be turned into the street with his family by Red Arm.

Further, Rudolph had involuntarily come upon some traces of an adventure in which the charlatan, Cæsar Bradamanti (perhaps Polidori), and a lady, who appeared to be of rank and fashion, were the chief actors.

And lastly, the Owl, recently emerged from the hospital, to which she had been taken after the scene in the Allée des Veuves, had some very suspicious communications with Mother Burette, fortune-teller and money-lender, who occupied the second floor of this house.

Having carefully noted these points of information, Rudolph returned to his house in the Rue Plumet, there to contemplate his next move in the mystery . . .

The Bat

BELA LUGOSI

*　　　*　　　*

Your fancy may crawl away from the tale I am about to tell you – in fact you may not believe it. But in order to tell you about the haunted house and what occurred there I must go back a little way in time. You know that I am married a fourth time. Yes, you know that.

You have heard about my – my other wives. You know that I come from the black mountains of Hungary where, in the arms of my old nurse, I heard the tales of vampires and saw their victims. Ah, yes, as I grew older and could take notice of things about me I saw many a young man and young woman pale and sicken and seem to die with no cause given. I had a sceptical mind. I read widely. I made a brave attempt to laugh off such nonsense. Folklore gone mad, I told myself. I would shake off the charnel-house odours of such foul superstitions . . .

And then, I met the woman. Her age was indeterminable. She was an actress. She was not outstandingly beautiful. Her hair was a pale brown. Her skin was deathly pale at times; at other times it was a blood, blood red – that was when she had been fed. Her mouth was thin and ravenous. Her teeth were tiny, and pointed. She had been married many times. There had been many lovers. One never asked what had become of them. Men feared her – and went to her at her command. Husbands left their wives because of her.

I had a wife, too, and two sons. Yes, I have two sons of whom I have never spoken. They are grown boys now. I have never seen them since I – I left. I have never, from that day to this, sent so much as a picture postcard home. Nor have I had one. How should I? I burned all my bridges behind me when I left more than fifteen years ago. It was safer to have no communication of any earthly kind. I wish I could say that I did not care, that the thought of those two young men of mine did not matter to me. But I do care, it does matter. However, to get back . . . At that time I was living the normal life of a young man of the town. I had played Romeo, with some success. I was said to be of outstanding appearance. I had a genial disposition and a happy outlook on life.

Then I met – her. The very first time I was introduced to her I broke out into a deathly cold sweat. My heart and pulse raced and then seemed to stop, dead. I lost control of my limbs and faltered in my speech. I was never happy in her presence. I felt always sick and dizzy and depleted. Yet I could not remain away from her. She never bade me come to her, not in words. There was never any of the conventional trapping of assignations. I simply went to her, at odd hours of the day and night, impelled by an agency I neither saw nor heard.

I lost weight. I hardly slept. I had seen other young men fade and wither before my eyes and had heard the village folk whisper the dread cause. But when it came to me, I did not know it for what it was.

It was my mother who forced me to flee the country and never to return to it again until that woman and every trace of her vanished from the sight of men . . .

This that I am telling you is the truth. It can be verified if you are curious or incredulous.

I came to America. After a time, my health returned to me. I tried, on two other occasions, to find human love, to marry and have a home as other men have. You have heard the results. One marriage lasted twenty-four hours ... The other ... I can only say she, the faithful one, was there and gave me to understand that if ever I felt love again, attempted marriage, she would stand between me and fulfillment.

For many months, for years I dared not think of love or of marriage. I was determined to stay alone.

And then I met my present wife. She was my secretary. She, too, is of Hungarian descent. She was born here. She, too, was raised on the folklore of the countryside, the tales of vampires and ghouls and unspeakable things.

She loved me, she has told me, at first sight. Something in her ached for me. I did not love her – not at first. I had put love from me. Then, day after day, as she worked for me and with me, did little things for me I had not thought to ask her, a craving for companionship, for a woman in my heart and in my home once more took hold of my very vitals.

But I wanted to put her to the test. For weeks before I dared to tell her that I loved her, wanted to marry her I – I tortured her. They were not nice things, the things I did to her. I cannot speak of them. Perhaps it was to test her ... perhaps it was an attempt to placate that – that other one. Whatever it was, and however shamed my heart, I caused her such suffering as made the tears stream down her face for hours and hours at a time ... but she never faltered, never turned away from me.

And so, nearly two years ago we were married and found this house. We thought, 'We will make it safe against invasion of any kind.' And so we have locks on all the doors, locks that cannot be unlocked by any hands but mine. And no one is admitted to this house unless that person is well known to us. No appointments are made over the phone. We have five hounds and one of them is white and his name is Bodri. He *knows*. The windows, as you can see, are screened and barred and locked. On the landing of each stairway is a large cushion upon which one of the hounds sleeps at night ... no footstep, human or otherwise, can mount or descend these stairs without their knowing it.

And there are times when they howl in the night ... howl fearfully though no eye, not even mine, can see what they are howling at. And so, in spite of all these precautions *the house is haunted!*

I knew it, first, when the dogs began to howl. I knew it when I first saw the white fur rise on Bodri's body, saw his ears flatten and his red eyes dilate.

I knew it when, in the dead of night, there came the sound of something dragging around the house.

And then, that first night in this house and every night thereafter the bat has come. The first night I saw that bat, monstrously big and with but one eye, flattened against the window.

'It began to be a monomania with both of us – to kill that bat. We had the feeling that if we ridded ourselves of that thing we would be free. We told Bodri to get it. We even hired exterminators to come up and watch for the creature and kill it. We had all kinds of men here lying in wait for it. They finally told us we were imagining it – there was no bat visible. We knew that they thought we were mad.

Months went by and then, one night, Bodri got it. We heard him howling in the darkness. He came into the house and he had it in his mouth, limp, dead, hideous beyond words. With a sick heart and shuddering flesh I went into the garden and there, in the dead of night, I dug a grave for it. I dug a hole deep enough to bury the Giant of Tarsus. I went back to the house, and to bed.

The next night came. We had a little festive dinner, my wife and I. We drank wine and were very gay. We even talked of the time when we might go back to Hungary, back to Lugos. In the midst of our happy talk, it happened.

My wife heard it first. I could tell that she had heard it by the look on her face. I went to the window. The bat was back again. Not the same one you say? But yes, it was.

I went into the garden with Bodri beside me. I dug up that deep pit again. The bat was gone. The ground was undisturbed but the bat – was – *gone!*

That is my story. In Lugos it would not be thought so strange, nor disbelieved. So often and so frightful is this sort of thing over there, even today, that the townspeople of Lugos often keep their dead for days and sometimes weeks to be sure they have died a Christian death and not the hideous, half-death of the vampires. But I do hope that I have not *frightened* you . . .

Cat People

VAL LEWTON

*   *   *

The church bells of Ghizikhan pealed out slow, lazy music to mark the end of the morning prayer. Kolya turned his head idly to look at the village. From his vantage-point in the open porch of the armourer's shop where he was engaged in polishing the swords and other weapons which his uncle had chosen to place on display that day, Kolya could see the entire length of Ghizikhan's single street. It was early and the long shadows of the Caucasian peaks fell like dark, irregular bars across the valley. Only through the gap between Mount Elbruz and the volcanic peak of Silibal came sunlight, falling squarely upon the village. In this pleasant light the folk of Ghizikhan went about their early morning tasks. At the well the maidens jostled one another, giggling as they drew up water. Kolya's eyes, although he had just grown to manhood, avoided this group, but turned with interest upon the shepherds who were having a last, long draught at the inn door before going on to relieve the men who had guarded the flocks through the night hours.

It was a sight that Kolya could see any time, and, yawning, he turned back to the task in hand, the scouring of a new sword blade with water and white sand. Diligently he worked the scouring-cloth back and forth, his long, fair hair falling down over his forehead as he bent to the task. Of a sudden a cry went up at the other end of the village, and Kolya's head was upflung as if by magic.

Two men were running towards the inn. Between them they carried a shapeless bundle. Kolya could only catch the colours of the object – red and white. As they ran they cried out: 'A Bagheeta! A Bagheeta! We have seen her!'

Kolya identified the burden which they carried between them. It was a sheep, torn to death by a panther. Dropping the scouring-cloth, Kolya ran to where a knot of men had gathered about the two shepherds. He forced his way towards the centre of the crowd until he could hear the words of one of the men: '– black as wood from a fire, bigger than any natural leopard – a monster, I tell you! Varla and I came upon her at her meal. With my own eyes I saw her – you can measure for yourselves – from here to here,' the shepherd indicated a huge, bloody rent in the flank of the slain sheep, 'she took one mouthful. A real Bagheeta – I swear it!'

The men around him crowded closer to see the evidence. It was true; an enormous mouth had made those long gashes in the carcass.

The *hetman* of Ghizikhan, pulling at his virgin white beard, questioned the shepherd: 'Fool, what did you do? Did you let the beast escape so that it may enjoy such a feast as this from our table whenever he wills it?'

The shepherd protested: 'It was a real Bagheeta, I tell you, *Hetman!* What could we do? Varla shot at her, but you know that no bullet can harm a Bagheeta – not even a silver bullet. She just snarled at us and walked away.'

'Walked away?' the *hetman*'s tones were dubious.

'Yes, *Hetman*, I have said it so: walked away, just turned and walked away. She knew we couldn't hurt her. Both Varla and I are married men, you know!'

'Aye, *Hetman*, I believe them.' It was Davil who spoke, Davil the old minstrel, who in his youth had killed a Bagheeta. 'This Bagheeta must be the same leopard we hunted all these last three days. If it had been a real leopard its skin would have been drying on the walls of your house by now, *Hetman*, but only a pure youth who can resist her blandishments can kill a Bagheeta. You must select a pure youth to hunt down this were-beast – a real St Vladimir, pure of heart as a virgin.'

'Nonsense! These are old wives' tales, falser than your rhymes, Davil,' Rifkhas the huntsman, whose very garments smelled always of the forest, spoke out heatedly. 'What is this beast, you say – a black leopard? To the east, beyond Elbruz, they are as common as black crows are in our land! It was the hard winter and the heavy snows which have driven them here. One good shot from my old rifle and your Bagheeta will be deader than the sheep he's killed. Do not forget, Davil, that I too have killed one of these black kittens, and with a rifle and a lead ball – I saw no signs of magic or sorcery.

'I have grown sick of these old lies which send our young men frightened into the forest. Believe me, it is safer in the forest than before the coffee-pots in the *khan*. King God has made man lord above the beasts and they all fear him.'

But by now the women of Ghizikhan had swarmed to the scene of the excitement, and their loud outcries drowned out the old huntsman's logic. Shrill voices explained the myth to those too young to know the significance of a black leopard among the spotted ones.

It is a were-beast, they said, half leopard and half woman, the reincarnation of a virgin who has died from wrongs inflicted upon her by sinful men, and who comes again to the world so that she may prey upon the flocks of the sinful. Only a pure youth, one who has lain clean and alone, can hope to slay the mystic beast. He must ride out against the Bagheeta with only a sword at his side and a prayer to King God upon his lips. The Bagheeta, so the women said, will change at his coming into a beautiful woman and attempt to coerce him into an embrace. If she is successful, if the youth kisses her, his life is forfeited. Changing again into a black leopard, the Bagheeta will tear him limb from limb. But, if he remain steadfast in his purity, then surely will he slay the beast.

Kolya listened eagerly. It was not the first time he had heard the legend. When they had done talking he looked again at the dead sheep. The bloody, mangled flesh, bearing clear marks of the enormous fangs which had rent it so hideously, sent little shivers up his spine. He had often heard Davil sing his song of the slaying of the Bagheeta, and standing in the warm sunlight, Kolya grew cold thinking on the dark forest and the dark beast, only its golden eyes visible in the night. He could see vividly the heavy, crushing paws, the curving claws, the red and rending mouth.

Suddenly the *hetman*'s voice rang clearly above the chatter of the women: 'Who among the *Jighitti* – the good, brave horsemen of our village – is pure of heart and free of sin? Let him stand forward, sword in his right hand!'

A silence fell upon the villagers, and all eyes were turned, first to the face of one youth and then to the face of another. All upon whom the eyes of the villagers fell turned blood-red and averted their faces.

The *hetman* grew impatient. He began to call the young men by name: 'Rustumsal? What! And you but sixteen! Fie upon the women of Ghizikhan! Valodja? Shame! Badyr? Shamyl? Vanar?'

All shook their heads.

Then Kolya, his heart pounding with excitement, stepped forward. In his right hand he held his sword, silent declaration of his intention. Behind him he could hear his mother shrilling: '*Hetman*, he is too young! It is but yesterday that he rode in the *Jigitovka*. Only two days has he worked as a man among men.'

The *hetman* paid no attention to her.

Bending forward so that he might look into Kolya's eyes, he asked: 'How old are you?'

Kolya answered sturdily: 'Sixteen.'

'And you have never laid yourself beside a woman, nor lusted after her with your eyes?'

'No,' said Kolya.

The *hetman* doffed his karakul *chapka* and with it still clasped in his hand, pointed to Kolya. A shout went up. Kolya the orphan, nephew of the armourer, had been chosen to hunt down the Bagheeta.

An hour later the men of the village, accoutred as if for war or holiday, rode out from Ghizikhan in a long cavalcade. Kolya, dressed in his best *kaftan* of Burgundy-coloured silk, a sleek black *chapka* set jauntily on his head, and wreaths of flowers about his horse's neck, rode at their head. At his side hung the best sword from his uncle's shop. The Silver Maid, his uncle called it, and for no price would he sell it, neither to prince nor commoner, saying always: 'Only by the grace of King God was I able to forge such a sword. One cannot sell God's gifts for gold.'

Beside Kolya rode the *hetman*, and behind them the two old enemies, David the minstrel and Rifkhas the huntsman, wrangling as they rode.

'I have lived in the woods my whole life,' the huntsman was saying, 'and not one, but many of these Bagheetas have I seen killed with bullets. The Russians pay well for their black skins.'

Davil silenced his arguments with a burst of song:

'I ride beneath the silver stars,
  All in my war array;
I ride beneath the silver stars
  To break Bagheeta's sway.

'The stars are bright and bright am I
  Clad in my war array.
The land about does gloomy lie,
  And Bagheeta's sway.

'I ride with flowers in my hair
  And grim sword at my side,
Among the youths I am most fair
  And in war foremost ride.

'To me unknown a maiden's wiles:
  For see, my heart is pure.
God looks upon my head and smiles:
  For see, my heart is pure.'

'Blah!' said Rifkhas, spurring his horse a bit so as to catch up with
Kolya and leave Davil to ride by himself, singing the song which he had
composed many years ago in celebration of his own victory over a
Bagheeta.

Kolya heard the song behind him go on and on as they rode forward
to where the shepherds had seen the leopard.

'Unfeared by me the Deva's call,
  The war's grim chance of death,
But here soft footsteps thud and fall,
  And quickly comes my breath.'

The lad shuddered. He could well imagine the sinuous body of the
beast, black as the night it walked through, creeping through the tree
trunks in the forest. How dark the forest would be after the moon had
gone down! Kolya's horse quivered. It was as if his master's agitation
had been conveyed to her too, and that she also knew of the trial ahead
of them. Davil's song went on:

'Of death alone I have no fear,
  Nor yet of sword hurt deep,
But now a silent move I hear,
  From darkness gold eyes peep.'

'My brave horse trembles in his fear,
   And tighter grows my rein.
Somewhere from night two gold eyes peer
   And mark his frightened pain.'

A restive horse in the darkness of the midnight forest; a silent and unseen foe, waiting to leap from ambush, to strike one down with huge paws, to rend one with enormous teeth; Kolya could almost smell the foetid, hot breath which was to issue from the gaping jaws. Yet all this must be true; had not the minstrel killed just such a beast in his youth? Was not this the very song inspired by the feat? Kolya gazed nervously into the green depths of the forest, crowding in upon the trail. Somewhere in its fastnesses was the Bagheeta, crouched, waiting, confident in its supernatural powers.

Rifkhas' voice was speaking to his ear: 'I'm sorry that they're not letting you carry a gun, lad. You could wait for the Bagheeta by the water hole. He must drink after his kill. Didst ever note how the cats go to the water but when they have eaten a rat in the granary? These leopards, black or spotted, are but big cats; they too must drink after they eat. You could shoot the beast easily if the light were good. But these fools, full of old wives' tales, they make it difficult for you. When the good King God has given us gunpowder, what sense is there to send you into the forest with but a sword in your hand? Likewise, when God gives mankind a full moon to hunt by, why in the name of the seven Peris must they make you wait until the moon has set before you go a-hunting? Why? Because old women like Davil are frightened of the dark, and they would have you be frightened also. Have no fear! There is no beast nor were-beast that will not run from a man. Have no fear, Kolya. I, who have been a huntsman for thirty years, tell you that.'

From behind them came the voice of the other old man. He had changed his tune. It was no longer slow, measured and fearsome, the words filled with dread. It came forth exultantly, as if he had just conquered fear. He sang:

'But now I tremble once again,
   For here a fair maid comes.
I tremble with no thought of pain
   For here a fair maid comes.

'Her lips are scarlet pomegranates,
   Her cheeks like Kavkas' snows,
Her eyes are tense as one who waits
   For sounds of ringing blows.

> 'Her speech is all of lovely things
> That are in other climes,
> Of butterflies with silver wings
> And bells with silken chimes.

> 'She lifteth up her laughing mouth
> And I bend down my own.'

Davil's voice fell. Deep and fearsome it pounded against Kolya's ears:

> 'What is this chill wind from the south?
> This noise of bone on bone?'

Kolya's heart skipped a beat. What if he were to have no warning? What if he were to be so entranced by the Bagheeta's charms that he were to kiss her?

Davil's chant answered the question for him:

> 'I fear, I fear and gaze at her
> Who looks with such a mien;
> I fear, I fear and strain from her
> Whose yellow eyes are keen.

> 'Out sword! Out sword! Bagheeta's eyes
> Look now into your own.
> Out sword! Out sword! He only dies
> Who must the kiss atone.

> 'With tooth and claw Bagheeta flies
> Straight at my armoured throat,
> And now so close his yellow eyes
> That I have falsely smote –'

Kolya's imagination conjured up the gleaming eyes, the hot breath of the beast, its claws sinking into his shoulder. He could feel the sense of helplessness as he was torn from the saddle – the weight of the giant cat upon his body.

Rifkhas' cranky voice, speaking in the calming tones of prose, allayed his fears.

'I'd like to have your chance at this beastie, Kolya,' Rifkhas was saying. 'One black pelt like that would supply me with wine and caresses for an entire year – aye, even an old fellow like myself could buy the soft arms of women with the price of such a pelt. It's a rare chance you have. If only these fools would let you go on foot. You can't hunt leopards on horseback. Why, the sound of your horse's hoofs will echo for miles about. Get off your horse and creep to the water hole, being careful to see that he doesn't get the wind of you; that's the only way you'll get close enough to Master Bagheeta to kill him with a sword.

'Mind what I tell you, Kolya, and forget all these old women who'd tell you that a leopard can change into a woman just because it happens to be black instead of spotted. Mind what I tell you, Kolya, and with the money you get for the pelt you can set up an armourer's shop of your own.'

Behind him, Kolya could hear Davil still singing, describing his own encounter with the dread and mystic beast long, long ago. The fierce half-joy of the conflict and the anguish of those long-healed wounds were in the voice of the old minstrel as he sang:

'Deep, deep I strike, again, again;
Deep do his talons rend.
I am oblivious of my pain
And fast my blows descend.

'With horrid shriek he falls aback,
And now my sword is free.
Again he leapeth to attack,
But now my sword is free.

'Half-way in air the leaping beast,
The cleaving sword, have met;
Now may the herdsmen joyful feast,
For sword and beast have met!'

'Stoi!' The hetman's command cut short both Davil's song and the movement of the cavalcade. The men grouped themselves about the leader as he explained to them how they could best aid Kolya in his adventure. They had arrived at the copse where the Bagheeta had been seen, he told them, and they would now surround the place in such a way as to turn back the Bagheeta if he, sensing Kolya's innocence, were to attempt an escape. None of the men, he warned them, must dare to engage the creature. This was safe only for Kolya, who was pure of heart.

With the point of his spear the hetman drew a rough map in the sand showing the copse and the hollow between two steep cliffs in which it was situated. To each man he designated a certain post at which to watch. He told them that if the Bagheeta approached their positions they must raise up their sword with the cross-like hilts uppermost and loudly sing the hymn of Saint Ivan. Thus, and thus only, could they turn the were-beast back.

At a word from their leader the men galloped off, shouting, to their positions. Only Davil and Rifkhas remained with Kolya and the *hetman* to wait for the coming of night and the dark of the moon.

It was still late afternoon and, although a pale slice of luminous white moon already rode high in the heavens – sure indication that it would set early – Kolya and the men with him still had a long while to wait before he could ride forth in search of the Bagheeta. Davil was all for passing the time in prayer and the singing of songs, but Rifkhas brought forth an earthen jug of wine and a pack of greasy playing-cards. Soon the three grown men were hard at it, playing one game of cards after another.

Kolya was left to his own devices. He fussed with his horse, watering it at the brook and removing the bridle so that it could graze at will. This took only a short time, and then Kolya was again left with nothing to occupy him but his own fears of the night's trial.

He turned his attention to the copse before him. It was dark with the shadows of the larch and fir trees growing on either side of the brook. This stream had, in the course of the centuries, cut itself a hard bed through the solid rock. Its either bank was precipitous. No animal, Kolya thought to himself, could drink from the stream unless somewhere there was a cleft in the rocky banks. If he were to follow Rifkhas' advice he would have to find such a spot where the leopard could come to drink and there await the Bagheeta's coming.

'But, there will be little need to find the Bagheeta,' he reasoned. 'She will come creeping upon me and, when she divines that I am pure of heart and have no knowledge of women, then she will turn herself into a maiden, and so lure me to my death.'

On whispering feet, darkness came stealing into the little glen in which they had halted. The beech leaves, quivering in the evening wind, lisped a plaintive song of nervous fear to Kolya's heart. The same breeze, straying through the pine boughs, struck deep soughing chords. Then, as the sun finally set, plunging the land into intense darkness, the evening noises quieted. Robbed of light by which to continue their card game, the three older men sat quietly. Even the horses ceased their trampling and champing in the place where they had been tethered. A cloud was over the slim, silver moon, shaped ominously, Kolya imagined, like a Persian dagger.

Some current of the upper air swept the cloud from before the moon's face. The *hetman*, looking up, remarked that the moon would set in another hour.

Kolya walked to where he had tied his horse. He saddled the animal carefully, glad to crowd fear out of his mind with activity. Putting his knee sharply against his mount's belly, Kolya jerked the girth tight. Then he bridled the horse, feeling with anxious fingers in the darkness to see that the check strap was properly set. When he had done all this he led the beast to where the *hetman*, Davil and Rifkhas sat about a tiny fire that they had kindled, more for light than for warmth.

The *hetman* lectured him: 'Pray earnestly, Kolya. Ask forgiveness for your sins. This is a creature of deep sin that you go to fight. Only through sin may it vanquish you. It will tempt you in many ways, but you must resist evil. The sign of the cross and the prayers of our people are most potent against magic. Keep your lips clean from its lips, and your heart clean from the evil it will try to teach you. Only in this way may you hope for victory.'

Davil spoke to him: 'Have no fear, Kolya. If your heart is pure, and you resist the blandishments of the Bagheeta – beautiful as she may become – then surely King God will send strength to your sword. I can see you now, riding back to us in the morning with the slain were-beast over your saddle bow –'

Rifkhas cut him short: 'I can see you too, Kolya! But I can see what a fool you will look if you follow the advice of this impotent old rhymester. There is but one way to hunt – whether you hunt leopards or were-leopards, it makes no difference – and that way is to go stealthily – and not on horseback with a clanking sword at your side. Do what I have told you to do and you will not fail to find the Bagheeta: go to the water hole and wait – else you will not see hair nor hide of the creature all the long night through.'

The crescent moon edged down below the horizon.

'It is time, Kolya,' said the *hetman*. 'May King God bless you, pure of heart.'

Kolya mounted, and wheeling his horse, rode toward the forest at a foot pace.

'Mind what I have told you,' Rifkhas shouted after him.

As the first slender saplings of the wood brushed against him, Kolya could hear Davil singing:

> 'I ride beneath the silver stars,
> All in my war array.

> I ride beneath the silver stars
> To break Bagheeta's sway.'

His sword swung reassuringly at Kolya's side. From behind him the second verse of Davil's song came floating to his ears.

> 'The land about does gloomy lie,
> And black Bagheeta's way.'

The distance muffled the other words of Davil's ballad. But Kolya could remember them. They sang through his mind as the wood grew denser and denser about him. He had often heard them before. Some verses brought him courage. He recalled:

> 'I ride with flowers in my hair,
> And grim sword at my side,
> Among the youths I am most fair,
> And in war foremost ride.

> 'To me unknown a maiden's wiles:
> For see; my heart is pure.
> God looks upon my head and smiles:
> For see; my heart is pure.'

Other verses brought him dread:

> 'King God, look on my woeful plight:
> Pity and give me aid.
> Hang out the moon to give me light
> And guide my palsied blade.'

The trees rustled in the light night currents. Each falling leaf, each snapping twig, brought sharp ice to the skin of Kolya's back. Clumps of deeper darkness – some fallen tree or jagged stump – denser than the overflowing night, caused Kolya to tighten his reins and grip fast the hilt of his sword. Out of earshot of the *hetman* and the others, Kolya drew his sword slowly from its sheath. The weight of the weapon, its fine balance, brought no comfort to his disturbed mind. The empty sheath banged now and again against his leg, making him wince at each contact. It would be just so softly, and with just such lack of warning, that the Bagheeta would spring upon him from the dark thickets at either side of the path.

Slowly, drawing rein again and again so that he might strain his ears for some sound of his mystic foe, Kolya traversed the wood. Now so frightened was he by the menacing stillness of the forest that he would have preferred to return to the men; but fear of the taunts which he knew to be the lot of a coward forced him on.

Again he rode through the wood. Again he peered right and left for some sign of the beast, fearful always of seeing golden eyes glow at him from the pitch blackness of the night. Every rustle of the wind, every mouse that scampered on its way, flooded his heart with fear, and filled his eyes with the lithe, black bulk of the Bagheeta, stalking toward him on noiseless paws. With all his heart he wished that the beast would materialize, stand before him, allow him opportunities to slash and thrust and ward. Anything, even deep wounds, would be better than this dreadful uncertainty, this darkness haunted by the dark form of the were-beast.

Near to the place where he had entered the forest, Kolya turned his horse about and rode through again. This time a greater fear had crept into his heart. What if the were-cat were to take advantage of its magical powers? It had done so with Davil. He remembered how he had gone, while still a student at the riding-school, to the village well to wash the blood from his face after a spill, and of how Mailka, the daughter of Davil, had placed her arm about his shoulder, so that with the corner of her apron she might wipe the blood from his forehead. He remembered now with a sense of horrible fear how he had longed to crush her to him, how some strange well-spring in his blood had forced him, against his own will, closer to her. It was only the passing of Brotam, the shepherd, which had prevented him from folding Mailka to his heart. And Mailka was not beautiful, nor willing for embraces. How then would he resist the Bagheeta, beautiful and inviting? He was sick with fear. His stomach was like a pit of empty blackness, as black as the night, as black as the Bagheeta.

It was with relief that he reached the opposite end of the woods and remembered that so far he had not come upon the Bagheeta. Somehow this thought gave food and drink to his fainting heart. If the Bagheeta were so strong, if these tales of supernatural power were true, why then did it not appear and make away with him? It must be, he thought to himself, an ordinary, spotted leopard which had frightened the shepherds in the morning. With this in mind, Kolya began to make plans to find and kill the beast.

'Thrice have I ridden through the wood on this side of the stream,' he deliberated; 'then it is reasonable that the Bagheeta, if it is such a creature, is on the other side of the stream. I will go there.'

Where the stream narrowed a bit, Kolya jumped his horse across, landing with a thud on the firm bank of the opposite side.

Twice he rode through the woods on this side of the stream, making, at intervals, little sorties through the forest as far as the cliffs which bound the copse on either side. He could find no trace of the Bagheeta.

Intent upon the hunt now Kolya had lost all fear. 'It must be,' he reasoned, 'just as Rifkhas told me, that I must hunt the beast on foot, waiting for him at the water hole.'

With this plan in mind, Kolya rode directly along the bank of the creek. The high walls of the creek bed, Kolya clearly saw, would prevent even a creature as agile as a leopard from going to the water's edge for a drink. Then, of a sudden, his horse shied back. Before him, Kolya could see where a slide on each side of the creek had made a sloping pathway to the water. Dismounting, he inspected the place. Hoof marks and paw prints were indubitable proof that the place was in use by all the animals of the vicinity. Kolya led his horse a little way from the bank and tethered it stoutly to an oak sapling.

He divested himself of his *kaftan* and sword belt, pulled his dagger from its sheath and stuck it through the waistband of his breeches. Then, sword in hand, he returned quietly to the water hole. Carefully he stole down half-way to the water and then, flattening his back against the wall of the cut, prepared to wait.

Even as he settled himself in a comfortable position, the falling of a pebble attracted his attention to the other bank of the stream. He could distinguish nothing. The water was as dark as the night. But from the water came a lapping sound. Something was drinking there at the edge of the creek. Kolya strained his eyes. He could see nothing. But as he continued to stare into the darkness he caught a gleam of eyes, yellow, round and burning as the burnished brass of the altar rail. Again Kolya heard the sound of water being lapped up by the rough tongue of the animal. The round, golden eyes were hidden as the creature drank.

Lifting his left hand to his mouth, Kolya ran his tongue across the palm and across the back of his fingers. Lifting it cautiously above his head he held it, palm forward, toward the Bagheeta. The palm of his hand felt colder than the back; the wind was blowing toward him. There was no danger of the Bagheeta taking his scent. But there was the danger that the Bagheeta might go back by the way he had come, without passing Kolya's ambush.

Slowly, ever so slowly, Kolya bent and picked up a large stone. With all his strength he threw it into the bushes on the other bank of the stream, then braced himself to cleave down his sword with all his might. The stone landed on the farther bank with a crash. Gold eyes turned up and, with the shriek, the Bagheeta flung herself across the stream and began to climb past Kolya.

With bated breath he waited until the powerful haunches had lifted the creature until its eyes were on a level with his own. For one moment the beast stared straight into his eyes; then Kolya's sword plunged down slashing the black leopard's shoulder. The Bagheeta shrieked piercingly and fell back a few feet. Again Kolya struck at it, but the beast, snarling, rolled free. Kolya gathered himself and lunged forward with the point as if toward a human opponent. A great feeling of satisfaction flooded his heart as he felt the blade sink deep into the thick neck of the Bagheeta. There was a choking sound, the quick pant and insuck of painful breathing, and then silence. The Bagheeta was dead.

'It was so easy. It was so easy!' Kolya repeated the phrase again and again in wonderment.

Dawn was breaking. Thin, grey light began to filter into the wood. Mists and vapours like grey wraiths whirled without rhyme or reason between the tree trunks. Stiff-legged, body and tail relaxed, with blood flowing over the sandstone on which it lay, Kolya could see the Bagheeta. The heavy jaws gaped wide open, and the boy could see clearly the long, thick fangs of the beast. Its paws were thrust out stiffly, the claws, cruel as Tartar simitars, still unsheathed.

Kolya laughed a bit hysterically. It had been so easy, it had been so easy to kill this fearsome thing of dreadful aspect and terrible strength. Two cuts and a single thrust of his sharp sword had killed the Bagheeta. Tough sinews, tearing fangs and rending jaws had been subdued by the steel of his sword. There had been no magic trial of virtue and morals. Davil was a liar, and Rifkhas a true man.

Kolya sat down upon a stone to rest himself, his eyes still drawn to the inert body of the leopard.

'How they will laugh at Davil when I tell them what a liar he is!' Kolya thought to himself. 'How fat and respected he has grown on that one lie these many years! That song of his – with its beautiful maiden and terrible struggle – why, every child in Ghizikhan knows it by heart, and even the *hetman* believes it. What a lie!'

But then doubts began to steal into Kolya's mind. He thought deeply: 'If this is untrue, if a Bagheeta is but a black leopard, no more dangerous than a spotted one, why then even the story about Lake

Erivan having been created by the tears of God as he wept for the crucifixion of his only Son might be untrue. And the story of Saint Ilya the Archer and his arrows of fire, giving courage to the pure of heart in perilous places, might also be a lie. Even God might be a lie!'

But the grey dawn was ghostly. The trees moved mysteriously in the light winds and the half-light of the morning, and the mountain towered dimly towards the sky. Who knew what dread creatures stalked abroad in the mist? The trees might fall in upon him, the mountains topple to crush him! Kolya put the unreality of God quickly from his mind. A ray of light touched the peak of Silibal and it shone, rose-coloured and white, against the blue of the morning.

Birds began to twitter in the bushes. A deer came to the water hole to drink, but, upthrusting her muzzle at the scent of the slain leopard, trotted off otherwheres.

'How they will laugh when I tell them what a liar Davil has been these many years!'

Stretching himself, Kolya rose, smiling, and prepared to return to where he knew the *hetman* and the *jigits* of the village awaited him.

He donned his *kaftan* and sword belt, replaced his dagger in its sheath, and started to cleanse his bloody sword with a wisp of grass. As he started on this task, a thought struck him. No, he must let the sword remain bloody – proof of the conflict. He laid it down in the grass carefully. Then, wondering at the weight and size of the animal, Kolya dragged the Bagheeta to where he had tethered his horse. The mare plunged and curvetted at the sight of the dead animal and at the smell of its coagulating blood. When he had secured the body to the high cantle with thongs, Kolya picked up his bloody sword, un-tethered the horse and mounted into the saddle deliberately.

As the horse nervously threaded its way under the double burden of victor and vanquished, Kolya rode slowly out of the wood with the reins held tight in his left hand. His mind was busy. A thought had come to him. For years Rifkhas had said that a Bagheeta was but a black leopard among the spotted ones. The people of the village had only laughed at him. Davil, the liar, they loved and respected. Rifkhas, they thought a strange man, a little mad from having lived so long alone in the woods.

'Even if they believed me,' Kolya was thinking, 'they would laugh at Davil only for a day, and then what? Then, no one would fear the Bagheeta any more. And so, no longer,' Kolya reasoned, 'would I be honoured as a man who had slain a Bagheeta.'

He said to himself: 'Surely there must be some reason for this lie.

Others have invented it so that they might appear brave and good in the eyes of the village.'

And Mailka, Mailka would certainly never give herself to one who had betrayed her father's secret. How warm and softly firm her arm had felt against his shoulder that day she had washed his wounds by the well.

'I will do as Davil has done.' Kolya spoke decisively. 'I shall tell them that I first saw the Bagheeta as a beautiful maiden, bathing at the water hole, her body surrounded by a white light. That she called me by name and spoke to me courteously – and that, enchanted by her beauty, I had forgotten all warning and bent to kiss her. Then, I shall say that an arrow of fire sprang through the sky. Knowing it for the sign of Ilya the Archer, I will say that I took warning from this and, springing away from the maiden, drew my sword. So fast that I could not even see the change, the Bagheeta transformed herself again into a leopard and sprang at me. I shall tell them that we fought for an hour and then, just as I was ready to drop my sword from weariness, a great strength surged through me and I killed the beast. Even as Davil has done, so will I do.'

At a sharp trot Kolya rode through the outskirts of the wood. Before him, cooking their breakfasts around little fires, were the men of Ghizikhan. With a great shout of triumph, Kolya struck heels to his horse and charged toward them. The men raised their voices in a hail of welcome which sounded thin and shrill among the mountains.

Kolya began to shout the words of Davil's song as he rode toward them:

> 'Half-way in air the leaping beast,
> The cleaving sword, have met.
> Now may the herdsmen joyful feast,
> For sword and beast have met.
>
> 'I rode beneath the silver stars
> And broke Bagheeta's sway –'

Kolya lifted his bloody sword high in the air, the cross of the hilt extended toward heaven, as if giving the victory to God. The men doffed their sheepskin caps and knelt in prayer at this proof of King God's all-powerful goodness.

'Blah!' said Rifkhas the huntsmen, as he knelt with the rest.

Vampirella

RON GOULART

*   *   *

Shortly after the manned space flight to the moon, a second flight was launched by NASA. Unlike her sister ship, the second craft's launch was shrouded in secrecy, and today is denied by the authorities. Officially, the ill-fated excursion never happened.

Some years earlier, an obscure scientist had mathematically determined the existence of a planet half a billion miles from Earth. Computers verified the findings. In the name of science, the planet must be reached and explored.

The Starcraft reached its goal. Drakulon was there – a planet of rare and alien beauty. Where burnished bronze spires rose majestically in the light of ancient twins moons. Where bizarrely twisted trees bordered rivers of flowing crimson. Blood rivers that nourished a gentle race who bent to drink.

Yet the Earthship came at the sundown of a once-lovely dream. Drakulon was dying – its scarlet waters drying and powdering to dust. The crew members died on the doomed Drakulon, but their spacecraft returned to Earth. When it crashed in a remote New England forest, it was empty save for a single stowaway traveller. A girl who had flown on alien wings to survive, the last of the Drakulon race. And she would survive. She had found new rivers of life-giving blood coursing through the veins of her adopted planet's inhabitants.

Earth people would call her a vampire, sharpen their stakes and mark her to die. But she would live. She was the huntress from the stars. She was: VAMPIRELLA.

Blood.

Blood raining down from the scarlet skies, flowing in streams down rocky hillsides.

Blood to drink, to give life.

Twins suns blazing in the sky. Burning away everything, killing the planet.

Not this planet, no.

A distant planet, in a distant system. Drakulon.

The double sun. Burning, burning.

The thirst, the hunger, the craving for blood.

Fireworks.

A rocket blazing away from Drakulon.

Alone.

The blood raining down.

No, not here. Here you must kill for blood.

Kill humans, people so much like yourself.

No other way. No other way, except to die.

I don't want to die!

Falling. Falling down through space and time.

Falling to Earth.

I don't want to die!

Falling toward the giant mountains.

The plane is going to crash!

No, that's not . . .

Everything is swirling, mixing, coming together and falling apart. Memories fall like snowflakes. Hundred of remembrances flickering.

Landing on Earth. That was . . . months ago.

Blood.

If I don't get it, I'll die!

The plane is going to crash! Crash into the jagged mountains.
I won't die!
A man in the snow. Saying something. Don't listen. Don't listen!
He's rising up.
He has no face! Not a man . . . some kind of beast. Huge, with great pawlike hands reaching out.
Don't touch me!
Falling. Falling down through darkness. Home is lost forever.
There is no home. Except here on Earth.
I didn't want to kill him!
No other way. It's that or –
'How are you feeling this afternoon?'
Someone out there. Is that a voice you can trust? Yes, but –
'I think you're looking much better. These past few days I've been very concerned, but I feel confident now.'
Days? Vampirella opened her eyes. A lean-faced blond man with rimless plastic glasses was watching her from the side of the bed. 'I'm afraid,' she said, 'that I don't – '
'We found you wandering in the snow, last week,' said the man. 'I'm Tyler Westron, a doctor.'
She sat up in the four-poster bed, looking around the room. 'Am I . . . is this the old house I saw?'
'Yes, you're a guest at the Westron Sanitarium,' explained the doctor. 'This house was built in the 1980s by a very wealthy, and very antisocial, copper millionaire. He had his reasons for wanting isolation; so do I.'
'A sanitarium? For what sort of patients?'
'Wealthy ones, mostly.' Westron smiled down at her. 'My speciality is orthomolecular psychiatry. Which is why your case is so interesting to me.'
Vampirella placed a hand to her breasts and noticed she'd been undressed and a lacy night-dress had been put on her. 'My case? You mean the effects of the exposure and the crash I – '
'I mean the vampirism.' Westron's smile grew a little strange around the edges. Seating himself on the edge of the bed, he began, 'It's been quite fascinating. So much of what we do here has become routine. A case like – '
She stiffened. 'How do you know about me?'
'You talked considerably in your delirium, Vampirella,' Dr Westron answered with a smile, 'aided at times by certain drugs. At first I thought it was nothing more than babbling, fever dreams. Then, after

a few tests, I became convinced that what you were saying was absolutely true.' He reached out to the carved bedside table to pick up a small beaker. 'Here, drink this.'

'What is it?'

'Medicine. Take it.'

Somewhat reluctantly, the dark-haired girl swallowed the thick, scarlet liquid.

'Very good,' said Westron. 'You are now freed of your greatest worry, Vampirella.'

'What do you mean?'

'Freed, I hasten to add, so long as you remain on friendly terms with me.' He smiled again, watching her. 'What you've just drunk is a blood-substitute serum . . . a little invention of my own. You must drink . . . let's not be too technical . . . let's say a short glass full every twenty-four hours. Do that, and you will have absolutely no craving for human blood.' He leaned closer. 'That will save you a good deal of embarrassment, won't it?'

She was not certain he was telling the truth. 'Why have you – '

'Why have I cooked up the serum? The challenge of the problem, of finding the right molecule, as it were. For another, I find you a very attractive young woman. I want to help you.'

'I see.'

'Yes, I imagine you do,' said Westron. 'The situation, to make everything perfectly clear, is this, Vampirella . . . you are to remain here, and to be, shall we say, obliging to me. Do that and you get your blood-substitute. Otherwise it's out in the snow with you.' He laughed.

'You want me to be your mistress,' said Vampirella. 'What did you do before I arrived?'

'I have been involved with . . . one of my nurses,' said the doctor. 'Lenore, I'm afraid, has grown increasingly tedious. Lord, if you knew how long I've actually had to . . . no matter. All you need concern yourself with is pleasing me. Since you're still recuperating I won't make any demands on you as yet.' Dr Westron put one hand on her shoulder, the other inside Vampirella's nightdress. He fondled her breasts as he kissed her.

She allowed that.

'Oh, and one other thing,' he said, getting off the four-poster. 'There have been some peculiar rumours about the recent crash of that airliner up in the mountains. The condition of one of the passengers was very strange. Seemed the poor devil lost an enormous amount of blood . . . and yet there was no blood at all around the place where he was found. Things like that do happen with a crash, I suppose, and yet . . .' He bowed in her direction. 'Ah, but so long as you're pleasant and well-behaved, Vampirella, no one need know what really happened up there in the mountains.' With a smile he left her.

She couldn't find her way out through the wall. The door of her bedroom was securely locked. Vampirella prowled the midnight room. She knew she was completely recovered from the effects of the plane crash and exposure and from the drugs which Dr Westron had administered to her while she was still only half-conscious. Westron must be aware of her recovery, too, and he'd soon be making further demands on her.

'Better find that formula right now,' Vampirella told herself, 'and then bid the good doctor a fond farewell.'

The leaded windows were barred. No one could get out that way. No person, at least.

Now that she was completely recuperated, Vampirella could use all her powers and abilities.

She opened one of the barred windows a few inches. Wind and drizzling rain rushed in from the darkness outside.

The dark-haired girl took a step back. She narrowed her eyes and concentrated.

Her voluptuous body seemed to shimmer. Then the girl was gone. In her place a large black bat hovered a few feet above the floor.

The winged creature flapped toward the open window and flew out into the rainy night.

www.ingramcontent.com/pod-product-compliance
Lightning Source LLC
Chambersburg PA
CBHW030406020726
47493CB00003B/970